To Anne and Adam

PART ONE

PART ONE

ONE

I tethered my horse and buggy in front of the Breitung House on the east end of Iron Street and started on my quest. Before I left Marquette I had been told that this was the shortest and busiest thoroughfare in the neighboring iron-mining town of Negaunee. I soon discovered it was also the booziest, certainly in the town if not in Michigan. I had already counted seventeen saloons and not yet come to the one I sought. Meanwhile I had encountered two dog fights and a street brawl and, while crossing an intersecting street, narrowly escaped getting run over by a team of runaway horses dragging a wildly careening dray. I paused on the other side to catch my breath. Doggedly pushing on I passed two more saloons, and was beginning to despair. The next one I came to was the one I sought. I sighed and stopped and mopped my brow.

"Long Jack's Saloon," read weathered twin signs painted on either window, executed with a fine if slightly faded Spencerian flourish. I pushed open the screen door—upon which hung long vertical strips of old newspaper, presumably to alert the waiting swarm of somnolent flies—and, entering the darkened boozy interior, walked up to the bar.

" 'Owdy, partner," the tall silver-haired bartender greeted me pleasantly. "Lavly summer day we're after 'avin'. Wot can I do for you, young fella me lad?"

"I'm looking for the proprietor, Mr. John Tregembo," I said. "Might you be he?"

"Not only might I be 'e, but I blawdy well is 'e," he said. "Glad you didn't ast for no drink," he went on, "cos av the new law aour legislative giants 'as recent passed wot says us 'ard-working saloonkeepers can't serve young lads under twenty-one no more. Blawdy nurse maids an' bookkeepers they now makin' outn us. . . . Me, I figger if a lad's ol' enough to earn 'is livin' toilin' ten-'leven hours a day at 'ard labor 'e's blawdy well old enough to spend 'is money 'ow 'e likes. . . ."

"I'm William Poe, the new lawyer over in Marquette," I said, both charmed and a little overcome by the colorful headlong rush of this man's extravagant vocabulary, which was rather less conversation than a kind of spilt exuberance. "I represent a young woman called Charlotte Kawbawgam," I explained, "and she said you might be able to help out with a legal case I'm handling for her. She said you once knew her father and had befriended him."

"Charlotte Kawbawgam?" Jack Tregembo echoed, pursing his lips and blinking thoughtfully, swiftly adopting the role of the thinker searching the shrouded mists of memory. "I'm afeared I don't knaow this 'ere young lydy," he said finally. "Ol' Jack's 'ad lots av parched customers these past thirty-odd years an' 'e can't 'spec' to 'member all av they. Was 'er ol' man an iron miner, might 'e been? Name daon't saound 'zactly Cornish to me. I wanst knew a Treboggin but 'e wos kilt up yonder mine by a chunk av falling ore." He swiftly hooked his thumb up towards the Jackson Mine, west of town, clasping his head and reeling drunkenly in pantomime of a man staggering from a mortal blow.

"No, the name's not exactly Cornish," I agreed, trying not to smile at his wild gesticulations and asides. "Perhaps I should explain," I went on. "Charlotte Kawbawgam is a young Chippewa Indian woman. Her given name in Indian means Laughing Whitefish, after the river by that name. Her dead father's name was Marji Kawbawgam and I thought maybe you—"

"*Marji Kawbawgam!*" Jack broke in, slapping the bar top with the palm of his hand. "Did I know ol' Marji Kawbawgam! Put 'er there, young fella," he went on, extending his big hand and burying mine in his grip. "W'y di'n't thee say so right off? Of course I knew ol' Marji. 'Chief' I used to call 'im. Guess maybe p'r'aps I was 'is bes' frien'—certainly amongst the w'ite folks I wos. A close-mouthed one 'e wos but 'e offen tole me sad an' confidential 'baout 'is little Laughing Whitefish. Closest ever I come to seein' an Hindian cry. Apple av 'is eye, she wos. An' naow she's a growed up young lydy—'ow time do fly."

"She's a fine handsome young woman," I said, recalling her grace and beauty. "She's just turned twenty-one."

"Muss be all of eight-ten years since poor ol' Marji got 'is. Le's see, naow—" he released my hand to do his sums as I gratefully flexed my aching fingers—"hit's 1873 naow an' take 1859 —w'en poor Marji passed—from 'e, leaves—w'y it's *fourteen* years! 'Ow the time *do* fly!"

"That's correct, Mr. Tregembo," I put in. "Marji Kawbawgam was killed just over fourteen years ago, early in July, 1859. His daughter is a fine young woman, you'll be glad to learn, and I'm trying to help her collect her just due. That's why I'm here, Mr. Tregembo."

"Don't keep Mister Tregembo-ing me," he ordered, deftly drawing a small beer for himself. "Everybody calls me Jack— that is, all but me ol' lydy, an' wot she 'urls at me ain't fit fer 'uman ears, hespecially for hinnocent young fellas like thee."

"All right, Jack," I said, eager to get on with my mission. "I do hope you can help her out."

Jack downed his beer in one neat gulp, wiping the ends of his flowing mustaches in a swift two-way movement, and confidentially lowered his voice.

" 'Ow kin I 'elp aout, young fella? Any frien' av Marji's is a frien' av ol' Jack?—even iffen 'e's a blawdy lawyer feller to boot, no offense meant, partner. Wott'll you 'ave to drink on old Jack? Compliments av the 'aouse."

"Do you have cherry soda?" I ventured, longing instead to order whiskey to show my vast maturity, but fearful of the consequences—after all, there was work to be done.

"Cherry soda?" he repeated, staring and blinking for a moment but rallying swiftly. "Ah, yes, I do. Keep some for the *Mining Journal* boy. 'Ere you are, young fella. 'Ere's mud in your eye."

"I'm really twenty-six," I explained hastily, sipping my soda, not going into the dreary fact that my extremely youthful appearance had long been my secret cross. "I never drink spirits—never, that is, when I'm working on a case."

"Every man to 'is taste," Jack said, "as the Dutchman said w'en 'e put salt in 'is tay." He motioned to a round-topped wooden card table standing in the far corner, with little shelved cubicles underneath to hold the players' drinks. "Le's set daown over yonder an' 'ave our talk, young fella—ol' Jack's legs ain't wot they used to be. This 'ere wos ol' Marji's favorite table," he said, rubbing his hand over the worn top. "Ah, yes," he sighed, looking at me closely. "Naow I hexpect your case 'as somethin' to do with Marji's ol' claim against the Jackson Hore Company, somethin' 'bout that ol' paper them first Jackson fellas guv Marji years ago."

"Yes, Mister—" I began. "Yes, Jack," I went on, "it certainly does. And it's going to be a tough case, that I see already, but I'm going to give it a good try."

"Good boy," Jack said. "Give 'em blawdy blue 'ell, lad.

Rollin' in money, they is, but nary a tuppence dud they 'ave for poor Marji wot shawed it all to um."

Somehow I trusted this man and spoke to him freely about the case, about my doubts as well as my hopes. I explained to him some of the handicaps I had to overcome: that my own client, Marji's daughter, knew very little about her dead father's past or his connection with the Jackson Mine or about the people who might be her witnesses. I told him I had already visited Philo P. Everett in Marquette—one of the original founders of the Jackson Mining Company and the man who had written and given the original paper to Marji—and that I had found a frail old man of failing memory and hearing.

I told him that while Mr. Everett seemed kindly disposed towards my client and the justice of her cause, I was fearful about his failing health and memory and concerned, most of all, whether he would survive until the trial, and be able to testify. I told him about my fears over the possible legal effects of Marji's various marriages, about which I still knew very little, of my apprehensions over the long lapse of time since the paper had first been given him—1845—before any action was being taken on it nearly thirty years later.

"But 'ow cud ol' Marji ever 'ave sued anybody?" Jack indignantly broke in. " 'E wos too much av a man to get after the ol' Jackson crowd w'en they wos daown on their luck, an' w'en finely they lost aout, 'e was far too broke an' unheducated to sue the new outfit w'en they tuck over. Moreover the only lawyer fella in the hull caounty not tied up wan way or tother with these 'ere minin' folks wos an ol' whiskey-drinkin' peg-leg lawyer daown at Marquette—I forget 'is name—an' 'e didn't come to these parts 'till long after poor Marji wos gone. So 'ow in 'ell cud Marji av sued? Wot wud 'e av sued with?"

"That's precisely what I propose to argue, Jack," I said,

somehow greatly buoyed that this uneducated but shrewd Cornish saloonkeeper should penetrate so swiftly to the heart of my case.

We talked along and he gave me the names of a number of potential witnesses I might see: among them McVannel, the livery-stable man, for whom Marji had occasionally worked; Benny Youren, the drayman; and especially old Captain Merry, now retired and a very old man but still "chipper as a chipmunk chasin' hacorns after an 'ail storm." He told me many other things and gave me other possible leads, all of which I gratefully wrote down in my notebook.

Just then I felt and heard a slow series of subterranean tremors, a sullen chain of booming earth thuds. The floor shook and the decanters on the back bar clinked merrily.

"*What's that?*" I asked in alarm, fearful that an earthquake had hit us.

"Oh that," Jack said airily, "that's only the day shift blastin' daown ore for the night shift up at Jackson Mine—'Old Rumbly' us locals calls it. Do it every evenin' 'baout quittin' time." He grinned at me. "First time's always a bit unnervin', Willy."

"Did Marji ever show you this old paper of his that Philo Everett gave him?" I asked when I was able to speak.

"Only wanst, Willy, a long time ago. Let me see naow, it wos right after 'e wos let go by they there new mine folks."

"Did he tell you what it was about?"

"That 'e did," Jack said with conviction. "An' 'ow 'e wos fired an' thrun aout of 'is cabin on yonder mountain an' I tole Marji, I did, I tole 'im 'e ought to go 'ire hisself a lawyer an' sue the bla'guards from 'ere to Ludgate 'Ill."

I put away my notes, thanked Jack, and prepared to leave. Suddenly the front screen door burst open and in piled all the waiting flies accompanied by a throng of freshly scrubbed iron miners just coming off the day shift at the Jackson Mine.

In they stampeded with their shining faces, alone and in twos and threes, shouting, swearing, jostling each other, clomping about in their mine-stained half-tied boots, hastily depositing their gleaming metal dinner buckets under the billiard table, on the weight-lifting machine, the penny scales, on the tall glass-covered music box, alongside the potted ferns in the half-curtained front windows, then shouldering up to the bar, ordering drinks, shouting insults, still mining ore. . . .

While busily fixing drinks Jack still managed to call out their names to me, in a kind of confused mass introduction, and when he paused for breath I had the vague impression that at least half of them began with the common Cornish place-name prefix of *tre*. There were representatives, I recalled, of the Tregembos, the Tregonnings and the Trebilcocks; the Trembaths, Trevarrows and Trelawneys; the Treloars, Tresedders and Trewhellas; the Tregears, Tremethicks and Trewarthas; the Tremberths, Trevellyans and the Trenarys—

"Get a move on thee, Jack, an' stow the hintroductions," someone shouted. "You saound like a train conductor back in ol' country, and you're makin' me bad 'omesick bawlin' all them bloomin' nymes."

"Pour the blawdy drinks an' cut aout the palaver," another shouted, eyes staring, clutching wildly at his throat. "I've jest 'ad ten hours av savage hamusement muckin' dirt up at they there Jackson Recreation Pavilion an' I'd dearly love to supprise me arid gullet with a drink. Do you think the lad 'ere needs to be *tole* we're a bunch av parched Cousin Jacks?"

" 'Old your 'orses, me 'earties!" Jack shouted back. "This 'ere's William Poe, the new lawyer—William, this is the thirstiest bunch av Cornishmen in Hamerican captivity—halso, I do believe, the world's best miners."

" 'Ear, 'ear—lissen to ol' Jack spreadin' the salve, will you? 'E's 'appy as an 'ore lydy on payday—ever'thin' comin' in an' damn little guven aout! . . . Ah, 'ere comes me lavly boilermaker

—daown the 'atch, Jack. . . . Naow 'ow 'baout fixin' 'nother for your ol' mate, 'Arry Penhale?"

I stood watching these men, fascinated by their swift pulsing talk and animal vitality. Cornishmen might also be Englishmen, I reflected, but there was a distinctly different quality in their lack of restraint, in the way they seemed compelled to act everything out. Hadn't I read somewhere that the Romans and Spaniards had long ago invaded Cornwall during their forays into Britain? Had not ancient Phoenician sailors once come in quest of tin from its mines? Had not the land once abounded with mystic Druid priests and still exposed their age-blunted burial stones? Might not all this account for the distinctly un-English dash and flavor of their talk and deportment? Even the act of drinking became a little solo drama: the anticipatory wetting and smacking of lips, the glass lifted reverently as a chalice, the long slow blissful tug—as at some vast celestial teat—the rumblings and gulpings and swallowings that accompanied it, the soulful "ah" which sprang unbidden from the inner man, followed by a calm beatific expression, with lidded half-closed eyes. . . .

Even the idlest bit of conversation was apt to bring on a full-dress drama: eager noddings of the head, shruggings of the shoulders, Gallic wavings of the arms and thrustings of the hands, thumbs suddenly hooked this way or that to indicate someone or something an inch or a thousand miles away; assorted whinnies, leers, grins of triumph and delight, grimaces of sympathy and sudden pain, wistful pauses; tugs at the neck, sudden digs in the listener's ribs. . . . I felt not unlike an uneasy Frédéric Chopin who, once finding himself marooned among the Scottish gentry, later told of "watching them talk and listening to them drink."

In a curiously inoffensive way these men plainly assumed they were squarely at the center of their universe; everything flowed and revolved around and about this pulsing central core. Their frequent detached references to themselves in the third person was all part of it. I found myself envying them their sturdy truce with their world, their fatalistic optimism—or was it optimistic fatalism? I also longed to feel just a fraction as sure of my *own* world.

And endlessly, obsessively they talked about their work: mining ore, burrowing drifts, erecting log cribbing, pushing heavy trams—which they called buggies, or rather "boogies"—crimping dynamite caps, 'ammering drills, setting off massive earth-shaking blasts—all this accompanied by vehement arm-wavings and strident neck-corded shouts. The din was incredible. Through it all a toiling Jack Tregembo beamed benignly as the little bell rang merrily on the wooden cash drawer.

The man they called Matt Eddy suddenly emitted a profound belch, and when the reverberations had died away all of them were eagerly off and away....

"Thar she blaws, mates! Steady the boat, lads, an' man the 'arpoon!"

"Jack must av pumped 'ot air 'stead av beer in me glass," Matt proudly declaimed, elaborately puffing out his cheeks. "Oney blawdy thing besides hinsults an' gab a body ever gets araoun' 'ere fer free."

"Saounds like the afternoon blast at ol' Number Two 'ole," another judiciously commented. "All kinds of ruction but damn little pay dirt."

"Mates," Jack cried out during a lull, "like I wos s'yin', this 'ere's young William Poe, the new lawyer fella daown at Marquette—where all the mining swells lives—a young gent who's fixin' to 'elp Marji Kawbawgam's daughter collect Marji's ol' claim against they there Jackson Company."

At the mention of Marji's name a hush fell over the company; those who spoke seemed delegates at an impromptu memorial service; I had the impression of suddenly being in church rather than in a noisy workingman's saloon.

"There wos no 'arm in Marji," one of them solemnly said. " 'E bothered nary a soul, that 'e didn't."

"Some says Hindians ain't no blawdy good," put in another, "but that Marji 'e wos true blue through an' through."

"For wanst you're right there, Matt Eddy," another said. "Poor ol' Marji wos 'is own worst enemy."

Others delivered their brief homely tributes and Long John Tregembo soberly added the final benediction. "Mates," he said, "effen more of us w'ites was 'alf as good a man as that there Chippeway Hindian Marji, this bloomin' ol' worl' wud be a better place for the hull of us." He raised his glass. "C'mon, partners, toss wan daown the main shaft for good ol' Marji Kawbawgam, may the Lard rest 'is wandrin' soul."

Before I could get away the proprietor had proposed still another toast, this time to "this 'ere William Poe, brave young lion av they legal profession!" and I speculated whether he was moved rather less by the solemnity of the occasion than the chance to stimulate business. Probably both, I concluded, watching the declamatory fervor in his pale blue eyes. I also perceived with a pang that the intemperate consumption of cherry soda would never become a problem in my life. . . .

"Go get um, Willy!" someone shouted.

"Sue they blawdy boogers, Willy," shouted another, "an' make um pay through the nawse."

"Sue an' sue an' make um rue the day they met the likes av you, Willy boy!"

"Jan's a poet, Willy, but 'e daon't knaow it!"

"Willy" they were already calling me, I ruefully perceived. Already my secret was out, my disguise penetrated—was there never to be any escape? Amidst all this jostling and shouting, during which I had uttered scarcely a word, these boisterous men had swiftly perceived that *this* William was a Willy.... Sipping my soda I marveled over the mass intuition by which the Willys of the world are spotted and recognized on sight; suddenly I saw that the essential chemistry of a man often spoke louder than actions or words. It was not a matter of goodness or badness or of strength or weakness, or yet of courage or moral stature or the lack of it, or of timidity or boldness or even impressiveness or modesty of physique. Rather there was a subtle emanation from the psyche, an invisible aura, that one wore always about him like a cloak. It unerringly marked the Willys from the Bills, and from its verdict there was no argument or appeal. I sighed and gulped the rest of my soda. Alas, the Bills were Bills and the Willys were Wills, and never the twain should meet....

"Twist their blawdy tails, Willy, an' give um an hextra turn for we!"

I took my leave amidst their shouted goodbyes and good luck wishes and several hearty thumps on the back. As I walked up Iron Street to get my horse and rig to return to Marquette I found myself strangely moved by what I had just witnessed. Their eulogies of Marji had been trite and sentimental, yet it was plain they had sprung from the hearts of these simple hard-working iron miners. Or were they so simple? They had managed swiftly to penetrate their Willy, hadn't they? And in their tributes to Marji, Lincoln himself could not have been more sober and solemn when he had delivered his Gettysburg Address. These men *cared* about this obscure Indian called Marji Kawbawgam. Could it be, I asked myself, that no man was truly dead while yet one person lived who treasured his memory?

It was one of those glorious Northern evenings I was learning to love, the tall reddish sky shot and aflame with great soaring rays and reflections from the dying sun. The Creation must have been something like this, I thought. As my rented horse plodded along the dusty ore-stained road I reflected about this elusive thing called success and material attainment. Who was ever to say with confidence that the Marjis of this world were failures? By and by I found myself thinking about the complex new legal situation in which I suddenly found myself—my first big case—thinking about it and all of its ramifications, thinking, too, about my new client, the withdrawn and aloof but strangely exciting young Indian woman, Laughing Whitefish.

TWO

Two weeks before on a lovely sunny day in early July I had been sitting in my new office on the third floor of the new brownstone bank building in Marquette. The address of my new quarters was regrettably rather more impressive to read— William Poe, Lawyer, Suite 317, Marquette County Savings Bank Building—than my quarters were to visit. "Suite 317" was an especially fine touch, I thought, my "suite" consisting of a small combination clothes closet and storage room and a single office room not much larger—the latter being divided into two still smaller rooms by a thin and not very soundproof partition for which my landlord had reluctantly shared half the cost. The larger of these contrived cubicles was my private office; the other, nearest the main hallway, served as a combination waiting room for my clients, and overflow library for my law books, and a place for my part-time stenographer, Miss Mugfur, to do her work in when I had any work for her to do. So far she had scarcely been overworked.

The new three-storied bank building was an imposing structure: tall, ponderous, fussily ornate, shrilly expensive, altogether executed in the most exquisite bad taste. No chance for ostentation and show had been overlooked; gracelessness and lack of imagination had been wedded into the structure in a kind of massive monument to mediocrity. It was the latest proud show place of the bustling young community of Marquette.

Little painted tin towers and turrets and onion-shaped domes fought for attention with native stone angels and plaster caryatids and gargoyles and toothy, ill-tempered lions; sudden minarets and wooden pagodas and fortresses of gilded scroll-work vied with oddly irrelevant eruptions in stone. This architectural fantasy was topped off by a gleaming golden dome, resembling nothing so much as a permanently captive balloon. The Marquette County Savings Bank had made good and was sharing its secret with the world.

The ground floor was entirely occupied by the bank; the second floor harbored the offices of the town's leading lawyer, Henry Harwood; the Michigan offices of the Jackson Ore Company; the "Art Gallery"—as he called it—of the town's leading photographer; then a dentist, and, finally—possibly as just retribution for his sins—the new offices of the architect who had designed the bank.

The third floor, where I roosted, was occupied by a curious assortment of tenants: Professor Leslie LeBaron Austin, "Voice Culturist and Professor of Pianoforte", the "Salon" of Ancell Orville Pruitt, the town's least successful photographer; Madame Dujardins, a dark handsome middle-aged woman, who modestly claimed to relieve by various manipulations and massages all manner of female pains and disorders, her special art being, I had vaguely heard, to ameliorate the pangs of the menopause. Farther down the hall dwelt two seldom-encountered male school teachers who simply roomed there; then Dr. Laird, an old physician; some mysterious railroad men who lived elsewhere but who at odd hours slept there during their layovers; and finally one William Poe, the town's newest lawyer, plain "Willy" to all who knew him more than ten minutes.

I had occupied my "suite" long enough to learn that the rental for the tenants—at least those on the third floor—apparently diminished as the tenant more nearly found himself relegated to the rear of the building. My office, Number 317, was the very last, at the extreme back, and from my window I commanded an unobstructed view of the rear of Hodgkins Livery Stable. But I also had a clear view of Iron Bay Harbor and beyond it cold, glittering, ever-changing Lake Superior. With so much time on my hands I was learning its every mood.

The lordly tenants up front, that is those who paid the most rent—golden-voiced Professor Austin and that angel of female mercy, Madame Dujardins—commanded only a narrow view of busy Front Street, with the new Masonic Temple looming boldly across the street—created by the same resourceful architect who had designed the bank. These front tenants were obliged to pay the highest rent, I gathered, because our landlord evidently calculated that any caller who had climbed the tall flights of stairs from the street could not fairly be expected to proceed much farther.

I in turn figured that anyone who had accomplished the initial feat of climbing all the way to my floor was under some compulsion to complete his mission to vindicate the trip; a matter of pride was involved. . . . The truth was I simply couldn't afford to pay any more rent; in fact, there was grave question whether I could continue to pay the rent I was paying.

The *Mining Journal,* the county's only daily newspaper, had welcomed me to town with a flourish. "YOUNG LAWYER CASTS HIS LOT WITH MARQUETTE," the glowing headline said. In my two months in town, to keep up my courage, I had re-read the article so often I had learnt it by heart.

William Poe, lately of Ann Arbor, arrived in town last week and has opened offices for the general practice of law in Suite 317 of the new Marquette County Savings Bank Building. Mr. Poe is a graduate of the law department of the University of Michigan, a member of the war-decimated class of 1865. His father, Professor Edgerton Beasley Poe, has for many years taught at the University and is a well-known authority on Elizabethan literature.

Following his graduation our young lawyer traveled extensively in Europe and upon his return to America saw considerable of our Far West, settling for a spell in Salt Lake City. Returning to Ann Arbor three years ago Mr. Poe became affiliated with a leading law firm of that city, resigning only last year so that he might seek a climate and locality more to his liking. Your correspondent made bold to ask him why he had settled on Marquette, and we think our readers will like the young man's frank reply.

"I decided on Marquette for a number of reasons," he said. "I like your people, I like your climate, I like your unspoilt woods and trout fishing, the romance of your early French and Indian history, and now the exciting unlocking of your vast mineral treasures. Moreover, when I learned that there was but one lawyer in the county not connected with the mining industry, I had an additional reason for coming here—the rather obvious one of making a living. But most of all I love being here. I never felt better in my life."

After considerable probing we elicited from this modest young man the information that he was one of the top honor students of his law graduating class and moreover one of the youngest ever to have graduated from the law department, having just turned eighteen. So it not only appears that we have a new lawyer in our midst, but also a smart one, and we wish Mr. Poe success and good health in his decision to cast his lot among us. Mr. Poe is unmarried and is temporarily residing at the Brunswick House. (*Take Mildon's Little Liver Pills*—Pd. Adv.)

What the generous correspondent of the *Mining Journal* had failed to reveal, largely I suppose because I had not told him, was that I had also left Ann Arbor because my mother had died the year of my graduation and my father had shortly remarried and that, gracious as his new wife was, I had rapidly discovered that my boyhood home had disappeared.

I had suddenly learned with my mother's death that home was an illusion, a wavering mirage that dwelt mostly in the human heart and, like it, could stop in an instant. My wistful boyhood pipedream that security was eternal and love forever abiding had vanished.

With my mother's death I learned in a rush one of the stark and bitter lessons of human existence; with terrible clarity I learned that all the places I would ever see, the books I would ever read, the music I would ever listen to, the people I would ever love—that all would one day disappear leaving nothing behind, nothing at all. If this gave me resignation and humility I hoped it also gave me a kind of daring, a daring to live to the hilt one's little span . . .

I had also not told the friendly newspaperman that one morning in Ann Arbor I had awakened to discover that I hated my work; that as I lay there contemplating this appalling fact I had asked myself some searching questions. Were the only adventures left in life inevitably concerned with the prosaic business of making a living? I could not believe it.

Of late I had thought I detected a massive tedium and joylessness all about me, a shrinking from life, a kind of snuffling mediocrity and relentless acquisitiveness which I for one regarded as an affront to the spirit, almost a physical violation of the person. But if I was depressed by the growing confusion of making a living with any fullness of living, I was appalled by the withering away of the spirit I thought I detected among the people around me: the deliberate stunting of talent, the smothering of latent abilities, the stifling of sleeping capacities, this slow leaking away of life. Willy Poe was lost among his own people and he had to flee to find himself.

Nor had I told him that one of the minor reasons I had come to the Upper Peninsula was that I had developed a passion for the new sport of fly-casting for trout—new in America, that is. For graduation my father had given me one of the exquisite new split bamboo fly rods made by Hiram Leonard of Bangor, and armed with this fairy wand even in the heavily fished waters around Ann Arbor I was growing quite proficient at the sport. The very act of fishing, I was finding, seemed to bring repose and a sense of kinship with nature. And the trout helped me to eat.

Nor had I so much as hinted to the pleasant newspaperman that I, William Poe, lawyer, nourished secret literary ambitions; that I probably read far more of Emerson and Poe and Whitman and Thoreau, of Hawthorne and Melville and the others— including the work of a promising young man called Henry James—than ever I read in my dusty law books; that a large part of my real reason for coming to the Upper Peninsula was my wistful hope that somehow I might gain the experience and time and repose to one day write lucidly and feelingly about something I had deeply lived and felt.

Meanwhile I had written reams of bad poetry and notebooks full of watery essays about Sunset Over Lake Superior and kindred fancies, all of which paper forget-me-nots I had at least possessed the courage to burn in my tiny office fireplace, watching their immortal ashes settle like snow on the roof of Hodgkins Livery Stable across the alley. Lastly, I had not told him, as I scarcely dared even to tell myself, that someday, somewhere, somehow, I hoped to meet a girl I deeply cared for, who for once would not call me Willy. . . .

Finally there was one more thing I had not told Pete Martin. I had not revealed to him that I had "resigned" from the Ann Arbor law firm because I had no other choice: I had been requested to resign; "fired" was the cruder word.

"Willy," kindly old Mr. Hayden the senior partner had told me the afternoon he summoned me to his comfortable, cluttered, book-lined office and gently broke the news, "all of us in the firm are genuinely fond of you, son, but it has become increasingly evident that your heart is not in your work. Nor, may I add, is your excellent mind."

"I know, Mr. Hayden, I know," I said.

He ticked off some of my more glaring recent lapses and shook his head. "All this is highly embarrassing, most embarrassing and expensive. Why, Willy, why? Your old law professors considered you one of their brightest students. What has come over you, son?"

"I don't know, Mr. Hayden," I answered truthfully enough, groping for words. "It seems that I lack any real interest in what I am doing," I continued. "There seems to be no sense of urgency, of accomplishment in my work." I put out my hands. "I cannot understand it, sir. I am as baffled as you."

"Your lack of interest has become all too evident, Willy," Mr. Hayden drily agreed. "Perhaps you are a victim of the old saying current when I was in law school—let me see—the bright students make the professors, the fair ones make the judges, while the poor ones make the money."

"The saying is still current, Mr. Hayden," I commented glumly, "and maybe it's the simple truth. I'm sorry, sir."

"Perhaps you might feel happier practicing by yourself, son," Mr. Hayden went on, "perhaps in some smaller community where you can pick and choose your own clients. In any case I'm afraid the time has come for the law firm of Hayden, Fowler and Hayden and Willy Poe to part ways. This decision was reached only after much discussion and soul-searching. I was an usher years ago at the wedding of my dearest friends, your mother and father. Perhaps in some new connection, in the proper environment, you may find yourself. But not here, son. I'm very sorry."

Mr. Hayden sighed and arose and came around and took my hand. "I have instructed the bookkeeper to pay you the balance of your month's salary in advance. You are therefore free to leave whenever you like." He cleared his throat and gently patted my shoulder. "Good luck to you, Willy—and do try to get hold of yourself. I couldn't feel worse if you were my own son."

"Thank you, Mr. Hayden," I said as I soberly took my leave. "You are most generous and charitable."

Whatever secret relief I may have felt over gaining my freedom, it was a wrench to have to face up to the fact that I had been fired from the first job I had ever held. For days I searched and groped to find the answer to my riddle. What *was* the matter with me? Was it true that I was cut out to be a professor? Or, dark thought, might I not have been meant for the law at all? Day after day I walked the woods and fields or boated the Huron River and pondered my dilemma. Gradually I felt better; at least a few things about myself and my profession were coming into clearer focus.

In a way I had not been entirely candid with old Mr. Hayden. For one thing I had neglected to tell him of my growing suspicion that I might simply have chosen the wrong kind of work—that and my further suspicion that among my fellow lawyers I was far from being alone. These dark doubts, I had since recalled, had even assailed me while I was still in law school. Then why had I kept on with the law? But what was a moderately sensitive and intelligent young man going to do with his life? Especially if he had also to make his way and yet lacked any taste for the prevailing getting and spending, for the new deification of money, for the increasingly commercial aspects of life? By and by I began to suspect the truth. In an age where everyone was expected to engage in some sort of gainful work, hadn't I, like many another young man, drifted into the legal profession simply because I found it the least offensive substitute for what seemed my unattainable true inclinations?

More and more lately I had come to suspect that the law was the great catch-all of the professions. It was the alluring beacon that beckoned those bewildered and uncertain individuals who didn't know precisely what to do. In these days, I reflected, a young man of good family could not choose to become an artist or poet. People would simply laugh at him, and moreover who was there to teach him these arts, where was he to learn these subtle crafts? Where were these young men to go, what were they to do? Almost naturally, it seemed, many of them turned in desperation to the law. More and more I was becoming convinced that the law attracted and harbored more dissatisfied dreamers, yearning malcontents and outright misfits in its ranks than any other trade or profession under the sun.

Part of the reluctant attraction of the law to these rootless wanderers, I sensed, was that not only did it offer a shelter of kinds, but perhaps more than any other calling it more easily allowed its votaries to escape gracefully into business or politics or diplomacy or *somewhere*. . . . Had not the great brooding Abraham Lincoln himself been a prime example of all this? And, to be fair, was not the law, of all the professions, the one that most appeased and comforted its reluctant pilgrims even as it frustrated them? The law, I saw, was the last of the romantic professions.

Whatever doubts I had about my own place in the legal profession, there was one thing on which my mind remained clear: I still nourished a profound respect for the law as an institution. That respect had if anything increased since I had got out of law school. Mr. Bumble had once called the law an ass, true, but for my part it was the myopic Bumble who was the ass for failing to discern that it was not the law that was an ass, but rather some of its practitioners for what they made of the law. Whatever imbecilities they might have foisted on their profession, it was the law—and only the law—that kept society from coming apart at the seams, the world from reverting to a jungle.

No other system than the law had yet been found for governing men than raw violence; it was society's safety valve, the most painless way for men to resolve their differences and achieve some sort of peaceful social catharsis; any other way lay anarchy and chaos. My doubts, then, were not about the worth of my profession; rather what Willy Poe was ever doing in it. It was bad enough for a young man to find himself adrift in a profession he hated; it was far worse to find himself miscast in a profession he revered.

In my doubt and soul-searching the farewell lecture of frail old Dean Lattimore came crowding back to me. "Always remember, young men," he had told our law school graduating class, "that the law is the busy fireman that puts out society's brush fires; that gives people a nonphysical way to discharge their hostile feelings and settle their violent differences; that spells the difference between a barroom brawl and a debate; that substitutes order and predictable ritual for the rule of tooth and claw. Never forget, young people, that the very slowness of the law, its massive impersonality, its neutrality, its calm insistence upon proceeding according to settled procedures and ancient rules, its tendency to adjust and to compromise, its very delays if you will—that all of these act to bank and cool the fires of violence and passion and replace them with order and reason. Ponder well, if you will, that this is a tremendous civilizing accomplishment in itself, whatever the outcome of a particular case. The law not only saves anarchy; it also saves face."

Here he had paused, blinking, and stood lost in thought so long that some of us thought he was ill. I wondered whether he was thinking of his only son whom he had but lately lost in the War. "Never forget," he went on, "that all the lofty Magna Cartas and constitutions and bills of rights in the world are only so much high flown rhetoric if we had not the law to buttress them, to interpret and reinterpret them, to breathe meaning and force and the pulse of life into them."

For a moment his voice had risen to an unaccustomed eloquence, stirred by the fire of his vision, but now it trailed away into a kindly old man's half-rueful, half-wishful meditations. "As you prepare to soar away, my eager fledglings," he said, "clasp to your hearts the wry knowledge that lofty abstractions about liberty and justice do not enforce themselves. These must be reforged in men's hearts every day. Every trial in the land is a small miracle of man's triumph over passion, a celebration of his escape from his ancient bondage to violence." Here his voice had trailed off to a mere whisper. "And so, my brave young eaglets, as you venture out into the heat and the fray of law practice remember above all else that your profession is man's oldest and noblest truce with *himself*. That way should bring greater peace to you. That way might bring greater peace to this old world. And so as I bid you farewell my prayers and hopes go with you, gentlemen."

These and kindred sombre thoughts had assailed me in the uncertain weeks after I had "resigned" from Mr. Hayden's law firm. They still did on my long leisurely lake voyage up to Marquette, and indeed since I had arrived. It was typical of my aimless state of mind that I had not planned even to stop at Marquette, much less settle there. I simply had to go somewhere, I had to get out of Ann Arbor, my funds were limited, so in a moment of mingled euphoria and desperation I had bought an excursion ticket to a romantic-sounding place called Copper Harbor 'way up on Lake Superior.

The weather had been unseasonably warm and we had

made an unplanned stop at Marquette harbor to discharge a sick passenger and replenish our dwindling supply of ice. I was immediately struck by the great natural beauty of the harbor, the bustle and stir of this raw new frontier town pitched picturesquely on a series of steep hills, with a rolling green blanket of forest looming beyond.

Clouds of strident gulls hovered noisily overhead, curving and dipping as though dangled from invisible strings. From the harbor I could make out carriages and drays crawling along the streets, a man pushing a high-wheeled bicycle up a steep hill, while closer, much closer, a householder sat on his back stoop in his undershirt, reading a newspaper and thoughtfully picking his nose. Below us, on the dock, a small boy stood relieving himself intently against a mail bag. Alongside him squatted a wise old hound—muzzle tilted, eyes half-closed, damp nose sniffing—rapturously drinking in the wondrous odors of the waterfront.

Presently two Indian squaws came alongside and sought to sell us their home-made baskets of sweet-grass and deer skin moccasins. In the distance I heard the slow tolling of a church bell and, looking townward, made out a large golden dome glittering in the sun—which only later I discovered was the captive balloon that graced the top of the new bank. Far over the town two kites bobbed and tugged at their restraining strings. I looked for but could not find the small boys to whom they were presumably tethered. I loved this place on sight; I liked its raw frontier quality and air of lusty informal living; its subtle suggestion of unplumbed romance and mystery. I found myself seized by a desire to stop here.

There was a sudden rush of passengers to the water-side rail. I joined them in time to see two stalwart bronzed Indians gliding by in a birchbark canoe, paddling away in graceful unison, their canoe cleaving the water like the blade of a knife, themselves disdainfully ignoring the copper coins some of our passengers flung their way, all the while whooping and clapping their mouths with their hands in taunting Yankee versions of Indian war cries. I hung my head in shame.

Rancor hung in the air like a fog and I sensed with dismay that my shipmates hated Indians—all Indians. It was true that in the past the Indians had practiced unimaginable cruelties on the whites and each other, and further west they still did. But somehow I felt—so far as I had ever seriously thought of it—that they did so largely because the whites had forced them to these desperate straits; they had forced them by coolly usurping their lands and relentlessly pushing them westward into inevitable collision with their own kind.

This blanket indictment of a whole race, this blind mass presumption of guilt, sickened and disheartened me. I felt that the bitter truth was that *we* had converted many of these children of nature into howling savages, and if some of them were ignorant and dirty and thieving and cruelly treacherous, we had made them no less so. And had we forever to appease our guilt for that bitter gift by an unrelenting hostility to a whole people? I could not believe it. Moreover it was contrary to the elementary tenets of any faith I knew of that men worshipped by . . .

I watched my Indians out of sight around a distant point, longing to follow them and apologize. Then I walked resolutely to my cabin and gathered up my things. I had reached a sudden decision: I would go look at this town and if I still liked it I might stay there. I heard a clanging of bells and I rushed out on deck barely in time to make it ashore. There was a series of shrill bleats from my departing boat and, panic stricken, I wheeled as though stabbed. I, Willy Poe, was being left behind! Mingled with my hope was a tantalizing sense of loss. What if I had *not* got off? I would never know . . . I stood staring after my slowly retreating home, suddenly filled with a sense of the enormity of all decisions, however small. I felt a cool thrust at my hand and looked down and the old hound was looking up at me. I could have sworn he smiled. I patted his head and grabbed up my luggage and started off. I felt better already.

But how could I ever have hinted any of this to Pete Martin, the newspaperman who had come to interview me? Indeed, how dared any young lawyer reveal that two disdainful Indians in a passing canoe had precipitated a decision that could change the course of his life? Were we not helpless slaves to chance and irrelevant circumstances? But who was to tell in life what precisely was or was not relevant? Ah, there was the rub ... So I kept my secret. Would sensible citizens ever dare trust their legal affairs to so impulsive a character? And so the newspaperman had come and asked the same safe old questions and I had given him the same safe old answers, each keeping his mask firmly in place. Now I sat waiting for some hardy clients to scale the stairs to Suite 317. I had been waiting for nearly two months ...

Sitting thus on this July day in a kind of reverie, watching the alluring lake, unable even to dream up the opening line of a tantalizing new poem that welled up inside me, half-listening instead to one of Professor Austin's aspiring young maidens singing *The Kerry Dance* remarkably off key, I became conscious of a measured rhythmic tapping coming from far down the long corridor outside my door. Someone was slowly ascending the long wooden staircase. This was the signal for me to start playing my little game. The game was to guess who the brave climber might be or, failing that, to guess instead into whose office he might turn off before he got to mine. That he *would* turn off had become a foregone conclusion.... It was a harmless if idle pastime and I was getting rather good at it. Already that day I predicted the goal of the wavering soprano, a shuffling caller at Doctor

Laird's, missing only on a substitute postman whose bold step I had not yet had time to learn.

Tap, tap, tap came the measured heavy tread up the creaking stairs. The tapping had ceased, the climber had gained the top, and I could picture him leaning against the head of the stairs, panting and exhausted, mopping his brow, clutched by fatigue and indecision, wondering whether the game had been worth the candle. Ah, the mysterious visitor had now resolutely started down the hall, tap-tapping on his way. Already poor Professor Austin and Madame Dujardins were out of the running. Now it simply had to be the doctor. But no, the steady tapping was now *this* side of his precincts—good heavens, could one of my anonymous railroaders have lost a leg!

There was a pause and a shuffling outside my office door and then it opened and there stood an unshaven and rather seedy-looking man wearing a wooden leg. The source of the tapping now stood revealed . . . Beside him stood the most striking young woman I had ever seen. I stared at her and blinked and then stared again.

"Come in," I said when I could arise and speak.

THREE

Her hair was long and intensely dark—giving off a sort of blue-black lustre—and was parted precisely in the middle, with two thick braids hanging down the front and over each shoulder, reaching nearly to her waist. Her dark eyebrows were shaped like the wings of a gull and gave her expression an inquiring and faintly surprised look. Her eyes were dark and smouldering, and these, along with her startling dark hair, made her face almost unnaturally pale. Her high cheekbones combined with strong features softened by womanhood, made me think at first she might be Spanish.

Except for her long dark braids and two narrow beaded bands she wore, one about her forehead and the other about her throat, she was dressed much like any other young American woman. That she was strikingly beautiful was evident at a glance, but she was more than that; hers was the rarer kind of beauty that radiated character and fire and intelligence. There was a grace and lissomeness in her bearing, a kind of relaxed poise and ease, coupled with a grave almost disquieting composure that—

"When you get through inventoryin' your new client, young man," her escort broke in drily, shattering the spell, "we might get on with the business at hand."

"I'm sorry, sir," I apologized, wrenching my eyes away

from this exciting young woman. "Please be seated—here, I'll take those books off your chair, Miss—"

"Kawbawgam," she said coolly, taking the seat I hurriedly cleared for her. "Charlotte Kawbawgam. Thank you, Mr. Poe, I'm quite comfortable."

"And my name is Cassius Wendell, young man," her companion said. "People call me Cash and wisely withhold the credit." He laughed heartily at his little sally and sat down heavily, thrusting his artificial leg straight out before him, holding on his lap a stuffed and bulging old leather briefcase. He was dressed in heavy black broadcloth, mostly in the pre-war mode, and his linen was untidy and he needed a shave; yet there hovered about the man an air of seedy gentility, a sort of raffish respectability, as though he were a poet masquerading as clown.

"Well," I said, rather inanely, looking from one to the other, and there was a moment's awkward silence and then he and I laughed hilariously, as though I had just told a funny joke. Charlotte Kawbawgam stared straight ahead and cracked not a smile.

"Ah me, oh my," Cassius Wendell chortled, sighing and wiping his eyes with a soiled handkerchief, finally regaining his composure. "I always say an occasional rousing laugh is good for the inner man"—here he paused and lowered his voice, half-looking around, as though he suspected eavesdroppers were lurking out in the hallway—"but what we're here to see you about is far from any laughing matter."

"Yes?" I gently prompted him, amused by his theatrical air of intrigue.

He sat studying me with his drooping pirate's eye. "How old are you, young man?" he suddenly demanded.

"Twenty-six."

In measured accents: "Do you *shave*?"

"Of course, sir," I blurted. "At least twice a week." I

glanced appealingly at Laughing Whitefish who regarded me unblinkingly.

"Hm," he said dubiously. "Laughing Whitefish here—Charlotte Kawbawgam is her American name—is the surviving daughter and only child of Marji Kawbawgam, a Chippewa Indian who died in 1859 leaving a possible interest in a valuable iron mine in this county. Charlotte's mother died shortly after she was born," he went on to explain, "and her father left no will. So far as can be determined, Miss Charlotte here is his heir at law—at least this is the premise I believe one must proceed on, else I'm afraid she had no case."

"Was his estate ever probated?" I ventured, the legal gears already creaking. "And wouldn't that be conclusive evidence of her—"

"No it wasn't probated," he snapped, glaring me into silence. "And please stop talking while I'm interrupting. Old Cash presently has the floor and he'll cover all that in good time. For the present all you've got to do is compose yourself and listen—the question period will come later."

"Yes, sir," I said meekly, again glancing at Laughing Whitefish, who sat intense and frowning.

Cassius Wendell went on to tell me, in his own good time, the story of her father Marji Kawbawgam: of how Marji had been working with the survey crew of William Burt when in 1844 the first iron ore was discovered near the site of what later became the village and then city of Negaunee; how the next year he showed this rich iron ore deposit to the white men from Jackson, including Philo Everett, who promised to reward him for his services; of the disastrous early efforts at mining by the original partners from Jackson; of their insolvency and failure and of the eventual taking over of the property by shrewd Eastern capitalists under the new corporate name of Jackson Ore Company; of the sensational success of the mine under the new

ownership following the building of the railroad and the opening of the Sault canal; of their failure to keep the old promise
made to Marji Kawbawgam and his discharge from his mine job
and his subsequent aimless drifting; and of Marji's ultimate dramatic death on the steep hill overlooking the mine property.

"So you see, young fella, we whites are still keeping up the
fine old tradition," he concluded. "As Rufus Choate so aptly put
it, 'When the white man came to America he first landed on his
knees and then on the aborigines.' Seems we're still at it."

I sat listening intently to this grizzled and fearsome individual, Cassius Wendell, horrified by the injustice of the tale he was
unfolding. Before I could ask a question he looked curiously
around my quarters and calmly passed judgment on what he
saw. "Dismal place as ever, I see," he said. "Squatted in these
very rooms for a spell the year this building was finished," he
explained. "Trust the spendthrift landlord has had a change of
heart."

"How do you mean, sir?" I said.

"About redecorating and things."

"How is he about that, sir?"

He waved his hand. "Prodigal, son, prodigal." Pointing
over my fireplace: "His idea of redecorating is to give you a
brand new calendar once a year to cover that spot on the wall."

"The bank redecorated some when I moved in," I said.
"That sooty spot is from my fireplace—sometimes the smoke
goes the wrong way."

He pointed out the window at the rear of Hodgkins'
Livery Stable. "Tell me," he inquired, "when the wind is favorable does the scent of trailing arbutus still waft in here from
yonder riding seminary?" He did not wait for an answer.

"Reminds me—time out for general asphyxia," he announced, rummaging in his pocket and filling a battered briar
pipe with a shredded evil-looking workingman's tobacco, which

he ignited—lit was scarcely the word—and then sat back, lost in thought, sending out great billowing clouds of smoke. I glanced in supplication at Laughing Whitefish and she motioned for me to raise the window, a mission I accomplished without arousing the ire of this unpredictable one-legged lion.

"Now getting back to this here case, we now come to the difficult and delicate part," he continued, going on to tell me about the first marriage of Marji Kawbawgam to Blue Heron; of his subsequent marriage to the mother of Laughing Whitefish, Sayee, while his first wife was still living; and, to my growing astonishment, of the possibility that there might even have been a third marriage. He also told me that Blue Heron, the first wife, had been childless; that Sayee, after also losing two children at birth, had died in 1852 shortly after giving birth to Laughing Whitefish, her only surviving child; how Blue Heron, the first wife, had devoted herself to raising the motherless girl; and of how Laughing Whitefish had gained her education in the Indian mission school at L'Anse and now herself taught in the new mission school at the Indian encampment on Presque Isle, just north of Marquette.

He then pointed out some of the perplexities of the case: whether Marji's claim, if one ever existed, might not now be barred by the long passage of time; whether it was better to file suit on the law or equity side of the court; whether one should start suit first and then talk settlement or whether it was better to talk settlement first and sue later; whether the legal pleadings should disclose Marji's first marriage or that be left for the defense possibly to raise; whether Marji's estate should not now be probated, to clarify and remove any question of Laughing Whitefish's status as heir, or whether. . . .

As he talked on I discerned that, for all his bizarre appearance, here was an excellent lawyer and one equipped with a shrewd and subtle mind. My only perplexity was why he was here discussing the case with me at all, the clientless and beardless Willy Poe.

"So you see, young man," he soberly pressed on, "there are many questions in the case, and two of them are particularly grave: one, whether the claim is enforceable at all and, two, whether in any case this Indian girl is in any position to enforce it. Are you following me, son?"

"I think so, sir," I said, my mind already in a whirl over this tangled legal situation.

"Put bluntly," he went on, "assuming the basic question of liability to *someone* there is the tantalizing question of whether that someone can ever be she. Put more bluntly there is the question of whether Laughing Whitefish is a lawful heir. Put even more bluntly there is the delicate question of whether, under our law, Laughing Whitefish might not be branded illegitimate and therefore without legal standing in our courts to enforce her father's claim. Are there any questions?"

"Yes, sir," I said, scarcely knowing where to begin. "Mightn't any possible question of lawful heirship be obviated," I plunged ahead, "if suit were brought by the first wife, Blue Heron?"

"It might indeed," Cassius Wendell commented dryly, "if it weren't for the regrettable fact that the poor woman passed away three years ago leaving neither chick nor child—at least of her own blood."

"I'm sorry, sir,—I didn't know," I said, glancing quickly at Laughing Whitefish, who sat gravely listening to our mystifying exchange. "Could not the first wife Blue Heron have made an assignment or, better yet, a will leaving her property—or at least this claim—to Laughing Whitefish?"

"She probably could have, Willy, but again the fact is she did not. I was not yet in the case when she died or I most certainly would have suggested some such course. But from what

Laughing Whitefish tells me about her step-mother, if I may for convenience call her that, she always took a decidedly dim view of Marji Kawbawgam ever having anything to do with the Jackson Mine, seems some old Indian superstition was involved. So all that is out of the case, Willy boy, water over the dam, as we lawyers love to say. But try again, son, you're doing fine—at least thinking and talking like a lawyer. The old law school at Ann Arbor still seems to be holding up, I see."

"Thank you, sir," I said, stealing a look at Laughing Whitefish, who sat staring broodingly out the window while we conducted this cold legalistic discussion about the kind-hearted woman who had raised her, the only mother she had ever known.

"Might not Laughing Whitefish," I went on, "be regarded as the adopted daughter of Blue Heron, so that she might sue as her adoptive mother's sole lawful heir even if she were a total stranger to her father?"

Cassius Wendell pursed his lips and stared up at my ceiling, stroking his bristly chin, reflectively blinking his faded blue eyes. "Very good, son," he said slowly, "that's one approach even I did not come up with—at least precisely in that form. Hm. . . . Very interesting. Now I don't say the possibility should be dismissed—it may ultimately be the salvation of the case—but from what I've learned from Laughing Whitefish no adoption was ever made—at least in any formal sense. There is also the further question whether the Indians ever practiced adoption, and whether our courts would recognize an Indian adoption if they had. Then there is the difficulty of proof after all these years. The one person who could surely know is dead—Blue Heron—and Laughing Whitefish was of course a small child when any adoption took place, if one ever took place." He sighed. "So adoption might be too slender a thread upon which to hang the case. But don't put it out of mind, Willy, and I grant you high marks for thinking of it. Any more questions?"

"Divorce," I said, trying not to wince too openly over his so unerringly calling me Willy. "If Marji Kawbawgam and his first wife, Blue Heron, were divorced then Sayee was clearly his lawful wife in any view of the case and the legitimacy and sole heirship of Laughing Whitefish could not then be questioned."

"It is the cleanest theory of all," Cassius Wendell agreed, "and reluctantly I keep coming back to it. I say reluctantly because again there is the difficulty of proof—both principals being dead and there being no records. And again there is the knotty question of whether the Indians ever practiced divorce, and whether our courts would recognize one if they had. But it still deserves the closest scrutiny. You're coming nicely, son. Will you enter the case?"

I turned and stared out the window at the calm glittering lake. I then looked at Laughing Whitefish, who regarded me intensely with dark questioning eyes. How could I help this strange withdrawn girl? I turned to Cassius Wendell. "There is much that I still do not know about this case, sir," I said, "and even more that I do not know about Indian tribal customs, but I think that somehow, some way—I am not yet prepared to say—this young woman should prevail." I paused and took a deep breath. "I'd be happy to enter the case."

"Fine, fine. Now how about the defense of polygamy?" Cassius Wendell suddenly shot at me, looking at me accusingly.

"How do you mean, sir?"

"I mean simply this, young man: suppose that when suit is started by Laughing Whitefish against the Jackson Ore Company they come charging into court piously claiming and prepared to prove that the plaintiff, this girl Laughing Whitefish, has no standing in court because she is the illegitimate child of a bigamous marriage? What then, Willy boy?"

"I don't know, sir," I answered truthfully. "This has all been so sudden—I've scarcely had time to think."

"Well you'd better start thinkin', son, because this case has landed squarely in your lap. Certainly you are aware that if there was no divorce and there was no legal adoption that the defense of polygamy and illegitimacy will be plump in the middle of your case. Any more questions?"

"Yes, Mr. Wendell, there are," I said. "You have just told me much about this strange affair. Obviously you have a broad knowledge of the case and its background. What I am curious about is why you now want to have a young unknown lawyer like myself associated with you?"

"Who said anything about your being associated with *me* in the case?" he stormed back indignantly. "Don't go jumping at rash conclusions, young man, it's flighty and unlawyerlike. I'm withdrawing from the case, getting out, *vamoosing*, turning the case over to you lock, stock and barrel. From now on the case is all yours, son, do you understand?"

"I understand, sir, but I still don't understand why you are withdrawing. Perhaps it's none of my business." I turned to Laughing Whitefish for help. "Is it really your wish that Mr. Wendell turn over your case to me and that I should be your lawyer?"

She stared for a long moment at Cassius Wendell, who sat looking stonily ahead. Then she turned her intense dark eyes upon me and I felt as if my very soul was being probed. Mingled suspicion and distrust and hope flitted across her face like passing shadows. I squirmed inwardly under her grave steady gaze. "Yes," she said, almost harshly, "it is my wish that you take my case."

"Thank you," I said, feeling almost reprieved.

"I am only a teacher in a poor Indian missionary school," she continued. "Any pay you will ever get from the case must come from winning it." Her face darkened. "Do you still want to be my lawyer?" It was more of a challenge than a question.

"Yes," I said, commanding myself to look her full in the eyes.

Her face softened almost into a smile. "I am only here because I hope if I win to help my school and my people. For myself I do not care."

"I think I understand," I said.

Cassius Wendell had risen and he now placed his bulging briefcase on my desk with a thump. "Here are a few notes and odds and ends I have gathered on the case," he said gruffly. He consulted his silver watch. "Must get back to the office," he said. "Duty calls and all that. Return the briefcase at your leisure." He turned to Laughing Whitefish and bowed. "Good luck to you, young lady," he said. "And good luck to you, son," he said, "for I'm certain you'll need it." Then with great dignity he limped and tapped his way out of my office and down the echoing hall. Laughing Whitefish and I were left alone. We listened in silence until the tapping died away.

"Well," I said, but this time neither of us laughed. "Why is Mr. Wendell leaving the case? Did you ask him to? I think I should know."

She regarded me gravely. "No, he wanted to leave."

"Why?"

"I don't know."

"Try and guess—it might help your case for me to know." She glanced at me quickly as though I was joking. I looked at her steadily. "Please try," I repeated.

"Well, there's lots of work still to be done on the case, I guess, and there is his leg—it's hard for him to get around."

"I thought of that. Anything else?"

"Perhaps he didn't want to risk all that time and work for so doubtful a chance of return."

"I doubt that—he doesn't strike me as one who frets about his fee."

She gave me a stony smile. "Aren't all you whites forever after the almighty dollar?"

This girl was deeply embittered and hurt, I saw, and I

weighed my next words. "Do you honestly think all whites are alike?"

"Aren't you?"

"Do you think all Indians are alike?"

Quickly: "No, of course not."

I smiled. "Then maybe you have your answer. When did he first get in the case?"

"Nearly two years ago—shortly after my mother, I mean after Blue Heron died."

"And he hadn't filed suit yet?"

She seemed to be relaxing a little. "No, it seemed he could never quite make up his mind. It seemed as though more than his leg was missing."

"His spirit?"

"Perhaps."

"Anything else?"

"I don't understand."

"Any other reason you can think of why he left the case?"

"Well," she began, and then hesitated. "I don't like to gossip."

"Neither do I but it could be important. Was it his drinking?" She regarded me with troubled eyes. "Was it?" I persisted.

"Yes."

"How do you know?"

She was talking more easily. "Often I went to his office and would find it locked and a sign on his door that he was gone. Yet I could plainly hear him snoring. It happened many times." She shrugged. "So what was I to think?"

"You have also heard of his drinking from others, I suppose, as I have?"

"Yes. I am afraid he has the same affliction my father had."

"Tell me about your father."

There wasn't much to tell. She had seen him but a few

times and barely remembered him. She told me of the last time she had seen him alive, only days before he was killed, when he had given her the paper that years before the white men had given him. "My people believe he was killed because he took part in desecrating the Haunted Mountain, the home of the gods of thunder and lightning."

"You mean the iron mine over at Negaunee he showed the white men?"

"Yes."

"Do you really believe that killed him?"

She half smiled. "I am Indian, you know."

I smiled. "I'm sorry—I keep forgetting all Indians are alike."

She arose, a flicker of smile crossing her face. "I want you to help me help my people."

"I'll do my best," I said, rising.

"And however long and arduous my case, you must enlist for the duration."

"I'm in till the bitter end," I said, putting out my hand.

"Thank you," she said, briefly taking my hand, and then she left. I sat for a long time lost in thought.

FOUR

During the next few weeks I worked virtually day and night on my new case, delving into yellowed and musty old law books, reading history, prowling the broad Peninsula interviewing witnesses, simply lying awake half the night brooding over the case. Getting it seemed also to be the signal for a turn in my fortunes; people at last became aware that a new lawyer was in town. Old Conkling, the music store man, turned over to me a ledger-full of ancient accounts for unpaid-for pianos he had sold years before.

The old gentleman didn't undertake to scale all the stairs to my office; instead he met me one day on the street and shooed me into his store and handed me the ledger of bad accounts. "Take anything you can get," he said. Since by some accident of good fortune he had sold all his pianos on a title-retaining contract, I was able to settle many of these stale accounts for fifty cents on the dollar. This I did mostly by a frank appeal to sentiment, pointing out to the laggard purchaser that it would be a pity to lose such a venerable out-of-tune relic. I delivered suave little lectures on proper ancestral respect: "Where," I would quaver, "where if you lost your piano would you put all the family knick-knacks, stereopticon views, sea shells and pictures of your loved ones?"

I had seen Laughing Whitefish only once since the first

time, again in my office. She wanted to discuss my fee but I put her off, pointing out that if we lost I would get no fee anyway, and if we won we would face that pleasant chore when the time came. My unconcern seemed to baffle her, but at the same time I felt she was becoming slightly more relaxed with me.

Little by little I drew from her the story of her girlhood: going to school in winter; helping with maple-sugaring in the spring; berrying in the summer; occasionally traveling westward to harvest wild rice in the fall; the usual things, I suppose, of a young Indian girl's childhood. She gave me the names of some of the Indians she had been raised with at L'Anse Bay and also friends of her foster mother, Blue Heron. She told me about Cosima, one of Blue Heron's oldest friends, and about old Osseo, who had known her father since his boyhood and who had been present the last time she had seen her father alive—shortly before his death when he had given her the fateful piece of paper, when Blue Heron was still alive.

"On that occasion old Osseo predicted my father's death," she said simply.

"But how could he?" I said.

"I can't tell you how he did it, but I was there and heard— and so it happened."

"You really believe this?"

"I am Indian," she said.

"Where is this Cosima and old Osseo?"

"They were at the Indian encampment at L'Anse Bay. I've heard since that Cosima may have moved away. Osseo may now be dead—he was very old."

"Then I must go at once to L'Anse Bay," I said.

She got one of her bright pupils, a teen-age boy called Mukwa, to accompany me to the Indian encampment on L'Anse Bay to act as interpreter. Ignoring my piano accounts we shortly set off on our mission. On the way the boy Mukwa, under my questioning, blushingly confessed that his name meant "the bear."

L'Anse Bay. The name beguiled me because, according to my shaky French, this was tantamount to calling the place the Bay Bay, a common enough redundancy, I was learning, in the headlong proliferation of American place names, a land where village storekeepers were more apt to bestow these casual christenings than linguists or scholars.

Here I met Iagoo—"his name means 'the boaster,'" Mukwa confided to me—the local Indian chief, a sly old party who seemed bent on molding custom to what he thought I wanted to hear—after being first adequately primed by gifts of twist tobacco. When I first raised the question of Indian divorce he replied with conviction that he knew all about it, that there was no such thing, and then, seeing my pained expression, quickly allowed for an occasional divorce. So I remained at sea.

Next I inquired closely for the Indian woman Cosima, old friend of the foster mother of Laughing Whitefish, Blue Heron, and in vague terms was variously informed that after Blue Heron's death she had moved to Minnesota or perhaps to Madeline Island in Lake Superior off northern Wisconsin or had probably died. No one had heard from or about her. On the verge of despair for the success of my trip I then met old Osseo. He looked skyward as he heard us approaching.

"The old man is blind!" the boy Mukwa told me in an awed whisper, clutching my arm.

He was sitting on a blanket in front of his wigwam, bare to the waist, blinking his sightless glaucous eyes up at the bright sun. There was a bird-like alertness about him, and yet he was incredibly old, seamed and weathered, as smoked and tanned with age as an unwrapped mummy, his large skinny frame and slack folds of skin showing that he had once been a powerful man.

The crafty Iagoo, his cheeks marvellously pouched with tobacco, mumbled an incoherent introduction and mercifully glided away, leaving the three of us alone: the old man, the boy and myself. I told him who we were and why we were there and we talked for many hours. When we were done I knew I had found a prime witness for our case. Moreover he volunteered to come to Marquette and testify if he was needed. I assured him he would be needed.

Yes, he had known Marji Kawbawgam ever since Marji was a boy, he told me through our young interpreter; he had helped Marji build his first canoe and taught him how to track animals and set snares . . . Yes, he had known Marji's first wife, Blue Heron, and had attended their wedding and had recounted old Indian legends for the assembled guests . . . He had also attended the wedding of Marji to Sayee, mother of Laughing Whitefish, and had again told stories of olden times; with advancing years it had become his accepted tribal role. He recalled that their young daughter possessed the beauty and grace of a running fawn. "That was before the light went out of my eyes," he gravely explained. I assured him she was still beautiful.

"How old are you?" I next asked him, but he didn't know; the Indians didn't keep track of time as the white man did; he guessed it must be well over a hundred summers because he had been told by learned white men that he plainly remembered events that had occurred and people who were known to have died—Indians, missionaries, white trappers, explorers—long before the turn of the century.

It gave me an eerie feeling, sitting there in the sun calmly talking with a man who had prowled these woods and waters before the Republic had been born, quite probably before the Revolution. I stared at this frail link with the past, this ancient man in whom a great spring had been installed and coiled tightly for a long run.

Indian divorce and polygamy? Yes, the Chippewa Indians practiced both—at least they had in his day—and he himself had once had three wives, forsaking one, I was charmed to learn, only when she stupidly scorched his favorite snowshoes near an open fire.

"Were Marji and his first wife Blue Heron divorced?" I asked.

The old man pondered for a spell before he spoke. "That I cannot say. I cannot say because I do not know," he finally said. "From some I heard that they were still man and wife, from others that they were not." His staring empty eyes seemed slyly to seek me out as he added: "I long ago learned not to pry between man and wife. What went on between them during Marji's infrequent visits I would not make a guess."

"Would it make any difference?" I persisted.

"It would," he answered with granite finality.

"At least he did not live with this woman and provide for her as other Indians did for their wives."

"No."

But he told me many other things I had not known and needed for my case and I made notes furiously. Had he ever seen the paper the white men had given Marji before he guided them to the site of the first iron ore discovery? Yes, he had not only seen it many times but had been present when the white men had given it to Marji. He had also seen Marji, shortly before he died, when he had turned the paper over to his daughter Laughing Whitefish up at L'Anse Bay.

"Was that when you told Marji he would die?"

"Yes, I warned him that if he did not forsake the haunted mountain, ancient home of the gods of thunder and lightning that had become the site of the iron mine, and return to his family and his own people he would shortly perish, that the violated mountain would surely kill him. He went back and inside of a week he was dead." He blinked his wet eyes and seemed lost in thought. "Soon old Osseo will join him," he added.

"How can you tell these things?" I asked boldly.

There was a pause, after much Indian conversation. Then: "The old man says he cannot hear such prying questions," the boy Mukwa said.

"But you *will* come to Marquette to be witness for Laughing Whitefish?" I said to hide my shame and confusion.

"As I already promised, insistent one, I will if I am still alive."

The sun was sinking behind the trees and the old man hunched his bony shoulders and plucked his blanket up around his frail body. I saw he was tiring of this long inquisition and we arose to take our leave. There remained one question I was burning to ask him. I turned back.

"Will Laughing Whitefish win her case?" I asked.

The boy Mukwa put the question to the old man. Osseo shook his head with weary annoyance. "I cannot tell. Why do people eternally ask questions about money and gain? With patience one occasionally gains some knowledge of these passing things. Perhaps I will know when next I see you—if ever again I should see you."

A breeze had risen and the leaf-shadowed sun made moving dapples on his lined face and withered body. I noticed how tautly the whorled skin was drawn across his narrow chest, like that of a wet drumhead dried too rapidly in the sun. His eyes were still watering and he rubbed them clumsily with his knuckles, simultaneously, like a sleepy child. His face cracked into a ghost of a smile. He said something in Indian to Mukwa and I saw that my young interpreter was deeply moved; sudden tears welled in his eyes.

"What did he say?" I asked the boy Mukwa.

The boy spoke in an awed voice. "He said, 'Is it not curious that eyes that are too old to see are not yet too old to weep?' "

I stared at the gallant old man and swallowed hard before speaking. "Tell him," I said softly, "tell him it is most curious —and also very sad." If old age was merely a stubborn postponement of oblivion, as a cynical Cash had recently told me, then the old man was putting up a brave fight.

We left old Osseo sitting on his blanket—secret, resigned, cowled by age—his head cocked sideways as though listening, still and unblinking as an old perched bird.

My young interpreter and I said our thanks and goodbyes and hiked back to the village of L'Anse and barely caught the late afternooon local train back to Marquette. Hours later I hired a buckboard to drive the dozing Mukwa—by then a mighty sleepy bear cub—out to his home on Presque Isle. There was a light still burning in the cabin of Laughing Whitefish; she had waited up for us. We led the somnambulistic Mukwa up to his parents' wigwam and later I glowingly told her of my long and encouraging session with old Osseo and how he had agreed to come and testify for her.

"He was a veritable mine of information," I ran on. Restrainedly encouraged by this good news, she insisted on walking me out to my tethered horse, where we lingered and talked of many things.

"Goodnight, William," she finally said, and before I knew it her cool lips had lightly brushed my cheek; it was far past midnight when I collapsed on my lonely cot where, dead tired, I lay for many hours in a kind of waking reverie about my case and my unpredictable client.

Our encouragement was short lived: three days later word came from L'Anse Bay that the lifeless body of old Osseo had been found slumped in the sun on his blanket in front of his wigwam; the great coiled spring had at last run down. A saddened Laughing Whitefish left for the burial and I remained behind to ponder how we might survive this harsh blow to our case. Though we might have Justice on our side, had we also Time? I worked even more furiously on the case, resolved now to file suit as soon as possible.

FIVE

I sought out the crusty Cassius Wendell for comfort and counsel; that and to return his briefcase and thank him for the great help it contained. I had not seen him in many days. A sign on his office door read simply "Gone Fishing," which I knew was a lie because he hated the sport—I'd already tried to lure him out trout fishing with me. "A pasttime fit only for children and dolts," he had snorted. "Moreover, since I loathe both eating and catching fish, I'd be unlucky enough to land a whale."

Should I leave the briefcase outside his door? I stood staring at it. Then from within I heard a prolonged reverberant snore. I softly tried the doorknob and lo, it yielded. An unshaven Cassius Wendell lay sleeping on a narrow leather sofa in a corner. He was clad in his underwear, was without his wooden leg, and scattered about him on the floor lay several empty bottles. The place smelled like Jack Tregembo's saloon; the old boy had been "on one."

I guiltily looked around. His bookshelves were empty save for a few old textbooks, among them a Tiffany on pleading, a Greenleaf on evidence and a battered old Leake on real property —that and a few others was about all. Of the bound state reports I saw none, which for a lawyer was akin to a carpenter plying his trade without hammer or saw. I marveled how the man had ever prepared the elaborate forms of pleadings and briefs he'd left with me from such a meager library; I'd leaned on them heavily in drafting my own bill of complaint.

The room was stifling and a swarm of flies buzzed crazily —or was it drunkenly?—at the inside of the closed window. I tiptoed over and tried to raise it. The window resisted. I tried harder. The window creaked and groaned and then suddenly shot to the top with a great clatter. Horrified, I let it go. It slammed back shut with even more din, bits of dried putty flying in all directions.

"That's a droll way for a rising young lawyer to enter a man's office," a voice said. I wheeled around. Cassius Wendell lay blinking up at me, wryly tasting his lips, yawning prodigiously, attempting vainly to scratch his back.

"I just returned your briefcase," I explained, again raising the window and awkwardly holding it. "Wanted to thank you for all your help. Was so hot in here was afraid you'd suffocate. Sorry, but the door was unlocked and—"

"No apologies, Willy. And don't stand there like a surprised felon—put a book under the window if you want it to stay open. Ah, that's fine, son. . . . Now sit down and rest yourself while I gather my wits—if any are left. Wait—before you compose yourself please get old Cash a drink of water out of the corner tap. Make it a big one and let it run cold. I swear old Sloat runs the pipe through his kitchen stove." Sloat, the harness maker, was his landlord, who occupied the ground floor.

With shaking hands Cash avidly drank his water and called for more, which he drank more slowly, now sitting half propped up on his sofa, surveying me out of furtive eyes as doleful and redrimmed as an old hound's. "Ah, there lad, I now think maybe I'll live. They say there's still hope for a man who craves only water after his bouts. Ah, me. . . . Well, Willy, at last my secret is out. How goes your big case?"

"I'm about ready to file suit," I said. "I wanted to see you and thank you for all the help you gave me." I couldn't resist stealing a glance at his empty bookshelves. "You did a really remarkable job of legal analysis, Mr. Wendell."

"Don't Mr. Wendell me, Willy. In my state I'm really not up to it. Call me Cash. If drunkards and sailors and barflies can call me Cash certainly one of my professional colleagues can. And thanks for the pretty compliment. You should run for public office." He glanced at his empty shelves and smiled. "To relieve your mind I didn't conjure my briefs out of my head. With a nice sense of irony I used the law library of Mr. Henry Harwood, over in your building. He's chief local counsel for the Jackson Ore Company, you know. He kindly allows me the run of his library and even showed me where he hides the key. I'm sure he'd have been charmed if he suspected what I was up to." He gestured at his own gaping bookshelves. "Drank 'em up four-five years ago." He grinned. "And if you ever see old Cash hobbling around on crutches you'll know he's pawned his wooden leg. Are you suing in law or equity?"

"I've decided to sue on the equity side of the court, Mr. Wen—Cash," I said.

"Why?"

"Well, for one reason, with the long passage of time in this case, I'd rather risk the more pliant defense of laches in equity than the more rigorous statutes of limitations that might apply on the law side."

"Hm.... But that way you lose the advantage of twelve good men and true—a good old sentimental jury, Willy. And you've got a mighty beautiful client—but a wildcat, I warn you, when aroused."

"I know, Cash, and I'd dearly love to have a jury pass on this case. But my biggest fear is I might never get to a jury if I took that gamble."

"What's your theory of recovery?"

"That my client, Laughing Whitefish, is the sole heir at law of her father, Marji Kawbawgam, and that she has brought suit as soon as she reached twenty-one."

"Are you claiming that the paper they gave Marji is an interest in the mine itself—an interest in land, in other words?"

"No, I'm filing my bill of complaint more in the nature of a bill for an accounting than anything else—that the original Jackson Mine people promised Marji Kawbawgam a certain percentage of the fruits of the property, which neither they nor the successor company have ever paid or accounted for."

"How you going to get around the fact that Marji got this paper fourteen years before his death and never filed suit or did a thing to enforce his claim?"

"By showing that the original mine operators were in increasingly dire straits until they sold out to the new owners and that Marji should not be penalized for his charity and forebearance in helping save the property; that Marji himself was an uneducated Indian who could not read and only barely spoke English; and further that up to the time of his death there was not a single lawyer in the county who was not connected with one or the other of the mining companies. Moreover I don't quite concede that nothing was ever done."

"How do you mean, Willy?"

"I mean, Cash, that with luck I can show that as late as the year of his death Marji made an effort to collect something from the new company."

"You *can?* Where did you ever dig up that morsel, boy?"

"From old Captain Merry, now retired, who was present when Superintendent Ira Beadle of the new Jackson Mine offered Marji thirty dollars for his paper."

"Good boy, you've been a busy lad since last I saw you. But why do you say that 'with luck' you hope to show this?"

"Because Captain Merry is now a very old man in failing

health and he may not survive until this case is heard." I then told him about my recent fruitful visit with old Osseo and of his sudden death. "Cash, I'm afraid this case will drive *me* to drink before it's done—it seems that all our best witnesses are either dead, fled or tottering on the brink of the grave. Ready or not, I've simply *got* to file suit. Last week I visited Philo Everett again and he, poor soul, acted as though he'd never heard of the Jackson Mine."

Cassius Wendell moistened his lips and glanced wistfully at the empty bottles lying around his sofa. "Can I go get you anything, Cash?" I boldly ventured. "It's the least I can do for all the help you've given me."

He shook his head. "No thanks, lad, let the old one-legged buzzard suffer." He sighed. "Perhaps there's some hope for a man coming off a spree who can't look a drink in the face and eyes, as the Cousin Jacks say. Not till he builds up a brand new thirst—and gets his next government pension. But thanks, Willy, it's mighty magnanimous of you, son."

"Then why do you drink the stuff, Cash?" I said.

"Ah, that's a good question, boy, a good question." He paused and rubbed his hand over the stubble of his beard. "I suppose really," he went on, "because like all periodic drunkards I have a secret sorrow and keep thinking with whiskey I can buy forgetfulness. I never can."

"I don't like to pry, Cash, but is it about your leg?"

"No, son, it's my heart," he said, putting his hand across his breast. "I merely left my leg at Chancellorsville; I discovered I'd lost my heart when I got home."

"I don't understand, Cash."

"It was one of the oldest casualties of war—any war. I found that during my absence the girl of my dreams had married another. Highly original, isn't it? Love, I discovered, is about one-fifth high blood pressure and four-fifths propinquity. The lion-hearted banker's son, who had thoughtfully bought his way out of the war—got himself an eager bounty jumper, you know—was Johnny-on-the-spot to comfort Clara when she was prostrated with grief over the news of the loss of my leg. So well did he comfort her he up and married her."

"I didn't know," I said, embarrassed by what he was telling me.

He pressed on. "At least out of it I learned one thing. I learned that the world is governed by one single truth: that when danger threatens some men draw their swords while others run away." He put out his hands. "And the sword-drawers frequently lose their lives and legs for their pains—and also their womenfolk to the wise ones who run away."

He paused and regarded his trembling hands. "With these two hands I am now fighting my way down to the gutter." He sighed and sipped the rest of his water. "When good old patriotic over-aged Cassius Wendell finally got out of the government hospital and came tottering home with his brand new leg and learned what happened he didn't even try to see her. What was the use? I had engaged Cupid in combat, lost the engagement, and was permanently missing in action. So without unpacking I simply said hello and goodbye to my maiden aunt—my only relative there—and took the first train to Detroit from Saline. From there I blindly took the first boat—which happened to be headed for Marquette." He smiled and put out his hands. "So I hung out my shingle and here I am. Please, some more water, son—I hadn't planned to make a speech. And why I'm telling you all this I know not, except maybe I guess I like you, Willy. My oh my, I'm getting to be a gabby old man."

"I'm sorry, Cash," I said, handing him the fresh water. "At least it's some small compensation that you are getting a decent pension, what with your rank as colonel."

"Colonel? *Colonel?*" he echoed. "Where did you ever hear such a wild story, lad?"

"Mr. Sloat downstairs called you 'Colonel Wendell.' Nearly

everybody around town calls you 'Colonel.' You're far too modest, Colonel Wendell—you never told me."

He grinned sheepishly and shook his head. "All sheer poppycock, son. I was never anything more than a common flea-ridden private. Pay no attention to such foolish yarns."

"But I don't understand."

"Look, boy, didn't you know that a remarkable proliferation of military commissions followed upon Fort Sumter? Scarcely a man on either side survived the conflict under the rank of lieutenant—all the mere foot soldiers had long since perished. The war simply had to stop when it was discovered there was no one left to do the fighting but officers." He frowned. "How can you possibly go on fightin' a war where there's all chiefs and no Indians?"

"You're pulling my leg, Cash. Were you or were you not a colonel in the War?"

He rubbed his raspy chin. "I was not—more than honorary, so to speak."

"What do you mean?"

"It's this way, boy. There was an unwritten law in our regiment—as in many others—that if a man lost a leg, say, he automatically became a colonel, both legs, he was raised clear to major-general. Are you following me?"

"I think so."

"So you see," he went on soberly, "if instead of my leg I'd lost my head, you'd now be talking to a full-fledged general. But, as you see, you've been reduced to toting water for a mere bogus colonel."

"You're still pulling my leg," I said, smiling and rising. "It's time for me to get over to justice court and remove a cloud of debt hovering over another of Conkling's ancient pianos. What do you think of my plans for the Kawbawgam case, Cash? I'm just about ready to file suit and I'd feel better if I had your views."

His face clouded suddenly and he held up both hands as though to stop my words. "Don't ask me, Willy, *please* don't ask me," he implored. "I'm just a silly uncertain old man who can barely make up his mind to shave in the morning. Forgive me, son, but I guess somewhere along the line I developed a hitch in my giddyap. Let's say that Cassius Wendell was killed at Chancellorsville and his ghost wishes you well on your case. What more can I say? That pesky case of yours plagued my every waking moment till I got rid of it. Oh yes, before I forget"—he pointed at his desk—"better you take that black book along with you when you leave. Read it."

"What is it?"

"One of William Burt's original field journals in the old man's copper-plate handwriting. Found and borrowed it from the Longyear historical wing of the new Peter White public library up on the hill." He grinned and loftily waved a hand. "Old Cash never wastes a moment, see—even combines browsin' with boozin'. Journal covers the period of the original discovery of iron ore—an' moreover proves your beautiful client's old man was accompanying William Burt when the discovery was made. Interesting reading. Must get it back tomorrow."

I moved over to his desk and picked up the weathered black book and eagerly flipped the yellowed time-stiffened pages. "I don't know how to thank you, Cash—" I began.

"Now stow the thanks and fetch me another glass of water before you go."

I was following instructions when I heard him let out a roar. "Willy," he bellowed at me, "be careful to strain out any tadpoles, mind—my stummick's awful queasy from something I et."

I stared at the old goat before I replied. "I always do," I said.

I brought him his water and he gulped it and lay back with hands folded benignly across his chest. "Oh me oh my," he sighed. "I'm not the man I used to be—what's more I never was."

"Thank you, Cash," I said. "Thanks for everything."

But his eyes were closed and already he had dozed off, or pretended to, so I tiptoed over and let myself out the office door and quietly took leave of "Colonel" Cassius Wendell—the man who'd left his leg at Chancellorsville and his heart in Saline. Here, I saw, was another misfit who had wandered into the inviting long corridors of the law—and rapidly found himself lost.

SIX

That afternoon I had to pursue old piano accounts over at justice court, and by the time I had prepared and eaten my lonely supper and tidied my quarters it was already growing dark. At last I settled at my desk and turned up my lamp and reached for the journal of William Burt.

From my school days and recent cramming on the case I already knew that William Burt had headed West from the state of New York shortly after the end of the War of 1812, in which he served; that after much wandering and working at odd jobs he had settled in the village of Mount Vernon near Detroit in the early 1820's, Detroit itself then still being a village on the very outpost of civilization, inhabited mostly by French-speaking settlers; and that once reunited with his wife, who had remained behind, he spent his winters teaching himself surveying and a smattering of astronomy, geology and mathematics.

The first real recognition of his ability had come in 1833 when he was appointed deputy U.S. surveyor of the vast Michigan territory, following which he surveyed roads and railroads, including the new railroad from Detroit to Ypsilanti, with time taken out to make the original survey of Milwaukee. Between times he invented the Burt solar compass, the main feature of which was that it could not be disturbed by local magnetic influence, the bane of accurate land surveys up to then.

I recalled too that after Michigan had become a state in 1836—at the price of yielding up to Ohio a hotly disputed strip of land near Toledo and reluctantly accepting in its place the sprawling and uncharted Upper Peninsula—Douglass Houghton, the new state geologist, had finally prevailed upon the federal government in 1840 to send a man up there so that the new state might learn the extent of what it owned. That man had been William Burt.

I reached for Burt's journal and opened it at random. There lay a pressed fern, perfect in all particulars, covering all of one page. Plainly it had been placed there years before by William Burt. Time had made it part of the journal and, though consumed with curiosity, I lacked the courage to try to read what was underneath. Or was it that I was afflicted with reverence? In any case I would leave to hardier souls the delight of one day boldly penetrating its secrets. Almost ruefully I realized I could no more have disturbed that fern than have spat on my mother's grave . . . I sighed and turned back to the beginning and began to read. The stiff time-rippled pages gave off the faint musty odor of freshly-picked mushrooms.

In a brief introduction, William Burt told of his new surveying assignment—"at an age when most men prefer to sit by the hearth I am about to embark on the most arduous job of my career," he had written. He quoted from his instructions, couched in the mystifying language of surveying: "It will be necessary for you to carry up one of the range lines to the Straits of Mackinac," they read in part, "and thence across the Straits by trigometrical process." This he had done in 1841, his survey being abruptly halted that autumn near the Tahquamenon River by hostile Indians of the Chippewa tribe. "Preferring to take the measure of unknown lands rather than that of unknown Indians, I returned home until it was safe to proceed," he had dryly written. On and on I read.

He was able to continue his survey in 1842 when by the Treaty of LaPointe, the last of the Indian land titles was extinguished in the U.P. I learned further that this historic treaty involved the transfer of more than twelve million acres, an area larger than most New England states; that in return the Indians were to receive seven cents an acre spread over a twenty-five year span of treaty payments.

I sighed and sat staring at my office wall. "Seven cents an acre!" I whispered, wagging my head in disbelief. The bitter words once uttered in Congress by a disgruntled Indian chief came back to me. "Behold the pious white man," he had scornfully declared. "Only he can perform the miracle of picking a man's pockets while both hands are folded in prayer."

I read on for hours in William Burt's journal, soaking up this fascinating history from the hand of this austere old man whose one passion was to calibrate and measure the empty places of the earth. I pounced on everything concerning Marji Kawbawgam, whom he occasionally mentioned, spelling his name "Margie Kobogum." I read of passing encounters with bears and hornets and of bogs and endless waterways.

I learned that even in the wilderness William Burt asked the Lord's blessing before every meal. I had earlier run across his picture in a book about Michigan pioneers: angular, beardless, dour-looking, with staring evangelical eyes, a member of that curious new American breed, the practical idealist, the self-educated jack-of-all-trades, the dreaming Yankee visionary who yet kept his eyes on the main chance.

Reading on I again encountered the pressed fern and again left it in peace. Presently I came down to the day that had sealed Marji Kawbawgam's fate: the first discovery of iron ore. The entry was almost casual.

This morning after breakfast I asked my men to accompany me over to a tall lone bald rocky hill looming up some

2 miles south-southwest of our campsite on Teal Lake. We had noticed it last evening, observing that it was curiously devoid of shrubbery save for a single tall white pine. Dr. Houghton has asked me to keep a lookout for interesting rock formations, and this looked interesting.

Our Chippeway guide, one Kobogum, led us there over what he said was an old Indian trail, though I saw not a vestige. For such a rugged powerful man he is as supple as an otter, gliding through the swampy tangle like a wraith. One hour later we stood panting on the top and I leaned against the lone white pine to catch my breath. This enormous tree stands on the very edge of the cliff, leaning out, and is scarred and ravaged by many a storm. Our Chippeway pointed at an eagle's nest in its topmost branches and then at the eagle, a black speck soaring and tacking far overhead.

When we had composed ourselves we spread out to explore the broad hill top. Soon I espied Mr. Ives staring incredulously at his compass. "Great Scott, Mr. Burt," he exclaimed, "my compass needle is pointing south but we know Teal Lake is to our north!"

I came and looked and it was true; we were standing on one of the most powerful magnetic anomalies I had ever beheld. "Look sharp, men," I said, and we scattered away from the crest. My own magnetic compass, which I now consulted, also gyrated furiously; only my solar compass held on true course. Suddenly our Chippeway ran up to me bearing specimens of loose rock. "See, see!" he cried.

I examined them carefully and they resembled remarkably specimens of blue hematite iron ore I had once encountered on apprentice survey in upper New York. I rubbed a piece against the back of my hand and it left the same telltale reddish-blue stain. "Where?" I said.

"Come," our proud Chippeway said, "I show."

He led us to a great uprooted stump of a white pine, doubtless a cone mate to the great tree still standing on the cliff's edge. The gaunt reaching fingers of its charred roots were clogged with ore specimens; when the vast tree had toppled it had exposed a veritable small mine of iron ore. In his halting way our Chippeway explained that the Indians regarded this rocky hill as the home of the gods of thunder and lightning and that the fallen tree had been struck by lightning in an ancient storm.

We shortly gathered more specimens than we could carry so I called a halt. Before descending I carved my initials and the date in the lone leaning pine. "Men," I said when we reached our main camp, "four years ago Dr. Houghton found copper in the Upper Peninsula. Today we may have been the first to find iron ore." Appropriately enough it is also my birthday—September 19, 1844—my sixty-second, alas. This country could not possibly be surveyed without my solar compass.

I paused in my reading and brewed some tea and then read far into the night. This was authentic raw history of my newly adopted homeland and I found it fascinating. There were several references to Marji Kawbawgam, and I noted all of them. Regrettably there was little I could use in my case—beyond showing that Marji was present and had participated in the discovery of iron ore—but still I read on.

William Burt was a bit of a scholar and from his journal I learned for the first time it was Ben Franklin who had saved the Upper Peninsula of Michigan to the United States. Franklin was then our envoy to France and it fell his lot to negotiate a peace with the British following the Revolutionary War. One task was to settle the international boundary between the United States and Canada. The canny Ben remembered having once read an account published in Paris in 1636 by one LeGarde describing the rich copper deposits he had found in the Great Lakes area "along the southerly shore of its greatest unsalted sea."

"That of course," William Burt's journal continued, "was Lake Superior, earlier known as *Lac Tracy*. Franklin remembered and held out for the Peninsula and so it happens that I am now surveying for a President instead of a Queen."

From still another entry I learned that the survey party had been abruptly snowed in on October 30, 1844 and for three days couldn't stir; that when the storm ended and the snow settled it was decided that the party return home via Wisconsin rather than risk uncertain water passage on Lake Superior, via the Sault, particularly treacherous at that season; that Marji Kawbawgam had accompanied the party to the Wisconsin border, where they parted ways; that William Burt and his crew uneasily walked across the pocked ice on the Menominee River while Marji headed back alone for L'Anse Bay.

Stayed at Kitsen's place 2 days to rest up [the journal continued]. So far took us 10 days, approx. 200 miles. Slept in real beds and ate at a table for the first time in months. Mr. Kitsen is agent for the American Fur Company and is married to an enormous Indian woman. Barney Ives of our party, an irreverent soul, opined a cow could graze on her ample bosom.

On 15 November 1844 Mr. Kitsen drove us by sleigh to Hall's sawmill on top of Green Bay, 3 dolls.; thence by sleigh with mail carrier to village of Green Bay, 5 dolls.; thence engaged a Frenchman to sleigh us to Fond du Lac, 4 dolls.—where I suspect our Mr. Holtzer swiftly found himself a bosom to graze on; thence by foot and sleigh to Milwaukee; thence by stage to Chicago; thence by stage to Marshall where Messrs. Ives and Holtzer remained; thence I proceeded home via the new Marshall and Detroit strap railroad. Total elapsed time: 23 das.

I marveled at his casual account of such an epic trek. A later entry showed that the state geologist, Dr. Houghton, assayed the iron ore samples William Burt brought him and found them the richest ever encountered in his experience. It was growing late and I was about to abandon my reading and go to bed when a still later entry caught my eye. It was dated April 2, 1845.

Had a most curious experience today [William Burt had written].

Two men came to my home from Jackson, a Mr. Kirtland and Mr. Berry, who introduced themselves as officers of the newly formed Jackson Mining Company. They said they had heard on reliable authority, which they did not identify, that my crew and I had discovered a valuable iron ore deposit on the Upper Peninsula the autumn before. I allowed I had. They said they would like to learn where it was; that they were prepared to give me 500 shares of stock in their new company if I would divulge the place to them.

I replied that as a government employee I could not give out such information to private persons and that in any case I could not accept a private reward for performing my public duties. I am puzzled where they learned of the discovery and I purposely did not mention it in my field report—no use unduly rewarding the politicians, who do quite well enough as it is! My visitors then requested a sample of the ore I had found and this I gave them. They then left. I am afraid I may have helped unlock the beautiful Upper Peninsula. It is ironic that a man who so loves the unspoiled wilderness should perhaps unwittingly conspire to deflower it. Am working on an improved model of my solar compass.

I closed the journal and sat staring at the far wall. My fire had gone out and my clock ticked crazily. Some pieces in my legal jigsaw were falling into place. Laughing Whitefish had shown me the old paper given her father years before by the Jackson Mining Company. I remembered it had been signed by three men for the Company; Philo Everett was one; the other two were one Kirtland and one Berry, president and treasurer respectively—the same men who had wooed William Burt.

I turned out my light and groped my way to my bed. "Small world," I murmured, and with that profound philosophical pronouncement, composed myself for sleep.

SEVEN

The die was cast, suit had been filed, and on a warm August day I walked out to my client's island to tell her about it, my brow filled with perspiration, my briefcase with papers, my heart with hope. Gaining the semi-island, attached to the mainland by a sandy strip, I found and followed a cool trail up through the woods to the Indian settlement.

Presently I emerged into a sunlit clearing around which were clustered perhaps a dozen wigwams. This was my first visit to the home of Laughing Whitefish and I looked around curiously. No one was in sight. The only sign of life was an old brown spaniel lying sprawled and panting before the nearest wigwam, regarding me with bulging, oiled, incurious eyes, looking rather less like a dog than a tattered old buffalo robe.

"Hello, old boy," I ventured placatingly—the eternal way of dubious man with strange dog—whereupon a dozen large yellow dogs sprang out of nowhere and advanced upon me, bristling and stiff-legged, venting curdling growls, even the old spaniel getting into the spirit of the thing and emitting a series of wheezy growls, like an old man clearing his throat.

"Laughing Whitefish?" I inquired nervously of a wrinkled old Indian woman who emerged from a wigwam to quiet the dogs, which by now were ringed about me, eyeing me with the slavering malevolence they might accord a haunch of fresh venison. "Laughing Whitefish?" I repeated, warding off the closest beasts with my briefcase. The old woman stood staring suspiciously at me as I pondered how I might make myself understood, as well as survive. Presently Laughing Whitefish herself came out of a small log cabin that stood somewhat apart from the wigwams in the clearing and, speaking sharply to the dogs, advanced toward me with her graceful free-swinging stride.

"Hello William Poe," she said, extending her hand and saying something in Indian to the older woman. The old woman stared at me sullenly for a moment and then grunted and disappeared into a wigwam. "The dogs are a nuisance sometimes but the children adore them."

"After facing that pack of canines I'm prepared to confront any battery of legal talent the Jackson Ore Company can muster against us. How are you, Laughing Whitefish?"

"Quite well, thanks," she said, "but please call me Lotti for short—all my children do. Only the older people seem able to manage the Indian for Laughing Whitefish."

"Very well, Lotti," I said, admiring her soft beaded deerskin costume, which set off her molded features and full lips. I pointed across the clearing. "Do you live in that little log cabin?"

"Yes. It's also my school."

"School? It seems scarcely big enough to hold you let alone a swarm of children."

"I rarely teach more than six at a time and have but a dozen. Come, I'll show you." She lead the way. I had never seen her appear so easy and relaxed.

Her school consisted of three wooden benches upon which rested a dozen or so small slates, while the teacher presided from the kitchen table near which a larger slate stood on an improvised easel. "How do you like it?" she said.

"Um," I said dubiously.

"It isn't much, I'll agree, but at least I'm able to teach the children passable English and to read and write and do their sums. Before I started teaching here these Indian children had no schooling, none whatever, and even the brightest could never qualify for the white school in Marquette. And some are very bright. This fall I'll have three starting school in town, including young Mukwa—remember?—your interpreter when you two went to L'Anse Bay a while back."

"Yes," I said, hefting my briefcase, "which reminds me of our case. I started it."

"That is good. Tell me about it."

I tugged at my neck to open my collar. "Can't we talk outside? I'm hot from my walk out here. Farther than I thought. Could I have a cold drink?"

"Of course. Let's walk to the spring where we can watch the lake. There are no dogs."

"By all means," I said, quickly following her.

The spring gushed out of solid rock, part way down a steep hill, and below us the vast lake glittered in the August sun.

"Now tell me," she said when I had composed myself beside her on the cool caribou moss.

I shrugged. "Well, I filed suit at the county clerk's office in the courthouse this morning. The sheriff is already on his way to Negaunee to serve the papers on the Jackson Mine officials. I also thought of praying a little but the words wouldn't come."

Her face clouded. "I hope something comes of all this, not only to repay you, but so I can help my people. They need help so desperately."

"But what more can you do? You're already doing everything you can, sharing your home with all those youngsters, devoting your time and probably most of your salary...."

"But I have no salary. The Indian mission can barely afford

to furnish books. Mr. Philo Everett has provided others." She put out her hands. "So when you ask what more I can do for my people, the list is endless. For one thing there is simply the matter of common hygiene, teaching the grownups as well as the children to keep themselves clean—their bodies, their teeth, their hair—to decently prepare and eat their meals. . . ."

"But can you hope to change the old ways?"

"I can try," she went on, "and I'm sure of one thing: if we Indians don't try to better ourselves no one else will. The white people seem intent on forgetting my people; they try to ease their guilty consciences of the fact that they robbed us of our homes." She looked out over the lake, her face a grim mask. "What the white people are doing to my people, William, is, after Negro slavery itself, the darkest blot on the conscience of America. They have robbed us, debased us, crowded the dwindling remnants of our tribes on the least desirable lands"—she turned back and looked at me—"and you ask what I can do for my people. Sometimes I hate all of you."

I could feel my face reddening. "I am ashamed of what we have done," I said, and I tried to tell her how moved and humiliated I was when I first landed at Marquette, when my shipmates had mocked and shouted at the two Indian braves in the passing canoe. "It's not that I make light of your trying to help your people," I went on. "It's only that you are so young and talented—it seems such a pity that you should bury yourself on this remote island—"

"Your people buried us here, William," she said harshly. "There had always been an Indian encampment along the banks of the Laughing Whitefish River. Wasn't it *your* people who fouled our river and herded us out to this unwanted island?" She gestured toward the encampment. "That wrinkled old Indian woman you just saw back there has but two surviving children out of a dozen confinements. Would you believe she is not yet fifty?"

I shook my head in disbelief.

"My father had at least two wives," she went on, "and I am the only seed to survive. I have no illusions I can bring back the vanished glory of the Noble Red Man, William, about which your poets wax so lyrical, but . . ." She shook her head. "I want simply to help my people so they may endure, so they may not perish from the earth. That's what I am trying to do." She reached for her throat. "Otherwise I would gladly burn this paper and let our white 'benefactors' celebrate still another victory over us ignorant savages."

There was nothing for me to say and I remained silent. She faced me, breathing deeply, her expression grown suddenly hard and bitter, her fists clenched. "But you could not understand," she went on scornfully. "None of you understand. None of you give a damn." Her breasts rose and fell and her breathing sounded like sobs. Glaring at me, she fairly hurled her next worlds. "I—I *hate* you ! I hate all of you!"

It was too wrenching to watch her and I turned and stared out across the lake, at its great slow pulse and heave, at this vast glacial sheet of hammered silver, at this deep brooding sea of intense blue—bluer even than the fabled mountain lakes of Italy —at this once unfettered highway of the ancestors of this tormented girl. A lone low-flying gull glided languidly along and, with flash of upthrust wings, lit on a slow swell, bobbing and dipping like a decoy.

I felt her hand on my arm. "William," I heard her saying, "I am terribly sorry. I could pluck out my tongue for what I just said. I did not mean it, I swear I didn't. Sometimes I'm about driven out of my mind I feel so helpless, because all of us Indians are so terribly doomed and helpless . . ."

I turned and faced her. "Of course you meant it and I can't blame you. Can I tell you something, Laughing Whitefish, something I've never told a living soul, until this moment not quite even myself?"

"Tell me."

"If I were an Indian I swear I would be so consumed with fury I would either be in jail or dead. That is truly how I feel. Do you believe me?"

"I believe you, William Poe." Her dark eyes burned into mine.

"And you must try to trust me because if I cannot have your trust and faith to help me I cannot stay in your case. It is too much for me to fight *them* and you too. I am not that strong."

"I trust you, William Poe."

"Good. I brought something for you." I fumbled at the straps of my briefcase. "In here, Lotti," I said quietly, "some books for you and your pupils. Mr. Philo Everett also sent some and wishes to be remembered warmly to you."

"Thank you. It's so hard to be fair when I think of what has happened to my people. Probably it would have been much the same had all the whites been saints—the old Indian life was doomed when the first white man stepped ashore." Her voice was flat with resignation.

"Why do you say that?"

"Because the white man found a primitive people still living in the stone age and, overnight, catapulted them into the modern world. Most of my people couldn't make the transition. It was like an invasion from another planet."

"I still don't quite follow."

"You whites were the source of all the new articles the Indians simply had to have if they were to survive among their fellow Indians who first got them. The need rippled inland in mounting waves. Crude flint tools could not match the axe, your metal kettles were far better than the fragile pottery of our nomadic people, the rifle made the bow and arrow obsolete."

"I never thought of that."

"Once my people began retreating back from the Atlantic, pushed westward by the whites, there started a sort of chain reaction, like rows of falling dominoes. Much of the undoubted ferocity of the Indians to the whites and each other sprang simply from that. They fought to survive."

"I think I am following you."

"Look, William, my people first had to fight the whites to save their ancestral homes. When they failed and were pushed ever westward they fell to fighting each other. In their stunned retreat, you see, the recently invaded now became the invaders. And all of them fought to get the new weapons of the whites at any price." She smiled at her earnestness. "At any price," she repeated. "But I guess your Henry Thoreau said it all when he wrote of my people, 'Steel and blankets are great temptations.'"

"He forgot rum," I said, not wishing to arouse her further by reminding her of the traditional ferocity of the Iroquois and other tribes to each other long before the whites arrived in America.

"Yes, and rum. That just about finished us. Just to help my people survive I must do what I can."

"I see, Lotti," I said slowly. "For the first time I really think I see."

"Tell me how Mr. Everett is. He seemed so poorly the last time I saw him."

I told her of my fears that Mr. Everett would ever survive to testify in our case, or surviving, remember what he knew about it. I told her of my plans and hopes for the case, how I had purposely not settled on any one theory of recovery in my pleadings—to avoid putting all our legal eggs in one basket—and how instead I had decided simply to narrate in legal terminology the story of Marji Kawbawgam and the Jackson Mine, depending upon the justice of the situation and perhaps also on the indulgence and good heart of the trial judge finally to prevail. . . .

She listened intently, occasionally making a comment or asking a question that showed she was closely following me. When I was finished the sun had sunk behind the trees, enveloping the rocky shore below us in blue shadows, while far out on the lake its rays still danced and glittered.

"There goes some of your father's iron ore," I said, pointing out in the lake, where far in the distance a low-riding ore boat ploughed its way down to the lower lakes with its heavy burden, its smoke plume folded behind it.

We sat for a long time without speaking, each lost in thought. I silently resolved that I would try to win this case. I was determined to help Laughing Whitefish and her people, but even more was at stake: my wavering faith in human decency. If rich powerful white men could successfully deal the Indians this final injustice. . . .

It was nearly dusk when we clambered up the steep trail to the top of the cliff, Laughing Whitefish leading the way. She paused at a fork in the leaf-littered trail. "Come," she said in a low voice. "I'll show you where my parents are buried. You will be the first white man I've ever taken there."

We climbed steeply for several minutes and emerged into a natural clearing in the forest, overlooking the lake, a secluded spot in which there were perhaps two score burial mounds, a few bearing crude wooden crosses or wooden markers. The early missionaries, she explained, had taught her people to bury their dead rather than place their bodies on elevated platforms as they had in the past.

"The body of my mother, Sayee, was taken from the old encampment and brought here," she said, pointing at a tangled grassy mound. "And here lies the body of my uncle, Sassaba, once chief of the Marquette Chippewa Indians. Over there are the bodies of my mother's parents. And here," she said, pointing at a mound covered with creeping groundpine and bearing a simple wooden marker, "here is where my father lies."

As I stood there beside her I was overcome suddenly with a feeling of the ephemeral quality of existence, of the vanity of all the eternal striving of men, of the essential anonymity of human life.

"I remember my father's burial," she went on quietly. "Some of the old men of the tribe spoke, lamenting our vanished way of life, and the injustice of my father's treatment by the white man. I remember particularly the words of old Osseo—he came for the burial—who had to be carried up here by two braves so that he could speak. He was brief." She thought for a moment and then spoke in Indian, her voice vibrant with bitterness.

Anamakamig
   Maiagwedjaganash,
Anokewag,
   Biwabikokeweg,
Anonigosiwag;
   Kitchimokomanag
Mamigewag.

I couldn't understand the words, but her passion was unmistakable. "Can you tell me what it means?" I said.

She reflected a moment and then said quietly:

In the bowels of the earth
   The foreign devils are working.
They are gathering our metals,
   They are the hired toilers;
While the Big Knives
   They are our despoilers.

EIGHT

Litigation is not one of the speediest activities to which mankind has devoted its energies, and I was doubly surprised therefore when the Jackson Ore Company not only acted with dispatch but entered its appearance and filed its first pleading in the case within a week from the time I had filed suit. It was as though they were ready and waiting for me; the battle had been swiftly joined.

I received my copies in the morning mail and was not surprised to learn that my legal opponent would be Henry Harwood, the county's leading lawyer. He had entered his appearance on behalf of the Company and also signed and filed the initial pleading, a general and special demurrer to our bill of complaint. This development at least lent a certain air of cosiness to the case; his law offices were under mine, on the second floor.

The general demurrer is an ancient legal device, the main office of which, while temporarily conceding but not admitting the truth of the plaintiff's claims, is to suggest that he still has not made out a case. It is a device that, when it succeeds, can end a case abruptly without the turmoil and expense of a trial. The special demurrer among other things points out in particular detail why the demurring defendant thinks the plaintiff is so misguided and wrong; it is a genteel guide to the judge; and it sometimes also gives the plaintiff, or rather his lawyer, a pretty good clue to what the defendant's real defenses will boil down to if his demurrer should finally be denied and the case proceed to hearing on its merits. From Henry Harwood's demurrer I gained such a clue.

In the quaint, repetitious and heavily Latinized prose to which all lawyers seem such helpless slaves, the Jackson Ore Company devoted nine paragraphs to criticizing my bill of complaint, and which in plainer English boiled down to this:

That since the original Jackson explorers did not own the mine property when they gave the paper to Marji Kawbawgam they could scarcely undertake to convey what they did not own, and anyway they had no right to bind the old partnership by any such high-handed action; that in any case the paper they gave Marji could not convey any interest in the original government entry permit under which they were exploring; that in any event the present Jackson Ore Company was not bound by any such ancient shenanigans; that moreover it had never recognized any such rights existing in Marji Kawbawgam; that Laughing Whitefish was estopped because she was complaining too late; that the defendant company owned the whole interest in the mining property and any usurpers were after so many years far too late; that Laughing Whitefish was guilty of fatal laches, that is, of sleeping on her legal rights; and, finally, that—and this was perhaps the gravest and most significant allegation of all— that whatever rights Marji Kawbawgam might have had under his paper, she, Laughing Whitefish, was no lawful kin of his and was therefore in no position to come into court seeking to enforce any of his rights—the demurrer concluding with the usual classical protestations of injured innocence and a prayer for dismissal.

I sat at my desk pondering what to do, wondering just how much the Jackson Ore Company and Henry Harwood knew about the informal domestic arrangements of Marji Kawbawgam and, especially, what, if anything, they knew about his successive marriages. I had not mentioned these in my bill of complaint. I had not because the burden was clearly on our side ultimately to prove that Laughing Whitefish was a person entitled to enforce her father's claim in court; if we failed to prove that, we had no case, and I saw no utility and some harm in warning our opponents in advance where our weaknesses might lie. But already the other side seemed to have smelled a rat. . . .

Still once again I read the demurrer and, revelation eluding me, decided to go consult the reluctant Cassius Wendell. Though I knew he was out of the case and shunned any responsibility, I felt I simply had to talk with someone. I could scarcely go to Henry Harwood, and the only other lawyers in town, and indeed in the county, represented still others of the burgeoning crop of new mining companies. So poor Cassius Wendell was elected . . .

At the bottom of the first flight of stairs on my journey earthward I almost collided with Henry Harwood, who had just climbed the ground floor stairs to his own office. Both of us smiled a little uncertainly and both were out of breath.

"You seem to be in quite a hurry this morning, Mr. Poe," Henry Harwood said in his mild way. "I can't imagine what has stirred you into such a flurry of activity."

"When your letter came this morning I hoped it might contain an offer of settlement," I said boldly, "or at least a suggestion that we might meet and discuss the possibility of compromise." I sighed. "Alas, I found only a declaration of war."

Henry Harwood pondered for a moment. He was a slightly built man of about fifty who wore a trim Van Dyke beard, beginning to turn gray. He also wore pince-nez glasses, which he had a habit of constantly removing and replacing. As I stood waiting for him to speak he daintily took them off and carefully clamped them on the tip of his upthrust thumb. They had dug deep furrows on either side of his nose, which gave him the air of a timid owl. He replaced them before speaking.

"The filing of timely defense pleadings never forecloses the possibility of compromise," he said in his precise rather high-pitched voice, "and the prompt filing of them may even occasionally facilitate a settlement." He paused and cleared his throat. "On the other hand, occasionally there are cases involving rights and principles of such magnitude"—here he paused and again removed his glasses—"that it is perhaps better to gird for war." He cleared his throat and smiled his shy diffident smile. "It was pleasant to run into you, young man. Now if you'll excuse me, I think I have a client waiting. Good day, Mr. Poe."

"Good day, Mr. Harwood," I said. "It seems I too have an appointment—to gird for war."

"A wise decision, Mr. Poe," he said, turning away.

I was more than halfway down the remaining stairs when I heard a voice behind me calling my name. I wheeled and there at the stair top stood Mr. Harwood, still holding his glasses poised on his thumb and peering down at me.

"I was just thinking, Mr. Poe," he called down to me, "that even in war there should be no lack of communication between the combatants else, once started, there could never again be any peace." He paused as I pondered the possible significance of his remark. "What I mean to say, Mr. Poe, is that though we may have to wage war, I have no objection to your availing yourself of my library to replenish your ammunition. My secretary, Miss Dyson, will show you where we keep the key."

"Thank you, Mr. Harwood," I said, moved by this kindness. "You are a generous opponent."

"The law, like the truth, must out," he said, and then once again he disappeared and again I heard his quick steps pattering down the corridor. As I continued on down the street to Cassius Wendell's office I tried to weigh the import of our conversation. Had he not been trying to tell me that there could not possibly be any settlement in the Kawbawgam case because the stakes were too high? And had he not at the same time told me that the issue was touch and go, either way, and that for his part, at least, his main concern was that justice should prevail? I shrugged and turned into the narrow weather-blistered doorway leading up to Cassius Wendell's office. Would I be lucky enough to find the old boy in?

There he was, sitting behind his desk, his wooden leg propped up on the top, leaning back reading the *Mining Journal* of the afternoon before. He smiled and unpouched his tobacco swollen cheek against a brass cuspidor. "Eases the stump," he explained, patting his leg.

"But supposing I'd been a paying client?"

"Could tell it was you by your footsteps," he said. "But anyway I doubt I'd have moved an inch. Most clients bore me. All they ever bring in is their eternal burdens of toil and trouble."

"Perhaps you are engaged in the wrong line of work," I said.

"Who isn't? Take yourself, Willy. *You* want to be a poet and writer."

"How could you know that?"

"Because, poor boy, obviously you yearn to express the inexpressible. Because compassion and wonder are written all over your face."

"Have you got a few minutes, Cash?" I said, trying to get him off *that* subject. "I'd like to bring you up-to-date on the Kawbawgam case."

The old boy was not to be deflected. "Compassion and wonder," he repeated. "It is compassion and compassion alone that makes you take on the dubious case of this poor Indian girl. That plus the fact that she's probably the comeliest young woman either of us ever laid eyes on."

"You don't think I have a chance to win, then?" I said, evading his shrewd analysis. "Is that why you palmed the case off on me—because you couldn't stand to lose?"

"I didn't say that," he continued blandly. "I mean only that you've got yourself a tough one—but you know that already. Anyway I see by the *Journal* here that you filed suit last week," he said. "Quite a little article, in fact. I trust you've come to tell me that the other side has just made you a generous offer of settlement."

"Not a chance, Cash," I said, and I told him about receiving the demurrer that very morning and of the rather revealing conversation I'd just had with Henry Harwood. "Looks like war to me, Cash. But it was nice of him to offer me the use of his law library, don't you think? One can't feel too bitter toward an opponent who between battles lets you come over and raid his ammunition dump."

Cassius Wendell gingerly eased his leg down off the desk, again spat, and leaned forward, linking his fingers and pursing his lips judiciously. "Henry Harwood is a *good* man," he said thoughtfully. "Fact is the legal profession would be better off if there were more like him." He turned and glanced out his sooted and dingy window and then back at me. "He is living proof that to be a good and successful lawyer a man needn't also be a cantankerous and scheming old goat. Moreover he refuses to accept the prevailing notion that any workman who dares sue a corporation he works for is a malingerer and a thief."

"Well, I don't know about the devious part. He just spoke to me pretty much in riddles."

Cash shook his head. "No, son, not precisely in riddles. My guess is that it's part of the man's effort to avoid bluntness and conflict—and, moreover, you've just told me you think you've solved his riddles. No," he continued, "Henry Harwood is both a gentleman and a gentle man. The two are not always the same. . . . He came here to Marquette from out East—Boston, I think it was—as a mere law clerk to the first lawyer in Marquette County, old Claudius Grant, now our esteemed circuit judge."

"That's another great comfort," I said gloomily, "having Judge Grant preside over the trial of a case in which the defendant is represented by one of the judge's former associates. A real cosy situation."

Cassius Wendell looked at me sharply. "Then you don't know old Judge Grant," he said reprovingly. "He'd rule against his own grandmother if he thought she was wrong."

"I hope so," I said, reaching for my briefcase. "Let me show you the demurrer he filed."

He shook his head. "I haven't finished telling you about Henry Harwood," he said. "When will you learn not to keep talking when old Cash is interrupting?"

"Yes, sir," I said, totally chastened.

"Henry Harwood has worked his way up to be the most successful lawyer not only in the town and county but perhaps the whole Upper Peninsula," he went on. "He does all the best legal work for all the best people. He drafts all the most elaborate wills for the wealthy, helping them to rule from the grave. And when they die he genteelly divides their loot among their inconsolable survivors. Moreover he is immensely rich himself. In a way I suppose I should envy him." He grinned and spat again. "Yet I wouldn't be in his shoes even if I got my lost leg back."

"Why, Cash?"

"Because the poor man doesn't get any fun out of life. All he does is work and sleep and race off to church and rush back and draft more wills."

"Doesn't it all boil down to a definition of 'fun'?" I said. "All of us can't be irreverent, cynical, hard-drinking, free-living characters who don't care a rap what their clients think or even if they have any."

"Don't be impertinent, Willy," he said, grinning his goatish grin. "But getting back to Henry Harwood—you have indeed drawn yourself a worthy opponent, as our more florid brethren so dearly love to put it."

"How do you mean?"

"His habit of winning the cases that he engages in is as monotonous as it is startling. Perhaps one reason for this is his reputation for not taking on a case unless he first thoroughly believes in it."

"You mean to tell me he'd risk losing his lucrative retainer with the Jackson Ore Company if he didn't believe in the purity of their position in the Kawbawgam case? Do you mean that justice and virtue have invariably been on the side of the Jackson Ore Company all these years? Nonsense."

"I mean simply that when Henry Harwood takes on a case it's because he believes in it. If he doesn't believe in it he won't take it. Why just last spring they had a bad accident up at the Jackson Mine in Negaunee—three miners were killed—and suit was filed by me and Henry Harwood bluntly told his Jackson people that they should settle and that if they didn't he would not represent them. They settled. So the mere fact that Henry Harwood has entered into your Kawbawgam case, Willy, means you're in the battle of your life. Gird your loins, son." He leaned forward and held out his hand. "Here now, let me see that there demurrer. Let's see how bad it is."

"Here it is," I said, fishing gloomily in my briefcase for the Kawbawgam file.

He sat reading the demurrer, with little twin rivulets of tobacco juice escaping from the corners of his mouth. Here was an intelligent sensitive man who went out of his way to make people think him a coarse and ignorant boor. The man was resolutely disdainful of the opinion of others. He didn't *care* how he looked or what people thought of him. He lowered the paper and gravely looked up.

"Gird your loins, son," he repeated. "If I read this thing right there will be no settlement—it will either be total victory or total defeat."

"You're a great comfort," I said. "What am I supposed to do?"

He looked at me quietly a moment before he spoke. "Why, son, you fight 'em, down to the bitter end. As some deceased admiral once said, 'Don't give up the ship till the water comes down the smokestack—then swim.'" He handed me back my papers and picked up the *Mining Journal* and, flouncing it a few times, quietly resumed his reading. I saw I was dismissed.

"Thanks, Cash," I said, dolefully gathering up my papers. "Thanks for your moral support."

NINE

"It took us a week to get from our homes in Jackson, Michigan, up to Sault Ste. Marie in the Upper Peninsula. We went by rail from Jackson to Marshall; thence to Grand Rapids by stage; thence to Mackinaw City by hired wagon—this last a ferocious trip along which we found only the most primitive accommodations. It tires me even to look back on it."

Philo Everett half sat and half lay on a complicated wooden rocking-chair, the kind that had an adjustable back and headrest and a footstool which slid out from underneath. These rockers were the latest rage, and Philo Everett looked every bit as relaxed as a victim of medieval torture being stretched on a rack. He paused in his discourse and leaned back in his rocker, which squeaked and the springs clanged, and passed a thin hand across his eyes.

This was the third time I had visited him at his home on Ridge Street to talk about the case; it was also the first time I had found him out of bed and likewise the first time he had summoned me. I felt encouraged; it was also the only time he seemed to have any coherent and continuous recollection of the events that were so important to our case.

"How was your trip from Mackinaw City to the Sault?" I gently prodded him.

"From Mackinaw City we proceeded by freight canoe to

Mackinac Island and thence by sail to Sault Ste. Marie. There we purchased a Mackinaw boat and had it hauled overland around the churning and still ice-clogged rapids of St. Mary's River to await favorable weather for our voyage up Lake Superior on our quest. We waited and waited. Remember, this was April of 1845, after one of the severest winters on record."

"And your Jackson associates accompanied you?" I asked.

"Yes, two of them—Mr. Kirtland, the president of the newly-formed Jackson Mining Company, Mr. Berry, our treasurer, and"—a faint smile lit his pale features—"and yours truly, Philo Everett, treasurer and erstwhile feed merchant and Yankee jack of all trades. We found hundreds of impatient copper prospectors ahead of us at the Sault, outfitting and planning, drinking and brawling, waiting for winter to relax its iron grip so they might coast up the lake in their assembled fleets of canoes and bateaux and heavier Mackinaw boats. There were yet no railroads in the Peninsula, you know, and the few roads and trails were still glutted with mud and snow. Going overland was unthinkable—so we too waited in the teeming and dissolute Sault."

"How was it that you three men were seeking *iron* ore while all the rest sought only copper?" I inquired, hoping that we might thus circumvent the Sault; I had heard *that* story on an earlier visit. I was also curious to find out how Messrs. Kirtland and Berry had learned about William Burt's discovery, as I had earlier read in William Burt's journal.

"Because the others didn't know William Burt had found a rich iron ore deposit in the Peninsula the autumn before. The presence of copper had been known for centuries but Douglass Houghton fanned a new interest when in 1840 he found rich new deposits along the south shore of Lake Superior. He was the young state geologist, you know." I nodded. "Ever since then prospectors had poured into the Keweenaw Peninsula area looking for copper. Rich finds had already been uncovered, new mines were opening, fortunes were being made—and so naturally we found the Sault teeming with copper prospectors. It was the country's first big mineral rush."

"But how did *you* men happen to know about William Burt's iron ore find when all the others didn't?" I persisted.

Just then Philo Everett's nurse swept in, a Mrs. Brown, a tall portly inexhaustibly cheerful woman wearing a watch pinned to the ample bosom of her starched shirtwaist. Mr. Everett was a childless widower living alone in his big brownstone house on the hill and she looked after him.

"It's past time for taking our medicine, you naughty man," Mrs. Brown sang out in that solicitous tone of maternal jocularity adopted by nurses the world over. She spooned him his medicine as she might a little boy—indeed, puckering up his face he seemed a little boy. After tucking the woolen afghan more closely about him—"There we go," she said—she swept starchily away; once again we were alone. He sat regarding me uncertainly.

"How did your party know about the recent iron discovery when the others didn't?" I prompted him.

He seemed to want to avoid the subject. "First I must tell you about our stay in the Sault," he said, and again he was away. Once again he told me about the huge mounds of rotting snow that had still glutted the streets there, this time also describing a dead yellow dog lying exposed in a melting snow bank, "its jaws hideously agape, curiously crumpled and empty-looking, more like a carelessly flung rug"—which I thought a nice macabre touch. He told me again about the gambling and brawling and fighting, about the prostitutes who boldly plied the streets and public houses, about the two hotels being crammed to the eaves with copper prospectors, some sleeping in the public rooms and corridors; about the bands of intrepid Indians teetering in their canoes over the spring-flooded rapids of the St. Mary's River, stoically scooping whitefish out of the angry depths.

I longed to interrupt and get him on with his account—the part I had not yet heard—but I was afraid I might disturb his uncertain train of thought, so I suffered in silence. Once again he told me about Henry J. Schoolcraft, Indian agent, geologist, explorer—in his younger days he had found the source of the Mississippi—writer, Indian grammarian, student of Indian lore; of how this colorful and talented man had graciously invited him and his companions to stay in his luxurious three-story palace-in-the-woods log home that possessed fifteen fireplaces, about the dark grace and beauty of his full-blooded Indian wife, Jane; of how Longfellow had drawn his epic poem *Hiawatha* from legends gathered by Schoolcraft; about how, when Philo Everett had chided him about the sin that stalked abroad in the Sault, Schoolcraft had smiled and replied that judgment was better withheld until he had seen the new copper region, adding, "It is said there is no Sunday west of the Sault."

Philo Everett paused and sipped some water and told me he had recently refreshed his recollection of those times from an old journal of his he'd run across since last he'd seen me. This I could well believe as he omitted nothing from his former account and added things I had not yet heard, including a detailed room by room description of the Schoolcraft mansion, down to the covered woodboxes which graced each bedroom, fashioned from unpainted red cedar. He also lovingly described the beautiful grounds and gardens about the Schoolcraft home, sloping down to the great churning river, with forested Canada looming in the distance, and I fidgeted and glanced at my watch, but nothing seemed to stem the flood of recollection. On and on he droned.

"How was your trip up Lake Superior from the Sault?" I rallied to venture, but he shook his head impatiently and instead

again told me about Schoolcraft's epic 1820 exploratory trip
with the then territorial governor Lewis Cass; of how earlier at
the Sault the unarmed and courageous Cass had defied a hostile
band of Indian chiefs with whom he had been meeting and had
boldly pulled down and stood upon a British flag they had taunt-
ingly run up. However stirring, I had heard all this before and
his voice sank to a reminiscent hum . . .

I raised my head with a start; the incredible was happening;
to my endless shame I discovered that while I had been half dozing Philo Everett had launched on a new tack: we were now
leaving the Sault! I leaned tensely forward: he was coming to
the part I was dying to hear, the part about Marji.

"After we rounded up these three cheerful brigands, these
French-Canadian *voyageurs*, these *les gens libres* whom the lust
for freedom afflicted like an itch, we set forth from the Sault in
our Mackinaw boat on May 18, 1845. Nine days later we
reached our destination, L'Anse Bay, nine of the most harrowing days of my life. I shall spare you the details, but our boat
capsized three times, once we stove it in on a hidden ice floe,
twice we were driven ashore in sudden snow squalls, and our
voyageurs nearly drove us mad with their singing and preening
and brawling and endless chatter. Poor Mr. Kirtland, whom I
had never suspected of excessive piety, spent most of the time on
his knees." Philo Everett closed his eyes and sighed over the
recollection. "The scenery was beautiful beyond words, especially the ancient sea-honed Pictured Rocks, but how can one
enjoy scenery, however lovely, when survival is constantly at
stake? Well, sir, we survived and reached L'Anse Bay."

"And there you saw Marji Kawbawgam?" I gently
prompted.

"We sent for him at once and he came immediately, a magnificent specimen of a man clad in buckskin, including a won-
drously soiled buckskin shirt that fit him like a pelt."

"Was he alone?" I said, remembering old Osseo.

"No, there was some inscrutable old Indian with him. Mr. Kirtland was our spokesman and he immediately got down to business and asked Marji if he had guided the William Burt survey party the season before, to which Marji answered yes. Mr. Kirtland then produced a sample of iron ore—which I then learned for the first time William Burt had given him earlier that spring—and handed it to Marji. Marji wordlessly took my arm and rubbed the specimen on the back of my hand. It left a reddish-blue stain. Then he produced a similar-looking specimen from a deerskin pouch he carried round his midrift and likewise rubbed it on the back of my other hand: the two stains were identical. My companions and I stared at each other; no words were spoken and none was needed; here was our man."

Philo Everett paused and blinked in recollection. "Next Mr. Kirtland asked Marji where the ore body was located. Marji smiled faintly and swept his hand vaguely eastward and said: 'By lone pine tree.' Since there are millions of pine trees in the Peninsula that helped us not at all except to demonstrate our Indian was no fool."

"So you made your deal with Marji," I prompted.

"Yes, but first we three conferred privately and Mr. Kirtland pointed out that soon the waiting hordes of prospectors at the Sault would be leaving there and swarming over the Peninsula—we had risked our lives by leaving earlier—and that we should reach an understanding with our canny Indian without delay. He pointed out that there were 3100 shares of partnership stock and he proposed that we offer Marji a 12/3100ths interest for showing us the site of the discovery; that this was less than a 1/250th interest of the whole, or approximately 12 shares, and far less than he and Mr. Berry had earlier offered William Burt to achieve the same end. To this we agreed." He smiled ruefully and then added: "That also was the first time I learned they had made an earlier offer to William Burt."

"How did they ever get to know about the Burt discovery and then about Marji?" I asked, hammering away.

Philo Everett shook his head. "To this day I do not actually know. I guess I didn't press my companions because I didn't want to know. I never felt proud of it. Mr. Kirtland was a shrewd banker and he had his connections."

"Do you think Douglass Houghton told him?"

"No, I am sure he did not; Dr. Houghton was the soul of probity and discretion. From vague hints from the others I believe it was some underling in Lansing."

"After William Burt turned them down how did they come to learn about Marji?"

He held up his hands. "Again I do not really know. It is my guess—mind, I said *guess*—that when William Burt turned Kirtland and Berry down on their stock offer they next made a trek to Marshall and visited upon the other men in Burt's survey crew, the two who wintered there."

"And made them the same proposition?"

"No, by then they'd learned their lesson and grown gunshy. As nearly as I can gather *this* time they were solely *copper* prospectors headed north, mere fumbling babes in the woods innocently seeking experienced advice on how to find a reliable Indian guide."

"Yes?"

Again he spread his hands. "So in turn quite innocently Burt's men told them to go see their guide, Marji Kawbawgam; that he could surely steer them to a reliable guide. It was as simple as that."

"I see," I said, for I saw. "So you made your deal with Marji."

"Yes, Mr. Kirtland outlined the terms, a Frenchman where we were staying interpreted them, and Marji asked only that we also give him a steady job at any mine we opened because he planned on marrying an Indian girl in the vicinity. We did not then know that he was already married to an Indian woman at L'Anse Bay. So I wrote out the agreement myself, tearing a page out of my journal." He reached over to a little table—clang, clang went the rocker—and got his old journal and opened and handed it to me. "For our records I wrote out a copy in my journal. Read it."

"Yes, sir," I said, and I read:

L'Anse Bay, Lake Superior
28 May 1845

This may certify that in consideration of the services to be rendered by Marji Kawbawgam, a Chippeway Indian, in hunting iron ores for the Jackson Mining Company under Permit No. 969 and discovering to us the ore body located near the lone pine tree, he is entitled to twelve undivided thirty-one one-hundredths parts of the interest of the said Mining Company in said location. Also a permanent job at any iron mine there so founded for life at mutually agreeable terms.

F. W. Kirtland, Pres
A. V. Berry, Secy

In presence of:
Philo P. Everett
Clovis Trepanier

I looked up and handed the journal back to Philo Everett. "It is exactly the same as the original you gave Marji Kawbawgam," I said.

"Good, but I knew it was, it had to be; I wrote both of 'em. See the place where I tore the page out of my journal for Marji's original copy?"

"I see," I said. "What happened then?"

"After the document was signed and witnessed Mr. Kirtland handed it to Marji who folded it away in his buckskin pouch and said simply: 'When do we leave for lone pine?'

" 'Tomorrow at daybreak,' Mr. Kirtland said.

" 'Tomorrow at daybreak,' Marji said, and bowing gravely he turned and left, followed by his old Indian companion."

Philo Everett seemed to be tiring and I made ready to leave. There remained one question I longed to ask him. "May I ask one more question?" I said.

"Fire away, young man," he said. "I'm as strong as a lion."

"Mr. Everett," I said, "I am puzzled: how did it happen that you men failed with the rich Jackson Mine while your successors made and are making fortunes out of it? The ore was always there, wasn't it?"

He smiled wryly. "A number of things conspired against us, young man, first among which was that we were utter greenhorns, babes in the woods, we knew nothing whatever about mining—which is no business for a tenderfoot. Another was that we were ahead of our time: proper equipment wasn't then available, the smelters then in existence weren't built to handle our high-grade ore. Another was that we were financially bled white because we began mining ore before we or the country were ready, instead of conserving our funds and directing all our energies at getting a railroad to Marquette and a canal built at the Sault. Both of these came eventually but by then it was far too late—we were broke, discouraged, and deeply in debt." He sighed. "Finally we were dogged constantly by plain bad luck. I could run on for hours with our harrowing tale of woe—floods, cave-ins, walkouts, premature explosions, high prices, panics, plagues, we had them all. When we gave up I was happy to go back to the feed business, a sadder and wiser man."

"And the new crowd had what you lacked?"

"Exactly, young man. They had experience, adequate capital, improved equipment, patience, vision and influence—especially influence. They also had a country teetering on the verge of civil war, alas. . . . About the first thing they did was pack a whole trainload of assorted local supplicants off to Congress—

including old lion-maned Peter White—to pray for government help to get a canal built at the Sault. They prayed eloquently: they got it—and the Pandora's box of the Peninsula was at last flung open."

"But hadn't you Jackson men earlier gone to Washington to seek the same canal?"

"Yes, the need was known for years—centuries, in fact—but for our pains we were able only to behold a scornful Henry Clay arise to his full five feet upon the floor of the Senate and in thunderous accents declare: 'This canal is sheer folly! Not one red cent will I vote on such a fantastic work, lying beyond the remotest settlements in the United States, if not upon the moon!' "

Mrs. Brown loomed in the doorway significantly fingering her watch. "I'm afraid it's time, Mr. Poe. The doctor said we mustn't tire Mr. Everett and it's now been nearly two hours."

I put my swollen notebook away and rose to leave. "One more thing, Mr. Everett. If we survive the defendant's pending demurrer will you come to court and testify for Laughing Whitefish?—and bring along your old journal?"

His reply was spirited and immediate. "I certainly will, young man, if it's the last thing I do. I want very much to help right that ancient wrong." He put out his fragile hand and I took it. "Good luck to you on the demurrer and on your case."

"Thank you, Mr. Everett, for all your help and encouragement. I already feel much better about our chances."

"Goodbye, young man."

"Goodbye, Mr. Everett, and good health."

TEN

After brooding over the demurrer nearly three weeks the circuit judge, Claudius Grant, asked both sides to submit briefs on the issue. This morbid task consumed virtually another three weeks, but at least served to soak me deeper in my case. It was nearly mid-December before Gad Smith, the county clerk and clerk of the court, got word to Henry Harwood and me to be in circuit court the next morning promptly at nine. Claudius Grant was ready to make his ruling on the demurrer. Would his Christmas present be coal in our stockings or victory?

I hurried out to Presque Isle to tell Laughing Whitefish the news and for my pains contrived to get caught in a sudden snow squall. For a time it looked as though I might have to spend my first night at an Indian encampment, but the pelting snow abated and I headed for town, Laughing Whitefish guiding me out to the town road. It was nearly midnight when I got home, tired and thoroughly wet, and threw myself on my cot.

After a troublous fretful night, during which I slept little, promptly at nine the next morning Henry Harwood and I were at our respective places in the circuit courtroom of the county courthouse: I at the plaintiffs' counsel table, on the right, nearest the empty jury box and facing the judge's bench; Henry Harwood sitting quietly alone at the defense table on my left.

Laughing Whitefish had snowshoed to town early that

morning over the drifted and snow-clogged road and she sat behind me in the first row of high-backed wooden benches, just
beyond the lawyers' rail, a fur-trimmed hood framing her face. I
wanted her to be there to see and hear what happened because if
we lost a big decision had to be made: either we would have to
appeal the ruling or abandon the case. If we won I wanted her to
see that too. Meanwhile our case hung in the balance.

I turned and glanced back at her and she nodded gravely.
She had removed her fur jacket and her only sign of nervousness
was that she kept fingering the little deerskin bag she always
wore about her throat as though it were a good luck amulet.
The courtroom was otherwise deserted and I speculated that
possibly people found little of interest in the claim of an obscure
Indian girl against the rich and powerful Jackson Ore Company.

The new county courthouse stood on the crest of a high
sloping hill overlooking the business section of town and the big
lake beyond. Patterned after Independence Hall, it was a one
story structure, dignified and imposing in the classical simplicity
of its lines. I was not too surprised to learn that the architect
who had designed the new bank, where I roosted, had had nothing to do with designing the new courthouse; it was mercifully
free of architectural frosting.

Off the long entrance corridor to the courtroom and on
either side were the various county offices: county clerk, regis-
ter of deeds, treasurer, prosecuting attorney, judge of probate,
and the like. Behind and separate from the courtroom was the
jury room, judge's chambers, and several conference rooms. The
new stone county jail stood by itself behind the courthouse, and
housed the sheriff's family and his office.

It was nearing nine-thirty and still the judge had not appeared. I arose and paced restlessly around the empty courtroom, studying the rather forbidding photographs of past

boards of supervisors and other county dignitaries, trying vainly
to catch a glimpse of the big lake out the tall courtroom windows to calm my nerves. This was an exercise in futility because
I knew that even a tall man would have to stand on a chair to get
a peek at the lake, the windows were so high. Shortly after coming to Marquette I had asked the clerk Gad Smith the reason for
blotting out this lovely view.

"We planned it that way, Willy," he replied.

"Rather obviously, Mr. Smith," I persisted. "But why?"

"So that the beautiful lake won't distract the jurors and
groundlings from the endless ham acting and burning eloquence
of you gabby lawyers," he shot back. Gad Smith, an old silver-
haired unbeatable politician, was a bit of a card. The first day I
met him he swiftly penetrated my armor and started calling me
Willy.

I heard the tall mahogany door of the judge's chambers
breathe open and I hurried back to my place, pressing Laughing
Whitefish's shoulder as I passed. Instead of the judge emerging it
was Gad Smith, nodding and rubbing his hands as he ap-
proached our counsel tables. Then he paused and spoke to
Henry Harwood and me in a sibilant stage whisper. Ham acting,
I saw, was not confined solely to lawyers. . . .

"Gentlemen, Judge Grant was delayed a little getting down
this morning by the heavy snow last night. He has just arrived
and asks that you bear with him another few minutes." Gad
Smith then retired to his little closed wooden cubicle immediately in front of the judge's high bench and busied himself shuffling papers. I again glanced back at Laughing Whitefish, but she
appeared deep in thought, or possibly prayer, and was shading
her eyes with her hand.

Again the door of the judge's chambers opened and this
time the judge himself emerged, tall and bearded, erect and aus-

tere, his black gown swishing silkily as he strode slowly across to the bench, climbed the little stairway, and, gathering up his gown, seated himself in the high-backed black leather chair.

"Please be seated, gentlemen," he said, nodding gravely. He glanced down at Gad Smith. "May I have the file in the Kawbawgam case if you please, Mr. Clerk?" The clerk arose and passed up the file and as the judge busied himself with it my nervousness increased. I could hear the courtroom clock ticking on the wall behind me, sounding like the hammers of doom. Although I had met the judge when I was admitted to practice in the circuit, and had watched him preside several times, this was the first time I had appeared professionally before him.

Claudius Grant was a transplanted New Englander in his late sixties, I judged, and had been circuit judge for nearly twenty years. His long full beard, worn in the square-cut pre-War style, was nearly white, as was the shock of thick coarse hair that pushed back abruptly off his high forehead in a kind of unplanned pompadour. As I sat watching the light glinting off the thick steel-rimmed glasses he wore under bushy eyebrows I couldn't help thinking that he looked for all the world like an austere and bespectacled Moses.

In his colorful irreverent way Cassius Wendell had summed him up for me. "Willy boy," he declaimed, "have no fears over Claudius Grant. You will find him meticulously fair, thorough to the point of exhaustion, and stiff as the proverbial stove poker—though he rarely exudes any of the latter's occasional warmth." About then I was inclined to agree.

The judge lowered his gavel once lightly to gain our attention. "Gentlemen," he said, "we will consider this special session of the circuit court convened and the clerk will so note. Are counsel ready to proceed?"

"Yes, Your Honor," Henry Harwood arose and said.

"Ready, Your Honor," I managed to croak.

"The court gathers from the pleadings," the judge went on, "and also from sources that might be said to fall in the realm of judicial notice"—he smiled slightly—"that this pending litigation is not only quite complex but highly important to both sides. But this seems ever to be the fate of even the most routine litigation—at least to the lawyers involved—and I may veer closer to my point when I say that this case appears to be one that could involve large sums of money. Now even the most modest case involving little money can present the most complex legal issues.

"Again some of the most important cases—financially speaking, that is—can present few and comparatively simple legal issues. The present case appears to present both complex issues and potentially large sums of money." He paused, removed his glasses, and, glancing up at the skylight, rubbed the corner of one eye and then replaced his glasses. "All this is preliminary to my informing counsel, as I now do, that since this case seems highly important on all counts, and an appeal seems likely whichever way I rule on the demurrer, I now propose to read the opinion I have prepared along with my ruling on the demurrer. With your kind indulgence, gentlemen, I shall now proceed."

It was not precisely a question; Henry Harwood and I remained silent. The judge sipped from a glass of water at his elbow, picked up some rustling papers from the bench before him, and clearing his throat and adjusting his glasses began slowly to read, his resonant voice echoing hollowly in the tall and all but deserted chamber.

"Charlotte Kawbawgam, an unmarried woman, also known as Laughing Whitefish, alleged daughter and heir of one Marji Kawbawgam, a deceased Indian, and herself a full-blooded Indian woman of the Chippewa tribe, has filed her bill of complaint in this court to obtain relief under the following circumstances: the defendant Jackson Ore Company is alleged to be a corporation that took over the iron mining property of the Jackson Mining Company, an unincorporated joint-stock partnership company formed by some Jackson business men in 1845, and by it later conveyed and sold to the defendant corporation. It is further alleged that incident to that sale and conveyance the defendant corporation agreed to take over, assume and pay 'all outstanding debts, claims, and demands of every kind and nature' existing against the original partnership company. This suit is brought to secure and enforce the rights alleged to have been contracted by the original partnership in a written agreement between it and Marji Kawbawgam, but never consummated or assured to him or his daughter, who now claims to succeed to his rights."

The judge frowned and paused and appended a notation to the opinion he was reading and I found myself mildly heartened to think that this severe perfectionist was occasionally prone to error or second thoughts. Or had his poor secretary erred? He resumed reading in his resonant droning voice. "The original partnership was formed for the purpose of mining in the Lake Superior area," he continued. "It is further alleged that the complainant's father, Marji Kawbawgam, was present in 1844 when iron ore was first discovered at the present site of the defendant's mine property in what later became Negaunee, and that the following year he discovered and made known to certain of the co-partners the mine property now known as the Jackson Mine, and that they then agreed to pay him for his services, which agreement was later ratified on the books of the original company. It is also alleged that the partnership had procured a permit from the War Department, in pursuance of which it subsequently took out a lease on the mine property, namely a section of land, that is 640 acres, by virtue of which it still later bought the land from the Government for $2.50 an acre, receiving therefore a deed of patent signed by the then President to which the defendant corporation has succeeded."

It came as a shock to be reminded that the fabulously wealthy and successful Jackson Mine property had been sold by an eager Government for a mere sixteen hundred dollars. Yet this was *twenty* times more than the Government had originally paid the Indians for the same property! Just then I heard a door open behind me but, absorbed, did not turn around.

"Marji Kawbawgam is alleged to have been an uneducated Indian who died in the summer of 1859," the judge pushed on. "The bill further alleges that his rights were recognized during his lifetime and that he worked for both companies pursuant to this agreement, which was later violated by his abrupt discharge by the defendant corporation. It is alleged that Marji Kawbawgam then and later tried to negotiate and settle his claim against the defendant company, but that his efforts were unsuccessful. Finally it is alleged that this complainant, the claimed daughter and heir of said Kawbawgam, has timely filed her bill of complaint upon reaching her majority."

The judge paused and took another sip of water and quietly resumed reading. "The defendant has demurred, generally and specially, relying on numerous grounds, which I need not detail here, including lapse of time. Another of its grounds for demurrer appears to be to question whether Charlotte Kawbawgam is a lawful heir of Marji Kawbawgam. But she plainly alleges that she is his daughter and heir, and it is elementary that at this stage of the proceedings the court on demurrer must accept as true all well pleaded allegations in the bill."

I sighed inwardly with relief as the judge droned on; this was the first small sign of victory. "The original agreement was in writing and however informally drawn contained an ascertainable description of land, and of Marji Kawbawgam's interest in it, and the consideration on which it rested. Does the defendant dispute that Charlotte Kawbawgam is a daughter of Marji Kawbawgam? It does not precisely say, and while the court may take judicial notice of some of the informal domestic arrangements that have prevailed and still regrettably prevail among many of our Indians, the complainant says she is his daughter and heir, and at this stage of the proceedings, at least, the court must accept her word as true."

I resisted an impulse to turn and look at Laughing Whitefish as the judge read on. "On the basis of the allegations in the bill the court is bound to assume that Marji Kawbawgam at least possessed an equitable interest in the property described which passed to his daughter unless already barred by lapse of time. While considerable time has indeed elapsed, the court cannot presently say as a matter of law that the claim has been barred. The defendant has not yet made answer and on this hearing the court must assume the allegations in the bill to be true. At least there is enough in it to call on the defendant to put in a defense and leave the merits to be tried on the facts. The court can scarcely anticipate what questions may be raised or issues projected when all the facts come out."

The judge looked up from his reading and lowered his voice. "The court accordingly holds that the defendant's demurrer must be overruled, with costs. Leave is given it to file an answer to the bill in twenty days." The judge looked down at Henry Harwood. "Is counsel now prepared to advise the court whether or not steps will be taken to appeal this ruling?"

Henry Harwood arose, stood silent for a moment, glanced back at the clock, looked briefly across at me, and then addressed the judge. "Your Honor, there will be no effort made to appeal your ruling on the demurrer," he said. "Our answer will be on file within twenty days." I sighed with relief.

"Very well," the judge said, and he lowered his gavel once and I had barely time to scramble to my feet before he had gathered up his papers, descended the bench and disappeared into his chambers, followed dutifully by Gad Smith.

I glanced over at Henry Harwood. "Thank you, Mr. Harwood," I said, stuffing papers in my briefcase.

He removed his glasses and half smiled at me. "Don't thank me, young man. Thank the judge and perhaps your instinct for rather inclusive if not rambling pleading." With that he gathered up his things and quickly pattered out the tall rear door.

Hefting my briefcase I turned to bask in the approval of Laughing Whitefish. Next to her on the bench, pantomiming his congratulations with clasped hands, sat a nodding and beaming Cassius Wendell. I hurried back to join them.

"Well done, Willy boy," the old boy cackled gleefully. "You have survived the first assault on your case."

"Thank you, William," Laughing Whitefish said gravely, and as I drew closer she arose and did a surprising thing: she kissed me, her lips barely grazing mine—cool, soft and tremulous as the wings of a moth. Never had victory tasted sweeter.

"My, my," Cassius Wendell said, rolling his eyes like an erring Santa Claus. "Guess poor lonely old Cash was a bit hasty in forsakin' his case." With that Laughing Whitefish quickly leaned forward and kissed him on the grizzled cheek, *winking* at me as she did so. I saw I was only barely coming to know this strange and unpredictable girl.

ELEVEN

A lawyer preparing for the trial of a difficult and complex case has much to do and many pitfalls to avoid if he is to get done that which needs to be done to win his case. Chief among these pitfalls is a rather helpless occupational tendency to become excessively enamored of some phase of his case to the neglect of the rest; to grow too much fascinated by one link in his necessary chain of proof; he is like a man consulting a dictionary who winds up chasing everything but the word he needs. Such was lately happening to me and, worse yet, the thing that obsessed me was a dead man: one Marji Kawbawgam, father of my client Laughing Whitefish. I could not get him out of my thoughts.

True, Marji *was* vitally important to our case, but yet he was only a link; it was quite enough if I could show in court that the man had lived and died, had meanwhile guided the original Jackson prospectors to the iron ore outcrop for a reward that was never paid, and had later fathered Laughing Whitefish, who was his heir. There was no need for me to prove an elaborate courtroom biography and indeed good reason why I shouldn't. Yet the man fascinated me; I wanted to know more about this anonymous Indian; who he was; how he had lived; to learn if possible by what quirk of fate this strange taciturn man had come to father the disturbing girl I knew as Laughing White-fish, Charlotte Kawbawgam—"call me Lotti for short..."

To this end I repeatedly went to see Jack Tregembo in Negaunee, the sickly Philo Everett in his big, empty brownstone house on the hill in Marquette, old Captain Merry, under whom Marji had worked for many years, now retired and living with a niece—anyone who had known him—probing them about the life and times of Marji Kawbawgam. I pored over the yellowed files of the *Mining Journal* and combed through old books and journals at the public library. While some of what I learned was helpful to the rest of my case—or so I hoped—much of it was clearly irrelevant, but still I kept on. Gradually I came to learn more about Marji Kawbawgam than perhaps any living person, clearly more than his own daughter had ever known.

From Jack Tregembo I learned that Marji had been abruptly discharged by the new management of the Jackson Mine in 1857; that thereafter, through the good offices of Jack himself, he had got a job as the ostensible chief apothecary of a traveling medicine show that featured an alarming decoction called Snakeroot; that Marji's main chore was to exhibit himself in the elaborate—if totally unauthentic for these Lake Superior Indians—feathered headdress and full regalia of a Plains' Indian, while the proprietor and real pharmacist, a crafty quack called Doc Halliday, hailed Marji as the great Indian healer who concocted Snakeroot. Jack had saved and produced for me one of Doc's old handbills, a model of professional understatement.

"Take that wonderful new Elixir of Life, that miraculous boon to Happiness and Glowing Health, Snakeroot, the original Indian herb remedy, that new Magic Potion made of a crafty combination of Snake Oil and secret Indian roots and herbs, mixed with care and cunning by a Genuine Indian Medicine Man, all according to an expensive and Ancient Tribal Formula."

Jack had attended Marji's maiden performance and in his dramatic fashion recreated the scene for me. Listening, I could see once again the bats circling in oiled flight over the muddy square in Negaunee, feeding greedily on the swarming moths and mosquitoes attracted by the coal oil flares of Doc Halliday's medicine show. After Doc's pretty wife, Dolly, had brought tears to the eyes of the assembled miners by a quavering rendition of "Annie Laurie," Doc had stepped forward and made his pitch. Jack had learned it by heart and, de-Cornished, it came out something like this:

"Ladies and gentlemen, I hold in my hand a bottle of precious Snakeroot made personal today by Chief Beaver Claw here"—pointing grandly at Marji—"that miraculous remedy sought even by the crowned heads of Europe. Locked in this bottle are the ancient secrets of the wisest Indian medicine men, passed on for generations, now known exclusive only to Chief Beaver Claw.

"Folks, do you ever wake up in the morning with spots before your eyes, gas on your stummick, pains in the small of your back, a strong and offensive u-*rine? Then take Snakeroot!* It banishes your aches and pains, releases the internal juices, tunes up the system, flushes the pipes and valves—in a word Snakeroot. Step right up, folks, a hi looky! All for one silver dollar, just ten silver dimes!"

After a one-night stand in Negaunee the show had moved on to L'Anse, then on up to the booming copper towns on the Keweenaw Peninsula, thence over to Ontonagon—and after that Jack had lost track of Marji the healer. Then one day nearly two years later—the summer Marji died—a gaunt and spooky Marji had shown up at Jack's saloon, minus his feather headdress, minus Snakeroot, minus Doc Halliday's medicine show.

"My Gawd, Marji," Jack had demanded, "where you been at? You look like a ghost." Over a succession of drinks on the house—Marji was flat broke—Marji told Jack the story of his adventures with Snakeroot.

After leaving Ontonagon the show had worked across northern Wisconsin, thence down the St. Croix River to the Mississippi River, thence downstream to Hannibal, where it had wintered. The following spring it had worked down the river to Cairo and then slowly up the Ohio River—always playing one-night stands and then moving on—a security measure Doc had early learned from bitter experience. Marji explained to Jack why Doc Halliday invariably ascribed the manufacture of Snakeroot to Marji; it was not modesty on Doc's part, nor yet merely to lend glamor and Indian authenticity to the concoction; it was mainly to save his own neck. "He was wife beater, bully, fake, and one big coward," Marji said.

"Allus knew it, Marji," Jack had agreed. "Never trusted no man what cudn't take his likker straight."

The blow had fallen just a month before at a bustling river town called Monkey's Eyebrow. Business had been so good that Doc had tarried yet another night and, business still thriving, for still another; a combination of greed and bourbon had conquered discretion. On the third night an even larger crowd was waiting, and when Doc went into his spiel a dozen men had leapt on the platform, visibly wan and shaken from their recent bouts with Snakeroot but determined on vengeance.

"Who made this here damned poisonous stuff?" their spokesman demanded.

In the past it had been Marji's job to take the blame and ward off any occasional complaints—between Marji's size and the debility swiftly afflicting any taker of Snakeroot, real crises had been few. Tonight the cowering Doc had quickly gotten behind

Marji and plucked away at his blanket, frantically whispering: "Tell 'em you made it, Marji, tell 'em you made it! If you don't, you thieving red drunkard, I'll fire you on the spot."

Something had snapped in Marji; all the gibes and insults he had taken from the bullying Doc came rushing back. Suddenly he rebelled and stepped aside and pointed an accusing finger at the cowering Doc and said: "Here is man who make bad medicine that make you sick, not well."

"Grab him!" the spokesman ordered.

Thereupon the men smashed the remaining bottles of Snakeroot—except one which they made Doc drink—wrecked the show, and tarred and feathered Doc Halliday and hung him in a tree by one leg while Snakeroot did its work—"took holt," as Jack described it. How did Marji get home? He had worked his way down the Ohio and up the Mississippi, and thence overland back to Negaunee—doing odd jobs on river boats and in stables along the way, scavenging when he was broke, occasionally being driven to pilfering. "So Marji come home," he concluded simply, downing his drink.

"Welcome home, Marji," Jack said. "Let's 'ave another on the 'ouse."

After Marji had returned from his medicine show adventures in the bad drought and depression summer of 1859 he was so ill and run down that he could not have worked at hard manual labor had he been able to get a job. Jack gave him odd jobs around the saloon and fed him and let him sleep on a cot in the back room. When Marji gained sufficient strength he caught a ride to Marquette on an ore train and walked out to Presque Isle to see his daughter. There he learned that Laughing Whitefish had gone to live at L'Anse Bay with his first wife, Blue Heron. Being weak and without funds, Marji had disconsolately returned to Jack's saloon.

" 'E wos terrible upset—'e 'ad a kind of hobsession to see 'is daughter," Jack told me. " 'E wudn't eat, only spirits 'e wanted. It was like 'e knew 'is end wos near."

Next I sought out old retired Captain Merry, one of the last white men to see Marji alive, and from him learned the next scene in the swiftly closing drama of Marji Kawbawgam. Shortly before his retirement Captain Merry was sitting one day in his tiny office in the Jackson Mine stone "dry" building—the miners' changing quarters—talking with Ira Beadle, the new superintendent under the new mine management.

"All of a sudden Marji Kawbawgam walked in," Captain Merry told me. "I hadn't seen him since I'd had to fire him on orders from my super Mr. Beadle two years before. He looked like a ghost."

Without a word of greeting Marji had tugged at the deer-skin pouch he wore about his middle, produced the old paper, thrust it at Captain Merry and said: "What will you give?"

Captain Merry saw at once how desperate and driven Marji was and tried to put him off. Years before he had told Marji to consult a lawyer to enforce his claim. " 'T'wouldn't be up to me, Marji," he said. "And you'd only drink it up anyway."

"Marji want money paid his daughter. What will you give?"

The alert Ira Beadle looked up over his glasses and arose and took over. "What will you take for your damned paper?" he said, winking at Captain Merry.

"Would hundred dollars be too much?" Marji replied ignoring Captain Merry's warning shake of the head.

"Pretty high, pretty high," Mr. Beadle murmured, again winking at Captain Merry. "Might be able to swing fifty dollars —no admission of liability, of course—just nuisance value."

"Will you really give fifty dollars?" Marji eagerly said. "Marji need money bad for little girl."

Old Captain Merry paused in his recital to me and shook his head. "That Ira Beadle was always a close one, he was. He winked at me again and I saw his eyes gleaming crafty-like behind his thick glasses. Then he said: 'I'll give you thirty dollars for your damned paper, not a cent more.' "

"What did Marji do?" I asked, horrified at such taunting muscular greed.

"Marji just stood there kind of numb looking and Ira Beadle came forward to take the paper away from me, but I pulled it away. I was mad and awful ashamed. Then Mr. Beadle turned real angry-like to Marji and said: 'Speak up, drunken redskin, or I'll make it even less.' "

"What happened?" I said, leaning forward in my chair.

"Marji kept staring kind of pleading at Ira Beadle. I thought he was going to cry. Then like a man in a dream he took a step forward, bent over, took careful aim, and *spat* in Ira Beadle's upturned face. Then he *slapped* him, twice, hard, once on either cheek—I heard the tinkle of Mr. Beadle's glasses smashing on the floor—and then Marji took his paper from me, carefully folded it away, and walked slowly off the mine property and down the new railroad track leading out of town."

"What happened then?" I asked.

"Ira Beadle hurried downtown and swore out a warrant for the arrest of Marji Kawbawgam. 'I'll see that murderous red devil behind bars!' he swore. 'Moreover I'll have him horse-whipped for this.' "

"Did they catch him?" I asked. "Was he ever horse-whipped?"

"Never," Captain Merry said. "Within a week poor Marji was dead."

From Laughing Whitefish herself I learned in halting bits and dribbles—she seemed almost reluctant to discuss her father

—that she and her foster mother Blue Heron had seen Marji during his one appearance with the medicine show in L'Anse; she was then a little girl.

"Did he see you?" I asked her.

Laughing Whitefish shook her head and turned her face away. Finally she spoke: "Small as I was I remember how filled with shame and compassion I was. I wanted to run up on the platform and take his hand and lead him away but my mother—Blue Heron, I mean—held me tight. So I stood there and watched my poor grotesque father and wept."

"Did he ever know?" I asked. "I mean later?"

"Yes, William, Blue Heron bitterly told him about the spectacle he had made of himself, this when he came finally to say goodbye, the last time I ever saw him alive"—her hand went to her throat—"the time he gave me this paper, when he hung this deerskin pouch about my neck—also the time when old Osseo predicted his death."

From others I learned other things: again from Jack Tregembo how he had hidden Marji from the sheriff when the fugitive Marji had returned from his final farewell trip to L'Anse Bay; I spoke to the night-watchman at the mine who, horrified and helpless, had witnessed Marji's death from the doorway of the dry building; I spoke also to one of the miners, now an old man, who had helped recover Marji's broken body with his worn and loaded packsack still over his shoulders.

I winnowed and pored over these fragments like a miser counting his gold. Little by little I began to *see* Marji Kawbawgam. I was not unlike a digger among ancient ruins seeking to recreate a vanished civilization out of bits of broken pottery. Such was my obsession that one wintry December night I sat down and wrote a story, my very first. I called it "Death of a Native Pine."

TWELVE

Marji Kawbawgam was awakened by a bright light shining in his face. For a moment he lay blinking, wondering where he was, where the streaming shaft of light was coming from. Then he saw the moonlight streaming in the window of the back room of Jack Tregembo's saloon. Memory came flooding back. He saw the cases and barrels and empty kegs piled about him, felt the frail cot creaking under him, and suddenly remembered that for days now he had lived in this hot and stuffy storeroom, only stirring late at night to stealthily prowl the alleys behind the saloon so that for a spell he might escape the intense heat and catch a breath of fresh air; that all this time he had been living virtually as a prisoner of his old friend Jack Tregembo so that he might not instead fall prisoner of the sheriff.

He recalled bitterly that the white men now sought to punish him and lock him away because he had finally dared stand up to one of them. Once again he saw plainly the staring acquisitive eyes of mine superintendent Ira Beadle gleaming out at him through thick glasses; once again he heard him hiss, "Speak up, drunken redskin, or I'll make it even less . . ."

Marji rose heavily from his cot and lurched to the window and stood staring up at the full moon. Tongues of heat lightning darted across the sky and he thought he heard a distant roll of thunder. Perhaps the long drought was about to end . . . He

112

swayed weakly and braced himself against the wall; he had not eaten for days, it seemed; all he had wanted was whiskey and more whiskey, which had sorrowfully been provided by his old friend Jack Tregembo—the only white man, he somberly reflected, who had ever truly befriended him.

As Marji stood thinking and watching a resolution formed in his mind: if the white men would not pay him his due, why should he not go himself and take it away? And if his days were numbered, as old Osseo had recently said, then wasn't the only safe way to provide for his daughter to go boldly to the mine and carry his share away—now, this very night? Yes, that was the thing... A purposeful Marji found his old packsack and unbarred the back door and stepped out into the moonlight. He pulled the door behind him until he heard the wooden bar fall into place. Then, keeping to the shadows, he hurried up the alley in the direction of the Jackson Mine. His plan was childishly simple—why had he never thought of it before?

All about him he could hear the hot click of crickets and grasshoppers shrilling their ancient rivalry. From overhead came the sharp cries of feeding nighthawks. And high over everything rode that ancient queen of the skies, the full moon, pouring its pale light upon the parched and dusty earth. "Laughing Whitefish," Marji whispered as he gained the fenced entrance to the Jackson Mine—*his* mine. He waited in the shadows until he saw the night watchman complete one of his nightly rounds and disappear into the dry building. Then, gathering himself, he darted across the open path of streaming moonlight and found the old weed-grown trail leading to the top of the rocky hill where he had once lived.

Gaining the summit Marji lay panting on the ground. Presently he arose and brushed the sweat from his eyes and lurched over to the lone leaning pine. He tried to make out the legend that had been cut in the ancient tree so many years before by

William Burt, but the first heavy clouds in months had risen swiftly and obscured the moon and he could not see. He ran his hand over the rough bark until he felt the old incision: "W. B. 1844." A strange peace came over him.

Then Marji felt the rain, the first in many weeks, and he sank to his knees alongside the tree and let the drops beat upon his upturned face. For a long time he knelt listening to the deep purr and murmur of the parched earth taking the rain in her like a woman taking a lover who had long been away, all the more ardently because in her secret heart she had feared he would never come back. Then Marji remembered there was work to be done, and he arose and splashed his way to the uprooted stump where, ignoring the pelting rain, he feverishly began filling his packsack with loose pieces of wet ore.

Then came the first flash of lightning followed by a great roll of thunder. It seemed a signal for the skies to fall open and the rain fell now in great slanting veils. In a kind of heedless fury Marji toiled until his packsack was full. He shouldered it with difficulty and staggered toward the lone pine, leaning to rest before making his long descent. The rain was falling in torrents now and the wind had risen. Marji could feel the old tree swaying and creaking under him. Once again he felt William Burt's initials and then, straightening, turned abruptly away.

Bracing himself under his burden, Marji started down the steep incline, slipping, almost falling, sliding to a stop. He turned and looked up at the lone pine, now looming almost directly above him. A low heavy mass of black clouds came rolling in from the northwest—ominous, convoluted, racing—seeming now to hang over the great tree. The forked tongues of lightning darted crazily everywhere; great booms of thunder shook the ground. Marji stood rooted and frozen, the wild rain pelting his upturned face like hail; never had he witnessed such an awesome spectacle. Then the rain suddenly abated and the lightning and thunder ceased; the fury was over; it grew ominously still. Marji stood staring in wonder.

Suddenly an enormous jagged shaft of lightning, a single bolt, blazed down out of the dark cloud bank, hovered for a frozen instant, like a poised eagle, and plunged to the heart of the ancient pine tree. For a moment the riven giant seemed to writhe like a beheaded serpent, its shattered top and raked sides emitting little puffs and jets of its suddenly vaporized life sap. As Marji helplessly watched, the great tree began to sway, gently at first, then in ever increasing arc, as though rocked by an unseen hand. Then with a great splintering sigh slowly and majestically the stricken tree came toppling off the cliff and hurtled down across the steep path where Marji obediently waited.

Marji thought he heard a horrified shout coming from below but he could not move. "Farewell, Laughing Whitefish!" he cried—then with a rending crash the prediction of old Osseo came true. Marji's crumpled body lay still, his eyes closed, a half smile on his face, like a dreamer dreaming a pleasant dream. All grew still save for the mutter of retreating thunder and the coursing rivulets of rain now mixed with human blood. The moon again looked out from between thinning, racing clouds. The ancient gods of the outraged mountain were appeased—Marji Kawbawgam had at last come home.

THIRTEEN

The ghost of Marji Kawbawgam had been exorcized ... I put down my pen and flexed my cramped fingers. I became conscious of the ringing of bells, the tumbling and frosty clanging of church bells, and presently I realized—magic phrase—that it was the night before Christmas. I heard the wind sighing in my chimney and I went to the window to see if it was storming, but I could not penetrate the clinging frostweb. Restless and exhilarated, I went to my tiny pantry and prepared myself an elaborate Christmas drink: rum, milk, eggs, grated nutmeg, more rum—lots of rum.

"Merry Christmas, Willy Poe," I mournfully toasted, but both the words and the drink clogged suddenly in my throat and I put down my cup. I felt horribly forlorn and lonely, on the verge of tears. I hurriedly got on my wraps and wound a muffler around my neck and, almost angrily, tramped my way down the hallway.

Arriving at the top of the stairs on my floor I heard a door open down the hall beyond me. "Oh," I heard a feminine voice saying, "I thought it was someone else. Merry Christmas, Mr. Poe."

Peering, I made out the dim figure of the lady doctor, Madame Dujardins, standing in her doorway. "Merry Christmas," I

116

said, tramping on down the stairs. What a droll hour, I thought, to be expecting a patient.

Fresh snow had fallen, and I scuffed it away from the street door so I could close it. Our thrifty landlord grew pained when we left it open.... The heavier snowfall had abated, and large lazy flakes, glistening like suspended jewels, floated slowly earthward, occasionally, when caught by the wind, flashing and banking like snowbirds. I toiled up Front Street hill and heard the music of a Strauss waltz coming from the Cozzens House. Pausing, I made out the dim figures of dancing couples gliding past the frosted windows.

The front door squealed open on its frosty hinge and a girl in a gauzy dress stood framed in a cloud of vapor, holding an open fan across her bosom, humming softly to the murmurous accompaniment of muted violins and voices and gay laughter. A young man came up—"Annie Isabella, you'll catch your death of cold standing there!"—and swept her away, the door slammed, the spell was broken. I turned away, numbed and bereft, and plodded on up the hill.

At the top I paused uncertainly and decided to walk east along Ridge Street. When I stepped off the curb I heard a sudden jingling of bells and quickly drew back. A team of dragon-breathed horses drawing a long sleigh box filled with blanketed and singing young people squealed round the corner and swept past me. The huddled driver, muffled in his buffalo coat, raised a bemittened hand in brief salute, his shouted "Merry Christmas" all but lost on the wind. I felt more lonely than ever. I had never been on a straw ride.

Trudging along I passed Philo Everett's big darkened house and, peering, saw a dim light glowing from the rear. I wondered how the old gentleman was and hoped he would be able to testify in our case. Most of the houses were dark and silent, each with its thin column of smoke curling up from the chimney and then suddenly caught and bent by the wind. I passed a lighted house and through the window saw a man teetering atop a step-ladder trimming a Christmas tree, reaching out desperately to-ward the tree top, a woman steadying him, clinging for dear life to the tail of his nightshirt. Pushing on I wondered how Cassius Wendell was and what he was doing. I thought of Laughing Whitefish and longed to be with her—just we two in a cutter drawn by a fast horse decked out with jingling bells . . . The snow fell harder.

Descending the steep hill at the far end of Ridge Street I came to the lake, now mysteriously veiled in swirling snow that gave the illusion of falling upward. I turned and took the dark-ened lakeshore road back toward town, following along the rail-road tracks. Two staggering men loomed up and passed me, going the other way. "Merry Christmas, partner!" they joy-ously shouted. "Merry Christmas," I shouted back, declining their kind offer of a drink from an open bottle. I came to the depot and saw a light burning in the ticket office. I peered in the window and saw the crouched figure of the night telegrapher, Miles Coffey, wearing his green eyeshade, bending over his key. I tapped gently on the window: two longs and three shorts. It was our signal and Miles hurried to the door and opened it to let me in.

"Merry Christmas, Miles," I said, scuffing the snow off my boots and entering.

"What's merry about it?" he demanded with fine Irish dis-dain. "All I bin doin' all evenin' is taking down Merry Christmas till I'm gettin' to hate the bloody words."

"Happy New Year, Miles," I said.

"Hate 'em even worse. Here, give me your wraps and set up the cribbage board while I go silence that chatter box."

Miles was not only night telegrapher for the railroad; his office also served the town. He was my new friend and a kind of mentor; he had not only taught me to fly cast better but was teaching me cribbage and fly-tying as well. Moreover he was initiating me into the delights of sour mash bourbon. He reached in a cupboard and drew out a bottle and we cut cards and settled down to play.

"Merry Christmas, Miles," I toasted him on the first drink.

"Up Ireland," he said, and we touched glasses and drank.

We played cribbage, drank, talked fishing, prayed for cuts and hurled friendly insults. When he had to stop to take a message I either played bartender or sat listening to the sputtering keys, to the kettle simmering on the stove, the wind grieving in the chimney, his cat purring in its box. It was nearly four o'clock when, girded and swathed against the weather, I cheerily bade him goodnight and took off down the tracks. My loneliness had vanished.

"Willy," a voice called after me. I turned and saw Miles standing in the open doorway. "Merry Christmas," he called out.

"Merry Christmas, Miles."

As I scuffed my way along—nearly a foot of new snow had fallen—I reflected that not only had my loneliness fled but that for several hours I had not thought about the obsessive Kawbawgam case: my blessings were coming in clusters . . . I came to my building and once again kicked the snow away and crept up the long creaking stairs to my floor.

The solitary gas light still burned at the top of my landing. I wondered sleepily whether I was the last one in and might safely turn it out. Leaving it on all night also pained our sensitive landlord. While pondering the problem I heard a door click softly farther down the hallway. Then I saw the figure of a man emerging from Madame Dujardins's quarters and stand whispering to someone in the door. Next I saw the bare arms of a woman reach out and draw him in for a long embrace. Embarrassed, I turned away and studied the gas light. I heard the door click and the man coming down the hallway. His walk had a familiar ring ... He came to a stop behind me and I wheeled around. It was Cassius Wendell. For a moment neither spoke.

Then: "Morning nausea?" I inquired politely.

"Fallen womb," he replied gravely, turning and thumping on down the stairs.

I was awakened by a great thumping and pounding at my outer door. Bright sunlight was streaming in my frost-etched window. I glanced at my watch—it was nearing noon—and, ah yes, this was Christmas Day. The pounding kept on.

"I'm coming, I'm coming," I called out, shuffling flannel-nightgowned and bare-footed to my outer door. "Who's there?"

"It's me, old Kris Kringle hisself," the cheery voice of Cassius Wendell answered. "Open up, I've got a special Christmas surprise for a Master Willy Poe. Does he perchance dwell in these ill-lit precincts?"

I turned the key and opened the door and started back when I saw Cash and Laughing Whitefish. She was carrying a long bulky package.

"Aren't you going to invite us in?" Cash said, stomping his way past me, pushing Laughing Whitefish before him. "Merry Christmas and all that twaddle, my boy."

"Merry Christmas, William," Laughing Whitefish said, thrusting the package she carried into my arms.

I stood awkwardly holding it against my flannel nightshirt. "Thank you. Please sit down," I said. "Excuse me—I'll get something on. Merry Christmas to you, Cash, Laughing White-fish."

I placed the package on my desk and retired behind my dressing screen to make myself presentable.

"Hurry, Willy," Cassius Wendell shouted at me from my

desk, which he had calmly appropriated. "We'll be late if you don't get a move on. We're all going to have Christmas dinner together up at the Cozzens House. Guests of old Cassius Wendell, no less—it's my little Christmas surprise. Put on a clean shirt for the occasion—another surprise."

"Sorry if I appeared stupid and inhospitable," I said, finally joining them, "but I played cards rather late last night with Miles Coffey over at the depot."

"What a way to spend Christmas eve," Laughing Whitefish murmured sympathetically, turning to Cash. "And how did you spend yours?"

"Yes, Cash," I joined in, "do tell us what you were up to last night."

"Oh, me?" he explained, darting me a quick look. "I spent the evening re-reading Dickens' *A Christmas Carol*. It's an old Wendell family tradition, you know—every Christmas I read it again, drunk or sober." He shot me another look. "Tends to keep me home mindin' my own business, Willy. By the way," he went on, changing the subject, "aren't we going to have a wee snifter before we dine? Season of gaiety and yuletide cheer."

Laughing Whitefish looked unhappy. "Oh, Mr. Wendell," she said, "don't you know drinking is bad for your health?"

Cassius reached over and patted her hand. "Trouble is, my dear, people always keep saying if you don't drink you'll live longer, but they're dead wrong—it only *seems* longer. Willy, can you succor a parched soul by giving him a little drink? Reading Dickens brings its solace, but drab sobriety as well."

"What would you like?" I said.

"Hm . . . What you got?"

"I'm afraid only a little left-over Tom and Jerry I made last night. It's a new drink I ran into when I was in New York. Are you familiar with the concoction, Mr. Wendell?" I inquired, elaborately polite.

"To my eternal sorrow," he dolefully replied. "The only

time I tried 'em I found that Tom and Jerrys not only furnish food and drink but, with the slightest application to their consumption, a free night's lodging as well. No thank you, son. Have you got a wee drop of plain whiskey? If so keep pouring till it runs cold."

"Sorry, Cash, I'm afraid it's Tom and Jerrys or nothing."

"Then it's nothing, thank you. Really didn't want anything anyway. Was just testin' Miss Lotti's loyalty and devotion." He pointed at the package on my desk. "Aren't you going to open your Christmas present?"

I looked inquiringly at Laughing Whitefish. "By all means open it, William," she said. "But don't get your hopes up—it's really very little."

For a moment I recaptured some of the magic thrill I used to experience as a child at Christmas. Never was the expectation greater than just before the last rustling wrapping was removed. Finally I exposed and drew forth a shiny new pair of handmade Indian snowshoes. I held them up before me. "Why, they're wonderful," I said, holding them out for Cash to see, clapping them delightedly together, longing to put them on then and there. "Look, Cash, look at the lovely red tassels tied along the frame—and the clever bead work along the crosspieces—"

"And the moose bindings that won't stretch or freeze," she added.

"They're really lovely," I said, touched. "Now when can we go snowshoeing?"

"I was hoping you'd ask that," she said. "When would you like?"

"How about this afternoon after dinner?"

"Fine, I'd love to."

Cash sighed and heaved himself to his feet. "Let's go eat. And don't think you're the only pebble on the shore, sweet William," he said, stomping across to the door. "Lotti gave me a deerskin jacket—made with her own hands, mind. And another of my secret female admirers presented me with a bottle of whiskey, so there. No, Willy, don't fetch your new snowshoes—you'll scarcely need 'em in the Cozzens House."

The new Cozzens House—rebuilt since the town's devastating fire of 1868—stood on one of Marquette's many bluffs, commanding a view of the lake. It was presided over by a retired lake captain, hale and stocky Captain Will Lightbody, who greeted us in person when we arrived at his door. The place was popular with seafarers all up and down the Lakes, and when the old captain wasn't entertaining his guests, he and his long glass were apt to be keeping the vigil in a little house he'd built on the rooftop.

After a sumptuous and leisurely dinner Cash sat with Laughing Whitefish while I hurried home to change into my outdoor clothes and get my new snowshoes. "What'll you be doing this afternoon, Cash?" I teased him when Laughing Whitefish and I were ready to leave. "Back re-reading *A Christmas Carol?*"

"No, Willy," he said dryly, "never on Christmas day." His eyes grew misty with recollection. "But for longer than you'd ever suspect, lad, it's been a well-kept tradition on Christmas eve. Now run along, you two."

Laughing Whitefish and I tramped entirely around her island, the trees sagging and beautiful under their glistening mantles of new snow. As I followed along behind her I imagined I was the rugged William Burt making his long trek from below snowbound L'Anse Bay to the Wisconsin border so many years before. Later she served supper in her little combination schoolhouse and home. Darkness had settled when she walked me down the hill from the Indian encampment to the main road to town, I proudly carrying my new snowshoes along the hard-packed trail. Arriving there we stood silently for a moment looking up at the stars.

"Thank you," I found myself saying, for some reason whispering. "Thank you for everything, Laughing Whitefish." She stood looking up at me mutely in the starlight and I put my arms around her and for the first time our lips met. I felt her arms urgently about me and we clung to each other, pouring into this sudden warm collision all our loneliness and hunger. Locked thus in close embrace, we swayed, reeled and nearly fell. Suddenly she broke away and ran swiftly into the darkness. I peered after her a moment and then, retrieving my fallen snowshoes, walked home as tall as the stars.

FOURTEEN

It was a crisp cold Monday morning, the first day of the second week of the regular February term of circuit court. Already I was at my place in the courtroom, champing to call my first witness and get the case underway. This time Laughing Whitefish sat alongside me at the plaintiff's leather-topped counsel table. The judge was still in chambers and my opponent Henry Harwood had not yet made his appearance.

Of the regular court attendants only the court reporter, old silver-mustached Audabon Bigbee, sat dreaming at his table, staring sightlessly at the opposite wall, surrounded by his rows of stenographic pads and batteries of sharpened pencils, resting before the impending torrent of rhetoric. I reflected that while the poor court reporter is the busiest person during any court trial, ironically he is least heard from. Mute inglorious Milton, I thought.

I had earlier requested the judge to set a day certain for the trial for some time during the February term so that I could subpoena my witnesses for an exact day. Many of my witnesses were Indians who lived in far places, more or less nomadic dwellers in the woods, who would have to travel there on foot. The judge had called in Henry Harwood and the three of us had conferred over the problem. The judge had consulted his tentative docket and pondered and stroked his square beard and finally suggested a date—today—and Henry Harwood had agreed. The latter had repeated his generous invitation for me to use his law library, again telling me where the key was hid. Yet I nourished no illusions that our trial would be any war of rose petals; for one thing, as Cash had said, the stakes were too high.

Meanwhile I had already given notice of and taken the deposition of old Captain Merry, who had lately become a patient in the Negaunee hospital, the most important facet of whose absentee testimony was to identify the written promise given Marji by the original company and the fact that it was never kept. He also recalled and told of the time Marji had tried to settle his claim with Ira Beadle, the superintendent of the new company, and of how Marji had slapped that grasping man when he had tried to reduce further the already ridiculously low settlement figure.

I craned around to glance at the clock—it was 9:15—and was surprised to see the benches behind me already well filled, mostly with Indians—men, women, children—although I had subpoenaed but seven witnesses for the first day. Some of these Indians were sitting in the unused jury box, their whispered conversations making a kind of piercing guttural buzz. I leaned over and whispered to Laughing Whitefish.

"Good heavens, Lotti, what brought all your people here? I know there was nothing in the paper about the start of the trial because I looked. Did you send runners around the Peninsula?"

She shook her head. "Of course not," she said. "I see you still don't know my people very well. They've been waiting for months for my case to start."

"Too bad we can't decide the case by ballot," I said, and then I thought of something new about the case and hurriedly reached for my notebook. By then I had so many thoughts embalmed in my swollen notebook that if I lost it we'd probably have to abandon the case.

During the weeks between the judge's ruling on the demurrer and today I had been far from idle. Once again I had been out prowling the Peninsula. I was all too aware that to make out an actionable case for recovery I had to prove the execution of the agreement between Marji Kawbawgam and the old Jackson crowd—the defendant in its answer had cagily pleaded no knowledge of Marji's agreement, leaving the burden up to me —and further show that Marji had done his part but that neither the original Jackson partners nor the present corporate defendant had done theirs. This proof alone would take a bit of doing. And since a finding of liability without proof of damages would be an idle victory, I had also done much scurrying to round up figures to show how much iron ore the defendant had mined and what dividends had been paid—in brief, how much money the company had made.

The results of my sleuthing were unnerving. I now knew that if I could win this case on the basis of Marji Kawbawgam's claimed share the quiet young woman who sat next to me would be wealthy beyond her wildest dreams. I had not dared tell her how much for fear she'd grow panicky and lose her nerve.

My biggest problem was to prove that my client Laughing Whitefish was entitled to her father's share—assuming that I could prove all of the rest. That proof hinged on divorce, I had concluded, yet this was the most tantalizing and frustrating aspect of my case, made all the more so by the fact that the Indians kept no written records. I still felt that the main thrust of my proof on this phase of the case was boldly to claim and try to prove that Marji Kawbawgam had married and then divorced his first wife, Blue Heron, and then had married Sayee, mother of Laughing Whitefish, who had died leaving my client the sole heir of her father Marji. I had gone over this strategy a thousand times. The time had now come to prove it.

My train of thought was interrupted by the courthouse janitor who came in and noisily shook down the ashes and refueled
the two tall Michigan Garland coal stoves that stood glowing,
their brass water kettles gently steaming, in opposite corners of
the large court chamber. The already heavy atmosphere now
grew mixed with coal gas. Perspiring, I longed to open my collar
but dared not; Judge Claudius Grant was a notorious stickler
for the proprieties.

Laughing Whitefish was leaning over whispering to me. "I
wish they'd start, William, this suspense is killing me."

"I know, I know," I whispered, sinking back with my
thoughts.

If my client had not been an Indian all I would have needed
would be to introduce in evidence a certified copy of her father's divorce from his first wife—and that would have been
that. But how was I to prove a divorce that was supposed to
have occurred many years before between unlettered Indians
who were members of a tribe which kept no written records of
births, deaths, marriages, or divorces? Particularly where most
of the knowledgeable witnesses had either died or moved away?

I stole another look at the clock, wondering what was de-
laying the judge and Henry Harwood. Nearly all the benches
were filled now, mostly with Indians, all seeming at the moment
to be staring stoically and unblinkingly at me. It occurred to me
that I had better be good . . . . I looked for Cassius Wendell but
could not find him in the buzzing crowd. Perhaps he's gone on
another of his periodic sprees, I thought, almost with a pang of
envy.

Someone was plucking at my sleeve and I wheeled around.
"You Mister Poe?" a breathless small boy said.

"Yes."

"This here is for you," he said, and he thrust a folded paper
in my hand and fled. I opened it and read.

Dear Wm. Poe:

Last night Mr. Everett had a terrible Spell and Doctor Barnett says he will be lucky to Live let alone come Witness for you. Am awful sorry but guess that is Life.

Resp. yours,
Mrs. Carrie Brown.

I silently passed the note to Laughing Whitefish who read it and looked anxiously at me. "What will we ever do?" she said.

"Pray," I answered bitterly. "First Osseo, now Philo Everett—our luck is holding steady."

"Poor Mr. Everett," she murmured, turning away.

The door of the judge's chambers suddenly sighed open and the first to emerge was Claudius Grant—tall, austere, gowned—followed by Henry Harwood, then by a tall, ruddy, distinguished-looking stranger, and finally by Sheriff Barney Langley and the court clerk, Gad Smith.

The judge mounted the bench and stood bearded and imperturbable behind his high-backed chair. Henry Harwood pattered over and stood at attention by his table, accompanied by the stranger. Both carried bulging briefcases. Sheriff Langley stood waiting in his little wooden cubicle extending out like a life boat off from the right of the judge's bench, poised gavel in hand. Gad Smith likewise waited attentively in his cubicle, doubtless calculating how many voters were out front. Cassius Wendell had told me that Gad Smith rarely went out campaigning; he did it in the courtroom, where voters came from miles around simply to behold him in action.

The judge now nodded at the sheriff, who pounded his gavel three times, craning his neck this way and that to see that all in the courtroom had arisen. Spying some laggards he pantomimed them up with both arms, palms up, until proper respect for the court was assured. "Hear ye, hear ye, hear ye!" he called out with the ardor of an auctioneer. "The honorable circuit court for the county of Marquette is now in session. Please be seated." Again he motioned all hesitant stragglers to be seated, palms down. His little drama done, he nodded up at the judge.

All were now seated, but still there was a general scuffling of feet and whispering from the crowded back benches. The judge spoke in a low voice to the sheriff, who again arose, scowling, and held a warning finger over his lips until silence reigned. I repressed an impulse to sneeze; I felt that just about then it might have cost us our case. The judge addressed Gad Smith. "The clerk will please call the next chancery case on the hearing docket," he said.

Gad Smith arose and, evidently spurred by the sheriff's stellar performance, called out our case as though announcing the Day of Judgment. "Charlotte Kawbawgam versus Jackson Ore Company," he bawled portentously. "At issue and ready for hearing." I secretly voted their oratory contest a draw; the sheriff had rather more volume, I concluded, but the clerk had tied him on style and general aplomb.

Judge Grant addressed counsel. "Are counsel on both sides ready to proceed?" he asked.

"The plaintiff is ready," I arose and said.

"The defense is ready, Your Honor," Henry Harwood said. "But first I have two preliminary motions to put to the court, if Your Honor please."

"Proceed with your motions, Mr. Harwood," the judge said. The stranger had now arisen and was standing quietly alongside Henry Harwood.

"Your Honor," Henry Harwood went on, "I should like at this time to present formally in open court my esteemed colleague and fellow lawyer from New York City, Guy Nesbitt. Mr. Nesbitt is chief counsel for the Jackson Ore Company and hopes to be associated with me in the hearing of this case. If

Your Honor please, I should like at this time to move the tempo-
rary admission of Guy Nesbitt to practice in this court for that
purpose and also move that the files and records of the case be
amended so to show."

The judge looked at me. "Any objections, Mr. Poe?"

I could hear myself taking a deep whistling breath as I
arose, my mind racing. What to do, what to do? To object was
probably idle, since I knew the judge could have granted the
motion without consulting me. And probably would anyway,
whatever I said. Was he testing me under fire? Or merely trying
to save my face?

"Mr. Poe?" the judge gently prodded.

"Your Honor," I began, but my voice came out in a
cracked falsetto and I tried again. "Your Honor," I repeated,
"the plaintiff has no objections to granting the motion. In fact
we deem it an honor to be opposed by such eminent counsel. Indeed we take it as a favorable omen for our case that the addition of such distinguished talent was deemed expedient by the
defendant. Ah-no, Your Honor, no objection."

"No need to make a jury argument, Mr. Poe," the judge
said dryly, "especially since we have no jury. The motion—or
rather motions—are granted. The clerk will so note." The judge
paused and looked out at the rapt audience of Indians. He produced a handkerchief from under his gown and damped his
forehead, glancing at the glowing coal stove nearest him. He
rolled his eyes and again spoke to the sheriff. "The sheriff will
please call the janitor to check the fires and air out this stifling
chamber," he said. "Meanwhile the court declares an informal
recess for five minutes. I suggest that nobody leave."

While the judge himself repaired to chambers, presumably
to catch a breath of fresh air, Henry Harwood beckoned me
over to meet Guy Nesbitt.

"Happy to know you, Mr. Poe," Guy Nesbitt said easily,

firmly shaking my hand. "And thanks for your flattering words. Better you watch out, young man, or you'll wind up in politics."

"I heard your visiting lectures on trial practice and examination of witnesses while I was in law school at Ann Arbor," I said, suddenly remembering him and reminding him of the occasion. "They were superb," I added, truthfully enough.

"Hope I didn't give away too many trade secrets," he said, chuckling genially, going on to explain that the reason court was late starting this morning was because his train from Chicago had been held up by a derailed ore train. "Doubtless some of your client's ore was on it," he added, chuckling over his little joke. "By the way, how is the health of old Dean Lattimore?" he inquired.

As we talked along I studied this man who was to oppose me. Guy Nesbitt was an imposing-looking man in his mid or late fifties, tall, white-haired and handsome in a big-shouldered florid sort of a way. While his hair was not thin it was so silky fine that each glistening hair seemed to have been installed with a needle. Through it glowed his pink shining scalp. In contrast his heavy eyebrows were a brownish-black, somehow giving him the appearance of an actor who had forgotten to remove all his makeup. The dramatic effect was heightened by a pair of candid blue eyes that looked out at me without a trace of guile. I had a strong intuition that I was in for the fight of my life.

I excused myself and returned to my table. Lotti looked at me inquiringly. "They've thrown one of the best trial lawyers in the country at us," I told her, lowering my voice. "Among lawyers he's known as the Silver Fox. But at least we've got them worried—they've brought him all the way from New York."

As I proceeded to tell her about the reputation and professional cunning of Guy Nesbitt, the janitor appeared and dampered down the coal stoves. Next he found a long window pole in a corner and opened two of the tall courtroom windows, one on either side, and I gratefully drank in the rush of cool February air. Then he padded into the judge's chambers, presumably to inform His Honor that general asphyxia had been averted.

Judge Grant emerged almost at once, rustled his way purposefully up to the bench, sat down and looked down at me. "Call your first witness," he said.

I arose and slowly moved forward, wondering as I did whether the Indians, who had fared so poorly against the white invaders in the past, would now fare any better in their courts.

PART TWO

FIFTEEN

"The complainant will call Octave Bissonette," I announced, and my new first witness—I had earlier planned on calling Philo Everett—arose and made his way from the back of the crowded courtroom up to the witness stand. The witness was a dark, rather flamboyantly handsome man of about forty, with touches of gray at his temples. Gad Smith intercepted him on the way and waved him down.

"Raise your right hand and be sworn," he ordered, holding up his own right hand.

"Very well, M'sieur," the witness amiably agreed, nonchalantly facing the clerk with upraised hand, all the while flashing his teeth, jutting out his dimpled chin, preening himself like a courting rooster.

"Your other hand," the clerk hissed. "That's your left!"

"Ha!—I'm—what you call?—a sout'paw?" the witness said, highly amused, quickly raising his right hand. There was a rumble of general laughter, especially from the Indians. The judge frowned and fondled his gavel. Quiet descended.

"You do solemnly swear that you will tell the truth, the whole truth, and nothing but the truth, so help you God?" the clerk demanded.

"You bet you boots, Octave Bissonette always tell the trut'—you know dat ver' well."

"Do you or don't you?" the clerk demanded. The judge looked away to hide his irritation.

"I do."

"Please sit down in the witness chair," the clerk ordered, pointing.

"Thank you, thank you—doan mind if I do."

The witness sat smiling at me, basking in all the suddenly focused attention, and I advanced upon him with my trusty notebook.

"Your name, please?" I asked.

"My name ees Octave Bissonette," he proudly declaimed, pronouncing it as elaborately as an elocution teacher correcting a dull pupil. "*Octave Bissonette!*" he repeated, pointing an accusing finger at me, "jes' lak I'm tell you before an' nevair lak I'm now hear you say."

He was one of those people with French accents, I was learning, whose most casual utterance tended to emerge as a full-blown nasal aria. I wondered what would happen if he got excited; we would probably have to send for an interpreter. I studied the man warily.

"Where do you live?" I said.

"On Gran' Island—'bout ten-twelve mile up from Munising, out in da Lake"—he grinned—"where I s'pose mos' islands is locate."

I ignored his sally and pressed forward. Why was it that even the soberest people so often tried to be funny once they got on a witness stand? "Did you know Marji Kawbawgam during his lifetime?"

"Sure, sure t'ing I did."

"Where and when did you first see him?"

"Why, at trading post of American Fur Company, lak I'm tole you before."

"Mr. Bissonette," I explained gently, "I well remember all

the things you told me before today, but you haven't yet told them to the judge. He is the man who must now hear whatever you know about this case for it is he, not I, who must decide it. Do you understand?"

"Sure, sure—I see, young fella."

"When did you first see Marji Kawbawgam at the post?"

Octave shook his head. "I can't remember—long tam ago— I was small boy, just starting to ride an' hunt an' shoot a liddle. My father he run post."

"Was he alone or with someone?"

"My father he run post alone."

"I mean Marji Kawbawgam. When you first saw him at your father's post was he alone or with someone?" I knew full well that Marji was with Sayee, Laughing Whitefish's mother, then a young bride, but since Octave was my witness I dared not put the words in his mouth.

"He was wit' his young Indian wife—he come dere to buy her some present. Dey coast down lake in his canoe."

"What was her name?"

"She was call Sayee an' she live up dere—well, I s'pose down from where I'm now sit—on Laughing Whitefish River wit' her pa an' ma."

"Did you ever see them again?"

"Many time—but not always togedder. I see dat Sayee more often than I'm see him." Gesturing: "Dat Marji he work somewhere yonder up da road. You see, I go visit often up where she live." He smiled in wistful recollection. "Dem days I know planty nice Indian girl up dere."

"Did they have any children?"

He pointed smiling at Laughing Whitefish. "She is only wan I know—I knew her since she was li'l papoose tied on a board." He wagged his head. "My, my—how tam he fly—now she big 'andsome girl." He regarded her with undisguised admiration and ran his tongue over his lips. "Fine big 'andsome girl."

"Go on," I prompted him, nettled by his boldness.

His face clouded. "Her mother she die, you know, pre' soon after w'en Charlotte here was born—I mean Laughing Whitefish. I'm remember my own mother he go up dere for burial an' help with dat little wan."

"When was that?"

He put out his hands. "I can't remember—fifteen-twenty year ago—maybe longer. Who can say? Her father him dead now too—guess dat Marji he got dronk an' fall off hill or somet'ing, I hear tell dat."

"Object to that last as hearsay," Guy Nesbitt arose and said quietly.

"Objection sustained," the judge ruled.

I paused and consulted my notebook. At least I now had Marji and Sayee safely married and the parents of Laughing Whitefish. It was time to get down to cases.

"You say your father ran the trading post at Grand Island? Was he an Indian?"

Proudly: "He was pure-blood Franchman from Quebec."

"And your mother?"

"She was pure-blood Indian, which I s'pose is 'ow I come be 'aff-breed." He smiled at his witticism.

"Of what tribe was your mother?"

"Chippewa. Mos' all Indian 'round here of Chippewa tribe. Few Cree and some udders, but mos'ly Chippewa."

"Are your parents living or dead?"

Hand shading brow he shook his head sadly, the dutifully contrite and bereft son. "Alas, bot' dead, dead."

"Are you familiar with the Chippewa Indian tribal rites and customs?"

Again shrugging. "Familiar? I see 'em Chippewa all my life. I fish, I hunt wit' dem, some still live today on our island, an' w'en I'm small some time dey come sleep our house or lie aroun' dronk on our yard or w'en is col' or wet, dey sleep on floor in store. I'm raise wit' dem. I'm part Chippewa myself, you know dat. Yes, I'm know dem people good."

I saw the judge frowning in distaste over this pastoral picture of tribal life. "Did you ever see a Chippewa Indian marriage?" I pressed on.

His eyes lit up. "Planty time." He held up his hands. "Big celebration, lots of eat an' drink, dance all bloody night, everybody broke an' hongry for long tam after dose wedding."

"I mean the ceremony itself?"

Shrugging, hands up. "Ceremony? Dere was no ceremony, if you mean lak preacher an' all dat. Everybody come, lak w'en Marji an' Sayee get marry, well, everybody come an' dey have wan hell of a big time. Maybe man he give her ol' man some present, dat's all."

The flushed judge tapped his gavel. "The witness will please watch his language," he warned, frowning.

Glancing: "Thank you, Jodge. Dey dance an' sing, dey eat an' drink—maybe wan two ol' man get up an' make big long speech an' bless young couple"—he rolled his eyes—"den by an' by pre' soon young couple dey sneak away to dere wigwam an' den—"

"Very well, Mr. Bissonette," I put in hastily, "then is it fair to say that the Indians had no formal wedding ceremony, like the whites, but—"

"No, no—no ring, no prayer, no marriage licings, no preacher, no papier—none of dat monkey business." He snapped his fingers. "Dey simply agree on get marry an' dat is dat." He frowned fiercely. "But no wan force. If dey doan get 'long dey part, if dey get 'long, dey stay marry"—again he snapped his fingers—"jus' like dat. Smart people, Chippewa Indian."

"Then the Chippewas did practice divorce?" I said, following this new scent. He had not told me this on earlier occasions.

Another shrug, both hands up: "Same as marry, **no**

preacher, no judge, no papier, no monkey business. If dey doan get 'long dey quit an' find new one dey can get 'long wit'. Dey doan"—he stole a sidelong look up at the judge—"dey doan sleep togedder or nossing after dat."

I paused and glanced at the clock. This talkative and unpredictable witness had already told me what I wanted to know from him and heaven knew what he might say if I launched any more questions at him in the dark. I walked back to my table and looked across at Henry Harwood. "You may examine," I said.

To my surprise Guy Nesbitt arose instead and came forward briskly erect, shooting his starched cuffs and buttoning the coat of his handsome salt-and-pepper suit. He was what my mother used to call "a fine figure of a man." He paused several feet from the witness, ran his hand lightly through his silvery hair, and then spoke in a low confidential voice. "How old are you, Mr. Bissonette?"

Shrugging airily: "Maybe t'irty-eight, maybe forty, who can tell? No papier, you know—same like get marry—an' bot' my parents he's die. Gone, gone."

"Hm, I see. And you say you knew Marji Kawbawgam?"

"Oh, yes, I knew Marji—beeg 'andsome man, queeck like wilecat."

"Did you attend his marriage to the woman called Sayee?"

"Non, non—lak I say, I was boy an' Indian wedding no place for kids."

"Then you only *heard* they were married?" Guy Nesbitt glanced at the judge.

He drew back, aggrieved, reproachful. "Of course, lak I know the jodge here is marry because I hear dat. 'Ow else you gonna know if somewan is marry? Anywan who admit marry mus' be marry."

"I see. And you say you are familiar with the practices and customs of the Chippewa tribe?"

The witness exuded confidence. "Like da back of my hand, M'sieur."

"Fine. Then you are doubtless aware, sir, that it was the common practice for an Indian to marry one wife and then put her away and take another and sometimes maybe still another?"

The question was dynamite and I held my breath. "Oh, yes," the witness cheerfully answered. "W'en Indian doan lak each other dey get new one, bot' man an' woman. Dey don't tie dem up an' drive each nudder mos' crazy lak you do; Indian have better way of marry, none of your 'umbug pretend you lak person wen you doan lak."

"*Touché*, Mr. Bissonette."

"Is trut', Mister Laywer," he said, solemnly crossing his heart.

My own heart sank. My witness had just blandly testified that the Chippewa Indians indescriminately practiced both polygamy and polyandry. Was our case flying out the courtroom window on my first witness?

Guy Nesbitt took a step forward, then suavely: "And how many wives did Marji Kawbawgam have?"

Loftily: "Oh, I doan know 'bout dat. All I'm hear 'bout is maybe two, maybe t'ree. I doan keep no count."

I leapt to my feet. "Objection, Your Honor," I thundered. "This is plainly hearsay. Move the answer be stricken."

"No more hearsay, Mr. Poe, than the marriage you're trying so hard to prove and about which your own witness just testified he had merely heard," the judge said quietly. "The objection is overruled and the answer may stand. Continue, Mr. Nesbitt."

"And of these two or three wives you say Marji had, was this Sayee the first?"

"Oh no, Marji he already 'ave wife up L'Anse Bay, but I'm never know her name."

Raising his bushy actor's eyebrows in mock surprise: "You mean that Marji and his first wife were not divorced when he married Sayee?"

I yearned to object but this was cross-examination and Guy Nesbitt plainly had the right to lead my witness where he could. And leading him he was—right over a steep cliff. I closed my eyes waiting for the answer.

"The witness will answer," the judge said.

Shrugging: "Divorce? I doan know 'bout dat—I always hear dey stay marry." He held out his hands indulgently. "But divorce or stay marry, what's diffrance? Indian can have wan, two, t'ree, maybe dozen wife if he can stan' dem an' afford for keep dem."

Again I closed my eyes, this time half in prayer. Would this talkative witness *never* get off the stand?

My prayers were answered. "Thank you, Mr. Bissonette," Guy Nesbitt was saying. "I think that's all."

"You're welcome," the beaming witness answered, rising and bowing like a courtier.

Guy Nesbitt smiled and nodded at me faintly as he walked past our table back to his seat. The Silver Fox had already shown his fangs.

"Back to you for re-direct, Mr. Poe," the judge gently prodded.

I arose and glanced at Laughing Whitefish who looked up at me anxiously—she sensed the swift turn in our case. "No further questions, Your Honor," I said, plumping to my seat.

"Then call your next witness, if you please," the judge briskly reminded me, taking up his pen and making some notes.

"May I have a minute please, Your Honor," I requested, rising and fumbling hastily through my notebook.

"Very well," the judge replied. The courtroom had suddenly grown hushed and the clock ticked horribly.

SIXTEEN

For several reasons I had wanted badly to call Philo Everett as my first witness: because of the precarious state of his health; to get the background clearly before the judge; and also to get the execution and delivery of the vital original Marji Kawbawgam agreement swiftly proved by the very man who had drawn and witnessed it, now the only remaining living person who could do so. Moreover Philo Everett had known Laughing Whitefish since she was a little girl and knew that she was Marji's daughter. There was no evading it—he was a crucial witness on a crucial phase of our case. Now he was gravely ill and could not come and my first witness, the voluble Octave Bissonette, had just unwittingly dealt our case a heavy blow. Guy Nesbitt aroused me from my doleful reverie.

"If it please the court," he was on his feet saying, "If plaintiff's counsel has some problem about the next witness to call, I think I have a suggestion that will give him more time to cogitate and yet permit us to get on with the testimony." I looked at him hopefully.

"The court is listening," the judge said, plainly vexed over my delay.

"We have a witness who happens to be here in the court today observing the proceedings and who must himself testify at some point during this trial," Guy Nesbitt continued. "If it is agreeable I suggest that he be called now. This would not only permit us to proceed with the case but also permit our witness to proceed with his plans for a European trip. In fact if he cannot testify now I am afraid we might have to notice the taking of his deposition in Ann Arbor."

The judge looked at me. "What do you say, Mr. Poe?"

"Who is the witness?" I inquired, suspecting some kind of trap. "And what does he propose to testify to?"

"A fair question," Guy Nesbitt smilingly agreed. "He is Professor Hugh Naughton, professor of anthropology at the University in Ann Arbor. Doctor Naughton will testify on the marriage and other related customs, rituals and practices of the Chippewa Indians, a subject upon which he is an acknowledged expert. Surely, Mr. Poe, you have heard of him?"

"Indeed I have, Mr. Nesbitt, although I must confess I was unaware that he was an expert on Chippewa Indian customs or I might have called him myself."

One thing was certain: I could not in any case keep Professor Naughton ultimately from testifying, so why not hear him now? If he was about to destroy our case wasn't it more merciful to learn it fast? Moreover neither I nor Guy Nesbitt could change the Indian customs; they had been fashioned centuries before either of us was born; they were what they were.

"What do you say, Mr. Poe?" the judge repeated, with more than an edge in his voice.

"The complainant has no objections," I said, taking the plunge.

"The defense will call Professor Hugh Naughton," Guy Nesbitt announced before the words were fairly out of my mouth. I recognized the towering figure of Professor Naughton —he was a ponderous giant of a man—slowly plodding up to the stand where, after being duly sworn by Gad Smith, he sat calmly facing us.

"Your name please?" Guy Nesbitt began.

"Hugh Sylvester Naughton," the witness boomed in a deep growl of a voice not unlike the low muttering of a church organ.

Guy Nesbitt then skillfully qualified his witness as an expert on the Chippewa Indian, deftly bringing out that he was an anthropologist by training and profession; had made a specialty of studying the Chippewa Indian and his customs, rites, myths and taboos; was the author of *The Vanishing Chippewa* and had written and delivered many monographs and papers on the subject of their folkways; had duly read the Jesuit *Relations* and other primary written sources, including the writings by and about Fathers Marquette and Baraga; also those of Schoolcraft, Parkman, Morgan, LeJeune and many others whom I had never heard of; and had for many years taken regular field trips among the Chippewas, studying their tribal customs, interviewing chiefs and sub-chiefs and the oldest survivors, endlessly probing and taking notes . . .

Guy Nesbitt turned to me. "Any questions on qualifications?"

"No questions," I replied, awed into submission by this massive display of erudition.

"Doctor Naughton," he pressed on briskly, "you have just heard the plaintiff's witness Octave Bissonette describe the informality of the Chippewa marriage ceremony. Would you care to comment on this phase of his testimony?"

"Yes, indeed," the witness rumbled. "In essence his testimony there was in all respects sound: as he said, there is no formal ceremony, no preacher, no written record kept. The heart of the Indian marriage depends upon two things—I am referring here to the Chippewa marriage ritual, but it applies as well to many other American Indian tribes—a mutual agreement of the parties to live together as man and wife plus a general tribal recognition that they are indeed man and wife. The crux is agreement plus reputation, as it were."

So far so good, I thought; this couldn't much hurt since it was no more than our side claimed.

"You may state whether or not the Chippewas practiced divorce," Guy Nesbitt pressed on. I leaned forward tensely; this went to the heart of our case.

The witness frowned thoughtfully for a moment before answering. "The Chippewas had no divorce in the sense that we view it," he began, "that is, as a formal dissolution of the marital status for grounds alleged and proven, conducted before some special tribunal. The Indian consulted only his conscience and one might better describe Indian divorce as a cessation of the marital state—I almost said hostilities—and marked this time by three principal factors: a physical separation of the man and wife; a cessation of all marital relations thereafter; and a common tribal recognition or acceptance of the end of the married state." He paused and smiled slightly. "I am speaking in lay idiomatic terms, Mr. Nesbitt, merely sketching the highlights. I could probably run on until the spring breakup tracing the historic, religious and symbolic subtleties implicit in the subject."

Guy Nesbitt held up both hands in mock horror. "By all means, please don't, Dr. Naughton," he declared. "Much as this clime enchants me the prospect of being marooned here till spring horrifies me. All we want—or at least all I want—is the distilled essence of your observations, the polished pearl as it were. Do you have anything further to add on the subject of Indian divorce?"

"Yes. I find it was rather more common several generations ago than after the whites came among them—especially the missionaries—many of whom frowned on divorce in principle and preached against it. Again I can cite you many sources, if you wish. Finally even those Indians who did not themselves embrace the Christian faith, or indeed any faith, less often divorced each other not so much because they didn't want to, but rather because the tribal practice had changed: the tribe came less and less to countenance and recognize divorce—using divorce of course in the loose sense I have described."

"How about polygamy?" Guy Nesbitt suddenly asked. "Did the Chippewas practice it?" Again I leaned forward.

"Yes," the witness answered, "and, ironically enough, even more so after divorce fell more into disuse. If they couldn't get rid of an undesirable mate one way—by divorce—they did it by another—simply by walking away and taking another mate. My investigations disclose, however, that the Chippewas practiced polygamy, and also polyandry—where the wife takes more than one husband—from the time of its emergence as an independent sub-tribe of the Algonquin stock. Nor do I imply that polygamy necessarily involved a 'putting away' of a first wife, as you earlier this morning phrased it, and taking up with another. I could cite many instances where Chippewa Indians, particularly men, had as many as three and even more wives living simultaneously in the same encampment, indeed in the same wigwam."

I glanced up at the judge, who sat thin-lipped and frowning with distaste over this calm account of barbaric profligacy. Guy Nesbitt pushed on. "Is polygamy still practiced among the Chippewas?"

"Yes, but rather less so than during the last half of the last and the first half of this century. The chief reason is economic: few tribal Indians can any longer afford to maintain more than one wife. As the hunting and fishing and trapping grew poorer, due largely to the Chippewas being pushed westward into collision with the Sioux, crowded into smaller and smaller areas, plus the growing influx and economic competition of the whites, plural marriages sharply dropped off. One wife was quite enough to provide for. Contributing factors to this decrease were the pressures of the whites, who of course do not practice polygamy—at least openly—and also doubtless the desire of many Indians to conform, to become Americanized. Another factor in the decline was the increase of mixed marriages between Indians and whites. Indeed I could go on for hours giving examples of the effect upon old Indian rituals and practices of the advent of the whites"—his face clouded—"not all of them happy, I assure you."

Guy Nesbitt was not to be lured down these scholarly byways. "But the Chippewa Indians occasionally still do practice polygamy?" he went on.

"Yes, occasionally."

"And they still did in the 1840's?"

"Yes, rather more so than now."

Guy Nesbitt looked at the clock. "Now gathering up the loose ends, Doctor, did I understand you to say that Indian divorce, as you defined it, is like the custom of polygamy on the wane among the Chippewas?"

"Yes."

"And was this also true in the 1840's?"

"Even more so, I would say, since then there was more polygamy practiced. Broadly speaking, the more polygamy you had the less need there was for divorce. It is difficult here to generalize."

This testimony was hurting, but at least the witness had allowed there could be an Indian divorce.

"And did you not say that a Chippewa divorce, where it existed, demanded three things: physical separation of the parties, cessation of all marital relations, and common recognition of the dissolution by the tribe?"

"That is correct."

"And is it fair to say that the lack of any one of those three elements would negate the idea of a divorce?"

"I would definitely say so, yes."

"I believe that's all, Doctor, thank you." Guy Nesbitt turned to me. "You may examine, Mr. Poe."

"Dr. Naughton," I said, arising and moving forward, "you would not say then that divorce, as you have defined it, no longer exists among the Chippewas?"

"I do not. Only that it has considerably dwindled."

"Or that it did not exist among them twenty-five or thirty years ago?"

"I do not."

"What about the children of divorced Indians—were and are they regarded by the tribe as legitimate?"

"They were and are."

I paused and pondered. What else should I ask this man while he was here? Maybe I should consult my notebook. I hastily riffled the pages, but everything seemed a blur. I closed it. Wasn't it high time that I consulted my own noggin instead of these cold old notes? The main issue of my case was childishly simple: was Laughing Whitefish legally entitled to sue and recover on her father's claim? Suppose for once I settled down and grappled with *that* problem.

"If you *please*, Mr. Poe," the judge prodded me.

"I'm sorry, Your Honor," I said. "Doctor Naughton," I went on, "do and did the Chippewas practice child adoption?"

"Objection, objection!" Guy Nesbitt was quickly on his feet. "Adoption is not relevant to any issue in this case."

"Mr. Poe?" the judge inquired.

"I think it is—or rather well might be. There is already evidence in this case that my client's father had more than one wife. I *know* there will be further evidence that the first woman who married Kawbawgam—one Blue Heron by name—virtually raised my client Charlotte Kawbawgam after her own mother's death. It is more than possible that this amounted to an adoption —that is if the Indians ever practiced adoption, which I am now simply trying to learn from someone who should know."

"Back to you, Mr. Nesbitt," the judge said, himself still plainly uncertain what his ruling should be.

"This is the first mention of adoption in this case, either in the pleadings or by any witness. Why didn't plaintiff's counsel ask his garrulous Octave Bissonette about adoption if he believed it was vital to his case?"

"Mr. Poe?"

"Because possibly plaintiff's counsel stupidly forgot," I truthfully answered. "Moreover I do not understand that Doctor Naughton was brought here especially as a rebuttal witness to the testimony of an unlettered backwoodsman whom the defense was unaware that I might even call. Or that I am limited in my present examination of this expert witness to what happened to be touched on by my own 'garrulous' witness."

"Mr. Nesbitt?"

"I renew my objection."

"Mr. Poe?"

Impatiently I crammed my notebook in my pocket—it was fast becoming a distracting nuisance—and took several steps toward the judge. "Look, Your Honor," I said earnestly, sensing that much might be riding on his ruling, "we are now examining a world-recognized authority on the marital and domestic customs of the Chippewa Indians—a witness doubtless brought here at considerable expense. Since he is about to leave for Europe it is probably our last chance. I again represent to the court that the question of child adoption can become important if not crucial to this case." I held out my hands. "I *beg* of you, Your Honor, to let me inquire of this expert authority while yet we may. I may add that I haven't the foggiest notion what his answer might be."

The judge put the tips of his fingers together and stared sightlessly out at the clock, which relentlessly ticked away. He looked up at the ceiling and then sat rigidly upright. "The answer will be received subject to the objection," he said. "The witness will please answer the question." I closed my eyes in relief.

Doctor Naughton looked up sheepishly at the judge. "I became so absorbed watching this professional duel that I must confess I quite forgot the question," he said.

"Let me help, Doctor," I volunteered. "My question was: 'Do and did the Chippewas practice child adoption?' "

"The answer is yes," the witness said, "though again, as with marriage, there is no undeviating practice, no formal proceedings to adopt, no record kept. Again it is a matter of determining the intention of the parties plus the understanding and recognition of the adoption by the tribe."

"And would an adopted child inherit from his adopting parent as though that parent were a natural one?"

"He would," he answered and then, glancing at Laughing Whitefish, smiled and added: "Or perhaps rather I should say, she would."

I paused and took a shot in the dark. "Doctor, did you ever run across an old Indian called Osseo in your travels?"

"Oh yes, I saw him many times," he answered swiftly, his face lighting up. "He was by far the oldest Chippewa Indian I knew or heard of and was a veritable mine of information."

"Veritable mine of information," I whispered to myself, charmed to recall that I had once coined the same daring figure of speech about Osseo. I felt more and more drawn to the witness: we shared even the same taste in clichés ...

"Was old Osseo one of those from whom you learned

about divorce and polygamous marriages among Indians?" I
pressed on.

"Yes, indeed—the old gentleman himself once had three
wives, ridding himself of one when she did something to dis-
please him."

"Such as maybe putting his snowshoes too close to an open
fire?" I inquired innocently.

"Precisely, and what a coincidence that you should have
guessed." He smiled. "But surely you already knew." I nodded.
"He was also a great student of foretelling the future," he continued. "The first time I saw him—let's see, that was back in '59
—he had recently predicted the death of an able-bodied fellow
tribesman. He said he would die within a week in a certain
place—and so it happened."

That would be Marji, I thought. "How did he do it?" I
asked.

"By a combination of capnomancy and spodomancy," the
witness replied.

"What in the world is all that?"

"Divination by means of smoke and ashes."

"How could he do this if he could not see?"

"It seems he had an assistant—perhaps I should say accom-
plice—an old woman who attended upon his ritual firemaking
and told him what she saw. I never saw him do it and he was
evasive about discussing it. It's all very mysterious and remarkable."

I lifted my eyebrows. "Do you believe in this sort of thing,
Doctor?"

He pondered his answer and spoke slowly. "As a scientist I
suppose not, but as a moderately observant traveler upon this
curious planet I sometimes wonder." He smiled. "Let's say I am
skeptically open-minded—or vice versa. When last I saw him
two years ago I told him I was looking forward to visiting him

again the following autumn—that would now be last autumn—but he replied that the omens had recently told him he might not survive till then." The witness sighed. "Alas he was right—old Osseo died but a week before I planned to visit him."

Guy Nesbitt had arisen and was pacing back and forth behind his table. The judge frowned and stirred restlessly, fondling his gavel, piqued by this mystifying exchange. I hurried to get on safer ground. "Doctor," I said, "what about the children of polygamous marriage—were and are they regarded among the Indians as legitimate?"

"They were and are."

"And may such children inherit from either parent as though there had been but one marriage by either?"

"Your question is rather over-simplified, but essentially that is correct. I warn you it might take days to trace the devious convolutions of Chippewa inheritance and descent. But the child would inherit."

"I would not wish to delay your European trip, Doctor," I said. "Now may I assume that you discussed this case with defense counsel before you testified here today?"

"Only in the most general way. I came here mostly to find out what I might learn." A slow quirked smile spread over his broad face. "If you are implying that I have trimmed my testimony to fit any defense theory of this case I can only assure you, sir, that my scholarship is not for sale. I have spent too many years learning the little I know for that. And let me remind you further, young man, that I did not create the rituals and customs of the Chippewa tribe—but a small fraction of which I have touched on today. They have evolved over many centuries, before any of us in this room was born, indeed before the white man launched himself in force upon this continent." He studied his big hands for a moment and looked up with an expression that was infinitely sad. "Though the white man may have failed to make the Indians good Christians he did succeed wonderfully in making them bad heathens. What is happening to the Indians of America is little short of tragic."

This earnest man *liked* the Indians, I saw, and I longed for the chance to talk privately with him, but ruefully acknowledged that after this brief collision I would probably never see him again; indeed to the lawyers this was one of the special fascinations of all trials. "I meant to imply no such thing, Doctor," I replied hastily. "In fact I was thinking much the same thing only a moment ago, and of how ironic it is that a white man living in remote Ann Arbor should today know more about their customs and folkways than the remaining Chippewa Indians themselves."

"If you are through making pretty speeches, Mr. Poe," the judge put in testily, "may the court venture to inquire whether you have any further questions of this witness?"

"No further questions, Your Honor," I quickly replied.

"Or you, Mr. Nesbitt?"

Guy Nesbitt arose and pondered for a moment. "Nothing further, Your Honor."

"Then we will recess for lunch and reconvene promptly at one o'clock. Mr. Sheriff, declare a recess."

SEVENTEEN

"Complainant will call Susan Gesick as the next witness," I arose and announced, getting the afternoon session underway.

An old woman dressed in the old-style Indian garb—moccasins and exposed leggins (as everyone in the Peninsula pronounced and spelled them) over which she wore a fringed blouse and a rather short skirt or kilt—arose from the back of the courtroom and, using a crooked homemade cane, hobbled her way toward the witness stand. "This witness speaks no English," I explained to the court as she painfully toiled her way up front, "and it will be necessary to use an Indian interpreter."

"Have you made arrangements for one?" the judge inquired.

"I have spoken with the sheriff, Mr. Barney Langley," I said, "and I am informed that during his boyhood he spent much time among the Chippewa Indians and is familiar with their language."

The judge smiled frostily and looked at the sheriff. "Mr. Sheriff, this is a facet of your talents I had been unaware of—you've been hiding your light under a bushel. Who knows, if the Indians would only exercise the elective franchise your tenure in office might approach immortality."

"Well, it's been a long time since I spoke Indian, Judge," Barney Langley explained sheepishly amidst a ripple of appreciative laughter. "I may be a little rusty."

"You can only try. Meanwhile you'd better get yourself sworn as an interpreter," the judge suggested, whereupon Gad Smith solemnly swore the sheriff "to well and truly interpret the questions of the court and counsel from the English language into the Chippewa Indian language and the answers of the witness from the Chippewa Indian language into the English language."

"I do," the sheriff declared after Gad Smith had triumphantly chanted this unwieldy mouthful by heart.

"Now swear the witness," the court ordered, whereupon Gad Smith gave the oath of witnesses to the sheriff in English, who repeated it to the aged witness in Indian, who grunted something in Indian, whereupon the sheriff said, "She does," and then helped her up onto the witness stand, where she sat staring out at us, occasionally wiping her watery eyes.

"What is your name?" I asked her.

The sheriff interpreted my question and when she answered he announced: "She says her name is 'Susan Gesick,' " he reported.

The judge shook his head. "Mr. Sheriff," he mildly put in, "it is neither necessary nor proper for you to preface your answers by 'She says' and words of similar import. It only clutters up the record in a case that already bids fair to be a long one. What we want are the actual replies of the witness, no more, no less. You are a mere neutral conduit whose sole job it is to transmit back to us precisely what *she* says. Perhaps it would be easier if you imagine that you are on the witness stand and are simply giving us her replies as though they were your own. Let's try again."

"Thank you, Your Honor," the sheriff said, perspiring freely. "I'll try to do better, Sir."

"I am sure you will." The judge nodded at me. "Once again, Mr. Poe."

"What is your name?" I dutifully repeated.

"Susan Gesick," the sheriff finally replied, basking in the judge's nodded approval.

"How old are you?"

"I cannot tell—old, old, very old. . . ."

I had noticed that she had cupped her ear and looked over at Guy Nesbitt's table as I asked my previous questions, and I suspected that both her hearing and sight might be impaired. "Is your eyesight failing from old age?" I inquired.

When the sheriff-interpreter conveyed this to her I saw her suddenly stiffen and sit very erect as she proudly answered, still looking straight at Guy Nesbitt: "The light in here is dim—I see very well." O vanity, thy name is woman, I thought as I pressed on.

"How is your hearing?" I continued, quite taken by this proud old crone.

"I can still hear the loon and owl a mile away and the *spung* of the nighthawk when he dives," she bravely lied.

"Did you know Marji Kawbawgam?"

"Yes. There was only one by that name. I danced at his wedding."

"Where was this wedding?"

"Why, right here below town—at our old encampment on the east side of the outlet of the Laughing Whitefish River."

"When was that?"

"I cannot remember—long, long ago." She spoke proudly, "I could dance all night in those days."

"To whom was Marji married at the wedding at which you danced?"

"To Sayee, of course, mother of the girl sitting there." She pointed a gnarled finger at Laughing Whitefish.

Maybe the old girl could see better than I guessed. Or had the other Indians earlier primed her?

"At whom were you just pointing?" I pressed on.

Spiritedly: "Why at Laughing Whitefish, daughter and only child of Marji Kawbawgam and Sayee."

"Did they have other children?"

"There were one or two others before Laughing Whitefish but they died in infancy. Most Indian babies died young. This child was the last and only one who lived. Her mother died shortly after she was born. I know because I was there and saw. Ah yes, Sayee, a good brave woman." I glanced at Laughing Whitefish. She had shut her eyes and was fingering the little deerskin pouch she wore about her throat.

So far so good, I thought. I knew that Guy Nesbitt would dig into other possible marriages of Marji once he got his hands on the witness, so I decided to anticipate him: avoiding the subject on direct examination would not chase these matrimonial goblins away and meeting it head-on might impress the court with my fairness and candor.

I swallowed hard and asked her a loaded question. "Did Marji Kawbawgam have any other wives?"

"There was one wife before Sayee up at L'Anse Bay. Her name—let me see—it was Blue Heron."

"I now ask you whether or not Marji Kawbawgam and this Blue Heron were divorced before Marji married Sayee?"

The interpreter blinked and looked distressed, looking pleadingly first at me and then up at the judge before he spoke. "I do not know the word for *divorce* in Chippewa," he confessed. "I never heard of it."

Guy Nesbitt was on his feet. "Possibly because divorce among Indians never existed," he suavely suggested.

"Is counsel now seeking to impeach the testimony of his own expert witness, Doctor Naughton?" I put in. "He testified only this forenoon that the Chippewas definitely practiced divorce. His only reservation concerned its prevalence."

"Gentlemen," the judge broke in, "we'll get nowhere if counsel keep launching general remarks at each other and into thin air. If Mr. Nesbitt has a specific objection to a question or answer let him address it to the court for a ruling. Do I hear any?"

"No objection, Your Honor," Guy Nesbitt said, smiling and sitting down.

"Perhaps you'd better rephrase your question, Mr. Poe," the judge suggested.

"Thank you, Your Honor, I'll try," I said pondering. Then: "Was Marji still married to this Blue Heron when he married Sayee?"

The old woman blinked her rheumy eyes before she answered. "No, I heard he had put her away before he married Sayee," she announced firmly.

"Objection, Your Honor," Guy Nesbitt was again on his feet saying. "Answer is manifestly hearsay. Moreover it is ambiguous—what is the legal status of a wife who has been 'put away'? Move answer be stricken."

"Mr. Poe?" the judge inquired.

"As Doctor Naughton explained here this morning a prime factor in determining the domestic status of the Chippewa Indian—whether marriage, divorce or adoption—was the common understanding of the tribe, in other words hearsay. As for the meaning of 'put away,' Mr. Nesbitt used precisely the same phrase this morning in questioning my first witness. Since a man of his skill and erudition cannot possibly be guilty of asking meaningless questions, I think it comes with bad grace that he now implies that the phrase has now suddenly become meaningless."

Guy Nesbitt shot me a swift smile as the judge turned the debate back to him.

"Your Honor," he began, "I did not and do not imply that

the phrase is without meaning; I question only that it means divorce. When I was questioning Mr. Bissonette this morning and used that phrase we were talking about polygamy, not divorce. So my use of the phrase could scarcely have implied divorce. If I had meant divorce there naturally would have been no polygamy."

At this juncture the witness Susan Gesick leaned suddenly forward and spoke earnestly to the interpreter, who tried to shush her up.

"Just a moment, Mr. Nesbitt," the judge said, frowning. He spoke sharply to the interpreter. "What did she say?"

"She wonders what she had just said that is making these gentlemen carry on so—the words are hers, Your Honor, not mine."

"Anything else?"

"She inquired whether they are about to fight."

The judge smiled his frosty mirthless smile. "Tell her," he said, "tell her that this is part of the standard dramatic repertoire that all lawyers feel periodically compelled to stage in court. Tell her she has nothing to fear and that there will be no fight. You might also tell her that I forbid her to again interrupt the proceedings of this court."

The interpreter delivered his message and the witness sat back with folded arms, her lined face breaking into an incredibly wrinkled smile, like the tracery on an old cracked pitcher. Hiding her toothless gums with her hand she giggled like a girl, all the while rocking to and fro. Our solemn antics had amused her mightily.

"Proceed, Mr. Nesbitt," the judge said tersely.

"The play goes on," Guy Nesbitt said *sotto voce.* "Your Honor," he went on, "this witness has just blandly said, and I quote, 'I heard he had put her away when he married Sayee.' Now gossip and idle rumor is one thing; common understanding by the tribe quite another. Whom had she heard it from? One

Indian? Three? Or indeed from a passing trapper who was no Indian at all? I renew my objection."

"Back once more to you, Mr. Poe," the judge said, blinking thoughtfully.

"Possibly all this indicates a fertile field for further inquiry, Your Honor," I said, and sat down.

The judge tugged thoughtfully on his beard, as he sometimes did when he was perplexed. Finally he spoke. "Counsel for the complainant may have a point there," he said. "I suggest he inquire a little further, subject to the objection. Meanwhile I'll reserve my final ruling. Proceed, Mr. Poe."

"What do you mean when you say Marji 'put away' Blue Heron before he married Sayee?" I asked the witness.

"I mean that the marriage was"—here the witness raised her bunched fingers, spreading them airily as she did—"over, done, flown, ended, no more"—here the interpreter paused and appealed to the judge—"and then she added another word, maybe slang, that sounded like 'phooey' or some such. I do not know this word."

"The reporter will please note the word," the judge said, nodding at me to continue.

"And how and whom did you hear this from?" I pressed on, treading boldly on dangerous ground.

"From many, it was common talk."

"Among whom was it common talk?"

"Among my people, of course. It was the common understanding of my people that Marji had put Blue Heron away before he married Sayee."

I sighed inwardly; for better or worse a possible divorce was now finally in the case. Or was it? "Your Honor," I said, "so that I may determine whether to keep flailing away at this subject, may I inquire whether the defense still sticks to its objection?"

"Up to you, Mr. Nesbitt," the judge said.

"One moment, Your Honor," he said, and he held a whispered conference with Henry Harwood—who had yet to say a word in court—and then looked up and quietly said: "With leave of court, Your Honor, the objection is withdrawn."

"Very well. Proceed, Mr. Poe."

I stood pondering, perplexed. Things were going along rather too nicely. What had come over my sly opponent, the fabled Silver Fox? Or was I wandering blindly into one of his hidden snares?

"Mr. Poe," the judge prodded. "Are you through with this witness?"

"Not quite." I advanced toward the witness. "Do you know who raised Laughing Whitefish after her mother Sayee died?"

"Blue Heron did—Marji's first wife who was put away. Blue Heron took the little one in and raised her as her own."

"By that do you mean that Blue Heron adopted this child?" I waited for the objection; it did not come.

Once again the interpreter appealed to the court. "I do not know of this word in Indian," he said.

"Try it another way, Mr. Poe," the judge suggested.

"What do you mean when you say that Blue Heron took Laughing Whitefish in and raised her as her own?"

"Objection, Your Honor"—this from Guy Nesbitt—"The question is not only leading and suggestive, but the previous answer speaks for itself."

"To you, Mr. Poe."

"Does counsel mean that he now concedes that the child was indeed adopted?" I inquired.

"Nothing of the sort," Guy Nesbitt answered spiritedly. "I renew the objection."

"The objection is overruled," the judge said. "Take the answer."

"I mean that Blue Heron raised the child as though it was of her own blood, her very own."

I pondered whether to pursue the subject further, but decided against trying to improve on perfection. Perhaps I'd better take a new tack.

"Where did Marji Kawbawgam and Sayee live after they were married?" I next asked.

"She stayed home at our Indian encampment near Lake Superior, near the mouth of the Laughing Whitefish River. Marji worked at some iron mine in the place they now call Negaunee. He was much away, sometimes for many weeks and months on end."

"Why did she not go live with him there?"

"Because he lived at the home of the gods of thunder and lightning, on what the Indians called the Haunted Mountain. But the gods took their vengeance and finally killed him."

The judge sat up, looking startled, and I decided to avoid injecting Indian mythology and superstition in the case on top of the rest, at least for now.

"Why did Marji live on this unlucky mountain and not with his wife Sayee?" I pushed doggedly on.

"Because his work was there—he was a part owner of this iron mine." I mentally cringed waiting for the expected objection. It did not come.

"How did you know he was part owner?" I pushed boldly on.

"I saw the paper the white man signed and gave to Marji before he showed them the Haunted Mountain. Marji himself later showed me this paper several times."

"Would you know that paper now?"

"Who can say? The light in here is dim."

I walked back to my table and facing front addressed the court.

"Your Honor," I began, "I am about to have a document marked for identification. It is the original agreement that, as the pleadings allege, was given Marji Kawbawgam by three of the original partners in the Jackson Mining Company in return for his guiding them to the ore deposit. My client was given this paper by her father on her promise she would never let it out of her possession. I accordingly ask leave of court to allow my client to accompany me up front to permit the reporter to so mark it."

"Do I hear any objection?" the judge inquired.

"None, Your Honor," Guy Nesbitt swiftly said, as my perplexity increased. This was one of the crucial documents in the case. Why all this benign agreeableness?

Laughing Whitefish arose and accompanied me up to the desk of old Mr. Bigbee, the court reporter. "I should now like to have this paper marked complainant's exhibit A for identification," I said, and Laughing Whitefish, her fingers trembling a little, removed from its deerskin pouch and placed on his desk the wrinkled and yellowed piece of paper originally torn from the journal of Philo Everett many years before. I remained silent while the reporter marked the paper and recorded this fact in his notebook. This done I again addressed the court.

"I have prepared several duplicate copies of this paper," I said, drawing them from my breast pocket. "After counsel has had an opportunity to compare them with the original, I request leave of court to substitute one of them in this case for the original and furnish counsel with another. That way we can let my client keep her promise to her father and also keep her trips up front to a minimum."

"Any objection from the defense?" the judge inquired.

"One moment, please, Your Honor," Guy Nesbitt said, and he quickly joined Laughing Whitefish and me up at the reporter's desk and carefully read the original paper and compared it with a copy. He looked up at the judge. "No objection to the substitution," he said, and retired to his table, handing his copy to Henry Harwood to read.

I advanced to where the witness sat, motioning Laughing Whitefish to join me. "I now show the witness the original agreement marked exhibit A for identification and ask her if she can recognize it?" I nodded at Laughing Whitefish who spread the wrinkled yellowed paper out on the flat rail of the witness box so that the witness might examine it. The interpreter delivered my message and the old woman leaned forward until her face nearly touched the paper. She finally looked up and wiped her watery eyes.

"I cannot see it well," she said, "the light in here grows dim—it is like trying to see in a smoky wigwam."

"Very well," I said, having expected as much. "The defense may examine."

"We'll first take a ten-minute recess," the judge said.

"How many husbands did you have?" was Guy Nesbitt's first question when court reconvened.

"But one, thank goodness. One man is quite enough for any woman, sometimes even too much."

"How many wives did your husband have?"

"Three."

"All at one time?"

"No, one he had earlier put away. There was but two at one time."

"Were you one of those two?"

"Yes."

"Were you on good terms with the other wife?"

She shrugged. "We had to get along—both of us lived in the same wigwam." I stole a look at the judge, who sat listening stonily, his lips compressed over such pagan goings on.

"Now why did your husband put away his first wife?"

"She was a witch—no man could live with her."

"So when he put her away you mean he simply walked out and left her and got himself a new woman—rather two—he could get along with?"

"Yes, I mean that."

"He didn't bother to end the marriage to the old one? It's just that they separated and didn't live together after that?"

"Yes."

"And that's what you mean when you use the expression 'put her away'?"

"Yes."

"And was it common for the men of your tribe to take more than one wife?"

"More common in my day than now, but only when they could afford it. My man was a good trapper. He also made and sold canoes and snowshoes—a good provider."

"But if a man got a woman he found he couldn't live with, he could just say 'phooey' and walk out?"

"Oh, yes. It's a man's world."

Guy Nesbitt glanced at me before he followed a new tack. "Now you said earlier that many Indian children died in infancy. Did many of the mothers also die in childbirth?"

"Alas, far too many."

"And who would raise their motherless children?"

"The women of the tribe, perhaps a relative—usually any woman with milk. Sometimes several women helped."

"Did you ever help?"

"Many times—it was the Indian way."

"But you have no children?"

"No, alas."

"So that nursing or helping raise a motherless Indian child did not necessarily make the child your own."

"Of course not."

"Even if that child stayed on with you or another woman until it was big enough to make its own way?"

"That is right—we Indians usually had troubles and children enough of our own without seeking more."

Again the quick backward glance, and I was beginning to see why Guy Nesbitt was called the Silver Fox. Once more I was encountering in an acute form the familiar problem I had already met in interviewing many of my prospective Indian witnesses: They could be led to say almost anything by an adroit questioner, and they tended to tell him what they thought he most wanted to hear. There was in them a curious mixture of guile and childish innocence. Guy Nesbitt pushed on relentlessly, like a winning gambler pressing his luck.

"Did you ever know Marji Kawbawgam's third wife?"

"I never met her. They say she was a lazy half-breed who swam in milk."

"What does 'swam in milk' mean?"

"She was a drunkard."

"Like Marji was?"

"Worse—she fell off a tall hill where they lived."

"Was she known as Old Meg?"

"I have heard her called that."

"Had Marji put Sayee away when he lived with this Old Meg?"

"It was my understanding he had not."

"So he was still married to Sayee when he took up with Old Meg?"

"That was our understanding, yes."

"Did you know Marji's first wife, Blue Heron?"

"Yes, I got to know her when she came to help with Laughing Whitefish after her mother died."

"So that Marji and his first wife Blue Heron always remained on good terms?"

"Oh, yes, she was a good and forgiving woman."

"But Marji did not regularly live with her?"

"No."

"Any more, say, than he ever regularly lived with Sayee?"

"That is right."

"And yet he had not ended his marriage to Sayee?"

"No."

"Any more than he had ended his marriage to Blue Heron?"

A slow smile spread over her wrinkled face. "You, sir, are a fox. It could be possible, as you say."

Guy Nesbitt straightened, shot his cuffs and addressed the court. "I believe that is all of this witness, Your Honor, please."

"Back to you for a re-direct, Mr. Poe."

I stood debating whether I should risk asking this aged witness any further questions. While she had come through beautifully on direct examination, Guy Nesbitt had shaken her badly on cross-examination, how badly only the man who had to decide our case could tell, Judge Grant himself. If I went over the same ground again I would not only exhaust her, as she was already plainly tiring, but possibly also risk leading the court to discount *all* her testimony. I decided against taking the risk. "Nothing further, Your Honor."

"The witness may stand aside," the judge said briskly. "Call your next."

EIGHTEEN

I was still going through my list of subpoenaed witnesses, preparing to call my next, when my attention was drawn to the judge, who was looking out anxiously toward the back of the courtroom. I craned around and saw old Mr. Philo Everett tottering slowly up the center aisle, leaning heavily on the arm of the tall buxom woman who accompanied him, Mrs. Brown, his nurse. He had looked bad enough when I'd last seen him; today he looked on the verge of death: pale, incredibly frail, little more than a spindly wraith.

As he drew near the lawyers' rail he stopped and looked uncertainly about him like a lost child. "Excuse me, Your Honor," I murmured, "there's been some mistake." I quickly moved back and joined him.

"Mr. Everett," I said, "what on earth are you doing here today? I had planned earlier to call you but when I learned you were ill I made other plans. My dear sir, you should be home in bed."

"Young man, I came to testify," he quavered in a thin, piping voice. "Can you take me now?" His black necktie was illy knotted, as though tied by a child, being both loose and the knot far out of line, giving him a curiously naked look.

"That's just what I told him, Mr. Poe," Mrs. Brown said,

171

"—that he should stay in bed. But he insisted on coming. I'm awful worried, Mr. Poe ..."

I turned to the judge. "I am deeply sorry for this incident, Your Honor," I said, "and I assure you it was not planned. If you'll give me a minute I'll try to persuade—"

"I came to testify," Philo Everett repeated in a petulant slurred voice. "I want to help Charlotte Kawbawgam and help right an ancient wrong. Where may I sit?"

I held out my hands helplessly toward the judge. "What can I do?"

Henry Harwood now arose and uttered his first words during the trial. "Why not let the poor man testify?" he said. "For better or worse he is here and it may be far worse to send him away."

"Gentlemen," the judge said, addressing counsel, "please step up to the bench a moment. Meanwhile, Mrs. Brown, I suggest you find your ailing patient a seat."

"Do fix his necktie," I whispered to Mrs. Brown before I hurried up front.

With the three of us lawyers clustered below him at the bench like stealthy conspirators the judge leaned over and whispered: "Mr. Harwood may be right—it may be more of an ordeal to send him away. Suppose we give it a trial? If he cannot proceed, as I fear, we'll face that when we come to it. What do you say, gentlemen?"

"I'm willing, Your Honor," whispered Guy Nesbitt, shaking his head. "I've encountered many strange things in court, but never quite this. The poor perplexed old gentleman ..."

"And you, Mr. Poe?"

"I'm agreeable to try," I said.

It took several minutes to get Mr. Everett out of his wraps and sworn and safely maneuvered up to and seated in the witness chair, where he sat facing us not unlike a truant schoolboy. Mrs.

Brown had indeed fixed his tie; it now looked even worse . . . I reflected that there were certain old men who, as the years pressed upon them, came more and more to look as they must have as boys. Philo Everett was one of them. His thin snow-white hair, his drawn and almost transparent skin, his fevered bird-like expression all reminded me of a delicate, tow-headed, angelic-looking choir boy. The judge nodded for me to begin.

"Your name, please?" I began.

"Philo P. Everett," he answered in the rather thick, slurred voice that I had never before noticed, as though he had a cleft palate.

"How old are you, sir?"

"Seventy-six, no, seventy-seven."

"Where do you live?"

"Here in Marquette."

"How long have you lived here?"

"Since the summer of 1845."

"Where had you lived before that?"

"Jackson, Michigan."

"What was the occasion for your coming to the Upper Peninsula?"

"Ah, young man, it's a long story," he began, and then, with frequent pauses, he related the story of the formation of the original partnership known as the Jackson Mining Company, organized early in 1845 for the purpose of exploring for and mining minerals on the Upper Peninsula; how some of his associates had learned of the fact but not the place of the discovery of iron ore by William Burt and his survey party the autumn before; and of how they had further learned that Marji Kawbawgam had guided the Burt party and concluded that very probably he could be persuaded to guide them to the site . . .

As he talked along in his slurred hesitant manner a slow trickle of saliva exuded from the corner of his mouth, forming a thin dangling string, which he occasionally sponged away with a handkerchief he held in his hand.

"And did you and these associates you have named seek out the Chippewa Indian called Marji Kawbawgam?" I went on, feeling a monster to be questioning this sick old man.

"We did," he replied, recounting how he and Mr. Kirtland and Mr. Berry had held their powwow with Marji at L'Anse Bay in the spring of 1845, and in return for Marji's promise to guide them to the iron deposit had promised him a reward for his services, which had been written on the spot by Mr. Everett and handed to Marji.

"And did Marji Kawbawgam keep his part of the bargain?" I asked.

"He did—he led us to what later became the rich Jackson Mine. Much later, I may add."

"And did your partnership keep its part of the bargain?"

"Alas, no, and it has haunted me ever since," the witness answered, again sponging his mouth and passing a thin hand wearily over his eyes.

"How did this happen?" I inquired.

Philo Everett then told of the early struggles of the partnership to get the mine started; of the persistent bad fortune that dogged the enterprise; of the crushing expenses and continual assessments. "We were bled white," he went on, "and were barely able to sustain our own families. When we sold our interests to the new crowd—the present owners—we insisted upon inserting a provision that they would assume and pay all outstanding debts and claims of every kind and nature. At least we did that much for Marji."

"And has the new corporation ever paid him?"

"Not a red cent!"

"Why?"

Twin spots of color glowed like rouge on either cheek.

"We didn't pay because we weren't able to," he said, his voice growing stronger. Then, looking straight at Guy Nesbitt and Henry Harwood, he continued: "Why they haven't paid I can only put down to swinish greed—nothing less can possibly explain it."

The witness was suddenly seized with a wracking coughing spell, and I was fearful he might collapse on the stand. The sheriff hurriedly brought him a glass of water which Mr. Everett dropped and broke. The nurse, Mrs. Brown, then helped him to drink from another. When he could go on I concluded I had better get him to identify the original agreement with Marji while he was able. Nodding at Laughing Whitefish to accompany me I went up to the witness and had Laughing Whitefish produce and spread out for him the original paper.

"Mr. Everett," I said, "I now show you complainant's exhibit A for identification and ask if you recognize it?"

Mr. Everett produced a little hand glass from his pocket to supplement his spectacles and, his hand shaking fearfully, scanned the paper he had given Marji Kawbawgam nearly thirty years before. The witness looked up: "I recognize it," he said. "It is the agreement I handed Marji Kawbawgam at L'Anse Bay in May of 1845. I wrote it on a sheet torn from my journal. Ah, if I were today but half the man I was then . . ."

"Do you have your old journal with you?"

"Yes, Mrs. Brown has it."

"May I see it?"

"Of course."

I looked up inquiringly at the judge, who nodded, and I then went and got the journal from Mrs. Brown and returned and handed it to the witness. Mr. Everett fumbled to find the place. "Ah, here it is," he murmured.

"I now ask you to place the original Marji Kawbawgam agreement against the page in your journal from which you say it was torn and see if they compare," I said, turning to invite defense counsel to view the matching ceremony, but Guy Nesbitt was already there. Even His Honor leaned over discreetly and deigned to peek. What if they *didn't* match? I thought in sudden panic. I bent forward tensely.

The witness looked up and made the only answer he could possibly make. "They fit like peas in a pod," he said.

"Defense concedes they do," Guy Nesbitt said, and quietly returned to his place. The judge straightened and made a note of the event.

After he had identified the signatures of the signers and various witnesses, I returned Laughing Whitefish her paper and excused her and pressed on. "After you had made and given this agreement to Marji and he had led you to the mine property, did you report your negotiations with him back to the partnership?"

"Yes, at a formal meeting held in Jackson during the following winter."

"And did they ratify what you men had done?"

"Yes, unanimously, and it appears on the books of the company. Some of the others thought we had done too little. Later still we agreed to vote him 12 shares from our reserve of nonassessable stock, but we never actually gave it to Marji because meanwhile we had sold all this reserve stock to raise money. This too appears on the books."

"And when you disposed of the company property what became of the old partnership books and records?"

"We turned them over to the new crowd—they were no longer any use to us."

"Including the record of the company ratification of your dealings with Marji and the further agreement to give him twelve shares of nonassessable stock?"

"Yes, indeed."

"And by the 'new crowd' you mean the present corporate defendant in this case, the Jackson Ore Company?"

"I do, young man."

"Was the unpaid company obligation to Marji Kawbawgam ever specifically called to the attention of the 'new crowd' when the old company sold out?"

"It was. I saw to that myself."

"To whom, if you recall?"

"I told Ira Beadle about it for one—he's still the superintendent at the mine in Negaunee—and one or two others."

"Do you recall their names?"

Again the palsied movement of the hand across his eyes. "Not at the moment—my memory has failed badly of late."

The witness was tiring rapidly before my eyes, and while there remained much that I still longed to ask him I thought it an act of charity to turn him over to the tender mercies of Guy Nesbitt—thus the sooner getting the sick man off the stand.

"I believe that's all for now," I announced.

"Mr. Everett?" the judge inquired.

"Yes, Judge Grant?" the witness replied, looking up at the judge.

"Do you feel able to continue or would you prefer to come back another day?"

The witness appeared agitated. "Oh, I must go on, sir. I must try to right this grave injustice if it's the last thing I do. *Please*, Judge, let me have my say."

The judge thought a moment. "Very well," he said. "Mr. Nesbitt, your witness."

"Did you ever know an old half-breed Indian woman called Old Meg?" Guy Nesbitt began softly.

"Ah, I've known many Indians, sir. The name sounds vaguely familiar."

"Would it refresh your recollection if I reminded you that she once lived in a shack on a hill on your mine property with and as the wife of Marji Kawbawgam?"

"Oh, that poor creature? Yes, I knew of her and her tragic end."

"And you also knew she was the wife of Marji Kawbawgam?"

"Well, that was my understanding."

"That she was his wife?"

"Yes, sir."

"And did you ever know the mother of that girl sitting there"—pointing at Laughing Whitefish—"one Sayee, also the wife of Marji Kawbawgam?"

"I never actually knew her, but I always understood she was also his wife."

"And she was still his wife at the time that Marji was living with this Old Meg?"

"Yes, sir." The witness paused and went on. "I was aware that many Indians practiced polygamy, but I did not think it my province to judge them." Looking straight at Guy Nesbitt he continued. "It struck me as being quite enough that we whites had robbed them of their ancestral lands without also robbing them of their ancient tribal ways. It was about all we left them."

Guy Nesbitt's ears had reddened a little as he pressed on. "But you did know Marji Kawbawgam very well?"

"I did, sir, and whatever weaknesses he may have possessed I found him to be a *good* man. Unlike some whites I know who practice monogamy but fail to keep their word, Marji Kawbawgam married his woman and moreover kept his word."

The flush increased, but the Silver Fox was not to be put off the scent. "And you know Blue Heron, Marji's first wife?" he pressed on.

"I did, very well—a gallant woman."

"And she also remained Marji's wife while he lived with Old Meg?" I held my breath for the answer.

"Well, that was always my understanding."

"Did you understand this from Marji?"

"I don't think we ever discussed it, but I always assumed she was still his wife."

I could see Guy Nesbitt's broad shoulders heave and fall as he sighed with satisfaction and relief. Then, after a pause, he was off baying along a new scent: that of the defense of laches, that is, that whatever claim Marji may once have had had long since vanished because he had slept on his rights.

"Did Marji Kawbawgam ever sue your old company to enforce his alleged claim?"

"He did not, because—"

"And did—"

"Objection," I hastily put in. "The witness hasn't finished."

"But he had answered my question," Guy Nesbitt shot back, "and making all due allowance for the precarious state of the health of this witness I was trying to discourage another gratuitous outburst on how we greedy whites have so basely robbed and cheated the noble red man."

"Tut, tut, gentlemen," the judge said. "Let's get this sick old man off the stand. Mr. Everett, did you have anything further to add?" The witness shook his head vacantly. "Proceed, Mr. Nesbitt, it appears that the ground of the objection has evaporated."

"Did Marji ever sue the new company?"

Vaguely: "Not to my knowledge."

"Yet he worked regularly for both companies, did he not, and could have well afforded to hire counsel?"

With a sudden show of spirit: "You did not know Marji, sir—he would sooner have cut off his arm than sue me or the old company, he knew how desperate was our plight." The witness paused and sighed. "Sometimes I wonder whether our failure was not retribution for our sharpness and cupidity in gaining the property as we had. If you are implying that Marji was rich, sir, he was not. There simply are no rich Indians, at least I've never known any. Moreover the few lawyers then in the county were to a man representing one or the other of the mining companies. To expect this poor uneducated Indian to have sued on his claim is nonsense, and you know it."

"Bravo!" I whispered to Laughing Whitefish, as Guy Nesbitt, a little groggy from this blast, rallied swiftly for the main business at hand—to defeat our claim.

"Did Marji ever ask you to do something about his claim?"

"No, you plainly do not understand an Indian's pride."

"In other words he did nothing about his claim?"

"For the reasons I have tried to state, no, he did nothing." The witness's head dropped forward and I feared he might be having another spell. "But *I* did something," he rallied to state. I perked up my ears; this was something he had never before told me. Guy Nesbitt sensed it too, and hastily launched another diverting question.

"So it is fair to say," he began, and I leapt to my feet.

"Objection," I thundered. "Again the witness was about to add something."

"Were you, Mr. Everett?" the judge inquired.

"I was, but already it has slipped my mind. What were we talking about? Oh, yes—whether Marji had ever done anything about his claim and I said that he hadn't to my knowledge, but that I had. It's coming back." I leaned forward tensely; all this was new. "I asked Ira Beadle many times to make a decent settlement with Marji. Then after Marji's death I stopped off specially in New York on my way to Washington to take up the matter with the then president of the present Jackson Ore Company."

"When was that?" Guy Nesbitt reluctantly prompted the witness, ruefully aware that he had committed the cardinal sin of the cross-examiner: he had asked one question too many. I recalled what our crimes professor had once told us in Ann Arbor. "On cross-examination the ideal witness will simply answer yes or no," he had said, then wryly adding: "But you will swiftly learn there are no ideal witnesses."

"When was that?" Guy Nesbitt repeated.

"It was I think in the late winter of 1865."

"What transpired?"

"I had made a copy of Marji's agreement and I showed it to your president—wasn't it Stewart?"—Guy Nesbitt nodded almost imperceptibly—" and I reviewed the whole matter with him in your company offices in the old Trinity building, since destroyed by fire. He said he knew nothing about the claim. At my request we went over the old partnership records and minutes stored in your offices and there found the ratification of the old agreement and also, on your own books, your company's undertaking to assume and pay all just claims and demands that were outstanding against the old partnership. Thereupon Mr. Stewart offered one hundred dollars in settlement of the claim."

"Did you take it?"

"No, sir, I did not. Instead I told him to take his money and have prayers said for his soul—that it obviously needed them far more than the poor Indians needed his niggardly hundred dollars."

"Had Marji Kawbawgam or anyone authorized you to take this action?"

"Nothing but my conscience and sense of fair play, sir. Marji was long dead and his daughter was but a young girl."

"How do you fix the date as being during the late winter of 1865?"

The witness thought a moment before replying. "Because that was the last time I ever saw President Lincoln—he was assassinated shortly after I saw and visited with him in Washington on the same Eastern trip."

Guy Nesbitt paused and pondered, and I felt sure I could read his thoughts. Should he continue to probe and perhaps again inadvertently refresh the memory of this unpredictable and outspoken witness? Had he not already asked too many questions? Already his defense of laches had taken some heavy blows, and if he continued might not . . .

"That's all," he said curtly, abruptly retiring to his table.

"Mr. Poe, back to you," the judge reminded me. "That's if you feel the circumstances warrant further examination of this ailing witness."

There were dozens of questions I longed to ask the witness; he had opened up whole new vistas of possible inquiry. Perversely enough, most of all I wanted to ask him about President Lincoln: how he had looked, what they had talked about, how this small-town feed merchant had ever come to know this great, brooding man. How could Guy Nesbitt have possibly turned his back on such a golden opportunity? But the hour was late, the witness was a sick old man, and, however fascinating the prospect, President Lincoln had nothing to do with our case. Moreover the judge had plainly hinted that I let the witness go.

"Your Honor," I said, "all things considered I shall pass redirect. No further questions."

"Gentlemen," the judge said, "we've all had a long day and I think we'll adjourn till nine tomorrow. Mr. Sheriff."

Barney Langley arose and stoically beat his gavel. "Hear ye, hear ye, hear ye!" he intoned. "The honorable circuit court for the county of Marquette is now adjourned until 9:00 A.M. tomorrow." The gavel fell once more, the judge hastily left the bench for chambers, and I rushed up to help Mr. Everett off the witness stand.

When I had seen him on his way I asked Laughing Whitefish to wait for me outside while I checked some papers at the county clerk's office. This done, I was about to leave his office when the clerk himself, Gad Smith, laid a detaining hand on my sleeve. He addressed me gravely.

"Willy," he said, "I'm afraid your last witness isn't long for this world." He wagged his head dolefully. "Philo Everett looks poorly, very poorly. Ah well, all of us must go some day."

"I hope you're wrong, Mr. Smith," I said, gently pulling away and hurrying to overtake my client. As I paced along I reflected that there were people in the world who went through life exuding gloom and dire foreboding; who were filled with dreadful prophecies and mournful cosmic intuitions; who derived their greatest joy from contemplating pain and sorrow. To them the best news was bad news, and the bustling Gad Smith appeared to be one of them.

Laughing Whitefish was helping Mrs. Brown tuck a buffalo robe around a swathed and muffled Philo Everett, the breath of the waiting horses steaming upon the frosty air. When he saw me Philo Everett put out a frail hand and I took it.

"Good luck, young man," he said. "If there is any justice left in this old world you will win."

I longed to ask him about Abraham Lincoln, but the poor man was in no condition for reminiscence; that could await another day. "Thank you, Mr. Everett," I said. "You are a brave man."

"Goodbye," he said.

"Goodbye," I said.

NINETEEN

Laughing Whitefish and I had supper at the Cozzens House and I walked her home. Only when we reached the trail to her island did we mention the case. "What do you think, William?" she said when we were about to part.

"I don't know," I answered honestly enough. "I thought some things went rather well, but that others may have hurt." I didn't tell her I was sure some of these had hurt badly; that I had seen the judge making rapid notes during several of them. "It's all up to His Honor and what he'll do is anybody's guess. As you can see, he's as inscrutable as the Sphinx."

"Maybe it's my imagination," she said, "but somehow I feel in my bones he doesn't like Indians."

I felt the same way but didn't say so; she still had to testify. "At least we've survived the day and will be back at it tomorrow." I unsuccessfully stifled a yawn. "Can I walk you up to your cabin?"

"No, William, I can make the rest of the way nicely by myself—I've done it many times. And you should get some rest."

I hated to see her leave. "Maybe one of your secret admirers is lying in wait."

"I'm intrigued. Who might he be? Young and handsome, I hope."

"Octave Bissonette is one of them—except he isn't very secret about it. He all but ravished you with his eyes in court today."

She laughed. "Poor Octave does that to all the Indian girls. I'd have felt neglected if he hadn't. *William*, you're pouting. I swear you're jealous. Now you run along and I'll handle any lurking admirers."

"Teacher's orders," I said with mock humility, and shortly we parted.

I had gone but a short distance when I heard her voice calling out of the dark. "William, William!" she called.

"Yes?" I called back, unaccountably alarmed.

"I thought you were wonderful."

"I think you are too."

"I don't mean that. In court."

"Thank you." I longed to follow after her and crush her in my arms. "Goodnight!" I called out instead, always the nice boy, ever the genteel, predictable Willy.

Her voice floated across the frosty air. "Goodnight, William. Pleasant dreams." Trudging along I thought I heard her faintly calling again but concluded it was the waves.

As I walked townward under the stars I resolutely put the disturbing Laughing Whitefish out of my mind. I wondered idly what had happened to old Cash. He had not been in court all day and I felt a little hurt that he had not at least dropped by to see if we had survived. At the foot of Ridge Street I took the low road so that I could stop at the depot and visit Miles Coffey. I was giddy with fatigue but my mind was churned and sleep was out of the question. Perhaps Miles and I could play a little cribbage; I felt I needed forgetfulness more than sleep.

"Ah, sweet revenge," Miles greeted me, rubbing his hands and diving for the cribbage board. Soon we were deep in our fifteen-twos and it was midnight before I reluctantly departed. I had lost every game and Miles was radiant. Back at my door I debated pushing on to see if Cash was still up but decided against it. I plodded on up the stairs. At my landing I almost collided with Cash. I couldn't resist glancing at Madame Dujardins's door.

"Midnight trysts seem to be getting chronic around here," I observed.

"Sh," he whispered, "I been huntin' an' waitin' around all evenin' for *you*. Where you been at?"

I told him as we proceeded down the hall to my quarters. I opened up and he coolly took over my desk while I lit a fire.

"What's up?" I demanded, finally joining him.

Cash rapped a folded copy of the evening *Mining Journal*. "Did you see that there article about your case?"

"I've seen nothing. I told you what I've been doing. What's up?"

"It's a long article, all about the case and its background, all about Guy Nesbitt and what a renowned lawyer he is, who took the stand today and testified and all that. After naming the white witnesses and detailing their testimony it says, 'An Indian and a half-breed also testified.' I love that magnanimous concession of their existence. Then near the end it says"—here Cash opened and consulted the newspaper— " 'According to an informed courtroom observer the case appears to turn mainly on the hotly disputed question of whether Miss Kawbawgam is her father's lawful heir, this in turn depending on whether or not she may have been the child of a polygamous marriage.' " Cash lowered the paper and looked at me triumphantly. "See what I mean?"

"Frankly no. Seems a pretty accurate appraisal to me. What you driving at?"

"To me it means that the reporter Pete Martin must have got it straight from the horse's mouth. He couldn't have dreamed it up. This is precisely what's botherin' the judge."

"You mean Pete Martin got it from the judge?"

"No. From Gad Smith, the clerk. The judge never tells nobody nothing."

"How would Gad ever know what's bothering the judge? And what's so secret about it? Fact is the same thing's bothering me."

"Because Gad knows the judge like a book and can read his mind."

"You're pipe-dreaming, Cash. You mean close-mouthed old Judge Grant would confide in gabby old Gad? You've been drinking."

Cash drew back offended. "Gad Smith can read *anybody's* mind," he repeated. "You just wait and see. But that's not what I mainly wanted to see you about."

I stretched and yawned prodigiously. "Let's have it, Cash. I got to get some sleep to be in shape for the Silver Fox tomorrow. He's hard enough to cope with wide awake."

"How did Henry Harwood do?" the old boy sparred. I told him that except for Henry Harwood's one brief suggestion that Philo Everett be permitted to testify he hadn't opened his mouth all day. Cash slapped his leg. "That proves it!"

"Proves what?" I said, both nettled and mystified.

"Proves his heart isn't in the case. My news is that Henry Harwood all along wanted to settle it."

"Too bad he didn't tell me about it. How do you know?"

"I've got my sources."

"Look, Cash, it's too late to play guessing games. Either tell me what I need to protect myself or tell me nothing."

"Steady, Willy, all in good time. The lady doctor told me."

"Madame Dujardins?" He nodded. "How could *she* possibly know? Has Henry Harwood now got a leaky valve and taken to visiting her?"

"One of her patients is Henry Harwood's secretary."

"Old Miss Dyson?"

"Precisely. Seems she has some chronic female disorder— indeed, to listen to Madame, half the dear ladies in town are coming apart at the seams—and she casually remarked earlier this evening to Madame that it was too bad her boss had to be tied up in court on the trial of a case he wanted to settle."

"And how did you find out? Were you at Madame's later for a treatment?"

"Don't be evil minded. Madame sent for me and told me— an' I been huntin' for you ever since."

I leaned closer; this *was* interesting. "How much did Henry Harwood recommend in settlement?"

"Don't know. All Madame knows is what Miss Dyson told her. Willy, it's the *fact* of his wanting to settle at all that's important, don't you see?"

"Guess I'm too tired, Cash—I don't see. What does it mean?"

"It means there's a fatal weakness in their defense that doesn't meet the eye. That's why their biggest gun Guy Nesbitt was hastily brought in. Your job is to discover that weakness, Willy. You gotta cogitate harder."

"If I cogitated any harder, Cash, I'd explode. I eat this case, I sleep it, lately I've even been dreaming it."

Old Cash came around and patted my shoulder. "I know, lad. Get to bed now. I just wanted you to know about this to keep your spirits up. There's a way to beat 'em and we gotta find it."

"Thanks, Cash. And please thank the Madame for me. With her rather restricted view of the world it's nice to know she keeps us in mind."

"She's an angel of mercy, lad."

He left and I sat listening dully as he thumped his way on

down the stairs. Then, ignoring the newspaper, I dragged myself off to bed.

There I dreamed the night away, a shuttling disordered dream about my case, one of those uneasy hallucinatory phantasms during which I remained half-skeptical and yet helpless to wake up or shut off the crazy flow. One moment an extravagantly costumed Guy Nesbitt and I would be furiously fighting each other back and forth across bridges and moats with clashing swords, another he and I were both pursued and pursuer, brandishing exotic weapons, galloping wildly across a broad plain. Henry Harwood appeared occasionally, his glasses over his thumb, a grave phantom thrusting bags of gold out at me and then regretfully pulling them away.

Throughout this chaotic dream flitted an underclad and darkly erotic woman, sinuous as a serpent. She sometimes drew near and breathed seductively in my ear and then glided maddeningly away. "Cogitate, Willy, cogitate my sweet," she would whisper. The woman, I was horrified to recognize, was Madame Dujardins ...

I overslept and awoke exhausted and after a hasty breakfast hurried down the creaking hallway. At the top of the stairway I paused and speculatively eyed Madame Dujardins's door. While the lady didn't know it, she'd had herself a busy night. "Angel of mercy," I murmured as I trudged on down the stairs.

TWENTY

The courtroom was already crowded, now with almost as many whites as Indians—doubtless the result of the article in the *Mining Journal;* sex had reared its winsome head. Many of the Indians, their seats coolly usurped by the whites, were squatting impassively on the smooth pine floor. Laughing Whitefish and opposing counsel were already in their places.

"Good morning, gentlemen," I said, bowing gravely to Henry Harwood and Guy Nesbitt, who as gravely returned my greeting.

"Did you have a good night's rest, William?" Laughing Whitefish inquired, regarding me closely with her dark eyes.

"Wonderful," I lied steadily. "Dreamless as a child. And you look radiant as ever."

I started riffling through my papers. I felt her touch my sleeve. She motioned me to lean closer. "William," she whispered, "after I left you last night out on the lakeshore I had a dreadful experience."

"What's that?" I whispered back.

"Octave Bissonette was lying in wait for me in the dark and when I passed he leapt out and grabbed and kissed me. He also tried to—to make violent love to me."

"The dirty dog," I said, clenching my fists. "Why, I—I'll—

Have you told the sheriff?" She shook her head no. "Why not, why not?" I insisted.

Her face broke into a tantalizing enigmatic smile. "My biggest hope, William, is that *he* won't tell the sheriff," she said.

"What do you mean?" I demanded.

She briefly held two clawed hands out at me. "I—I'm dreadfully afraid I almost killed *him*." She drew back and sat absently fingering the pouch at her throat. I stared at her in wonder.

"Lotti," I whispered hoarsely, "I think you're a lovely disturbing wildcat." I longed terribly to take her in my arms.

My longings were rudely interrupted when Gad Smith glided over to our table. "Did you hear the news, Willy?" he whispered sibilantly so that Laughing Whitefish could hear. "Philo Everett passed away during the night."

"Dead?"

Gad rolled his eyes up toward the courtroom skylight. "Gone," he replied mournfully, piously folding his hands. Then he slid back to his place. His day was a wild success: he'd scored a complete obiturial triumph. Moreover he'd predicted it.

Lotti grasped my sleeve. "The poor man," she murmured, biting her lip and half turning away. "The poor brave little man."

"He knew he was dying," I said, "but still he came to testify." We sat silent and lost in thought.

The judge suddenly swept in and rustled his way purposefully up to the bench, the sheriff swiftly hammered us to our feet and bawled out his piece and court was once again convened. The world must go on, I reflected; the obscure northern feed merchant who once knew Lincoln would take his little secret to the grave; Octave Bissonette would mutely nurse his wounded vanity; rancor and hostility were once again to reign. "Call your next," the judge said brusquely, nodding at me.

"Complainant will call Charlotte Kawbawgam, also known as Laughing Whitefish," I said.

The lamb goes eagerly to the slaughter, I thought as she glided quickly up front, was duly sworn by Gad Smith, and sat calmly facing me, a picture of feminine composure, her hands demurely folded on her lap. If they only knew, I thought.

"Your name, please?" I asked, trying to put Philo Everett and Octave Bissonette out of my mind.

"Charlotte Kawbawgam is my American name," she answered. "My parents called me Laughing Whitefish, after the river...."

"And who were your parents?"

"Marji Kawbawgam was my father, my mother was Sayee. She died shortly after I was born."

"Were both your parents members of the Chippewa Indian tribe?"

"They were."

"Did you know your father during his lifetime?"

"Yes, though I saw him seldom. I last saw him shortly before his death. I must have been about seven."

"Did he give you the paper that has been referred to here as complainant's exhibit A for identification?"

"Yes, the last time I ever saw him."

"And have you kept it in your possession continuously ever since?"

"Yes." She fondled the little deerskin bag about her throat.

"Will you please produce it?" I said.

She removed the bag from around her neck and finally held the yellowed paper in her hand. I turned to the court.

"Your Honor," I addressed him, "complainant now offers this paper in evidence as complainant's exhibit A."

"No objection," Guy Nesbitt quickly arose and said.

"It may be so received and marked," the judge said.

I nodded at Laughing Whitefish who stepped down from the stand and placed the paper before the court reporter, who duly marked it. Then she returned the paper to her pouch and returned to the stand.

I continued to address the court. "May it be understood that the copy may stand on this record as the original, and may it also be so marked?"

"No objection," said Guy Nesbitt.

"It may be so marked," the judge said.

This done, I again faced Laughing Whitefish. "Did you know an Indian woman called Blue Heron?"

"Very well. She raised me and was really the only mother I knew."

Guy Nesbitt arose as though to object, and then, evidently thinking better, held his fire.

"Is she living or dead?"

"She died some years ago, when I was a girl. I was fourteen."

"Were you still living with her when she died?"

"Yes."

"And had you continuously done so as long as you can remember?"

"Yes."

"Did she leave any children or other relatives of her own blood?"

"No."

"Now Miss Kawbawgam," I pushed on, trying to anticipate and soften the expected frontal attack of Guy Nesbitt, "had you known that your father was once married to the woman called Blue Heron?"

"Yes. It was well known."

"Do you know of your own knowledge whether your father and Blue Heron were divorced before your father married your mother?"

Guy Nesbitt arose but again held his fire. Laughing Whitefish glanced at him.

"You may answer," I prompted her.

"No, I do not," she replied. "I would not even have been born when that happened."

"What was your understanding on that score?"

"I have heard it both ways," she answered steadily, and I admired her candor though it was doing little to help our case.

"What is your honest belief?" I said, glancing expectantly at Guy Nesbitt.

"That they were divorced," she replied. A smile crisscrossed her lips as she went on. "But perhaps this is wishful thinking since I may profit by this view of the case." Her smile broadened. "And naturally I hate to be thought illegitimate."

I heard a horrified gasp from the onlookers. I glanced back at the clock and saw the outraged ladies whispering away. I admired my client for her frankness. I paused to take stock of the situation. I had been asking a series of questions which quite probably could not have withstood serious objection by opposing counsel. My perplexity increased. Why was Guy Nesbitt letting all this in?

"Did you know the late Philo P. Everett during his lifetime?" I pushed on. "I mean the last witness who testified here yesterday and who died during the night?"

There was another gasp, this time of astonishment, followed by an excited buzz of whispering which the judge swiftly put down with a glare. Gad Smith seemed to be frowning. Was it because I had stolen his thunder?

"Did you know Philo Everett?" I repeated.

"I knew him well," she answered. "He was most kind to me

and my mother—I mean Blue Heron. He gave us food and clothing and at times offered Blue Heron money, which she declined. He has also sent me books for my school. I shall miss him greatly."

"Did you know before yesterday that Mr. Everett had tried to realize on your father's claim?"

"Yes, Mr. Everett later told—"

"Objection, Your Honor," from Guy Nesbitt. "Clearly and obviously hearsay."

"Objection sustained," the judge swiftly ruled.

"Move that the question and answer be stricken," Guy Nesbitt pressed on.

"They may be so stricken," the judge ruled. "Mr. Poe, why do you persist in this objectionable line of questions?"

"Sorry, Your Honor," I murmured contritely. "I'll try to mend my ways."

"See that you do," the judge came back, plucking away at his beard like a gardener thinning an overabundant crop.

"How old are you?" I asked, moving to less sensitive ground.

"I was twenty-one last June 15th."

"And did you take immediate steps to enforce and collect upon your father's unpaid claim?"

"Yes, even before that."

"And before that did you and Blue Heron ever take any steps in that direction?"

"Yes, over at the Sault. It was probably two years before Blue Heron died. We were on a visit to the Sault. While there we saw a lawyer about the claim."

"What did he say?"

"He said that while it was not impossible to commence action then it might be better to wait until I could sue in my own right and name."

"Anything else?"

"Yes, he said that he could not very well represent me in any event, because of the distance from Marquette. He also added that it might be well to wait until I could obtain a lawyer who was not tied up with one of the mining companies."

"And to your own knowledge neither you nor your father ever received anything on the claim?"

"I know we did not," she answered with spirit.

"One more thing," I said. "Did your father and Blue Heron receive their respective shares of their annual treaty payments from the Government during their lifetime?"

"They did," she answered, "although Blue Heron usually collected my father's share as he was much away."

"And who got your father's share after he died?"

"Blue Heron."

"And who got both her's and his share after she in turn died?"

"I did," she said, adding, "but since then the Government treaty payments have ended."

"Your Honor," I announced, reaching a swift decision, "the defense may now examine."

"We'll first take a five-minute recess," the judge declared.

"Miss Kawbawgam, did you ever know an Indian woman called Cosima?" Guy Nesbitt began softly, getting his cross-examination underway.

"Yes, she was one of my mother's—I mean Blue Heron's—oldest and closest friends."

"And do you know what has ever become of her?"

"No, she moved away westward after Blue Heron died, and I have not seen or heard from her since."

"Have you tried?"

"I've made several inquiries, yes."

"Of course you told your lawyer, Mr. Poe here, about Cosima, did you not?"

"I did. He wanted to know about any of the older Indians who might know about my father and his background."

"Like about whether your father and Blue Heron were really divorced when your father took your own mother Sayee as his second wife?"

"Well, yes, we considered that important."

"And did your lawyer ever try to reach this Cosima?"

"Yes, Mr. Poe has worked hard on my case, sir."

"But he too was unsuccessful?"

"Yes, the best he could conclude was that she was probably dead."

I felt a sudden chill grip my spine. These were not idle questions; I knew they weren't because this man didn't ask idle questions. He pressed on.

"I see. Now the fact is that this Cosima, if she were alive, would probably be in the best position of any living person to tell us whether your father and Blue Heron were ever divorced?"

"Oh, yes, sir. She lived with Blue Heron, and then with both of us after Blue Heron took me in."

"In your opinion would she not be a far better witness on that score than, say, Susan Gesick, who testified here yesterday?"

"Why naturally, sir—she was in a far better position to know."

Guy Nesbitt took a deep breath and stared up at the skylight. Then once again he was back at the witness: "So would it be a fair statement, then, Miss Kawbawgam, that you would be willing to let your case stand or fall on the testimony of a witness like Cosima—provided she were still alive and could appear and testify?"

"Of course," she answered before I could get on my feet.

"Objection, Your Honor," I belatedly said, my mind in a whirl of ominous conjecture. "The question calls for a legal conclusion by this lay witness," I groped on. "And there are other issues in this case besides divorce."

"Possibly, Mr. Poe," the judge said evenly, "but since your client has already responded, we'll let her answer stand—subject of course to your objection. Proceed, Mr. Nesbitt."

Guy Nesbitt studied the skylight. "Treaty payments," he finally announced portentously. "If the Government continued to pay Blue Heron your father's share after his death it must have been for the reason that the Government considered her his surviving widow, would it not?"

It was a nice question and Laughing Whitefish blinked thoughtfully before she answered. "I hadn't thought of that," she replied. "It could have been."

Guy Nesbitt drew himself as erect and corsetted as a reviewing general. "No further questions," he said.

"Back to you," the judge said briskly.

It was my turn to study the skylight. "Treaty payments," I announced. "If the Government continued to pay you both your father's and Blue Heron's shares after their deaths it must have been for the reason that the Government considered you their lawful heir, would it not?"

"I suppose so, but I hadn't thought of that either," she replied.

"No further questions," I said.

"Call your next," the judge said, and Laughing Whitefish looked at me anxiously as she resumed her place at my side.

"Jack Tregembo," I said, reflecting bitterly that the grim reality of the day could sometimes be far more harrowing than any dream. What was Guy Nesbitt up to? Had they finally found the elusive Cosima?

"Your name, please?" I asked the waiting witness, who

seemed to have grown taller and leaner and his mustaches more silvery since last I'd seen him.

"Jack Tregembo," he answered, somehow injecting a rich Cornish accent into this brief reply. Was not accent often as much a matter of intonation as of pronunciation? I speculated.

I was suddenly oppressed by the futility of what I was doing; a pall of defeat seemed suddenly to hang over the case. "State your business and place of residence," I continued briskly, trying to affect a confidence I scarcely felt.

"Saloonkeeper, Iron Street, Negaunee, Michigan," he answered equally briskly.

"Did you know Marji Kawbawgam during his lifetime?"

"Did I knaow Marji, chum? I wos wan av 'is best friends in a seldom sort of way—at least among the whites. Used to call 'im Chief—fine powerful figure of a man."

A startled Guy Nesbitt was on his feet addressing the court: "I mean to inject no levity in these proceedings, Your Honor," he was saying, "when I suggest that we may also need an interpreter for this witness. I scarcely understand a word the man is saying."

Before the judge could comment, a red-faced Jack drew back offended and earnestly delivered himself: "By the same token, me fine 'earty, ol' Jack can scarcely hunnerstan' your fancy 'igh-toned Heastern haccent. Saound like a bloomin' fake Lon'on swell to me, if you wanna knaw the plain facks of it."

The judge, flushed and deeply vexed, rapped his gavel sharply, glaring at Jack, who glared back. "The witness will remain silent until questions are directed at him by court or counsel. One more such outburst and—and I shall be obliged to take steps."

"Your Honor, please!" Henry Harwood was on his feet. "I understand the witness perfectly," he said quietly, "and I promise to keep my associate fully informed."

"Proceed, Mr. Poe," the judge said harshly, still rankling, plucking away furiously at his beard.

I drew from Jack that Marji had worked for both the old Jackson Company and briefly for the new; that the new company had abruptly discharged him; that during his leaner years Jack had helped Marji keep body and soul together; that, yes, he knew of Marji's "paper," and had been shown it by Marji; that he knew that Marji had tried to settle his claim with the new company because shortly before he died he had got in an altercation with Ira Beadle during one such session and struck him, and Jack had finally had to hide him from the cops. . . .

"What's that?" the judge broke in sharply. "What's that last you just said?"

"I said I 'ad to 'ide 'im from the bloomin' cops so they cudn't harrest poor Marji. Worked, too, hexcept poor Marji went an' got hisself kilt."

The judge clucked his tongue helplessly over this bland confession of an ancient obstruction of justice. His thin lips pursed into his familiar look of almost permanent vexation, the picture of a perfect man alone and adrift in a regrettably imperfect world. With a weary wave of his hand he motioned me to proceed so that—he somehow eloquently conveyed—this unlovely creature would the sooner be banished from his sight . . .

"To your knowledge, Mr. Tregembo, did Marji ever consult or retain counsel to press his claim?" I pressed on.

"If by counsel you mean lawyer, that 'e did not, more's the pity, though I urge 'im to manys the time."

"Why didn't he?"

"Ha! First place, Marji was mos'ly broke—spent all 'is hearnings on booze—a bit av a steadfast soak, you might say. Moreover, Mister Poe, w'ile Marji wos smart enough, 'e didn't knaow Henglish good like the likes of we"—I longed to steal a look at Guy Nesbitt, but cravenly lacked the courage—"an' moreover in 'is day there waren't no lawyer 'ere in the caounty but wos to a man courtin' an' makin' hup lovin' an' purty to they there mining companies. 'E 'ad no proper chance." Jack closed his eyes and shook his head sadly. "Fack is, chum, Marji never 'ad no proper chance—hit was like they wos an 'aunt on 'im drawin' 'im to 'is fate hup on that cursed 'ill." Jack dolefully shook his head. "Poor Chief, 'e wos an 'armless sort."

I nodded my thanks to the witness, not daring to look at Laughing Whitefish. "You may examine," I said, abruptly sitting down, numbly nursing a growing conviction that something dreadful was about to happen to our case.

"Were Old Meg and Marji formally married or did they just take up living together?" Guy Nesbitt suavely opened hostilities.

Jack glanced swiftly at me as though to say: " 'Ow much do this 'ere bounder knaow? Wot'll I say, Willy?" I could have objected to the question on the grounds that it was not relevant to the matter brought out on direct examination—the rule of evidence in some jurisdictions—but I knew this would be a vain objection in Michigan, where the question needed only to be relevant to any issue fairly in the case. I shrugged my shoulders, releasing Jack from his quandary.

"They just tuck hup together—it was the Hindian wye—kind of frank an' fearless, no sneakin' aroun' back alleys an' aout in buggies an' buckboards like us 'umbuggin' w'ites."

"Were they customers at your saloon?"

"Steady. Night after night they'd come set at their reg'lar table in the back room, silent as sentries at their posts, drinkin' somethin' fierce."

"I see. And you knew Marji once served time for stealing oats from the company?"

"Yes, I knew that—an' I halso knew that 'e cud 'ave stull all the oats you ever owned an' 'twouldn't near pay 'im back a fraction for all the fortunes you an' your ilk 'ave made outa wot poor Marji went an' done for you."

"And that he served still another jail sentence for selling a canoe that didn't exist?"

"Yes, I knew 'baout that—but I don't see wot that's got to do with w'ether you howe 'im money nor not."

"And that he was attempting to carry away a sack of the company's ore the night he was killed?" Guy Nesbitt pressed on. Again I dared not look at Laughing Whitefish.

" 'E was 'alf rummy from drinkin', 'e wos—an' if it'll hintrest you, mister, I daon't blyme 'im wan bit."

The judge frowned and raised his gavel and held it poised. Witnesses were not supposed to comment gratuitously on counsel's questions or their own answers.

"That's all," Guy Nesbitt abruptly said, resuming his seat.

"No more," I said, a feeling of futility now all but oppressing me.

"Call your next."

Guy Nesbitt was on his feet. "If your Honor please, we would like to call another witness out of turn. This witness has been hard to locate, she has come a great distance, she is now here in the building, she is old and not too well, she says she cannot stay, and in view of recent developments—I refer to the swift and lamentable passing of Mr. Philo Everett—I'd like to take her testimony now while yet we may."

"Cosima," I whispered to myself.

"What do you say, Mr. Poe?" the judge inquired.

"No objection, Your Honor," I arose and dully said. There was no use objecting; however bad the news it had to be faced, perhaps the sooner the better; moreover the judge would probably grant the request anyway, whatever I said.

"Proceed, Mr. Nesbitt," the judge briskly said.

"One moment, please, Your Honor," and Guy Nesbitt

whispered to Henry Harwood, who arose and pattered out a rear door and shortly returned with an old Indian woman. "She won't need an interpreter, Your Honor," Guy Nesbitt announced.

"*Cosima!*" Laughing Whitefish whispered, clutching my arm.

TWENTY-ONE

The witness sworn, Guy Nesbitt wasted no time in directing his heaviest fire against our case.

"Your name?" he began softly.

"They call me Cosima—it is my only name." She was short, dark, plump, and had a broad amiable ageless countenance with slanting intensely black eyes.

"And to what Indian tribe do you belong?"

"The Chippewa."

"Where did you spend your girlhood and younger womanhood?"

"At the Indian encampment near L'Anse Bay on Lake Superior."

"Where do you live now?"

"On Madeline Island off the Wisconsin shore, also on Lake Superior. I have dwelt there since shortly after the death of Blue Heron, surviving widow of Marji Kawbawgam."

"Have you lived there since you left L'Anse Bay?"

"Yes, there was no other place to go."

Guy Nesbitt pointed at me. "Have you ever seen this man?"

She peered my way. "No, he seems a stranger." She peered closer. "He seems but a boy." I squirmed and hoped she could not see me blushing.

"Or the young woman sitting next to him?"

"I cannot see that far—I am old, old. She is pretty." The coal-black hair of the witness was severely parted in the middle and hung over her shoulders in two long braids. At first glance one might have thought she was wearing a black cloth babushka of the kind worn by immigrant women. She smoothed back her hair and I was further confirmed in my growing suspicion that one could not ever safely guess an Indian's age.

"You have spoken of the widow of Marji Kawbawgam— Blue Heron," Guy Nesbitt purred on. "You knew this woman?"

"Very well. She was my closest friend. She took me in when I was widowed, alone and ill."

"She took you into her wigwam?"

"Yes, she was kind and good."

"Did you know Marji Kawbawgam?"

"Very well—I knew him since he was a young boy. My husband and old Osseo taught him to make his first pair of snowshoes and his first canoe."

"To whom was he married?"

"Blue Heron—I danced at their wedding."

"Did Marji have any other wives?"

"Later he married Sayee, down the big lake near what is now Marquette, just east of where I sit."

"Were you living with Blue Heron when Marji married her?"

"I was."

"Did you continue to live with her after he married her?"

"Oh, yes, the wigwam was a large one."

The judge was rapidly taking notes, and at this he looked up, frowning, and paused to listen. Guy Nesbitt, the consummate actor, waited before asking his next question so that its import would surely sink in. I leaned forward tensely.

"Now I ask you, Cosima, did you continue to dwell in Blue Heron's wigwam after Marji married Sayee, his second wife?"

"I did. It was my only home."

"Did Marji ever visit Blue Heron at L'Anse Bay *after* he married Sayee?" Guy Nesbitt was phrasing his questions carefully, leaving me little room to object.

"Oh, yes, I remember several occasions," she answered.

"And did he ever spend the night?"

"Oh, yes, he always spent the night. It was too long a trip there and back in one day."

"Where did he spend it?"

"In Blue Heron's wigwam, of course."

"And where did you sleep?"

"Why, in the same wigwam of course."

Guy Nesbitt turned and looked back at the courtroom clock, as though to mark the very minute he would administer the fatal blow to our case. He faced the witness and spoke softly.

"What did Marji and Blue Heron do when they spent the night together in the same wigwam where you slept?"

A slow smile spread over the witness's features. She glanced slyly up at the judge. The judge had put down his pen and was regarding the witness with mingled incredulity and distaste. The witness spread her hands, palms up, her smile now increasing. "What does a healthy man and his wife *do* who have long been parted? They, they—how can I put it?"

"Say nothing," the judge put in curtly, gathering up his silk robe about him as though he were crossing a muddy lane. "Your point has already been made abundantly clear."

The witness was not to be denied. "They—they performed the final act of love," she blurted, then put a hand over her mouth to suppress a giggle.

"*That's enough!*" the judge ordered curtly, banging his

gavel sharply. Guy Nesbitt used the occasion to steal a slow glance back at me and nod. His was a masterful performance: my optimistic claim of a divorce had just gone a-glimmering.

"Are you through, Mr. Nesbitt?" the judge demanded harshly.

"Presently, Your Honor, but I do promise we'll now emerge from the communal wigwam." He faced the witness. "Now I ask you what relation Blue Heron was to Marji Kaw-bawgam when Marji Kawbawgam died?"

Innocently: "Why, his wife, of course."

"Did Marji ever put Blue Heron away or did you ever hear that he had?"

The question was objectionable as leading and suggestive, but a victorious objection now would have been academic—the mischief was done. I remained glumly silent.

"Of course not, though I wouldn't say he was a good husband—he drank too much and, worse yet, spent too much time away." She glanced uncertainly at the judge. "But I must say he made up for it when he came home to visit Blue Heron. Why, I remember—"

The judge ominously raised his gavel, and the witness clapped her hand over her mouth, like a child caught stealing cookies. Guy Nesbitt relented; his cake did not need two coats of frosting... "Complainant may examine," he said, making a courtly gesture toward me as he retired to his table.

I sat there stunned and dejected, not daring to look at Laughing Whitefish—she was far too intelligent not to discern what was happening to our case.

"Do you waive cross-examination, Mr. Poe?" the judge crisply demanded.

I arose and advanced toward the witness, as much to disappoint His Honor as anything. At least I would clear Laughing Whitefish and myself of trying to suppress Cosima's testimony.

"If you speak English so well why didn't you answer the letters I sent you at Madeline Island?" I said.

"Because I never learned to read or write English," she answered simply. "My learning to talk it was a kind of a gift, like the raven imitating the fox. I also speak French," she added proudly.

"Why didn't you get someone else to read and answer for you?" I gloomily pressed on.

"Alas, the only one who could have was the schoolmaster, who dwells on the far side of the island." She spread her hands. "I meant to do something, but I am old and forgetful." She peered at me closely. "I hope no harm was done—I have told only the truth."

I was curious how the opposition had found her. "How did you come to answer the letters of these others?" I inquired, gesturing at the table of opposing counsel.

"There was no need. They came and talked with me."

"Who did?"

Pointing at Henry Harwood. "The man who guided me in here today—I forgot his name. I trusted him."

"When did you first talk with him?"

"Oh, 'way last fall—before the first good snow had fallen."

So Henry Harwood had known all along, I thought glumly. Then why had he still later wanted to settle the case? My mind raced, seeking some mental sunburst that would reveal to me the missing key to our case . . .

"Mr. Poe, are you through conducting your inquest?" the judge now demanded, the merest trace of a smile flitting across his grim features.

More and more I was growing to dread the mercifully rare occasions when the judge smiled. To me his smile was more of a fleeting muscular contraction than a smile, reminding me more of a nervous tic or the grimace of an infant afflicted with gas pains.

"Are you through?" he demanded more sharply.

"Not quite, Your Honor," I answered, turning back to the witness. "Do you know why you were brought here?" I asked her, taking a shot in the dark.

"I was told that my testimony might be of help in a matter involving Marji Kawbawgam." She spread her hands. "So I came."

"Of help to whom?" I pressed doggedly on. If this case was to be lost, I would expose the whole shabby business to the light of a heedless world. Or was I trying mostly to save the face of Willy Poe?

"Why, of help to Marji's family, I always supposed," she replied, looking anxiously across at Henry Harwood, who sat staring down at his table. "I *have* helped, haven't I? Doesn't the truth always help?"

It was a good question, I thought bitterly, and one I had ignored far too long.

"Was it ever explained to you," I pressed on, "that you were brought here to testify *against* the family of Marji Kawbawgam?"

Clapping her hand over her mouth. "Oh, no, no, no. . . ." She glanced wildly about. "Have we been deceived once again by *them?* Have—"

Guy Nesbitt was swiftly on his feet, cutting off the witness. "I don't see the drift of this cross-examination, Your Honor, and—"

"You mean you see it all too well," I burst out, suddenly stung to bitter anger, as much at myself as anyone else. "You have—"

"That will be all, Mr. Poe!" the judge harshly broke in,

pounding his gavel. "How dare you break in on counsel when he is addressing this court! Once more and I warn you... Continue, Mr. Nesbitt."

"I'll withdraw my remarks," Guy Nesbitt said, returning to his seat. Well he might have, I thought, as already he had accomplished more than he sought: not only had he interrupted my train of thought but, worse yet, set the judge even more against me. I again felt a wave of futility over what I was doing.

"Are you through?" the judge again demanded.

"Not quite, Your Honor," I said, elaborately polite. I paused and then added: "I may be inexperienced and weak on courtroom deportment, but at least I am aware that counsel usually announces when he is done with a witness. I'll try hard to remember that, sir."

The judge clutched his beard with one hand, and glared out across the courtroom, eyes staring, the light glinting ominously from his glasses, evidently debating whether I had gone quite far enough for him to discipline me for having committed a contempt in open court. That he longed to do so I could feel in my bones. Then he picked up his pen and began rapidly making notes. "Go 'head, then" he said gruffly, evidently even more concerned to defeat my case.

Again I addressed the witness. "Did you know that Laughing Whitefish, daughter of Marji Kawbawgam, had brought suit in this court against the people who are now mining the iron ore that Marji originally showed the white man?" Win or lose I was determined to pour salt on *that* wound so all the world might see.

She rocked in her chair and spoke almost in a wail. "Oh, I did not know, I did not, I swear I did not know."

"Did you know that you have instead been brought here to testify *for* the mining company and *against* Laughing Whitefish?"

"You've been all over that," the judge quickly broke in. "The witness need not answer." Cosima had bowed her head. I waited for her to look up. When she did there were tears in her eyes.

"Have you been ill?" I said, remembering Guy Nesbitt's statement why she should be called to testify out of turn.

She wiped her eyes and patted her ample bosom. "Cosima ill? Nonsense, I am strong as a horse. I am ill only that I have been fooled."

"Where did you learn to speak English so well?" I pushed on, prolonging the agony.

Proudly: "I once clerked at the trading post in L'Anse," she answered. "I guess I had a kind of parrot's knack."

"Who raised Laughing Whitefish?" I asked, suddenly taking another tack. Out of the corner of my eye I saw Guy Nesbitt arise and quietly edge his way forward.

"Why, Blue Heron, of course."

"Did Blue Heron treat Laughing Whitefish as her own daughter?"

"Objection, objection," came the expected thrust from Guy Nesbitt. "Plainly leading the witness."

"What do you say, Mr. Poe?" the judge demanded.

"Why, I'll of course abide by the court's ruling—though I may reluctantly have to note an exception," I said. I looked at the judge, wide-eyed and trusting, and he glared back at me, his eyes magnified and staring. Then a frightening steely smile passed over his face. He suddenly saw through my little snare: I was trying to trap him into reversible error on appeal for failing to let the witness answer a proper leading question on cross-examination on a crucial issue of the case.

"I remind you that this is cross-examination, Mr. Nesbitt," the judge said, almost apologetically. "I'm afraid I shall have to overrule your objection. The witness may answer."

"I don't remember the question," the witness said.

"Mr. Poe, ask her again," the judge ordered.

"I got so lost in the intervening maze of legal rhetoric that I don't remember either, Your Honor," I lied apologetically. "Possibly the court reporter might."

"Mr. Bigbee," the judge grimly ordered, "read back the last question asked the witness by complainant's counsel before the objection."

Stoically flipping the pages of his notebook, finding the place, clearing and re-clearing his throat, then reading: "Did Blue Heron treat Laughing Whitefish as her own daughter?" he chanted wearily, confirming my suspicion that all court reporters secretly hated their work as well as all lawyers and were to a man wretchedly and permanently bored.

"She did," the witness answered.

"Why?" I asked.

"Because she *was* her daughter; Blue Heron had—what's the word?—adopted her from the first day she took her in. All of us at L'Anse Bay knew that."

I affected surprise. "You mean that the Indians practiced adoption just like the whites?"

"Well, they never had papers or records, if that's what you mean, but otherwise, yes, just like the whites."

"And under Indian custom Laughing Whitefish would get whatever her adopting mother left behind just as though she was of her own blood?"

"Yes, it is the old Indian way."

"One more question, Cosima," I said. "Did Blue Heron leave any other children behind?"

"Alas, she did not. Her babies all died at birth. I know because I was there and took care of her, poor broken reed."

"Or any other relatives?"

Shaking her head sadly: "Blue Heron was all alone. All she

left behind was Laughing Whitefish. Hers was a sad lonely life."

"Back to you, Mr. Nesbitt," I said, it now being my turn to accord him a fine, courtly gesture.

"No further questions," Guy Nesbitt arose and said, whereupon Henry Harwood pattered up front and beckoned the witness away.

"Call your next," the judge ordered curtly.

"One moment, Your Honor, please," I said, flipping my notebook. I had intended to call another Indian as my next witness, but I decided to revise my plans. For one thing I felt the case had reached a crucial point and that before anything else happened I wanted to get into the record the enormous stakes that were involved—thereby also possibly impressing the judge with the gravity of the case. To this end I had subpoenaed the bookkeeper from the Jackson Mine, as well as his books and records, to show the vast tonnage of ore that had been mined, a necessary step in our proofs. I suddenly decided to call him now. Next I would put in the astonishing record of the cash and stock dividends and then . . .

"The complainant will now call Eric Kellstrom for cross-examination, as provided by the rules of practice," I arose and announced.

There was a rustling in the back court as the witness arose bearing an armload of heavy ledgers.

The judge held up a staying hand. "Just a moment," he announced. "The court has a few preliminary questions to ask complainant's counsel." The judge's eyes bored glinting into mine. "Mr. Poe," he asked evenly, "is the court correct in assuming that the main thrust of the evidence you now seek from this witness goes largely to the measure of damages and extent of money liability, assuming basic liability?"

"That is correct, Your Honor," I answered truthfully.

His eyes gleamed as he lowered his voice and continued:

"And may the court further understand that you have now completed your proofs on the issue of basic liability?"

"Yes, Your Honor."

"Including the right of your client to bring suit here at all?" he carefully pressed.

"Yes."

"And bearing on the related question of whether her father and his first wife were ever legally divorced?"

This is it, I thought, now it is coming... "Yes, Your Honor," I answered, because it was the only honest reply I could make. "I had subpoenaed additional witnesses but I have decided against calling them because their testimony, where not inconclusive, would only be largely repetitive and cumulative. I propose henceforth to inquire into the measure and extent of the relief that should be granted."

The judge glanced at the court reporter as though to reassure himself that this exchange had been taken down. "Very well," he said quietly, "then at this time I ask you, sir, to address yourself orally to the issue of why the bill of complaint should not forthwith be dismissed, with costs awarded the defendant."

There was a gasp from the audience; at last the blow had fallen. "Why, Your Honor?" I asked dully. "Why may we not finish the proofs in our case?"

"The court does not propose to submit itself to cross-examination, Mr. Poe. If you failed to hear what was just said I'll have the reporter read it back to you." I stood staring up at this cold and devious old man. "Do I take it, Mr. Poe," he continued, "that you waive the court's offer to let you speak to that question?"

"No, Your Honor," I feebly fought back. "It—it's only that this is all so swift. I've barely had time to comprehend what you have said let alone argue the question."

The judge looked out at the courtroom clock. "Very well,

if it's time you need, I'll give you slightly more than an hour. We'll take a recess now until one o'clock. If you please, Mr. Sheriff."

In the scrape and scramble of departing people that followed the sheriff's declaration of the noon recess, I turned to Laughing Whitefish, whose wide dark eyes looked anxiously into mine. "This is it, my dear," I said. "You are about to witness another glowing triumph for the downtrodden white man."

She touched my arm and managed to smile. "I have never admired you more than now, William," she said softly.

"Nor I you," I said, suddenly aglow in the moment of imminent defeat.

I arose and glanced back at the exodus of milling people and saw Cassius Wendell sitting in the front row. He raised his hands, palms up, and closed his eyes and mournfully wagged his head. Laughing Whitefish was moving uncertainly toward the rear of the courtroom.

"Where are you going?" I inquired of her.

"Back to see Cosima," she said simply. "I must go and comfort my mother's old friend."

"I'll join you soon," I said. "First I've got to receive the condolences of old Cash." And maybe also congratulate him, I thought; maybe the old boy knew what he was doing when he'd ducked this haunted case.

TWENTY-TWO

"See, Willy," Cash said excitedly when I joined him. "Despite Henry Harwood's knowledge of the whereabouts of Cosima, and precisely what she would say—particularly about there being no divorce—he nevertheless still *later* wanted to settle the case. Don't you see? That means there's surely a grave defense weakness he must be aware of but that still hasn't met our eyes."

"Whatever it is, Cash, I wish he'd impart the secret to His Honor during the noon recess," I said gloomily, "because it sure hasn't dawned on me."

"But we must find it, Willy, we must, we must." The old boy was quivering with concern. "One more thing," he ran on, "while I can't bet with you about what the judge is going to do with your case, because I agree with you he'll probably dismiss it, there's one thing I will bet."

"What's that, Cash," I said absently, my mind in a whirl.

"A new beaver hat that in doing so he will quote from or at least mention his tin god Blackstone. You see, His Honor has a favorite author for every day in the week. His name is Blackstone or rather Blackstone's *Commentaries*." Cash blinked in recollection. "*Cave ab homine unius libri*," he intoned.

"Don't go showing off. What does it mean?"

"Of course, I should have known you wouldn't have

known. It's from an old Latin proverb that, loosely translated, means—let's see now—'Beware of the man of one book.' Well the *Commentaries* is the judge's favorite book and Blackstone is his favorite boy, he thinks the sun rises and sets in his"—he paused and glanced appraisingly at a woman standing near by—"right eye."

"It's a bet," I said, eager to get back to work.

"Fine. Now wrack your brains, Willy. Find that weakness, go find it, boy."

I shook my head. "Too late, Cash, 'way too late. Don't delude yourself as I have all along—we're beaten. At least I now have the courage to face up to that. Up to now I've acted about this case like the addled unbeliever who knelt every night and thanked God he was still an atheist. I too have not faced up to my situation—and now that it's too late I'm about to . . . Excuse me, Cash, I must go send my witnesses away and find Laughing Whitefish." I managed a small smile. "And if the judge acts fast today I might still have time to get over to justice court and lose a collection case."

"Don't give up the ship, Willy," Cash said, patting my shoulder as I left to pay off and discharge the remaining subpoenaed witnesses I'd no longer need. Most of them were Indians, there for the duration of this courtroom show, squatting cross-legged on the floor and stoically eating their lunches. I'd heard the sheriff say earlier that many of them had been his overnight guests in the empty cells in the jail. "Lotsa room, lately," the sheriff had explained. "Postholiday slump, I guess." As I paid them off I reflected that subpoenaing these Indians had been an idle gesture; they couldn't have been kept away with a club.

On the way to the back of the courtroom I ran into a disconsolate Octave Bissonette, both eyes blackened, his face a mass of bandages and criss-crossed patches of court-plaster. One arm was dangling limply from a sling.

"What's the matter, Octave," I inquired politely, "did you have a fight with a wildcat? "

He regarded me mournfully. "You bet you boots, Mist' Poe," he said. "An' wilecat she wan. Octave awful 'fraid for scare dat wilecat."

"Sorry, Octave. Better luck next time."

He sighed and shook his head, gesturing with his good arm. "Is bettair man never try for force wilecat—is bettair let wilecat firs' come to man."

"I'll try to remember that, Octave."

Reaching the corridors back of the courtroom looking for my client I encountered Henry Harwood, who nodded gravely and silently pointed to the closed door of a lawyers' conference room. Opening the door I saw Cosima and Laughing Whitefish sitting on a bench against the far wall, laughing and crying in each other's arms.

Laughing Whitefish fought to compose herself. "This is my lawyer, William Poe, Cosima," she finally said. "He is my friend."

Cosima arose and curtsied and briefly pumped my hand. At closer range I could see the tiny hieroglyphics that time had etched about her eyes. "I could cut my tongue out if I said anything that has hurt my dear girl," she said. "Oh why didn't I answer your letters? I'm just a stupid forgetful old woman."

"It wouldn't have made any difference, Cosima," I said. "This case was apparently decided by things that happened before she was born. Nobody can alter that."

"You are kind to say so, young man. Ah, we must go now and drive to catch my train back home—that little lawyer is waiting to take us to the depot. It's a long journey with many waits and changes."

Laughing Whitefish looked mournfully at her, seeming again on the verge of tears. "Cosima don't leave me, please don't leave me," she almost wailed, at the moment looking as appealing and plaintive as a little girl. Watching this revealing show of loneliness, my heart was wrenched. I longed to take her in my arms.

Instead Cosima put her plump arms about Laughing Whitefish, holding her close and patting her. "There, there, child, but I must go. Children still keep getting born and foolish old Cosima must still be on hand to help. Take heart, little one, you will always have Cosima on your side. You know I love you, my little orphaned fawn."

My glance wandered from this poignant scene and for the first time I noticed a tall slender man standing quietly over by the window, arms folded, his back towards us, looking out over the lake. I looked at him inquiringly and Cosima saw my look.

"Metoxon," she called out, and he turned around, and I saw a lean swarthy young Indian with a face like a curved dagger, probably my age or younger. "Meet William Poe," Cosima continued, "lawyer for Laughing Whitefish in her case." She spoke briefly in Indian, apparently saying the same thing, since I again heard my name.

"How do you do," I said when she was done.

He looked me up and down slowly, disdainfully, as though I were a gnat. Then he nodded gravely without speaking and coolly turned back to his contemplation of the lake. I could feel myself flushing.

"Metoxon is a sort of distant relative I discovered on Madeline Island," Cosima rattled on, "and he came along to take care of this silly forgetful old woman." She paused and smiled so broadly that her eyes became wrinkled slits. "He reminds me so much of Marji Kawbawgam in his younger days that I brought him along in the hope, too, that he and Laughing Whitefish might get married." She laughed at her resourcefulness and rocked on her bench and slapped her knee.

"*Cosima!*" said Laughing Whitefish.

But Cosima the match maker was not to be put off. She appealed to me. "Before his death Metoxon's uncle was chief of the Madeline Island Indians, just as Laughing Whitefish's uncle once was here. They'd make a handsome pair, don't you think, William Poe?"

"I—I'm certain they would," I managed to say. "Sort of a union of Indian royalty."

"And their children would be beautiful, don't you think?"

"I'm sure they would be very beautiful," I said mechanically, longing to turn and bolt from the place.

"Cosima, stop it at once," Laughing Whitefish said.

I held out my hand to Cosima. "Thank you for coming and now I must leave. I've less than an hour to dream up a way to save this case." I turned to my client. "Meanwhile you might pray." I glanced toward Metoxon, who was still studying the lake. As I hurried on my way, my cheeks burning, I kept wildly thinking that this could be the lucky day when I might not only lose my case but my client as well.

TWENTY-THREE

Even before one o'clock the courtroom was jammed with people: whites, Indians, and colorful mixtures of the races, both young and old, men, women and children, seated, standing, squatting...During the noon hour the word had evidently gotten out that the Kawbawgam case had reached a crucial stage; it seemed the whole town had turned out to witness the imminent slaughter.

As I took my place my eyes idly swept the front row. There was good old Cash, nodding and giving me a silent handshake, and even His Honor the mayor—ah yes, and my landlord, the president of the bank—besides a number of stylish women, corsetted and elegantly befurred. Even the town's oldest pioneer was there, resolute silver-haired Peter White, half-dozing, looking like a somnolent lion in his inevitable suit of black broadcloth, his great powerful hands rigidly clasping his knees, his heavy gold watch chain sagging across his barrel chest, his vast bulk occupying the space of two normal-sized persons. He was, by tacit consent, oral historian of the area; he settled disputed questions on the spot out of memory, not out of books...

Laughing Whitefish seemed lost in thought, sitting at my side. I leaned over and touched her arm. She started and looked at me inquiringly. "Did she mean it?" I whispered.

"Did who mean what?" she whispered back.

"Did Cosima really bring the silent one over here to marry you?"

She shrugged wearily and briefly closed her eyes. "You heard what she said, William. It's all I know."

"But had you known him before?" She shook her head. "Are you going to marry him?" I persisted.

She half smiled. "How can I tell—for one thing he hasn't asked me."

"But, look, you scarcely know the man. He may be brutal and never take a bath—and even *drink!*"

"He hasn't asked me yet," she coolly repeated. "As for my not knowing him before, that is the old way of my people. Often the first time an Indian bride ever sees her man is on her wedding day."

"But Laughing Whitefish, all that is in the past. It's the sort of thing you're trying to change, don't you see? You can't possibly be serious about—"

Just then the judge swept briskly in and strode rustling up to the bench. After hostilities were declared reopened he looked in my direction and said quietly, "You may proceed, Mr. Poe." While the words were couched in request the voice was one of cold command.

I arose in the hushed courtroom. "Your Honor," I began, my mind in a turmoil, "I shall not waste time reviewing the background of this case. I came in here on a theory that my client should prevail because she was the sole surviving lawful heir of her father, Marji Kawbawgam. Candor moves me to concede that the last witness who testified here has shaken that theory. But in doing so I submit she has measurably strengthened still another theory implicit in the case."

I took a deep breath and plunged desperately on. "I mean this, Your Honor: if the court should find that my client, Laughing Whitefish, has no standing in this court to sue as the lawful and legitimate heir of Marji Kawbawgam because she is the issue of the second and polygamous marriage of her father to her mother Sayee—in other words, that there never was a valid divorce between Marji and his first wife, Blue Heron—then I submit that the court should nevertheless find for her on the alternative theory that she is the lawfully adopted child and sole heir of her who, for want of a better phrase, I shall call her foster mother, Blue Heron.

"Let me try to put it another way, if the court please. If there was no lawful divorce between Marji Kawbawgam and his admitted first wife, Blue Heron, then it follows that this same Blue Heron, who survived him as his widow, as such also took his property, since no one questions the validity of *her* marriage to Marji. If the court reaches this point, then I submit it follows that my client can still maintain this action as the surviving adopted daughter of Blue Heron—and this even if we were obliged to regard her as a total stranger to the blood of Marji Kawbawgam, which of course she was not."

The judge stared down at me impassively through his glasses. I paused, seeking to find some way to enter the cranium and possibly the heart of this inscrutable mid-American Moses. Was there no hidden reservoir of compassion in the man I might tap? Was there not some way I could pierce this granite complacency? Or was I butting myself vainly against a rigid armor of prejudice that couldn't be penetrated or dispelled?

"That the Chippewa Indians practiced both adoption and divorce has been shown here by the defendant's own expert witness, Professor Naughton," I pressed on. "Both domestic states appear to be as informal in their nature—that is devoid of record and formal ritual—as Indian marriage itself." I held out my hands. "If the court finds by the testimony of the last witness Cosima that there was no divorce because intimate marital relations continued with the first wife, then I submit that precisely the same witness had equally shown that my client should prevail and her case continue here because she is truly the adopted child of that surviving widow, Blue Heron."

Again I paused, groping for inspiration. "If the court is oppressed by the informality of the adoption in this case, I earnestly submit that it is no more informal than the Indian marriage ritual itself. So if the court hesitates to find a valid Indian adoption here because of informality and lack of ritual and written record, must not the court also take the position that no Indian *marriage* can ever be valid for precisely the same reason, that all Indian children are therefore illegitimate and may never sue in our courts on any claims of their parents? Yet that would be manifestly absurd. That is all, Your Honor," I said, abruptly taking my seat.

Guy Nesbitt was quickly on his feet. "Does His Honor wish the defense to argue to the question?" he inquired.

"His Honor does not, thank you," the judge replied, compressing his lips.

"Very well, Your Honor," Guy Nesbitt said, bowing and resuming his seat.

"Gentlemen," the judge continued, "with your forbearance I have decided to read my remarks so that I will surely say—and be credited with saying—precisely what I mean." He then picked a manuscript off the bench and clearing his throat and adjusting his glasses prepared to read. Then, remembering, he glanced at the court reporter, smiled faintly, and again spoke: "It will not be necessary for the court reporter to take down my remarks unless he feels the need of further practice in his craft. A copy will be furnished him later."

A titter of amusement rippled through the courtroom over this demonstration of judicial wit. Again the court reporter was dutifully convulsed. I frowned and averted my eyes. Such devoted hilarity was not only excessive, I thought, but far beyond the normal call of duty.

At length old Mr. Bigbee, the reporter, so far recovered himself that he was able to nod gratefully up at the judge for the respite. He then closed his notebook, folded his arms, shut his eyes, and appeared promptly to fall asleep. Court reporters, I reflected, were probably the most disillusioned and put upon souls at any trial; in their quiet despair that any witness might ever be moderately coherent, let alone lucid, they were forced to cultivate a kind of protective professional stupor. After all they had to endure it was perhaps uncharitable to deny them their occasional snatches of oblivion. I prayed only that this one wouldn't snore; I had an intuition Claudius Grant wouldn't like that.

Now more than ever I was convinced we were about to lose. The judge could not possibly have prepared his written opinion while I was talking, so rather obviously nothing I had just said had even faintly changed his mind. Moreover, to have an opinion ready at all meant he must have worked on it even longer than today; in fact he must have pretty well made up his mind against us from the first hour of the case. I slumped in my seat, gloomily composing myself to hear the worst.

"In the summer of 1844 a Chippewa Indian called Marji Kawbawgam worked as a guide and tote man for the survey party of William Burt," the judge began reading. "In late September of that year the first iron ore was discovered by this party on a rocky hill near what later became Negaunee. The following spring three officers of a partnership association formed in Jackson and known as the Jackson Mining Company, having learned of this mineral discovery but not its whereabouts, sought out this Indian at L'Anse Bay and treated with him to guide them to the site of the discovery. Terms were reached, the agreement reduced to writing and handed the Indian, and he guided the party to what later became and now is the Jackson Mine, the first and possibly the richest iron mine in the Lake Superior area. Nothing substantial was ever paid this Indian. So much for these background facts, which seem undisputed by all concerned."

The judge glanced out at the clock before he resumed reading in his monotonous and rather weary voice, like a preacher manfully embarking on a four-hour sermon. "Nearly thirty years elapsed before any suit was filed on this claim, if claim indeed it was. Meanwhile this Indian had acquired himself at least two additional wives to the one he already had, only death perhaps mercifully preventing him from engaging with a fourth. Suit has now been filed in this court by one Charlotte Kawbawgam, sole surviving issue of the second marriage, on the theory, one gathers, that she is the sole surviving heir of Marji Kawbawgam.

"The defendant corporation urges a number of matters in defense, not all of which are necessary for me to review at this time. One of these defenses, however, goes directly to the issue of the complainant's right to sue. Now manifestly it is idle for us to spend time listening to testimony on limitations and laches, measure of damages, or related matters, or even speculating about these and other things if Miss Kawbawgam lacks the basic right to sue. I shall therefore proceed to examine that vital preliminary question.

"The complainant's bill of complaint filed in this case is sometimes known as the 'shotgun' variety among the legal profession, wherein the pleader attempts to erect an umbrella of general allegation which he hopes is sufficiently broad to cover a variety of theories of recovery. At the outset of this hearing it rapidly became manifest that the complainant was pinning her hopes largely on a theory that she could sue because her father had divorced his first wife before he married her mother. This was an inviting theory because it would neatly have disposed of the little matter of polygamy, illegitimacy, bigamy, and any possible rival claim by the first wife or any relatives she might have left."

The judge flipped over a page and glanced down at me. I suppressed a sudden wild impulse to stick out my tongue. "Regrettably for her, however, this theory does not appear to fit the facts," he droned on. "Rather manifestly, too, there never was a valid divorce from the first wife in this case, and the court so finds. If neglect and desertion and wilful nonsupport and a swinish devotion to whiskey by the husband can amount to a valid divorce then it might equally be argued that Marji Kawbawgam had as well divorced his second wife, Sayee, mother of this complainant. So far as this record shows he equally ignored both women except when he felt an occasional pagan impulse to go spend the night with one or the other of them. On one such occasion, not bothering to leave town, he appears to have taken up with a compliant creature called Old Meg, who died later in a drunken fall."

Again the judge paused and took a sip of water and again the front benches obediently tittered in appreciation. I now saw a pattern emerging from these pauses and sippings: they were his genteel signal that another pearl of judicial wit had been unveiled; his disciples had to be alerted. His Honor, I saw, thirsted not so much for water as for applause. He pressed on. "If the complainant in this case were a white woman instead of being a Chippewa Indian clearly she could not sue here as her father's lawful heir. Citation of authority should be needless on such an elementary proposition, but cite some I shall.

" 'Polygamy is not only a vicious arrangement but is utterly incompatible with any notion of civilization, refinement and domestic felicity,' 2 Kent Commentaries 48. Again in Warrender versus Warrender, reported in 9 Bligh's New Reports

112, Lord Brougham well observed, 'No Christian nation can possibly recognize polygamous or incestuous marriages or the issue thereof and long remain Christian.' In addition our own Michigan statutes forbid polygamous marriages (Revised Statutes of 1838) and make violation thereof the crime of bigamy (Revised Statutes of 1848). Moreover we think it unseemly for a court of law to have to sit and conduct sober investigations into precisely what talk or bargains or primitive blandishments may have preceded a casual collision between unlettered savages many years ago. Such a grotesque state of affairs cannot be the law."

The judge paused—I leaned tensely forward—but this time he didn't take a sip of water; the front benches remained obediently silent. Still he hadn't mentioned his boy Blackstone. Perhaps, I dismally reflected, perhaps if I couldn't win my case I might at least win myself a new hat. The judge quickly dashed even this forlorn hope. "Finally Blackstone himself, on page 164 of the fourth volume of his celebrated commentaries, had this to say: 'Polygamy cannot be endured under any rational civil establishment, whatever specious reasons may be urged for it by the Eastern nations, the fallaciousness of which has been proved by many sensible writers: but in Northern countries the very nature of the climate seems to reclaim against it; it never obtained in this part of the world, even from the time of our early Germanic ancestors, who, as Tacitus informs us, "*prope soli barborium singulis unoribus contenti sunt.*" ' "

The judge looked up to let his little shaft of erudition sink in. Brushing up hastily on my rusty Latin I gathered vaguely that the early Germanic tribes almost alone among the barbarians had been content with a single wife. I thought it nicely typical of the plausible and windy Blackstone that he had invoked the one exception to prove the rule.

I longed to turn and look at old Cash who, on a small tidal

wave of legalistic Latin, had just won himself a new beaver hat. My monotonous habit of victory was reaching epidemic proportions...

"Why, because she is an Indian, should the rule be any different?" the judge droned on. "I can discern no single reason why, and none has been shown me. It strikes me that those who seek redress in the white man's courts should at least be willing to have their deportment tested by the white man's ways." The judge paused and shot a quick look at Laughing Whitefish, who sat very still at my side. "Perhaps it is true that the sins of the father should not be visited on his innocent children, but this court cannot elevate that principle, however charitable, into a guiding rule of law permitting recovery in this case. He cannot do so because by his solemn oath he may not let charity blind him to the law.

"If Marji Kawbawgam did not divorce his first wife Blue Heron, which fact the court has already found, and if she indeed survived him, as the court also now finds, then she or her heirs or personal representatives would seem to be the proper parties complainant here, not Charlotte Kawbawgam, boldly suing alone and in her own sole right. At the very least there would appear to be a fatal nonjoinder of necessary parties complainant in this case. This alone would be reason enough to dismiss this case, but there is more.

"As the hearing in this case progressed, and it became apparent that the theory of divorce was untenable, complainant then tried to bring her case under the broad umbrella of adoption, resourcefully urging that she was now the adopted daughter of the first wife, Blue Heron, and as such would inherit her adopting mother's interest in this claim. This also was a neat theory, if it worked, but again it cannot hold water. One simple reason it can't is that this court has always understood that where two persons are married to each other both must consent to the adoption of a child for any such adoption to be binding on either. I find not a shred of evidence in this case that Marji Kawbawgam ever knew of any such claimed adoption, much less assented to it. But the court has a broader ground for not permitting any theory of adoption to prevail in this case. It is this."

Again he cooly flipped a page and pressed on. "That the Indians occasionally practiced both adoption and divorce seems clear from the expert testimony in this case, and the court so finds. But that is not precisely the question presently before this court. Rather it is this: Granted, arguendo, that there could be a valid Indian adoption, must such an informal adoption be recognized in our own courts? I am not persuaded that it must, and again no authority has been shown me that it must. Again if this complainant were a white woman suing on such an informal claimed adoption she could not possibly prevail in this court. She could not because the adoption would not have been conducted according to our settled procedures and rules. Again the court suggests that those who seek redress in our courts should be willing to submit themselves to the rules and laws governing those who dwell within the jurisdiction of those courts. It therefore follows, as the day the night, that the complainant, having failed to qualify as a proper party litigant, may not prosecute her claim further in this court. Therefore, with some reluctance, the court is obliged to dismiss and now dismisses the complainant's bill of complaint, with costs awarded to defendant."

The judge glanced at the court reporter, whose head was now resolutely sunk on his heaving chest. He tapped his gavel lightly and Mr. Bigbee awoke with a start and automatically reached for his bristling crop of pencils. "Call to arms, Mr. Bigbee," the judge said, again flashing the steely mirthless smile I was growing to love so well. Mr. Bigbee's shoulders shook with instant merriment. With a manly effort I managed to restrain my own hilarity.

The judge now looked out at Laughing Whitefish and spoke in a low voice without manuscript. "The loser in this case may draw some comfort from the fact that she had no knowledge of or control over the events that have contrived to defeat her," he said. "She may further console herself by the knowledge that she was ably and spiritedly represented by her counsel. That the court might privately feel that the defendant in this case might well have met its moral obligation to Marji Kawbawgam and his kin, regardless of the law, might also comfort her." He sighed and looked at the sheriff. "Mr. Sheriff, we will now adjourn for the day."

When court had been adjourned, and the judge had swiftly retired, an Indian in the crowd arose and spoke briefly to the other Indians in Chippewa. Immediately there was an ominous rumble of voices and a milling of Indians in the body of the court. Gad Smith quickly glided out a rear door and reappeared shortly with three armed deputies. No one spoke or moved; the scene seemed frozen, spellbound, carved out of ancient wood. Then a woman screamed and swooned. Laughing Whitefish arose and spoke briefly and earnestly in Indian and, after a pause, the Indians and then everyone began slowly filing out.

"What did you say?" I turned and asked her anxiously.

"First I'll tell you what the Indian said. He merely said 'White man win.' All I said was, 'White man win here, maybe lose in Lansing.'" Her eyes searched mine. "Or did I say too much?"

"No, my dear," I said quietly. "We will appeal this case to hell and back. I've made up my mind."

I felt a hand on my shoulder and turned. It was Guy Nesbitt. He nodded pleasantly at Laughing Whitefish and offered me his hand and I took it. "Well, I must say you extended me, young man," he said. "But don't feel too badly—we can't win 'em all. Hope we meet again some time."

"Congratulations, Mr. Nesbitt," I said. "You are a worthy opponent, as the saying goes. As for our meeting again we may do so sooner than you think—on the appeal of this case. As some patriotic soul whose name now escapes me once said, 'We have just begun to fight.' "

Guy Nesbitt laughed easily. "What your elusive patriot really said—if you don't mind my correcting you—was this: 'Strike my colors, sir? Why, I have not yet begun to fight.' "

"Thank you," I said, feeling my ears burning. "However it should be phrased I assure you, sir, that I mean to fight."

Just then I caught the eye of Henry Harwood, who was hovering in the background, and while it may have been my churned imagination that made me think so, I thought his eyes lit up with a sudden glint of approval.

"I'll look forward to seeing you even earlier then," Guy Nesbitt replied with his air of invincible aplomb, turning away and almost immediately turning back, this time bowing deeply and addressing Laughing Whitefish. "And if I may say so, young lady, much as I love to win my cases, today's victory was tempered by a certain ruefulness that the loser had to be the comeliest litigant I have ever opposed." He looked at her admiringly. "By far the comeliest," he added.

"Thank you," Laughing Whitefish said, frowning and dropping her eyes. When Guy Nesbitt had again given her a courtly bow and turned finally away, she added swiftly to me: "That man, William—he collects women as you might gather pretty pebbles along the beach."

"Since I'm not very proficient at either," I said, "I'm curious to learn how you know?"

"By his eyes," she said. "They are the kind of bold male eyes that undress a woman—slowly, totally, piece by piece." She clasped her dress at the throat. "I'd sooner Octave Bissonette..."

"Sooner what?" I said, pierced by a swift shaft of jealousy.

"Sooner have him after me. A woman can cope with such crude admiration.... Why William, you're put out and you're blushing. The whole thing is silly—I despise both of them."

"Just as you despise Metoxon?"

She clucked her tongue and shook her head despairingly. "William, sometimes you're simply impossible. I scarcely know the man...But men like Guy Nesbitt make a woman feel naked." She shivered. "I feel I'm standing here without a stitch."

"In that case I'd better rush you out of here," I joked feebly to hide my jealousy. "Some men have so many enviable talents, undressing women with their eyes, winning all before them, while others find only ugly pebbles and lose their big cases. Guess I should stay in justice court where I belong. Or better yet take up harness making."

"Don't talk that way, William," she said quickly, touching my arm. "You were wonderful and, as you say, we've only begun to fight."

Disconsolately I finished stuffing my files in my briefcase and we slowly made our way out of the courtroom through a sort of impromptu honor guard of watchful smoky-eyed Indians silently lining the long exit corridor on either side. Laughing Whitefish, carrying herself proudly as a princess, greeted some of them by name and paused to chat briefly in Indian with one or two.

Plodding along behind her I was suddenly jostled from behind. I turned and saw two Indians restraining a third, a stranger, who stood glowering at me with fierce unblinking eyes.

Laughing Whitefish had not seen the incident and I shrugged and continued on my way, resolving not to tell her. She had troubles enough of her own...

I thought wryly of the old drawing by Daumier depicting a plump French advocate proudly leaving the courtroom with his weeping clients, comfortingly telling them: "You have lost your suit, it's true, but you have had the pleasure of hearing me argue." At least Laughing Whitefish was not weeping and of arrogance Willy Poe felt not the faintest trace.

TWENTY-FOUR

That Thursday afternoon Cassius Wendell—looking very dignified in a new beaver hat—and Laughing Whitefish and I attended the funeral services for Philo Everett held at the big brownstone church on Ridge Street where for so many years he had been so active and which in his younger days he had helped build. Later, amidst the somber tolling of church bells, we accompanied the procession out to the new Park cemetery, the shining narrow black-tasselled sleigh hearse being drawn by four spirited black horses wearing tall black plumes, all of which had been rented by the undertaker from Hodgkin's Livery Stable, the rear end of which my bachelor "suite" commanded such an excellent view. During the brief graveside services it began to snow. I observed a knot of blanketed and round-hatted Indians standing off by themselves as wooden and inert as totem poles.

"I wonder why they came," I remarked to Laughing Whitefish as we rode back to town, the sleigh bells muted, the runners squealing frostily on the glistening new snow.

"For the same reason we did, William," she replied softly. "Because they loved and respected the man."

"Must be that," old Cassius joined in thoughtfully. "Cause when I hates a man I hates his corpse. But I'd rather have a wisdom tooth out than attend most funerals. Fact is I have plans afoot to avoid attendin' me own. Yet somehow I *wanted* to go to this one." He wagged his head. "A most curious and soberin' thing...."

Cash and I planned to dine together at the Cozzens House so that we might talk over the case undisturbed—our first real chance since the swift courtroom events of the Tuesday before —and I invited Laughing Whitefish to join us.

"I'm sorry, William, but I've persuaded Cosima to stay over for a few days, and tonight I promised to make her a venison supper. I'm really very sorry."

"Were you able to persuade her talkative relative to remain over, too?" I couldn't resist asking.

"While I didn't especially ask him, Metoxon is staying over, as I assumed he might since his job is to take care of Cosima," she coolly replied.

"One of his jobs, you mean."

"Yes, one of his jobs, William. Thank you for reminding me. And now I must go."

When she had left Cash and I started walking to the Cozzens House, and I tried to put the cool disdainful Metoxon out of my mind. Cash had other ideas.

"Who's this here Max Toxin or whatever you and Lotti were just sparrin' about?" he demanded. I told him. "Is he young, single and Indian?" I nodded. "Is he figgering to marry her?" I nodded glumly and held the hotel door open for the shrewd old boy to enter. "Well, at least he ain't marrying her for her money," he said comfortingly. "Sounds like a real love match to me."

Cassius was drawn to the hotel bar as by a magnet, where I reluctantly accompanied him. Was this to be a drinking bout instead? In a way I somehow suddenly didn't much care.

"What's yours, Mr. Poe?" the bartender politely inquired, briskly snapping his ruffled armbands.

"Cherry soda, please, Jake," I ordered.

"And for you the usual, I suppose, Mr. Wendell," the bartender inquired. "Double bar whiskey an' a snit of beer?"

"Cherry soda," Cassius answered firmly.

"Cherry soda?" the bartender repeated in a small voice.

"Cherry soda," Cash repeated. "A new era has dawned in my drinkin', Jake. From now on it's straight cherry soda whatever old Cash may say."

"Are you *sick?*" I asked old Cassius, when the bartender had served us and retired in a state of shock.

"Here's to the future, Willy," Cash said, clinking glasses. "Old Cash is about to embark upon what may be a life-time project."

"What's that?" I inquired, fearful that the old boy had departed his wits.

"Reading all the law books in the library of Henry Harwood," he calmly announced, draining his glass and making a face. "And I'll bet my wooden leg it holds the golden key."

"The key to our case, you mean?" I said, dimly following.

"Of course, Willy—because it's *got* to," he said, wistfully eyeing and all but sniffing an open decanter of whiskey at the elbow of a customer standing next to him. "C'mon, Willy," he announced, plucking at my sleeve, "there goes the dinner bell. Let's go eat so I can avoid temptation and get started early on my search."

"You mean you're going to start hitting the books tonight?"

"This very night, lad," he solemnly announced. "As you told Guy Nesbitt in court the other day, 'We haven't begun to fight!' "

Dinner over, Cash pushed his things away and stuffed and lit one of his evil pipes and leaned back and proceeded to envelop me in its billowing, acrid fumes.

"I've been thinkin' about the judge's opinion," he mused dreamily. "It's really quite a document."

"How do you mean?" I asked, waving a menacing storm-cloud of smoke away.

"For one thing few people will ever find themselves called a bastard to their faces with such infinite grace and delicacy as Laughing Whitefish was called one the other day by the judge. Such was his genteel gallantry that he managed to call her a bastard seven times without once using the word, a new courtroom record in dainty legal euphemism, I swear."

"Ssh," I warned him, scandalized, "some ladies are sitting behind you."

"Well, maybe only six times, then," he indulgently conceded. "An' I been thinkin' something else about his decision, in case you'd faintly care to learn the reactions of an old one-legged soda-drinkin' veteran."

"What's that, Cash?"

He sat forward suddenly, putting his elbows on the table and fixing me with unwavering blue eyes. "I been thinkin'," he began slowly, "that in all honesty I can't much blame Judge Grant for reaching the decision he reached."

"How's that?" I swiftly came back, smarting at hearing such disloyal sentiments from my friend.

"Because he got no help from you to reach the right one," he shot back. "Look, Willy," he pressed on earnestly, "be honest with yourself. A lawyer with a meritorious case should not expect the trial judge to show him the way to win it. That is the lawyer's job, not the busy judge's, who has quite enough to do preserving decorum, taking notes, ruling on objections, and avoiding the clever snares and traps that both sides are forever settin' for him so maybe they can dump him on appeal should they happen to lose before him. Face up to it, lad, you didn't help the judge one smidgin to reach a right decision, now did you?"

"Well no, I guess not very much, Cash," I finally admitted.

"And when you appeal this case to Lansing the state supreme court will be in the same boat if you fail to help them," he pressed on. "Clapping a black nightshirt on a lawyer and packing him off to the state capital and thenceforth calling him 'Mister Justice' makes him no less fallible and uncertain than he was when he was back home drawing five-dollar wills. He still can't carry all the law in his head, it doesn't burst upon him like a sonnet—either he must look it up or somebody must tell him about it; otherwise he can only guess. Look, we've been livin' with this case for months and we still don't know the answers. Do you expect the poor overworked judges in Lansing to pluck 'em out of thin air?"

"I—I," I began, but he held up his hand.

"The floor is Colonel Wendell's and he's tryin' to help you, lad," he said gently. "You've got to think anew about your case, think down into its very bone and sinew, so that *this* time, when you get to Lansing, the judges can't help but reach a right result. Don't expect them to do your work, Willy. This time you got to show 'em the light."

"Look, Cash," I fought back, stung by the sharp nail of truth in his swift hammer blows. "I'll agree that I didn't much help Judge Grant with the law—simply because I couldn't find any—and I'll further grant there is a certain surface logic to his ruling. But if the man had any doubt in his mind about the right course to pursue, why in God's name didn't he resolve it in favor of continuing with the case rather than abruptly ending it, in favor of a poor orphaned Indian girl rather than a fantastically rich mining company, in favor of elementary justice rather than flatly against it?"

"Go on, boy, you're doing fine," Cash said, smiling and nodding approvingly. "*That's* the way you got to feel over your case—all riled up an' rarin' to go. As for Judge Grant, I think he was simply an innocent victim of his personal code of morality.

Not knowing what the law was, he simply called it as he thought it ought to be called." He gave me a wry smile. "Or possibly as his *wife* thought it ought to be called."

"Twaddle!" I came back hotly. "What can any unbiased person possibly think who watched this case unfold? That right is a matter of retaining canny counsel, that justice depends upon the state of the judge's liver?"

"The judge only held what he felt in his heart—what I'll wager nearly all of the white onlookers felt in their hearts."

"What do you mean?" I demanded.

"Look, Willy, as a people we are not notably tolerant of the customs and folkways of others, and especially are we reluctant to believe that the domestic and marital arrangements of a handful of savages can possibly equal much less surpass the God-given sublimity of our own." He grinned malevolently. "Brace yourself, Willy, but we share with the English an intolerable affectation of superior virtue. God may love everyone, possibly, but in our hearts we *know* he adores us."

The old boy was off on one of his cantankerous philosophic talking sprees, and I tried to divert him. "The biggest thing that gnaws me, Cash," I said, "doesn't concern the judge at all—it concerns Henry Harwood."

"How do you mean, boy?"

"You tell me he wanted to settle this case, that he knows something we don't know, that right may all along have been on our side. I'm more than half inclined to agree with you, and if so, why wasn't the case settled, why didn't Henry Harwood insist upon it, and why if it wasn't settled didn't he inform the court about the true state of the law when he saw the judge heading hellbent into error and a bad decision?"

"Would *you* have, Willy?" Cash asked quietly.

"Who, me?" I asked, pausing thoughtfully and then smiling over my one-sided earnestness. "Well, maybe no, Cash," I admitted, "perhaps it's still not the job of a lawyer publicly to point out the weaknesses of his client's position—at least while our trials remain adversary proceedings. But it's a nice problem in legal ethics, isn't it? At least I insist he could have told his client what he knew and prevailed on it to offer us a half-way decent settlement."

"We already know he told his client, but his people turned him down."

"But how *could* they, Cash?" I almost wailed. "How could they possibly have not wanted to settle this case with the daughter of the very man who unlocked and showed them—or rather the men they succeeded—their glittering treasure house?"

"*Auri sacri fames*," he intoned.

"Translate!" I said, nettled by his ostentatious show of erudition.

"For you 'lust for gold' is close enough. Greed might be closer." He rubbed his thumb and index finger rapidly together. "Money is even plainer."

"How do you mean?"

"Because the stakes have gotten too high. Look, Willy, if they'd up an' offered you say twenty thousand to settle, you'd have smelled a rat and have probably demanded forty. Then if they turned you down on that what would they have accomplished? Nothing. They would not only have weakened their defense of laches but also have tipped you off that there surely must be some fatal weakness in their defense."

"I still don't see it," I said, shaking my head.

"Moreover, Willy," Cash went on, "you are forgetting that corporations are organized primarily for profit. The special genius of the corporation is that while it possesses a kind of immortality and can never die, it is never bothered by a heart or soul or any qualms of conscience. Corporations can do—and omit to do—things that their stockholders would be horrified to do by themselves. They can do so because the responsibility is finally dispersed among so many that no one is to blame because all are. That is the great fearful power of the modern corporation."

"You make them sound like creatures out of Edgar Allan Poe," I said. "You mean you are against corporations?"

He shook his head wearily. "No, Willy, not against them, just realistic about them. And while I mercifully won't be around to see it, I predict that one day in this country there will be corporations so vast and so powerful—yes and so helpless to restrain their own giantism—that they will rival and possibly even challenge the Government itself."

"Sounds like a bleak prospect," I murmured.

Cash sat squinting at me through billowing clouds of smoke. "Willy, if you don't mind my gettin' personal, son, why don't you relax more? You're all tensed up over this case. Tain't good for you or it."

I laughed. "Maybe I ought to take up serious drinking."

"No, I mean it, son. Why don't you meet some of the young people of the town—there's lots of 'em—and maybe find yourself a nice girl?"

"Too busy. Moreover I never seem to get around to meeting any."

"You mean you've never been invited up on the Hill?—a nice eligible young bachelor like you?"

"Now that you speak of it, no, Cash, I never have."

He nodded sagely. "Ah, I'm beginnin' to see the light. Wanna know why you haven't? I should have realized it before now."

"Why?"

"Tain't alone the fact you're suin' a big mining corporation, and one in which all the best people on the Hill own stock—though that's bad enough."

"Why then?"

"Because you've dared to take the part of a despised Indian

against *them*, the whites, your own kind, that's why. Win or lose they'll never forgive you for that. *Never*."

"Alas, my future appears desolate. Please pass the hemlock."

He clucked his tongue. "No, son, you'll never draw their wills, never squire their daughters, never ever darken their doors. You're a pariah, son, a renegade, a traitor to your tribe."

I shrugged. "Guess I'll have to turn Indian, Cash."

"Looks like. At least you aren't apt to be one of those lawyers sellin' out his profession for a mess of pottage."

"What do you mean?"

He leaned forward earnestly, elbows on the table, holding his smoking pipe aloft like a poised dart. "I mean the trouble I see loomin' ahead for our own profession, the law."

"What in the world are you driving at?" I scented a new lecture.

"I mean that each year more and more of the cream of the crop amongst lawyers is surrendering lock, stock and barrel to the world of business."

"What's wrong with that?" I said, bridling. "Do you expect a business man in trouble to go out and hire the worst lawyer he can find?"

The old boy was away and running. "No, of course not, Willy, and I'm not necessarily blaming business—I'm blaming us lawyers for our almost gleeful abdication of our traditional independence, of our ancient role as guardians of the common weal, enemies of injustice, protectors and defenders of the underdog. And it still wouldn't be so bad that business is getting all the best legal talent if our legal brethren did more to shape the new business world once they got there. Instead they are mostly being shaped by it. Worse yet, since our courts and legislatures are fairly bulgin' with lawyers, with their help our very statutes and judicial decisions are being shaped by it."

"I don't think you're being quite fair, Cash."

With aggravating slowness he packed and relit his pipe and accusingly pointed the bit at me. "Not being fair, eh, young fella? Not fair, you say? Then take Guy Nesbitt there—he's a beautiful example of what I mean. Here he is, using all his great talent and brains and charm to defeat what in his secret heart he *knows* is a just case. He's one of the new breed of smilers—get yours but smile, smile, smile." He gloomily shook his head and rapped the table to accent his words. "For all his elegant airs, his fancy finery, his fat fees, he's nothin' but a whore—a painted, smirking, sashayin', street-walkin' *whore!*"

"Ladies!" I again warned him, a finger over my lips. "Remember those ladies behind us."

"Ladies?" he murmured, leaning out and stealing a furtive look. "Hm, can't quite tell from here . . . Ah well, if they are ladies they won't know what I'm sayin'. If they aren't I'll have to speak to the management."

I stared at the old goat. "Cassius Wendell," I said, "you are a wilful wicked depraved old man."

He bowed gravely as though acknowledging a fine compliment and coolly pushed on. "Take this very case. One reason suit on it was so long delayed—and that fact alone may finally defeat it—was that for years it wasn't possible to find a single lawyer in this whole bailiwick who wasn't beholden to the mining companies. To a man they were contentedly nuzzling at the bountiful corporate udder."

"Lawyers must eat," I said sententiously.

"But not surrender," he came back at me, pointing a plump forefinger in the air. "Who," he intoned, "who among the great lionhearted lawyers in this county dares speak up for the Indian?" He shook his head dolefully. "A *boy*," he bawled in a kind of prolonged oratorical wail, "nothing but a callow, beardless *boy* barely out of law school—yes, and one hellbent on losing his first big case." I hung my head as he glared at me scornfully. "An' I suppose you're jest dyin' to go over to the camp of the enemy."

"I haven't been invited," I said, my face burning, stung by his harsh indictment. For a long time we sat lost in thought and tobacco fumes. Could there be a grain of truth in his extravagant charges?

Cash finally spoke. "Don't take it to heart, Willy," he said softly, grinning over at me. "I'll come down off my high horse. Air's too rare up there anyway. It's the way things are, lad, and neither of us can change it." He peered anxiously across at me. "Perhaps we'd better get back to our case."

"Let's," I said, feeling listless and discouraged.

"The thing is you've got to *think* anew about your case, Willy—and then go dig up the law to win it."

The blows were coming thick and fast. "*Think* about my case! That's all I've been doing. I've barely slept a wink for two nights, thinking and brooding over this damned case."

Cash was unrelenting. "Then give me just *one* reason why on appeal you think the supreme court should reverse Claudius Grant?" he challenged me. He paused for a moment, his blue eyes regarding me anxiously. "You are going to appeal, aren't you, Willy?" he inquired in a small voice.

"Yes, of course, Cash," I answered, affecting a confidence I scarcely felt. "I've already ordered the transcript of the testimony from the court reporter, Mr. Bigbee, and he's already gone to work on it—so I guess I'm committed." I paused and frowned. "And I'll probably have to start chasing old piano accounts clear up to Negaunee and Ishpeming to pay for his services. No wonder old Mr. Bigbee can keep a fine team of bays—the estimated expense of this item alone is faintly staggering."

An aroused Cassius was not to be side-tracked. "You still

haven't told me one good reason why you think the supreme court should reverse His Nibs on appeal," he pressed on with his cross-examination, boring me with his blue eyes.

"Adoption," I ventured. "I think Judge Grant was dead wrong in rejecting adoption."

"Why?" he demanded. "Can't you see any sense in holding that a parent must consent to the adoption of his child by a stranger, even if that stranger happens also to be his wife?"

"Possibly, but not when the parent has virtually abandoned his child, as Marji did. Moreover Blue Heron could plainly have adopted the child alone and on her own *after* Marji died. Moreover it seems utter nonsense that Marji should be held to have to consent to an adoption of Laughing Whitefish—who was already his daughter."

"Good, good, boy," Cash said slowly, nodding and relenting a little. "But where's your legal authority?"

"I haven't found it yet. After all it's only two days since I lost the damned case and I'm still clutched by defeat. Give me a chance, Cash."

"What else?" he demanded.

The old boy was determined to probe me, and I had to be frank with him. "I really don't know yet, Cash," I admitted. "As far as I can now see—it's all still very nebulous—this time it's got to be a theory of adoption, plus . . ." I paused, groping for words.

"Plus what?" he pressed me, at the moment reminding me of a rather seedy but equally persistent Guy Nesbitt.

I pondered before answering. "Here is my thinking," I said slowly. "We now know that there can be Indian marriage, Indian divorce, Indian adoption, and all the rest. All that is now firmly in our case—and their own witness, Doctor Naughton, was at some pains to put it there."

"What then?" Cash prodded me.

"So the big question on appeal, as it's vaguely shaping in my mind, is not so much whether Marji divorced Blue Heron, or didn't divorce her, or whether Blue Heron adopted Laughing Whitefish, and if so when—although all these things and others are important—but whether a state court can reject and fail to recognize and apply Indian tribal customs once they are established. If it can then it strikes me that our courts could equally reject *any* Indian marriage, which is nonsense. In other words, Cash," I vaguely concluded, "was Judge Grant right or wrong in deciding, as he did, that when an Indian sues in our courts his status and rights must be tested only by rules applying to whites? I think he was wrong, Cash, and God willing I hope to prove him wrong."

"Aye, aye, lad, you must be readin' my mind, I'm moving that way myself," he said softly. "But what's your legal authority?"

"That's for me—I mean for us—to bloody well find out," I concluded, looking him straight in the eye.

"And I'm starting right now, Willy," Cash said, arising and smiling down at me. "And I really didn't mean that about your wantin' to go over to the camp of the enemy," he added softly, bowing gravely at the ladies. Then he wheeled abruptly and thumped away, leaving me with my troubled thoughts—and also the dinner check.

TWENTY-FIVE

When I left the Cozzens House I emerged into a wondrous glistening winter night. A great high moon lit up the sky and lake and I decided to walk down to visit Miles Coffey. I paused as I passed the darkened house of Philo Everett—the man who knew Lincoln. The night was so eerily beautiful I purposely took the long way around the moon-drenched lake shore, with its gleaming and jagged mounds of ice looking like frozen waves.

I found Miles wearing his green eyeshade and crouching over his vise, contriving to look like a counterfeiter, although he was merely tying up some new trout flies. In my clumsy way I helped him for a spell and then we fell to playing cribbage. It was past midnight when we finished and he saw me to the door.

"Sorry you lost, Willy," Miles said.

"Don't give it a thought, Miles. You usually beat me, it's nothing new."

"I don't mean at cribbage, I mean your case."

"Thank you. I'm naturally sorry too."

"Good luck on your appeal."

"Thanks, Miles, but how did you know I was going to appeal?"

"Well, lawyers have to tell their absent clients when they've won, you know."

"Guy Nesbitt sent a victory telegram, you mean?"

"I ain't really supposed to say, Willy."

"And I guess I shouldn't have asked. Goodnight, Miles."

"Good night, Willy, and good luck."

Clouds had risen and obscured the moon and on the way home I got my feet wet walking into lurking water puddles in the pocked and snow-covered road. Carrying my soggy over-shoes I crept stealthily up the creaking stairway in the dark— our impoverished landlord had lately imposed a midnight cur-few on the hallway light—and I felt like a footpad as I groped my way down the darkened hallway to my quarters.

I stood at my door fumbling to fit my key. Suddenly I heard the soft sound of swiftly running feet, like someone run-ning barefoot. The sound was rapidly coming my way. I flat-tened myself against the wall. Someone was groping at my door, impatiently wrenching at the knob, muttering in a lan-guage I could not understand. Then he brushed against me and touched my arm and drew away. I could feel his hot breath on my face. It smelled strongly of whiskey. Clutched by sudden fear I grabbed for him and held on for dear life.

Wordlessly we grappled in the dark, in a kind of crazy dance, swaying and thumping violently against the walls and my door. Again I heard a guttural phrase I could not fathom and then I felt a sharp glancing blow on the side of my head that staggered me. Rallying, I fought for my life, aware now that my assailant was carrying some sort of weapon.

I tried to pin his arms but with another angry grunting cry he strained and broke away. I quickly crouched, still half dizzy from his blow, and I could hear him futilely hitting the wall where I had just been standing, grunting with each savage blow. I dove for his legs and heaving mightily, tried to upset him. If I could only hold him till help came. . . . Suddenly I beheld a great sunburst of light, a shooting cataract of light, as though tor-rents of stars and exploding meteors were raining earthward in a vast celestial downpour. . . .

I opened my eyes. It was daylight. I was undressed and in bed in my office. My head was throbbing and I felt it gingerly and discovered it was heavily bandaged. Bright sunlight poured in my window. Before it stood Laughing Whitefish, silently looking out.

"Lotti," I said.

She came over swiftly and knelt beside my cot, her eyes dark-ringed, looking anxiously into mine. "Who did it?" she asked fiercely, her fists knotted.

"I don't know," I answered truthfully.

"Was—" she drew a deep breath—"was it one of my people?"

"I don't know, Lotti. I cannot say."

"If it was you must get out of my case—we cannot let the Haunted Mountain destroy you too."

"No, Lotti, I'm not getting out of your case. I enlisted for the duration and we haven't begun to fight, remember?"

"But it isn't worth it, William. I know my people, I know them. . . . I have a dreadful feeling it was one of them."

"If someone wants to harm me, Lotti, my getting out of the case won't help. And if I stay I might just win, you know."

"Oh, William, I'm so terribly worried. Thank goodness it wasn't Metoxon—he spent the evening with Cosima and me and slept on a cot in my schoolroom."

"It hadn't occurred to me that it was. Why should *he* attack me?"

"I don't know, William." She looked away and then back at me. "Maybe he regards you as a possible rival."

I tried to affect a casual smile. "The idea is sort of preposterous, isn't it?"

She looked at me steadily. "I didn't say so, William, you did." She arose and went over and stood by my desk. "I do hope Mr. Wendell returns soon. I sent him out for food. You haven't eaten anything since you were hurt. Actually I found little or nothing to eat. I don't know what you've been living on."

I bunched my fingers and airily opened them. "Fairy dreams, I suppose, as becomes an imaginary rival."

She held up her hand. "Please, William, don't. . . ."

"Is Cosima and this Metoxon still here?"

"No—they've left for home."

"Did he ask you to marry him?"

She sighed. "Yes. He spent half the night asking me. That's how I know he wasn't the one who attacked you."

"Are you going to?"

"Am I going to what?"

"Marry him, of course?"

She shook her head wearily. "Oh, I don't know, William. Most Indian girls are married in their teens. Yet after all he *is* a perfect stranger to me." She looked away. "I—I put him off. Please don't talk so much, you must try to rest."

"I feel better already and I want to talk."

"I'm terribly worried, William. Do you have any enemies you haven't told me about? Where had you been that night?"

"Well, my piano debtors occasionally get a little riled, but none has ever threatened to do me in. Actually I don't think my attacker meant to kill me—he could easily have stabbed or shot me. His idea seemed rather to maim me."

"He might have killed you and nearly did. Where were you that night?"

"After dinner last night Cash and I talked about the case a while and parted. Then I went and played cribbage with Miles Coffey. About midnight I walked home alone and while opening my door was suddenly attacked by someone in the dark. That's all I know."

"Not *last* night, William. It was the night before, on Thursday. It's now Saturday afternoon."

"Saturday! You mean I've been unconscious all that time?"

"Most of the time. Sometimes you half came to and babbled incessantly about our case—and other things."

"Like what?"

"Oh, about your boyhood in Ann Arbor and—I swear I'm not making this up—how you've never been on a straw ride. You said lots of foolish things."

"Well, at least there I was talking sense—I *haven't* ever been on a straw ride and I yearn to. How long have you been here?"

"Since early yesterday morning when Mr. Wendell drove out to tell me about your accident. He'll be along shortly to spell me. I must go change my clothes."

"But where have you slept?"

"I haven't. I dozed some in your office chair."

"You poor girl. How did Cash learn about me?"

"Madame Dujardins went and got him. She heard the scuffling and then your moaning and found you lying by your door in a pool of blood. She got Doctor Laird out of bed and it was he who attended you and sewed up the gash in your head. She may have saved your life—she and the fur hat you were wearing. Ah, he's coming now."

I heard the familiar thump-thump and then a rattle at the door, and in burst Cash carrying a load of groceries in a striped paper bag. "You've come to at last, I see, Willy. Thought sure for a spell we was goin' to lose you. How's the old noggin'?"

I felt my head. "Fine, fine. Probably feels no worse than your own on certain mornings."

"Ah, he'll live, Lotti—you see how bold an' sassy he's gettin' already? Now you run along for a bit, my dear, and I'll torment the patient for an hour or two."

She left shortly, and Cash quickly drew up a chair. "Who did it, Willy?" he asked me earnestly.

"I don't know."

"Honest?"

"Honest, Cash."

"Could it have been an Indian?"

"I wouldn't want to say unless I was sure. Laughing White-fish feels badly enough already. Does the sheriff know?"

"No, we've told no one. Wanted first to talk to you." He glanced around stealthily and leaned closer. "Willy, I'm pretty sure it *was* an Indian who assaulted you."

"Why do you say that?"

"You were still clutching this in your hand when Madame Dujardins found you lying out there in the hall." He fumbled in his pocket and drew forth and dangled by its broken drawstring a deerskin pouch of the kind usually worn by Indians. "In it is a piece of twist tobacco and three rusty gang fishhooks and a spare length of rawhide for fixing snowshoes on the trail. There's no doubt in my mind it was an Indian."

"Have you told Laughing Whitefish anything about this?"

"Not yet—again I wanted to talk with you."

"Then don't."

"Why?"

"First will you promise?"

"Well, yes, if you really don't want me to tell her. Now tell me about it. . . ."

"I think it was an Indian, too, Cash," I said, and I told him how I had been jostled by a strange Indian while leaving the courtroom the day we lost the case; of the soft padded running footsteps, the guttural curses, the remembered feel of deerskin leggins—and now the typical tobacco pouch with its broken drawstring.

"But Willy, why don't we tell Laughing Whitefish? Maybe she can put a stop to this dangerous nonsense. The man might have killed you. He might even yet."

I shook my head and the pain stabbed me. "No, Cash. Remember you promised. Not a word."

"All right, Willy, but why?"

"Look, Cash, telling her will do no good and only distress her. Perhaps with some idea of saving me it might even make her forsake the appeal and we can't let that happen. She has no one left to turn to. I've simply got to stay. Also I want to."

He blinked thoughtfully. "There's still old Cash," he said bravely.

"No, Cash, it's my fight and I'm determined to stay in the case. Naturally I hope you'll help all you can. And in a way I can't blame the Indians for wanting to hurt somebody. I'd feel like hurting someone, too. I suppose he thought I threw the case. I guess in a way he wasn't so far off."

"Nonsense, Willy. Nobody was to blame for losing the case unless it was old Cosima, a full-blooded Indian herself. So don't talk that way, boy. But as I promised, mum's the word." He held up his hand. "Sh . . . I think I hear her coming back already. She's been here day and night, Willy. I think she's mighty fond of you, boy. Try as I might I couldn't drive her away . . ."

"I feel much better already . . . And thank Madame Dujardins for me till I can myself. Hello, Lotti, please chase this evil old man away—he's killing me telling his stale Army jokes. Let me at some food—I'm hungry as a lion."

TWENTY-SIX

Laughing Whitefish returned to her school the following Monday, at my insistence, and after nearly ten restless days of enforced idleness and convalescence, under the doctor's orders, I went out to see her to report on our progress on her case, or rather the lack of it. I was greeted by the usual reception committee of slavering yellow dogs, which I held at bay with a heavy sapling I had thoughtfully cut on the way. A sullen Indian woman appeared and silently watched me defend myself, staring with undisguised hostility when during a lull I asked for my client.

"She gone, gone," she finally grunted, pointing ambiguously at the sky.

"Mukwa?" I then said, remembering my youthful interpreter. She disappeared behind a wigwam and presently the boy Mukwa showed up alone.

"Where's Laughing Whitefish?" I said.

"She's gone away, Mr. Poe."

"Yes, I know." Anxiously: "Is she all right?"

"Yes, she's fine."

"Where did she go?"

"I don't know."

"How long has she been gone?"

"Nearly a week. Took her snowshoes and a packsack and left—that's all I know."

"Did she go to Madeline Island to see Cosima?" I said, thinking of Metoxon.

"I don't know—she may have. She didn't say."

"She didn't tell *anyone?*"

"Not that I know of."

"When is she coming home?"

"Sorry, Mr. Poe, I don't know."

"Who's teaching in her place at your school?"

"Nobody. She closed it."

"I suppose that greatly grieves you, Mukwa?"

He grinned. "I love it—all the others do too."

"Thank you, Mukwa. Please tell your teacher I was here."

"I'll tell her. Mr. Poe, could I please ask you a question?"

"Surely, Mukwa. I've been asking you plenty."

He pointed. "That bandage. What's the matter with your head?"

"I fell on the ice and conked it. It's nothing at all."

"Conked?"

"Conked, Mukwa. I've suddenly been conked on the head."

"Does it hurt?"

"A little, but I guess my heart hurts even more."

"I'm real sorry, Mr. Poe."

Upon leaving the encampment I cached my sapling against possible future canine emergencies and as I trudged back to town I thought of everything but the case. Why hadn't she told me she was leaving and where she was going? Supposing I had needed her for something important concerning the case? Had she gone to Madeline Island to marry Metoxon? What other powerful lure would have made her abruptly close down her school and so mysteriously disappear? Worst of all, what business was it of mine that my client should visit or marry whomever she bloody well pleased? *That* was the bitterest pill....

Back at my office I plunged furiously into the neglected appeal. Maybe the therapy of work would keep my mind off Lotti. During an interlude I discovered I had been scrawling absently on a scratch pad. I stared at it in horror. Over and over I had written "Charlotte Kawbawgam Metoxon versus Jackson Ore Company." I crumpled the paper and flung it away and sat gazing moodily out the sooty window.

Late one afternoon I heard a timid knock on my office door.

"Come in," I said, and my client entered and sat quietly across from me. "Hello, Lotti," I said casually. "I hear you've been away."

"Yes, William, I had to go visit a friend who was sick."

"My, my, he must be as dear as his illness was dire for you to so abruptly slam the door on your precious school. I trust he has recovered uneventfully."

"*She* has, thank you," she answered coolly. "Mukwa told me you were out to see me."

"Yes—nearly a week ago. I wanted to bring you up-to-date on your case."

"Well, I'm here, William," she said simply.

I told her what little there was to tell and then both of us sat in silence. Presently the air of constraint between us grew so strong we avoided each other's eyes. I pretended to take some notes and then looked up and once again we sat in awkward silence.

"Look, Laughing Whitefish," I finally blurted huskily, "have you been to Madeline Island?"

"Yes, William, I got that far."

Like a triumphant public prosecutor: "Ah, your poor sick friend lives there, I suppose?"

She colored and looked away. "No, but she lives so close I decided to push on and visit Cosima."

The pursuing district attorney went baying along the scent. "Isn't it a little odd you neglected to tell your pupils or anyone your reason for leaving?"

Her color deepened. "I left in a hurry."

I could feel in my bones she was lying. "And you also saw the talkative Metoxon, I suppose?"

She faced me defiantly. "Well, naturally I saw him."

"And he again asked you to marry him?"

"Naturally."

I held my breath as I asked the next question. "And you *did* marry him?" I cleared my throat professionally and picked up a pencil. "I'm not merely prying—I'd have to suggest your marriage on the appeal if you *are* married. Are you?"

She sat looking at me with a crumpled expression. Tears filled her eyes and her lips trembled. Suddenly she got up and rushed to the doorway. She turned and tried to smile. When she spoke the words seemed torn from her. "No, no, no—you are such a blind foolish man, William," she almost wailed. Then she turned and fled. I heard the street door slam and I walked over and stared out the window at the rear end of Hodgkin's Livery Stable. Mr. Hodgkin's winter accumulation of manure, I gloomily observed, was by way of assuming magnificent proportions.

This was my first appeal to the supreme court, and I shortly found myself so wrapped up in the sheer legal mechanics of perfecting our appeal that I found little time to concern myself with how I might win once I got there. Wrestling with form books, text books, convoluted mazes of court rules, talking with Cash, and writing a few old legal hands in Ann Arbor who had been along that rocky road before me, in a piecemeal fashion I gradually penetrated the mystery of how it was done.

I also learned that the five-man supreme court held four formal terms of court a year—in January, April, June and

October—at which time the respective lawyers appeared and made their oral arguments, their briefs having already been filed; and that at this oral argument they submitted themselves to any questions that might be asked them by the assembled justices, a fairly awesome prospect in itself.

This ordeal over, the appealed case was considered submitted, its fate then squarely up to the court. After that the justice to whom the case was assigned, and whose identity meanwhile remained unknown to the arguing lawyers, at his leisure wrote an opinion expressing his views on the case, including his decision whether the result reached below should be affirmed or reversed, with his reasons for so deciding. Copies of his opinion were then circulated privately among his brethren who, at a later closed session of the court, either signified their intention to join in his decision or else indicated they might "hold" it so that they could ponder further or possibly even write a dissenting opinion of their own.

If agreement was unanimous at this first conference the opinion was forthwith signed and filed, the respective lawyers informed, and the outcome made public. This ended the appeal, the opinion ultimately winding up with the other opinions of that term in the bound and printed court reports as the settled law of the case. It was these printed state reports that constituted the backbone of any lawyer's library, though he needed more, much more, besides.

It soon became apparent that it was not possible to perfect our appeal in time for the April term, so the June term became my goal. Then, as the weeks passed and I still found myself grappling with the appeal, I began wondering if I could be ready in time for the June term. Blustery March came and dragged along interminably—"the only month in the year two months long," Cash mournfully described it.

I had prepared a draft of my all-important brief in skeleton form: the statement of facts, the propositions of law I deemed controlling, my step-by-step argument why I considered that Judge Grant had erred in dismissing our case. But I still badly needed sound legal authority, actual decided cases, to flesh out the skeleton and breathe it to life. Beyond vague general propositions, however persuasive to Cash and me, this crucial legal authority maddeningly continued to elude us.

Meanwhile I saw very little of Laughing Whitefish; she was busy with her pupils and I with my appeal. The case was now beyond her power to help or hinder me, since our appeal like most other appeals would make its long journey to the supreme court in a "frozen" state to be decided solely on the testimony given and rulings made during the proceedings below. Moreover a constraint had grown up between us, a constraint whose name I feared was Metoxon. . . . Cash usually dropped by every day, as much to show me he was still on the wagon as anything, I suspected, because his slow mastication of Henry Harwood's law library had so far produced little result.

"What are you doing down there?" I asked him. "Reading novels?"

"No, writing one," he answered dryly. "On the dubious therapy of pink soda pop."

After quizzing him once or twice on the progress of his research I learned to hold my peace. "Don't keep askin' me, Willy," he declared testily after one such session. "If and when I find anything you'll hear me bellowin' clean from the little man's library below you, don't worry."

"But aren't you finding *anything* I can put in my brief?" I pressed him. "If I don't finish and file it soon the case will simply have to go over to the October term, which will only mean more delay."

He fixed me with a baleful look. "Findin' anythin'?" he demanded scornfully, rolling his eyes up to the ceiling. "Am I findin' anythin', you ask! Willy, you are now in the presence of the world's greatest legal authority on all the law ranging from Arson to Zinzer's Rule—all the law, that is, but what we need and seek. Like the firefly, what we want continues to elude me, though occasionally I get a little flicker."

"Like what?" I pressed, ready to clutch at any straw.

"Well, like the general American rule that the validity of a marriage, say, is generally to be construed by the laws and rules of the people among whom it occurred, not of the court where any question concerning it might arise."

"Well, that's something," I said.

"Then I'll look a little further and run smack into the opposing English rule—followed by a few pretty respectable American courts—that the validity of a marriage or divorce or similar domestic arrangement is to be tested by the law of the forum, that is of the court where the case is being tried, not by the law of the place or people where the marriage or whatever took place. You see, Willy, the English, with their lofty assumption of superior virtue are not going to let any damned heathen foreigners tell *them* how to view the holy state of wedlock ... So it's Tweedledum and Tweedledee, you puts up your money an' you takes your choice. It's exasperatin', I calls it," he said, shaking his head. "Moreover," he pressed on, "I find that virtually all English and American courts agree on one thing: in flatly rejecting all polygamous marriages and in refusing to recognize the legitimacy of any children born of them. That won't win us much pink soda pop down in Lansing."

"But no case involving Indians, for or against?" I inquired.

He dolefully shook his head. "You'll know soon enough when I do, lad. I'll bray like a lovelorn ass."

In our daily sessions Cash and I had between us gradually evolved a kind of rough working hypothesis for our appeal that ran something like this: the American Indians were not to be treated like the average white citizen of a state; they were essentially a separate race and people, with their own traditions and customs, and were not properly to be judged by the white man's laws; that proof of the soundness of this view was the fact that the United States Government had in the past always treated with the Indian tribes as though each were a separate nation, indeed calling these agreements "treaties," all of which had like treaties with foreign countries to be signed by the President and ratified by the Senate, and in which the idea of separate nationhood was implicit; and that finally, in our case, the Government had already demonstrated that it countenanced and recognized Indian custom by paying Marji's treaty payments to Blue Heron when he died, and both of their remaining payments to Laughing Whitefish after Blue Heron died—thus, in her case, at least tacitly also recognizing the validity of an Indian adoption. But still we lacked solid legal precedent to back up our arguments and hunches. Meanwhile time was flying.

Then one morning I received in the mail a formal notice from Henry Harwood that he was withdrawing from the case and that the appeal would henceforth be handled solely by Guy Nesbitt. When Cash dropped around to conduct our daily wake I told him the news. "What do you make of it?" I said.

"Tantalizin', tantalizin'," he said, blinking his eyes thoughtfully. "All the more proof that Henry Harwood feels so strongly about this case he can no longer even silently remain in it."

"Then why did he stay in it in circuit court?" I demanded.

"Because he was stuck, that's why. As I've told you before the man simply couldn't up and leave Guy Nesbitt all alone to grapple with strange witnesses in a strange case before a strange judge. Now that he knows the Silver Fox is well up on top of the case he promptly got out." Cash lifted up his eye glasses with one hand and wearily rubbed his tired eyes with his thumb and index finger in toward his nose, meanwhile blinking up at the ceiling. "It only serves to spur me on in my search—that's if the old eyes hold out," he concluded arising and tapping on his way.

It was a blustery afternoon toward the end of March. I was sitting alone in my silent office absently going over my boxes of trout flies, pondering my case, trying to determine whether I should go out and eat or, more frugally, stay home and prepare one of my own dismal meals. Lately I had been thinking so much about my case that my mind seemed to have gone utterly numb; endlessly I had gone over the latest working hypotheses, especially the one I had dreamed up: that since the Government had dealt with the Chippewa Indians by treaty it no longer lay within the province of a state court to treat Indian litigants as though they were bound by the same state laws that bound the average white resident of a state.

"Treaty?" I mused out loud, startled at the sound of my own voice. "What, Willy, *is* the precise legal effect of a treaty with the federal government?"

Abruptly I pushed my fly boxes aside. Suddenly it dawned on me that the *federal* Constitution might have some interesting things to say on the subject of treaties in general and quite possibly on the power of state courts to rule on treaty provisions in particular. At least it was worth a look.

I moved over to my bookcase and pulled down a volume containing the U.S. Constitution. Knocking the dust and soot off it I resumed my seat and flipped open the pages.

"Preamble, preamble," I murmured. Nothing there. "General powers—la de da dum dum . . ." Nothing there. Next Congress, and lots of big resonant phrases, but even colder. Executive branch—"Dum tee dum dum." Section 2 of Clause 2, Article 2. Ah, the President has the power to make treaties by and with the advice and consent of the Senate "providing two-thirds of those present concur." Warmer, but still no great help. So far, no good. My eyes wandered to my intriguing fly boxes. Thank heaven in another month I would be fishing . . .

I had now waded through the first five articles with no results. Should I give up and go out and eat? I sighed and decided to keep on. Then, reading on in the very next Article, the sixth, Clause Two suddenly leapt out of the page at me and smote me as though carved from granite blocks. "This Constitution," the electrifying passage read, "and the laws of the United States which shall be made pursuant thereof; and *all treaties* made, or which shall be made under the authority of the United States, *shall be the supreme law of the land; and the judges of every state shall be bound thereby, anything in the constitution or any laws of any state to the contrary notwithstanding.*" I whistled and read the passage again to make sure it was there.

I sat staring at the opposite wall, my mind racing. In a vague way I knew that the old Indian treaties frequently had provisions in them guaranteeing the Indians continuing fishing and hunting privileges, rights to occupy certain lands, to harvest wild rice and similar provisions. The thought now suddenly assailed me that these old treaties also might have something in them about the right of the Indians to continue to practice their old tribal customs and ways of life.

What lay in these old treaties, of course, could only be determined by consulting the treaties themselves, and they were doubtless moldering away in some forgotten vault in Washington. But since all treaties were public documents that had been ratified by the Senate their text simply must be in existence elsewhere. How about the local public library? I grabbed my hat and coat and ran for the door, not even waiting to put on my overshoes, and clattered down the stairs and headed up slushy Front Street past the Cozzens House and straight for the new Peter White public library, my trout flies and pangs of hunger forgotten.

TWENTY-SEVEN

"Can I help you, Mr. Poe?" one of the lady attendants finally asked me, observing me lurking back among the gloomy stacks, man totally at sea, plucking helplessly at all the wrong books.

"I hope so," I said. "Do you happen to have a book containing copies of the Government's old treaties with the Chippewa Indians of this area?" I held my breath for her answer.

Putting the tips of two fingers against her lips as though she were daintily removing a fish bone, she blinked thoughtfully. "I think we have," she answered graciously. "Just a moment, I'll go see."

Presently she came back staggering under the weight of a big black leather-covered volume which sagged my arms down when she turned it over to me. "I knew where this old book was because I remembered getting it out for your colleague Henry Harwood not too long ago," she explained.

"Oh," I said with a casualness that would have done credit to the Silver Fox himself, "how long ago was that?"

"I think it was just before Christmas . . . Yes, I'm sure, because at the same time he brought us some new children's books for our Christmas party—he's such a kind generous man . . . Perhaps you'd rather sit up at this table where the light is better," she suggested.

265

"Oh, thank you," I said, wanting to give her a hug. "Thank you very much," I murmured, burying myself in the musty old volume.

It was nearing nine o'clock when I found a champing Cassius Wendell waiting at my office door when I staggered home with the precious volume under my arm. He too was toting a large book, only slightly smaller than my own.

"This time I think I've got it, Cash," I whispered triumphantly, "I think at last we're on the right track."

"I *know* we are, Willy," he whispered back, lovingly patting his own book as though it were a colicky infant. "This time we got 'em dead to rights. Open the door, lad, let me in, this weighty tome is killin' me."

"Hold your horses, Colonel Wendell," I said, fumbling for the key.

"It may feel like lead but its contents are pure gold," Cash ran happily on. "You'll see, lad. Open up, open up!"

I lit my gas lamp and poked up the fire and at length we faced each other warily across my littered walnut desk, like rival duellers using books as weapons. I raked my fly boxes into a drawer. "What've you got?" I demanded, opening hostilities.

"Show me yours first," he countered. "With my helpless lust for melodrama I've got to wring every ounce of suspense out of this golden moment. Boy oh boy, Willy...."

"First I'll read you the so-called 'federal supremacy' clause from the United States' Constitution," I said. Noisily clearing my throat and tugging on an imaginary beard in imitation of Claudius Grant I read him the clause I had found that afternoon. I looked up. "Don't you see, Cash, any and all treaties made by the federal government are the last word, and our state judges simply must follow 'em or they're bucking the Constitution itself. See, that gives us a brand new ground of error—old Square Beard defied the federal Constitution."

Cash looked mystified. "I hear what you're sayin', lad, but I don't quite see what it's got to do with our case."

"I'm just coming to that. Now I'll show you a copy of the second Treaty of Mackinac, executed between the U.S. Government and the Chippewa Indians." I hummed as I traced with my finger down to the part I wanted. Finding it, I began reading:

" 'It is further solemnly agreed by and between the parties to this treaty that the Chippewa Indians may continue to exercise, observe and carry on all tribal practices, customs and usages common to the tribe without let or hindrance from the United States or any state or territory in which they may dwell, and further this provision shall be binding upon and shall be recognized by the United States and all states and territories in which said Chippewa Indians may now or hereafter dwell.' "

I looked up. "What do you think of that, Cash, straight from the horse's mouth? I've read at least half a dozen other Indian treaties, made both before and after this one, and they don't vary one jot or tittle, even to a persistently lovely misspelling of 'solemly' in the first line, an eloquent tribute to the soaring originality of the bureaucratic mind."

"Frosting on the cake," Cash said, fluttering his eyelashes. "It completely dovetails with my little prize."

I closed the big book and sat back. "Now what've you got?" I repeated.

Cash hefted his volume in one hand, as though he were displaying a prize cabbage. "I hold in my hand an elusive and erudite new volume fresh from the law library of one Henry Harwood, Esquire, called 'Musgrove on Marriage.' The very latest word on this lovely romantic subject. Don't you like the beautiful alliterative poetry inherent in that name, Willy—'Musgrove on Marriage'?"

"It shatters me," I conceded. "Almost as sublime, say, as 'Wendell on the Water Wagon.' "

"Or perchance 'Poe on Pink Soda Pop,'" he fought back. "The book's got a whole section devoted to Indian marriages."

I eyed him owlishly. "Cash, you're killing me," I pleaded. "Open and read that damned book before I expire."

Cash, wringing every drop of suspense from his little triumph, placed the book on the desk before him, opened it, peered and frowned, moistened a finger and daintily turned some pages, backed up a few, now paused to clean his glasses with a soiled handkerchief, took an enormous chew, worked it up like a reluctant wad of taffy, cleanly missed the coal scuttle, and began finally to read.

"Lissen to this lovely preliminary statement by Musgrove," Cash ran on, virtually cackling with glee: "'The political status of Indians residing in the United States and the consequent policy of the Government to allow them to be governed and their tribal and domestic questions to be controlled by their tribal laws and customs, in a semi-independent state, and the notion that to refuse to recognize Indian marriages contracted under Indian custom, which generally tolerate dissolubility of marriage at will and polygamy'"—Cash looked up beatifically. "Isn't that lovely, lovely?" he crowed—"'would be tantamount to subjecting them to the state laws contrary to that policy and have consequently influenced most leading American courts to recognize such marriages, whether first or second.'"

"Why that's wonderful, Cash. That gives us two big cannon shots at blasting Judge Grant's decision—adoption and now polygamy as well. Don't you see, Cash, Laughing Whitefish is *legitimate!*"

"And no less lovely despite that, lad," he observed dryly. "Lissen to this comment by Musgrove on a recent New York case," he ran on: "'Here the court, on a question involving legitimacy of children, upheld the validity of a second marriage while there was an existing first wife, saying: "There is no doubt that permanency enters into the idea of marriage among all civilized and Christian people. But where there is cohabitation by consent among Indians for an indefinite period that in a state of nature would be regarded as marriage 'in the sight of God' we must recognize it as a valid marriage, and all marriages that may follow it, else all Indian children must be regarded as illegitimate, not merely those born of plural marriages. Our research discloses that it has long been the policy of the Government and Congress to permit the personal and domestic relations of our Indians to be regulated by tribal laws and customs. In retrospect it could not very well have been any other way." ' "

"That's great, Cash, I—"

"Don't interrupt, Willy, lissen to this further comment by Musgrove, citing a flock of cases: 'Most American courts, and in our view the better-reasoned cases, where legitimacy of children of plural Indian marriages is called in question, especially after the death of the parents and after a great lapse of time, indulge every reasonable presumption in favor of legitimacy.' "

"Any more?" I ventured.

"Here's a dandy from Ohio—great, forward-looking state, Ohio. 'While most civilized nations in our day wisely discard polygamy, and it is probably not lawful anywhere among English-speaking nations, yet it is recognized as valid among many other nations. As for Indian marriages we must either hold that there can never be *any* valid Indian marriage or we must hold that *all* Indian marriages are valid where by Indian usage they are so regarded. There is no middle ground so long as our own laws are not binding on the tribes. The Indians do not occupy this country by our grace or permission but because they were here first. We are the usurpers, not they. Moreover they were placed by the Constitution of the United States beyond our jurisdiction and we have no more right to dictate or control their domestic usages than those of Turkey or India. We cannot interfere with the validity of such marriages without subjecting them to rules of law they never lived by.'" He looked up, blinking thoughtfully. "That there constitutional reference must refer to the 'federal supremacy' clause you just read me." He glanced back at the book. "Ah, yes, here a footnote cites and quotes the very constitutional clause you just read me. The pieces are falling in place."

"Wonderful, Cash," I murmured. "You got anymore?" I said, totally awed by this sudden avalanche of authority.

"Lots more, I'm just skimmin' the highlights. Don't you see what this means, Willy? It means our native Indians are an *exception* to the general English and American rule against recognizing polygamous marriages or their issue. It also means that when he dismissed your case old Judge Grant had a bee up his—"

"Bonnet," I suggested helpfully.

"Precisely." Crooking a finger he silently beckoned me over by him. "Come look and see what's in the margin of many of these passages I've just been reading," he said, triumphantly pointing. I looked and there were the neat pencilled initials "H. H. 12/24/73" appearing in several places. "So this means," Cash continued triumphantly, "that for once old Cash was right—as early as last Christmas Henry Harwood *did* know that he had himself a loser, that right was on our side, and that the case ought to be settled."

"This is great, Cash, but how come you took so long to find such a spanking big book, especially one on marriage? Seems to me you would have tripped over it by now. Or had Henry Harwood hidden it on you?"

"Not exactly. All the time it was lyin' on his desk in his private office and I didn't know it."

"How come you found out today—did you finally get desperate and raid his private office? Wasn't that a little beyond the call of duty, Colonel Wendell?"

"No, I was toilin' away in the library late this afternoon, same as usual, when his secretary Miss Dyson stopped by on her way home to say goodnight and remind me to be sure and put out the light—also same as usual." He pompously cleared his throat and gave me the leering sidelong look of an aging satyr. "Fact is I believe the old girl has a bit of a crush on old Colonel Wendell. Fine figure of a man—at least those parts not contrived of wood."

"Go on, go on," I urged. "Let's have facts, not woodland fancy."

"Half beside myself with lack of success I gave her my most languishin' smile and inquired whether perchance Mr. Harwood might not himself have the one book I was lookin' for. 'What book is that?' says she. 'On marriage,' says I, and with that she blushed like a young girl and said he usually kept his newest books on his own desk while he read them. She invited me to come with her and look, so we went and looked and, lo, good old Musgrove all but leapt off his desk at me. Our treasure was there all the time, mind you, gathering dust and gaily eludin' me. I was tempted to give Miss Dyson a hug, but compromised by giving her a fatherly pat, an' I swear the old girl was all a-tremble."

"All you got to do now, Cash," I put in, "is cast your spell over some gal down in the bank below us and you'll have a poor woman enslaved on every floor of my building."

"A good idea, lad," he said briskly, "but right now we got to get busy and copy out Musgrove so Henry Harwood won't miss him in the morning. Anyway, I promised Miss Dyson I'd return the volume tonight."

"Will she be awaiting you at a midnight tryst?" I asked.

He looked over his glasses at me: "Precisely," he said, grabbing up a pad and falling into a declamatory tone of voice, "reeking of musk and oil of cloves and consumed by the smouldering fires of unrequited passion. Let's go to work, lad," he concluded dryly. "Where's some better paper and—miracle of miracles—a pen that actually writes?"

TWENTY-EIGHT

The ancient supreme court chamber on the third floor of the domed capitol building in Lansing looked more like the inside of an eccentric old church than a courtroom. Worn red carpeting covered every inch of the creaking floor; ill-assorted chairs lined the walls on both sides, supplementing the plain highbacked wooden benches that looked rather more like the uncomfortable pews of some austere religious sect; a faded flag hung inert and listless from a floor staff standing near the court crier's wooden cubicle; and huge dusty portraits of bearded bygone judges—seeming mostly rows of staring cataleptic eyes peering out from great thickets of whiskers and billowing yards of black silk robing—lined the walls like the forbidding images of obscure and vanished saints.

It was an unseasonably hot morning in mid-June, the kind of sticky enervating heat one rarely encountered farther north. Several of the tall windows of the courtroom had been cautiously raised—supported by the most unimpeachable authority, bound volumes of Michigan law reports—and some of the reaching leafy branches of the stately capitol elms seemed almost to nod in our laps. Birds twittered and squirrels scolded noisily with a fine contempt of court and occasionally from far below I could hear the distant clopping of horses' hooves along the cobbled streets.

273

Mercifully there was a little breeze, and as the trees' branches creaked and swayed, occasionally a dust-moted shaft of sunlight penetrated the tall chamber and wavered and winked out, like the fitful beam from a revolving beacon, all adding to the atmosphere of ecclesiastical gloom.

Despite the eager crowd of assembled lawyers, each full of disputation and hope, there hung over the place a dusty and bated hush, the kind of stifled uneasy silence one might encounter at night in the deserted mummy room of a museum. Continuing this morbid fancy I bandied the notion that all of us in the courtroom were wax figures sentenced to sit forever in this melancholy chamber. I longed to rip open my constricting starched collar; instead I ran my finger under it to admit a little air.

A red-faced perspiring Cash leaned over and whispered hoarsely in my ear. "Guy Nesbitt just walked in followed by a train of young gun bearers lugging bulging briefcases of reserve ammunition. Ah, the safari has now settled down about two rows behind us."

I nodded nervously and resisted the impulse to turn and look. Ours was the third case set to be orally argued that morning, and two Detroit lawyers were up at the counsel tables, one of them earnestly arguing the second. I gathered vaguely that the client of the appellant, a hapless pedestrian, had been struck and run down on Woodward Avenue by an equipage consisting of a span of skittish horses and a shiny new carriage carelessly driven by the defendant.

The five black-robed justices sat in high-backed chairs behind an elongated slightly curved judge's bench in various attitudes of attention ranging from rapt to skeptical on through undisguised boredom. One bewhiskered justice on the end was either concentrating mightily or had fallen asleep.

Some of the justices occasionally asked a question of counsel, and Chief Justice Isaac Marston, seated in the center, occupied himself by mopping his brow and jotting an occasional note. I idly speculated that he was probably doing so because in the judicial lottery of assignment he had already drawn the case, fruitless speculation on this subject being a kind of tormenting perpetual guessing game among all appellate lawyers.

The plaintiff's lawyer was rounding into the home stretch. "Your Honors, you are today privileged to be present at the unveiling of a brand new defense in the law of personal injuries," he declared, his voice throbbing with scorn; he fairly spat his words. "Stripped of its convoluted rhetoric the defendan''s argument boils down to this: that my poor maimed client should consider himself already amply compensated by the éclat, the renown, the inestimable social advantage that has accrued to him by his enormous good fortune in getting himself run over by an Alger."

The Chief Justice smiled, rolled up his eyes, and wearily mopped his brow with a limp handkerchief. I admired and envied the lawyer his fine corrosive irony and made a mental note to remember it; his voice faded away and swam back. "We view with alarm this growing tendency of our trial judges to take the plaintiff's case away from the jury," the arguing lawyer ran on in ringing tones. Then, so full was I with my own case, his voice again trailed away into an unintelligible hum.

It struck me that if some of the justices looked bored it was probably simply because they were bored. I was rapidly learning why boredom was an occupational hazard of the job; every lawyer who ever came to argue before them assumed that *his* case was unique in all jurisprudence, by all odds the most absorbing and important in the long annals of adversary litigation...

"So in the name of justice I ask that you reverse the patently erroneous action of the trial judge below, I thank you," the earnest lawyer was saying, whereupon he sat down, mopping his face and neck, and then, with jaundiced and skeptical eyes sat watching his opponent arise and begin pleading with equal fervor for an affirmance. Justice meanwhile found herself caught firmly in the middle of this ceremonial tug of war.

Following our joint discovery of a vast new area of law favorable to our case, Cash and I had worked virtually day and night to get my brief out and served on the supreme court and opposing counsel in time for the June term.

"How will Guy Nesbitt ever possibly answer us, Cash?" I asked, caught in a wave of euphoria when our brief was done.

"Don't worry, lad, he'll answer us right enough," he said. "We'll be pelted with cases against us."

"But how can he?" I insisted. "How can he possibly get around Musgrove?"

"Because there are few propositions of law, however weird, for which one can't find some legal authority somewhere," he replied. "If you can dream it, lad, some judge has held it. Don't I keep tellin' you judges aren't infallible? Old Professor Durfee once defined the breed thus: 'A judge is simply a law student who marks his own examination papers.' And all of 'em aren't John Marshalls by a long shot. Judges are just as groping and uncertain as the rest of us. In fact I suspect the best ones are mostly that way."

Because of the distance and added expense, Laughing Whitefish had decided not to accompany us to Lansing, much as she longed to. I wondered if she was instead off visiting the silent Metoxon . . . On the long train ride down I had yielded to Cash for the only remaining Pullman berth available and, having sat up all night in a crowded coach which included a colicky infant, now kept stifling tormenting impulses to yawn. This compelled me virtually to sit with my hand clapped over my mouth, like a man self-consciously wearing new dentures. There, I wanted to yawn again . . .

Old Cash had long since abandoned any pretense that he was not in the case with me up to his ears. The clincher came when, after I had personally seen our brief through the local printers, I handed him the first copy, scarcely yet dry. He examined it and let out a startled yelp.

"Whaddya mean, Willy, putting my name on the brief along with yours as 'Of Counsel'?" he indignantly demanded.

"Because I wouldn't have had a chance to win this case if you hadn't stuck by me, and you know it," I coolly replied. "Moreover," I continued, "if it hadn't been that I was the only attorney of record at the hearing below I'd have listed you as full co-counsel. Thank you, thank you, my loyal friend, and now let's go celebrate up at the Cozzens House. We'll hoist a cherry soda. Maybe two."

He stood blinking his faded blue eyes at me, a little mistily I thought. "I don't mind if I do, counselor," he said in a small voice. "Cassius Wendell, of counsel," I heard him murmuring as we clattered down the hall. "Now I'll be a ring-tailed son of a bastrich!"

In due course after our brief had been served on Guy Nesbitt we received a copy of his own thick brief, a monumental argument exhaustively annotated with cases, all directed solely at one thing: why the decision of Judge Grant should be upheld. Cash and I spent the better part of one day just going over the highlights. In it, among other things, he endlessly reiterated the defense of laches; now added adverse possession as well; urged that Marji Kawbawgam could not have claimed any interest because he had not paid any stock assessments; now for the first time claimed that we had waived our newly-discovered constitutional grounds for recovery by not first raising the question below; urged that Marji Kawbawgam's estate administrator and not Laughing Whitefish should properly be bringing the suit; that on appeal we had changed our theory from that originally alleged in the bill; that at this late date it would be inequitable and scandalous to penalize innocent stockholders who had invested in Jackson Ore Company stock without knowledge of this ancient dormant claim—all this and much more besides.

Cash had been right; there *was* a good deal of legal authority against Musgrove and our line of cases, and Guy Nesbitt had apparently found and marshalled all of it.

At the end of our first session poring over Guy Nesbitt's mammoth brief, Cash closed and thoughtfully hefted it in one hand. "Between five and six pounds," he gravely estimated. "Fact is, Willy," he continued, "the Silver Fox has backed off forty paces and thrun the hull Harvard Law School Library at us."

So Cash and I got down to work on our reply brief and shortly hurled back at him the remnants of the more modest law library of Henry Harwood. Today the supreme court would have to weigh both briefs and make its choice. I for one hoped that at least one potential John Marshall sat up there among them.

"Charlotte Kawbawgam versus Jackson Ore Company," the court crier was calling, putting the best efforts of poor Sheriff Barney Langley to shame. I sat forward tensely. Here at last was the real thing in court announcers, a genuine professional hog caller whose rasping bored nasal voice was penetrating as a station master's. "Appeal by complainant-appellant from court's dismissal of bill of complaint below," he bawled. "At issue and ready for hearing. William Poe, Esquire, for complainant-appellant, Guy Nesbitt, Esquire, for defendant-appellee. Counsel will please come forward."

Guy Nesbitt shook hands and greeted me amiably as we moved up front. "And so we do meet again," he said in an easy undertone, exuding in equal parts, or so it seemed, an aura of confidence and cologne. "Meanwhile, son, you seem to have been hitting the books. Fact is you've kept me and my young law beagles up nights grappling with that pesky brief of yours. Mighty fine job, young man, and I congratulate you."

"Thank you, Mr. Nesbitt," I said rather inanely. "Your brief kept me up too."

Swiftly taking in the elegance of his attire I felt like a country bumpkin: the handsome new suit, so rich, so exquisitely tailored, the high stiff flare of his gleaming wing-collar, the scarved elegance of his flowing cravat, from the center of which glowed a large solitary pearl that all but cried: "I came from Tiffany's!"

We had reached our tables and stood stiffly at attention. The chief justice wearily mopped his brow, whereupon with the flourish of a conjurer Guy Nesbitt—it all seemed one motion— reached for his breast pocket, drew forth a flowing undulant handkerchief, delicately patted his brow, ran it grandly through his thumb and forefinger to refold it, and—presto—returned it impeccably to its place, giving it a farewell pat. Despite his superb performance I felt a pang of disappointment; after all that it seemed a pity he had not produced at least a rabbit.

The chief justice nodded for us to be seated, whereupon we sat poised at our respective counsel tables like runners awaiting the signal to be off. Then Chief Justice Marston again damped his face with his wilted handkerchief and looked down at me with glazed eyes. "You may proceed, Mr. Poe," he said, almost visibly bracing himself for another avalanche of rhetoric.

TWENTY-NINE

I arose and moved mechanically before the lectern. "May it please the court," I began, getting immediately down to cases in the brief time allotted me, "the sole question presented on this appeal is whether the chancellor below was wrong when he dismissed my client's bill of complaint. I think he was.

"It is said that confession is good for the soul and at the outset I have a confession to make. It is this: I went into circuit court below on the wrong theory. At that time I thought I must prove a divorce between my client's father and his first wife for my client to prevail. I thought that otherwise she would be held to be the illegitimate child of a polygamous marriage and therefore unable to sue. Indeed that is the prevailing rule in England and America, and I erroneously thought it applied to Indians as well. I was wrong. I have since found that the American Indians are an exception to the prevailing rule, and that my client had a perfect right to sue even though now concededly she is the issue of a plural marriage. The authorities cited and analyzed in my brief show this beyond any doubt, I submit, and I shall not weary you by repeating them now.

"I have another confession to make. It is this: My worthy opponent also came into court below on an equally wrong defense theory—but the difference now is that he still stoutly adheres to his wrong theory. He still insists that there are no valid exceptions to the general rule that polygamous marriages are unlawful and that the issue of them are invariably illegitimate and may not sue as heirs in our courts. He further insists that my cases are bad law, that the chancellor below was right, and that the sanctity if not the future of all matrimony hangs anxiously on your decision. It is a grave responsibility he has sought to impose on you, Your Honors. It also happens to be wrong."

The dozing justice on the end now sat up with a start, gingerly tasting his lips like a parched inebriate in the night, fixing me with a baleful eye. "Did I just hear you say, young man, that polygamous marriages are lawful and should be upheld by this court?" he querulously demanded.

"Not precisely, Your Honor, please," I explained. "At least I meant to say that those polygamous marriages among certain Indian tribes which are regarded as lawful by the tribe may not be ignored by our state courts because, if you will pardon my bluntness, sir, they are simply none of the business of our state courts."

"Why, I never heard of such an outlandish proposition," my bewhiskered questioner muttered, shaking his head in disbelief.

"Would you like me to explain, Sir?"

"I'd like you to *try*, young man," he said witheringly. "So far your argument has totally eluded me."

All of the justices were supposed to have read all of the briefs in advance of the oral argument, but this one rather plainly hadn't read mine, I guessed, or if so had promptly forgotten it. So seizing the opportunity to make a convert I went to work on this unabashed skeptic, talking at him as if he sat alone on the bench, quoting the federal constitutional "supremacy" clause regarding treaties, quoting from various of the Chippewa Indian treaties—duplicate originals of which, I pointed out, were on file in the secretary of state's office just below us in the same building—and of which consequently the court was bound to take judicial notice—quoting at length from our life-saving Musgrove and from the leading cases Cash had rounded up.

"While the facts in this case may be complex, perhaps a trifle exotic, and cover a wide reach of time, the basic issue confronting you is really quite simple," I pushed on. "It may help isolate that issue if I now point out what I conceive are *not* proper issues in this case."

I stepped forward and raised my voice. "Gentlemen," I said, "I am not asking you to put the stamp of approval of this court on polygamy, polyandry, bigamy, illegitimacy or any other of all the dire and dreadful things my opponent says I am asking in this case. I am not asking you to approve these things because they are not and never were issues properly before you in this case." I paused and collected my racing thoughts. "The sole burning hard-core issue before you is not whether Indians dare take extra mates but rather whether—if you will again pardon my bluntness—that subject is any concern of yours in this case."

I stepped back and lowered my voice. "I say it is not. My authorities say it is not. I now ask you to put aside your natural prejudices and say it is not."

Altogether my eloquence was so burning and persuasive that when next I looked at my questioning justice to mark my progress I found he had so admirably contained his rapture he had again relapsed into sleep. I yearned to join him in this enterprise; again I wanted dreadfully to yawn; I felt my mouth yawing open; at the last moment I converted it into a discreet sneeze and throat clearing, murmuring an apology.

Still doggedly talking at my dozing justice, on the off chance that a remnant of consciousness remained, I moved on to the argument that, polygamy or no polygamy, Laughing White-fish should prevail in this case because, even if she were a total stranger to the blood of Marji Kawbawgam, she was plainly the adopted daughter of Blue Heron, again under settled Indian tribal custom, and that such an adoption was equally as entitled to recognition as Indian marriage itself, and for precisely the same reasons.

I dwelt heavily on the adoption theory for several reasons: one, as a safety gap in case the court still wouldn't swallow my theory of a valid polygamous marriage, despite our impressive legal authority; again to meet and defeat the canny and resourceful argument of Guy Nesbitt, first made on appeal, that if the court should be persuaded that my polygamy theory was sound (of which perish the thought), Laughing Whitefish still would only be entitled to but roughly one-half of her father's claim; this because Blue Heron would herself have already inherited the other portion; and further that, since she had died childless and intestate, her share would escheat, that is, only the state might claim it—the comatose state conveniently having failed to come forward. The Silver Fox was now trying to hedge his losses; if he couldn't win all at least he'd try to salvage something . . .

"It shows we got 'em scared," Cash had gloated when we first received Guy Nesbitt's thick impressive brief. "They're so scared now they're arguin' half a loaf is better'n none."

"Maybe so," I agreed dubiously.

I paused in my argument and glanced out at the nodding elms at my right. I was not saying precisely the things I had long planned to say. Where was this orderly passionless cold elucidation of the law getting me? Was this any way to convince the favorable, or persuade the uncommitted, or switch the skeptical among these weary high priests of the law? This was the crucial moment, the instant of ultimate confrontation—why hold back now?

I thought of Laughing Whitefish, of brave little Mr. Everett, of the earthy Cosima. I thought of Marji Kawbawgam and of the whole long procession of nameless shuffling Indians. A knot of vipers seemed suddenly to writhe in my gut. Chief Justice Marston gently prompted me. "Mr. Poe, if you please. . . ." I breathed deeply and again squarely faced the court. I had made up my mind: even if it meant certain defeat, there were things in this case that simply cried out to be said. . . .

"Your Honors," I resumed, "as I sat here this morning waiting my turn it came over me as in a dream that every lawyer who ever argues before you somehow thinks *his* case is the most important in the history of Anglo-American jurisprudence." This raised a weary smile from perspiring Chief Justice Marston and a small ripple of pained recognition from my waiting brethren. "I will not say that about my case, whatever I may feel about it. For the cold truth is that if the defendant here gave the Chippewa Indians a *hundred* Jackson Mines it wouldn't repay them even a small fraction for all that we whites have stolen from them during the past centuries. We have left behind us an unbroken wake of broken promises, broken hearts and broken people. Henry Thoreau spoke poetic if not literal truth when he wrote: 'The Indian has vanished as completely as if trodden into the earth. . . .' To this I may more bluntly if less poetically add that what has happened to the American Indian is one of the most disgraceful blots on our history; it is our eternal shame."

This statement so startled my slumbering justice that he opened one eye. Encouraged, I pressed on. "We boldly took his choicest lands; we crowded him into smaller and smaller areas; we shot his game, caught his fish, felled his forests, fouled his waters, stole his women; we brought him strange gods to worship and fiery water to drink; we debauched and corrupted him and bestowed upon him our choicest imported diseases. The cold truth is," I said, pointing at my heart, "we have all but destroyed the American Indian here."

I lowered my voice, talking straight at my justice, who had now cautiously opened the other eye. "It seems passing strange that we whites in our vast power and arrogance cannot now leave the vanishing remnants of these children of nature with the few things they have left." I held out both arms and tensely shook them. "Can we not relent, for once halt the torment? Must we finally disinherit them from their past and rob them of *everything?* Can we not, in the name of the God we pray to, now let them alone in peace to live out their lives according to their ancient customs, to worship the gods of their choice, to marry as they will, to bring forth their children, and finally to die?"

I straightened and sighed. "An obscure Chippewa Indian called Kawbawgam once showed some eager restless white men the first iron ore ever discovered in the vast Lake Superior area. The white men promised him a pittance for his efforts, but even that promise they will not keep, even that pittance they will not pay, though they made and are making fortunes from what he trustingly did for them that distant day. So we are here a generation later still fighting for that pittance, and mighty and resourceful are our adversaries. Can we, who for centuries have treated the Indians as dogs, only now treat them as equals when they dare seek relief from injustice in our courts? This, gentlemen, is the gnawing question you must answer, a question as gravely moral as it is legal."

My voice sank even lower. "I am the first to concede that whatever you may decide here will be but a passing footnote in the long history of jurisprudence, that the pittance we are jousting over is but a minor backstairs pilfering in the grand larceny of a continent." I held out my hands, my voice barely audible.

"Gentlemen, the destiny of that pittance now rests in your hands. Do with it what you will." I turned away suddenly and slumped to my seat, quivering to my very spine yet feeling strangely purged. Come hell or high water, I had had my say.

Guy Nesbitt arose and moved slowly before the lawyers' lectern. He drew himself erect and corsetted, smoothing down his hips, regally standing there with all the negligent grace of at least a Plantagenet. Then, beginning slowly, he gradually unloosed the throbbing organ pipes of his voice. "Esteemed members of this distinguished court," he began impressively, and again the jousting was underway.

His oral argument was a masterpiece of righteous indignation and suave avoidance, of calculated flattery and artful persuasion, during which he extolled the sanctity of the monogamous state, quoted from the Scriptures, drew upon the marriage ritual, and invoked the eminently quotable Blackstone—both in Latin and in English.

"Speak-for-yourself, John" was the tenor of his opening salvo, during which he adroitly reminded the court that if a young backwoods lawyer arguing his first high court case wanted to admit he'd been dead wrong in circuit court, all well and good, but that he should scarcely presume also to speak for opposing counsel or his client. . . .

"A little humility in a fledgling lawyer is always gratifying to behold," he suavely declared, glancing over at me and swiftly winking his off eye. In full cry now the Silver Fox swiftly took me over the course.

He pointed a finger at the high ceiling. "Confession may be good for the soul, yes, but the truth is that my candid and resourceful young brother has changed legal theories in midstream," he declared, "and I for one cannot help feeling that such a course is equally as dangerous, if possibly somewhat dryer, than changing horses in midstream." This brought a faint smile to the face of the chief justice; on smiles we were now running even.

In a vein of indulgent irony he told the court that he was unaware until today that his client was to be held guilty for all the inequities and injustices that might ever have befallen the American Indian at the hands of the white invaders. "Must my client now account for every beaver pelt ever stolen from a drunken Indian?" he oratorically declaimed.

His chin sank on his chest and the modulated rich organ tones of his voice grew low and murmurous. "Must we forever assess blame and weigh fault?" he intoned. "Is it not enough to say that if the plight of the American Indian was partly the white man's fault, was it not also, once given his presence, equally the Indian's fate?" I found myself nodding helplessly in agreement.

Guy Nesbitt glanced my way and once again pointed up at the ceiling. "Who," he demanded, "who is this young Lochinvar from the north who comes boldly before you learned men of the law and dares make an impassioned jury argument?" I hung my head. "But enough of his ringing rhetoric and evasion of issues and appeals to emotion—I shall dwell on the law."

He then dwelt on the venerable English and American cases which held that neither polygamy nor the issue of it was ever recognized in our courts, quoting sonorous and ringing indictments of the proposition from famous high court judges of the past. "The exception that my resourceful young opponent here speaks of is an exception born of desperation, a bold syllogism built upon shifting legal sands, a law fit only for the jungle. I am confident that the good sense of this esteemed court, for which it is far renowned, will reach a sound and equitable result."

He paused, turned sideways, stared raptly out the nearest window at the nodding elms, and ran his hand lightly through his silvery hair, disturbing not a lock, like an old actor about to launch a soliloquy. "How?" he demanded of the elms in ringing tones, "how are the great businesses and corporations of our nation to expand and grow, and bring undreamed of prosperity to reds and whites and blacks alike, if the progeny of a casual backwoods coupling between two unlettered savages can maintain this belated suit so many years after the fact?"

He again faced the court and raised his hands and lowered his voice. "How, gentlemen, I ask you, how can my client ever be sure, if this complainant succeeds here, that in another few years another natural child of a woodland collision with still another compliant squaw does not come into our courts clamoring for his share of the booty? How can our great business enterprises survive such a chaos, our investors dare continue to risk their capital?" He lowered his hands, and the vibrant tremulo of his voice sank to a beguiling purr. "Gentlemen, I now rest our case in your hands and await your decision—as does indeed all free enterprise—with every confidence in the result." He turned away and sat down with bowed head and folded hands. I resisted an impulse to applaud.

"Mr. Poe," the chief justice said, "you may close." Then he added with swift hopefulness, "That's if you so desire."

I half rose and spoke from a crouch. "Thank you, nothing further, Your Honor," I said.

"We'll take a ten-minute recess," he said devoutly, already loosening his constricting gown at the throat. "Mister Crier, declare a recess if you please." Then: "Jesus, Jeff, it's hot!" I heard him whisper to an associate, rolling up his eyes, pushing himself wearily to his feet. Guy Nesbitt looked slyly over at me and winked and shrugged and again reached for his flowing silk handkerchief.

Fascinated, I watched him execute his flourishes. Maybe this time, I thought, he'll come up with that rabbit.

No rabbit came forth and I sat staring up at the now vacant

judges' bench. I heard a tapping and felt a hand on my shoulder. I looked up. It was old Cash. There were tears in his eyes, his lower lip trembled, his face was ashen with emotion. He squeezed my shoulder. "Son," he said huskily, "win or lose you did one hell of a job."

I nodded and smiled brightly and slumped forward in my chair. Suddenly I was assailed by an immense fatigue, it swept over me in engulfing waves, and I leaned back with closed eyes and succumbed to an orgy of yawning—prodigiously, unabashedly, repeatedly. Win or lose, my work was finally over.

THIRTY

The summer dragged by on leaden wings and as the oppressive uncertainty increased I discovered that a lawyer awaiting a decision in his big case is like an accused murderer waiting for the jury to come out—in both, wistful hope mingles inevitably with gloom and foreboding. Old Cassius had known the supreme court clerk during his boyhood in Saline, and before we left Lansing, had arranged with him to telegraph us when the court next convened for an opinion day and again when the decision was reached. We could not abide the thought of having to wait for the slow and uncertain mails.

July came and went, and then part of August—and then one morning, just as I was sneaking off for a day of fishing, a telegram came and was delivered to me by Miles Coffey's nephew, who helped out as messenger boy during the summer months. The telegram was not from the clerk of the court; instead it was from Guy Nesbitt.

"Would you consider a fifteen thousand dollar settlement if I can persuade my client to pay it?" it read.

I got out of my fishing clothes and hunted up Cassius Wendell and broke him the news. "What would you do, Cash?" I inquired, torn between taking this bird in the hand or possibly nothing at all.

Cash considered all of ten seconds before he spoke. "I'd tell him to put on his best salt-and-pepper suit and go jump in Lake Superior," he said firmly. "He now knows he's licked and he's trying to crawl out of a loser for marbles, he so hates to lose his cases. As for his *persuading* his famished client I'll bet a new hat he's already told them the worst."

"But seriously, Cash, I've got to answer the man."

"Regrettably the decision isn't up to me, lad, or you either, it's up to Laughing Whitefish," he said soberly. "But for my part I'm hoping and betting she won't take it." He looked over his glasses at me craftily. "Would you like to bet a new hat on that?"

"Not on your life," I said, grabbing up my own hat. "C'mon, Cash, let's go hire a buckboard from Hodgkin's and ride out and see Laughing Whitefish. It's up to her, as you say."

"What would you do, William?" Laughing Whitefish asked after I'd shown her the telegram, her dark eyes searching mine. "Please tell me honestly as you know—I could do so much for my people with my share of so large a sum of money."

"Share?" I said, puzzled. "What do you mean?"

"I long ago made up my mind that you and Cash—I mean, Mr. Wendell—must take half of anything we ever realize on my claim," she said. "Tell me what you honestly think, William."

"We won't argue about that now," I said, looking out over the lake searching for an answer. Far out on its glittering surface I discerned an out-going ore carrier riding deep with its heavy burden—could it be some of Marji Kawbawgam's ore?—down the lakes to the fiery destiny of its cargo. I took a deep breath and turned back and faced Laughing Whitefish.

"I would tell Guy Nesbitt," I said solemnly, "to go jump in Lake Superior."

"Wearing his best salt-and-pepper suit," Cassius chimed in.

"Very well, that is my decision," she said quietly.

During our silent drive back to town Cash finally cleared his throat and spoke softly. "I was just thinkin', Willy," he said, "I was just thinkin' that maybe I'll take and buy *you* a new hat."

"Why, Cash?" I inquired politely, rousing myself from my racing thoughts.

"Ah, lad, just for the hell of it is why. I guess maybe I like your pluck. Moreover you *need* a new hat—your old one reeks to high heaven of fly dope."

"Thanks, Cash," I said, relapsing into my reverie.

"Onward to Ormsbee and Atkins!" Cash chanted. "Gents furnishings, shoes, cravats, genuine beaver hats . . ."

The fateful word came to Cash early in September. "Erudition assembles here next Monday forenoon" the telegram read. "Good luck. Spider," it ended cryptically.

"Who's Spider?" I inquired.

" 'Spider' is what we used to call the court clerk when he was a boy back in Saline," Cash explained.

The following Monday Laughing Whitefish and Cash and I met at noon at the Cozzens House to take up the vigil. During the meal we spoke little, each being preoccupied with the one big question: what was happening to our case in Lansing?

Afterwards Cash, nervous as a cat, resolutely marched me into the bar while Laughing Whitefish waited in the lobby. There he manfully downed two cherry sodas in rapid succession. "Habit formin'," he said, putting down his glass with a grimace, "but tonight, win or lose, I'm fallin' off the wagon."

"What's the big occasion, Mr. Wendell?" inquired the bartender, overhearing him.

Cash pondered the question before answering. "It's the anniversary of the lucky day I didn't get married," he replied, "the day my best girl jilted me. Celebrate it every year. See you later, Jake." He plucked at my sleeve. "C'mon, Willy, let's go down to your quarters—maybe the messenger boy's already clamorin' at your door."

Nobody was waiting for us, and we three sat around and morosely resumed the tense vigil.

Three o'clock came; then four, and still no word. "Maybe they couldn't agree," Laughing Whitefish finally suggested.

"It's a possibility," I said nervously, by then almost wishing that might have happened.

"Win, lose or *draw*, I'm fallin' off the wagon," Cash put in, hedging his bets.

Supper time came, but none of us had any stomach for food so we sat there waiting. At seven-thirty I arose and reached for my new hat.

"Where you goin', Willy?" Cash demanded.

"Over to see Miles Coffey at the depot—they don't deliver messages after supper, and Miles can't leave the place on the nightshift. Maybe one just came."

I was back shortly. "Nothing," I said. "Nothing one way or the other. Miles said no messages have been coming through from Lower Michigan all evening—seems there's a line down below us somewhere. Said he'd somehow get word to us if anything happens." I turned to Laughing Whitefish, who had anxious dark circles under her eyes. "Why don't I take you home? I'll bring you whatever word comes through first thing in the morning."

She shook her head. "No, William, I'm staying," she said quietly.

Nine o'clock came, then ten, and then it began to rain, the wind slanting it dismally against my dripping windowpane. Cash and I started playing cribbage—during which he contrived to skunk me three times and win back more than the price of the new hat he'd presented me.

At eleven it was still raining. Cash arose, collected his winnings, and prepared to leave. We looked at him inquiringly. "Just going up to Jake's and catch me a cherry soda," he explained, coolly appropriating my umbrella. "Be back in a half hour."

"I'll go with you part way and slip down to the depot and check again with Miles Coffey," I said, rummaging for my raincoat. I turned back to Laughing Whitefish, pointing at a magazine on my desk. "There's a spine-tingling new story by Henry James in the latest *Atlantic Monthly*. I've also just got his first novel, *Roderick Hudson*, but haven't had time to look at it."

Laughing Whitefish shook her head and smiled ruefully. "Thank you, William, but right now I couldn't read my own name, my spine is tingling so. *Please* hurry back."

We opened the office door to leave and there stood a breathless and dripping Miles Coffey. In his hand he held aloft a damp telegram.

"You either won or you lost," he blurted excitedly, waving the telegram. "At least the decision was unan-unan—aw, what the hell, they all agreed."

"What do you mean?" Cash demanded. "Come in, come in—here, hand me that there telegram. Did we win or didn't we win, man?"

"I—I can't tell by the fancy language. You lawyers can't even say yes in plain English," Miles stammered, still standing in the doorway holding the telegram away from Cash who, dancing about on his wooden leg, kept darting his hand up at it ineffectually.

Miles entered and closed the door and, glancing around stealthily, lowered his voice to a stage whisper. "This telegram's not for you," he breathlessly explained. "It's a copy I made of one that came for Henry Harwood. It's longer'n a mass for a bishop—been mostly two hours gettin' it all down. Ain't never supposed to do that. Could cost me my job if it ever got out."

I suppressed a wild impulse to dive for the telegram. "What it says is no secret," I said silkily, edging toward him. "It's now in the public domain for all the world to see." Miles glanced nervously at the door.

"All hell couldn't change it," Cash chimed in, edging doorward himself. Suddenly he lurched forward and backed against the door, facing us, legs resolutely apart, arms thrown up, looking as though nailed there. "Moreover, my fine hearty, you're getting out of here with that there telegram only over my dead body." The old boy glared across at me. "Go block the window, Willy!"

Since there was a three-story drop to the cobbled alley below I instead moved closer to Miles, Cash now forsaking his door and closing in from the other side. We continued our stalk, Miles taking quick little steps backward.

"*Gentlemen!*" Laughing Whitefish's eyes were flashing. "Stop it at once! You're acting like children—all of you." She turned to Miles. "Please, Miles, please—can't you see how this suspense is killing us? Take your telegram away if you must, but we've simply got to know how it came out."

Miles stared at her uncertainly. His words came in a wild rush. "Shouldn't even of left the place ... Messages pourin' in right an' left—clack-clackety-clack ... Knew how anxious you all was. Could cost me my job ... Aw hell, take the damn thing!"

With that he thrust the damp telegram in my hands and turned and fled. The bunched telegram fluttered to the floor where Cash pounced on it and sank to a chair at my desk, swiftly turning its pages to the end. I felt for Laughing Whitefish's hand. Cash looked up. There were tears in his eyes.

"Of counsel Cassius Wendell is happy to announce," he said, "that by a unanimous decision of the supreme court, justice at last has triumphed." His voice rose. "We won, *we won—*

Willy, Laughing Whitefish—*WE WON!*" With that, half laughing and half crying, he was about to fire the telegram in the air, thought better of it, and spread it out on my desk, fighting to compose himself. "Ah, come, Colonel Wendell, all this is utter nonsense," he said to himself. He looked up at us with blinking eyes. "Compose yourselves, my dears, and I'll now read you the word according to St. Wendell—traditionally the ancient prerogative of all of-counsels. Are you ready?"

"Cash, *please*," I begged him, putting my arm about Laughing Whitefish, who stood quietly at my side making quick panting intakes of breath, fighting back her tears. Cash scanned the first few pages, uttering not a word. "Please, Cash," I implored.

"The opinion is written by Mr. Justice Campbell," he said, looking up at me over his glasses. "That was the old beaver with the mutton-chop whiskers who sat on the right—the one I feared had slept through the best part of your argument, lad." He blinked thoughtfully. "And while I'm sure it had nothing to do with his decision, he came to the bench from an even smaller backwoods town than Marquette. 'Member Guy Nesbitt referring to you as a 'backwoods' lawyer?"

I nodded and Cash resumed his study. "First few pages is a detailed statement of the facts," he said. "Now I think we're all moderately familiar with them by now so I'll skip that part. Then it outlines our arguments on appeal and quotes your 'federal supremacy' clause an' some clauses from the old Indian treaties an' . . . Ah, here we're getting to the good part—we're now drawin' near the mighty Musgrove." Clearing his throat importantly he began to read.

THIRTY-ONE

" 'Many and ingenious are the reasons advanced by the defendant company, appellee here, why the complainant Charlotte Kawbawgam should not prevail in this case. One is that the original co-partners had no right to execute the paper they gave her father, Marji Kawbawgam. To examine this argument only casually is to defeat it. The president and secretary and treasurer of the original joint stock mining partnership at considerable pains and expense traveled to the distant Upper Peninsula expressly to obtain mineral lands for the company. They obtained them. If these men could not propose and execute an agreement whereby for a song they were shown one of the richest iron mines yet discovered in the Lake Superior area, we are at loss to divine who might have acted in their stead. The argument is entirely without merit; it must be assumed that these officers were expected to execute such papers and to do those things necessary to achieve their goal, in which they so richly succeeded. Least of all should anyone expect an unlettered Indian to go behind or question the authenticity of an agreement bearing the signatures of the only persons who usually act for such bodies.

" 'It is further urged by the defendant that probate intervention is first necessary to determine heirship and settle the estates of Marji Kawbawgam and that of his first wife, Blue Heron, before any suit can be brought on this claim. This strategem of delay is also without merit. For reasons which we shall presently dilate on at greater length, the Indian tribes are not within the ordinary state jurisdiction and the interests of tribal members pass directly to their heirs. Such is the doctrine laid down in Davis versus Shanks, 15 Minn 369 and also in Dole versus Irish, 2 Barb. 639 and, as we shall presently see, it is also the settled usage of the Government under Indian treaties.'"

Cash looked up. "Congratulations, Willy, those two lovely cases they cite from our reply brief were dug up by you."

"Read on, read on," I urged, chilled with relief and delight.

"'It is further suggested by the appellee Company that whatever rights Marji Kawbawgum ever had were lost by his failure to pay any assessments and by the passage of time and long inaction,'" Cash read on. "'As already noticed, Marji Kawbawgam was recognized on the records of the old company as entitled to a certificate for twelve *paid-up* nonassessable shares of stock. While he never got that certificate, nothing further was needed on his part to perfect his holdings or to acquaint the old company of his rights, they stood plainly outlined on its own records. These records then passed to the new company, which had assumed all outstanding debts and liabilities of the old. That is where the matter rested. Did this act to extinguish the Indian's rights? We think not. We are aware of no law or decision that terminates the right of a stockholder without some adverse action by the corporation asserting its extinction or denying its existence. Merely burying its corporate head in the sand is not enough.

"'Again it is suggested by appellee that the complainant has waived the constitutional question she first raises here because she failed to assert it below. This is a new wrinkle in constitutional law. The constitutional inhibition that concerns us here lies without the power of any individual litigant to waive—as, for example, she might have waived her right to a jury trial in a criminal case. But this one is enjoined upon all state judges by the Constitution itself and were complainant to sign a waiver in her own blood she could no more negate or waive this provision than she could waive the power of the President to make treaties. It is imposed as part of the pact of statehood. Defendant in effect suggests that judges may now ignore a plain constitutional mandate aimed squarely at state judges because an Indian girl remained silent. The argument is so clearly without merit that we shall charitably say no more.' "

Cash looked up. "Wow!" he said. "The proud Silver Fox ain't gonna like that."

"I suspect that one of his eager young stable of honor graduates will like it even less," I said. "Lay on, MacWendell."

" 'It is also ingeniously suggested by appellee that since Marji Kawbawgam was once prepared to surrender his original paper to the new company for a small sum, this should now be the sole measure of recovery, if any recovery is due, which it denies. Now it is undoubtedly true that Indians may be easily led to make bad bargains and, when made, usually stick by them; our history bristles with sad examples. But because Marji Kawbawgam made a bad bargain originally, and was prepared in desperation to make an even worse bargain later on, this is no reason to deprive his daughter of the true value, provided she could inherit his rights. The fact is that he held on to his paper through thick and thin, and passed it on to his daughter, who has clung to it through a lonely fatherless childhood. The only remaining question that concerns us is whether his interest passed to his daughter and whether she may sue on it in our courts.

" 'According to the testimony of defendant's own expert witness, Professor Naughton of the University at Ann Arbor, and the recent monumental work on marriage by Professor Musgrove, both wives of Marji Kawbawgam were lawful wives by Indian usage and the child of the second wife, Charlotte

Kawbawgam, complainant here, was clearly a lawful child by Indian usage and was so recognized by the Chippewa tribe. If this were not enough, the Government itself has by many treaties guaranteed these particular Indians full freedom in following their ancient customs, and we are further enjoined by the Constitution itself from ignoring such treaties.

" 'The United States supreme court and many respectable state courts have recognized as law that no state laws have any force over Indian tribal relations.' " Cash looked up. "Here they cite a flock of our cases, Willy, and a few we never found. Thirty lashes for Musgrove." He resumed reading. " 'In addition and as already observed, the United States by solemn treaty granted the Indians full self-government in following their old customs, and as noted we are bound by the Constitution itself not to hold counter to such treaties.' "

Cash read on to himself for a moment, and then looked up in triumph. "Speaking of adoption, the court adopts the lovely language of our prize Ohio case word for word. That's the one that said, 'The Indians do not occupy this country by our grace or permission but because they were here first. We are the usurpers, not they. We have no more right to dictate or control their domestic usages than those of Turkey or India.' " Cash then reread the whole long passage, savoring every word. He then demanded and got a cold glass of water and, after much lip smacking, again resumed reading.

" 'If this complainant were an Oriental visitor to our shores it would be unthinkably offensive and possibly internationally provocative for our courts to question her legitimacy if she were already considered legitimate at home. There is all the more reason for respecting the rights and dignity of an ancient native people who dwell lawfully within our borders under rights which the states are expressly forbidden to interfere with or control. We hold because we must hold that Charlotte Kawbawgam was a legitimate child of Marji Kawbawgam and has every right to sue. Such a view not only accords with the law; it happens also to accord with elementary concepts of justice.' "

Laughing Whitefish turned and looked up at me, her eyes swimming with tears. Cassius glanced up at her and pressed on. " 'The many treaties made between the United States and this very tribe not only provided tribal self-determination but also recognized heritable relations among them. The evidence further shows that the Government paid this very complainant the balance of her father's share of his tribal annuities upon his death, thus itself recognizing her as his daughter. Implicit in all this is the Government recognition that the Indian tribes have the right to say who should share in tribal benefits. Since white men cannot withdraw themselves from state law, we have not only the jurisdiction but the duty to determine their legal status. But Indians are not obliged or indeed permitted to look to state law in governing their tribal affairs.

" 'If we will not recognize their own customs then we must in effect deny our native Indians their existence as human beings, and this we refuse to do. The authorities already cited clearly show this view to be the only sound one and there is no respectable authority against it. We are aware that there are some decisions which undertake to apply to Indian relations the rules of jurisprudence of the states where the Indians live, but we cannot think that such precedents are good law or safe guides. Certainly they do not express the prevailing sentiment on the subject.' "

Cash looked up. "Guy Nesbitt's ears will burn when he reads that. Justice Campbell is really laying it on."

"I revere every gray hair in the good justice's whiskers," I said.

" 'The learned trial judge' "—Cash began, and then he grunted and looked up and delivered an aside. "It's a theorem as immutable as one of Euclid's that the harder poor trial judges are reversed the more learned they become," he pontificated, resuming his reading—" 'The learned trial judge also rejected the theory of adoption and the appellee now suggests that in any case, whatever our decision on polygamy, recovery to the daughter must be limited to her own share, and should not include the first wife's. We reject this theory for the same reason that we must sustain the validity of the second marriage and the issue thereof. If there was a valid second marriage there was also a valid adoption, for precisely the same reasons, and we must recognize both.' " Cassius shot me a quick glance. "That last is stolen almost word for word from your oral argument, lad."

"Arrant plagiarism in its most forgiveable form," I said, fluttering my eyelashes modestly.

Cash paused and blinked thoughtfully and delivered himself of a pearl. "Judges in their opinions," he said, "dearly love to soar off on little rhetorical flights, flashing their erudition like a pawnbroker's diamond, affecting a dispassion and detachment marvelous to behold—all the while ever so discreetly wooing the law reviews." He wagged his finger. "But there comes a time in every case when rhapsody must cease, the judge come down out of the clouds, and the contest be resolved. Litigants crave results rather than rhetoric; for their part the poor toiling judge might better have saved his wind and simply voted yes or no. For however crass and wrenching such partisan goings on may be, it is the main business of a judge to decide his bloody case. I detect faint signs that we are reaching that point in this one."

"Amen," I said. "I too am for less rhetoric and more decision."

Cash glared at me reproachfully and resumed reading. " 'We have here plural marriages and an adoption between members of an Indian tribe unquestionably good by Indian rules. The parties were not subject in those relations to the laws of Michigan, and there was no other law interfering with the tribal determination of these personal relations. We cannot interfere with the validity of such marriages or such an adoption without attempting unlawfully to subject them to rules of law that never bound them.

"It follows that the decision below must be reversed and the cause remanded to the circuit court so that the bill of complaint may be reinstated and the proofs proceed on the question of the amount of recovery. Since Marji Kawbawgam was also promised a permanent job at the mine, additional damages for this further breach should be reckoned to the date of his death.

" 'The other Justices concurred.' "

THIRTY-TWO

"Looks like we won everything but the county court-house," I murmured, stunned by the magnitude of our victory.

Cash pushed aside the telegram, arose and grabbed his hat, and started thumping toward the door.

"Where you going?" I demanded.

"Home to bed," he said. "It's too late to start drinkin' and too early for church. Moreover I don't want to disturb you two love birds—you've had your arm around her, Willy, all the time I been readin' the word according to Mister Justice Campbell. Goodnight."

I looked down, and lo, the man had told the simple truth. "Wait," Laughing Whitefish said, and she ran up and kissed his unshaven cheek. "That's simply on account, dear friend—we'll discuss drab business on another day." She turned to me. "And as for you, William, next winter we'll go on a straw ride."

Just then there came a timid knock on the door. "Come in," I said, for a moment wondering fearfully whether our telegram had been some sort of monstrous hoax.

Miles Coffey popped his head in the door, holding another telegram aloft. "Telegrams, *telegrams*, TELEGRAMS!" he declaimed. "Here is a brand new one for you, Mr. Wendell," he apologized.

"What does it say?" Cash demanded. "An' don't pretend you haven't read it."

"Sure, sure, Mr. Wendell. It says: 'Unan—unan—' ah, that word again—'victory is yours and congratulations to the bogus Colonel. Spider.'"

Miles Coffey handed Cash his telegram and turned to leave. "Miles," I said, "I've got one question to ask before you go." He turned back. "Do you mean to tell me," I continued, "that Henry Harwood actually ordered the first telegram you gave us and has to pay for it?" I hefted it. "Why it's as long as a small novel."

"I mean that, Willy," he said. "He does it in all his appeal cases. Some's even longer. Guess it's his one big extravagance."

"But, Miles, I can't believe it, man—it must cost him a fortune."

"He's got a bigger fortune," Miles came back. "Moreover he owns a good share of the bloody railroad."

"Them as has gits," Cash loftily put in. "Let's not quibble over shillings in our hour of victory."

Miles turned to Cash and eyed him speculatively. "Speakin' of victory, Mr. Wendell, would you after be comin' an' joinin' poor Miles in a wee victory drink? I'm awful parched from runnin'. Would you, Mr. Wendell?"

Cash struck a Daniel Webster attitude, hands clapped against his body fore and aft, pondering the problem. Finally he spoke. "My young friends," he answered, "you are now gazing upon a man who has just conquered his iron will power." He nodded at Miles. "The equally parched Colonel Wendell will gladly join Mr. Coffey in a victory drink—mebbe two."

Laughing Whitefish reached out her hand toward him. "Oh, please, Mr. Wendell . . ."

He faced her, lips pursed, eyes blinking reflectively. "Forgive me, my dear," he said softly, "but there seems to be a law of nature that when a man's right he's most apt to go wrong. After residin' with rectitude too long there comes a wild compulsion to kick over the traces. I feel a powerful urge tuggin' at me now, pullin' me under. And if I must drown in somethin' I'd prefer it'd be booze rather than virtue."

"Oh, Cash, Cash," she said, sorrowfully shaking her head.

Cash coolly lit his pipe and blew out a billow of acrid fumes. "Fear not, my friends," he announced loftily. "Always remember that two of the oldest preservatives known to man are smoke and alcohol." He waved his hand languidly like a strolling baron. "Lead on, Mr. Coffey, lead on."

"Have one to the memory of Philo P. Everett," I called after him in farewell.

The old man paused and half turned. "True, lad," he soberly agreed. "And another to Cosima and another to Dr. Naughton—who in a way really saved us—and, ah yes, another to Mr. Justice Campbell and still another to Laughing Whitefish and—ahem—her brilliant lawyers." He again turned to leave.

"Mr. Wendell," Laughing Whitefish said, "before you go please tell William the real reason why I took that sudden trip after his accident last winter."

"But you made me promise not to," he said, once again arrested in flight.

"I now release you from your promise. Please tell him."

"Very well," he said, facing me. "Willy, after you got conked on the head last winter Laughing Whitefish set out alone and visited just about every Indian encampment and settlement clean from the Straits of Mackinac to Northern Wisconsin telling them to lay off you. She told them how much she trusted you and how loyal you were and how hard you were working. For good measure she warned them that if any of them again did you harm she'd personally hunt him down and kill him."

"*Punish* him," Laughing Whitefish hastily corrected him.

He shook his head. " 'Tain't the way I heard it, my dear—and moreover I believe you would have. I also heard tell that a few Indians got so scared just listenin' to you they up an' fled across to Canada."

"*Mister Wendell!*" she said.

"Facts is facts, ma'm," he said.

"Well I'll be damned," I said.

With that the old boy resolutely squared his shoulders and stomped out after the waiting Miles, leaving us alone. We stood listening until the sound of tapping faded down the hall.

I moved closer and lifted her chin and looked in her eyes. "Then there never was any sick friend?"

Contritely: "No, William," she said, backing away.

"You did it for me?"

"Yes, William."

"But dear girl, why didn't you tell me?—especially when you knew I was lashed and corroded with jealousy?"

"I guess I should have, William. I've never been any good at lying."

"Then why didn't you?"

She spread her hands. "Your pride, William. A man has his pride. I didn't tell you because of that. I didn't want you to think you had to hide behind a woman's skirts. So I made up that clumsy story you never quite believed." She paused. "Then maybe I *wanted* you to be a little jealous . . . Anyway, I had to do something to save you from my people."

"You knew all along it was an Indian."

"I was certain it was. Especially when I met such sly evasion during my travels when I tried to find out who had done it. But try as I might I could never discover who it was." She shrugged. "So I warned *all* of them." She smiled wanly. "And now you're here safe and sound and finally we've won."

I stared at her and shook my head, the eternally baffled

male. There were deep circles under her eyes and she stood rubbing them like a sleepy child. I put my arm around her and led her to the door. "Come, my dear. It's been a crowded day for both of us. I'll walk you home."

"Poor old Mr. Cash," she murmured. "Now he'll go and make himself sick and spoil everything."

"I'm not so sure," I said, taking her hand. "Any more than I'm sure that one should ever meddle with the divine right of everyone to be a damned fool in his own way. Come, sweet Lotti."

The rain had stopped and the skies had cleared and once past the town's outskirts we beheld the eerie shafts of the Northern Lights glittering far out over the lake. A breeze had sprung up and occasionally we heard the waves searching against the sandy shore, their subdued slap-slap sounding like distant applause.

"I think maybe I'll go visit Cosima before school starts," Laughing Whitefish said musingly. "She made me promise and anyway I want to."

"And also Metoxon?" I could not resist saying.

"No, William," she said quietly. "Poor Metoxon lost any possible chance of ever interesting me when he was so rude to you when you met. He's now found himself a good Indian wife and left Madeline Island. I wish him well."

I restrained an impulse to whistle. Walking along slowly we came to Presque Isle and climbing, continued past the dark and silent Indian encampment on up to Laughing Whitefish's favorite lookout high above the rocky northern shore. There we stood hand in hand.

"Look," Laughing Whitefish said, pointing out at the sky.

Far out over the lake the filmy smoky shafts of the Northern Lights wavered and raced in trailing scarves of light, shifting and melting across the flaming sky in great dripping organ pipes of silent melody—folding, leaping, coiling, gliding vaporously like gauzily-veiled dancers on a vast celestial stage. We stood watching the awesome spectacle until I reluctantly broke the spell.

"What will ever become of you, Laughing Whitefish?" I asked huskily. "What are you going to do?"

She was silent for a time before she spoke. "Well, William, after I return from visiting Cosima I plan to paint and redecorate my school. That's if there's time before our case comes back from Lansing."

She had not precisely answered my question. "There will be time," I said, wondering how I might better speak what was crowding upon my mind and heart. The haunting couplet of Matthew Arnold came rushing back to me: "Alas, is even love too weak," he had written, "To open the heart and let it speak?"

"What are you going to do, William?" she asked me.

It was my turn to fall silent. Then my words came in a wild rush, in a tone of compulsive banter I was far from feeling. Were there occasions in life too serious ever to be serious? "I think I'll go visit Cosima, too—but I want to do it as part of our honeymoon, Lotti," I began. "I've always wanted to marry an heiress and write a book—and now I've discovered I'm in love with one and have just lived through the other," I ran on. "Perhaps you can even teach me to spell. Will you, Lotti?"

"Will I teach you to spell, William?" she inquired softly.

"Will you let me go with you to see Cosima?" She remained silent. "Will you, Laughing Whitefish?" I pleaded. "Please, please, I do so much want to, believe me, my dear."

Under the pallor of strange light she stood looking out over the lake. Far out the whistle of an unseen ore boat sounded a distant throaty bleat. In the stillness I heard a dog barking back at the encampment. The slow rocky thud of the surf below sounded oddly like the clatter of falling boards. When finally she turned back to me and spoke her voice too had a certain huskiness. "There's an old Indian custom, William, that when an orphaned Indian girl is asked to marry she should consult her mother's oldest friend before deciding. Are you willing to go visit Cosima and see what she says?"

"It's a bargain," I said, "for I've now learned that old Indian customs have the mighty force of law, that your idlest custom is a command. You see . . . That is . . ." I paused and then blurted the words. "I love you."

"I know, William," she said. "I've known all along—ever since I nursed you and in your delirium over and over you told me you did. It was the first time I ever dared let myself dream of loving you. And I do, oh I do."

She had loosened her hair and the breeze caught and lifted it and I reached out and felt it vibrating under my hand. I thought of Stephen Foster's Jeannie, she of the hair that was "borne like a vapor on the soft summer air."

"I do love you so," she murmured.

I moved closer and took her in my arms, her flowing hair brushing my face. "There's an old white custom that the man kisses the woman he loves when he plights her his troth," I said. "Is it a bargain, darling?"

"It's a bargain—darling," she whispered, lifting her face up to mine in the eerie glow of the Northern Lights.

AUTHOR'S AFTERWORD

I first heard the bare outline of this story many years ago from the lips of my old circuit judge, Frank A. Bell, when I was a struggling young district attorney practicing before him—struggling, that is, not to lose the courthouse and jail along with most of my cases. Judge Bell then gave me the citations of the legal cases and I read them avidly and resolved then and there that I would write this story one day if I was able.

While the general historical background of the times and of the case are pretty accurate, I have not hesitated to change things occasionally for the sake of my story. Thus I am aware, to take a passing example, that Schoolcraft had left the state long before any of these events occurred. Yet his name is so closely linked with the history of the U.P. and the Chippewa Indians I simply felt compelled to drag him back, however briefly. More-over his beautiful wife Jane Johnston was not a full-blooded Indian; she was of the half-blood, her father being Scotch-Irish. Now I hate to spoil the fun of the ancient order of fly-speckers, but there are many other instances.

A writer best learns his craft by writing, I suppose, and from this book I learned that dressing up fiction in a bustle doesn't make it any easier to write. Harder, if anything, because there is additionally the constant problem of authentic idiom, dress, furnishings and all the rest. And constantly one must be on guard against the illusion-shattering anachronism. One swiftly learns to avoid describing a character as possessing a nose like W. C. Fields', even if he was so blessed. ... I learned too that research on a book of this kind is important largely so that one can omit with confidence. If one put all of it in it would read like the inventory of an antique shop.

While most of the characters in this novel actually existed, my treatment of them is in all respects fictional. This is particularly true of the principal characters, who are purely creatures of my imagination. So with the various excerpts from journals, diaries and newspapers, these seemed a hopefully painless way to inject a little history and get on with my narrative without also inducing sleep. So any similarity between my characters and actual people, living or dead, is purely coincidental, as the saying goes, including that of their appearance, ages, actions, conversations, motives, appetites and assorted romantic and domestic arrangements. Since most of these people were long dead before I was ever born I simply had to make them up. In doing so I learned that there is a vast gulf between the cold reports of ancient litigation, however absorbing, and the pulsing striving people who once engaged in it.

The case itself actually got in the state supreme court not once but three times. Now my passion for Lansing is as tender as it is unappeasable, but three journeys there in one book seemed a trifle excessive. Lawyers, law buffs or readers simply curious to trace the wayward course of fiction in collision with raw fact may find the original cases reported as follows:

49 Mich 39, 12 NW 901 (this is lawyer talk for volume 49 of the Michigan supreme court reports beginning at page 39, and also means that the same case can be found reported in volume 12 of the Northwestern Reporter system beginning at page 901); 50 Mich 578, 16 NW 295; and 76 Mich 498, 43 NW 602.

Upper Peninsula of Michigan, 1965   Robert Traver

ABOUT THE AUTHOR

Robert Traver (John D. Voelker) was for fourteen years the District Attorney of the rugged glaciated iron mining community of Marquette County, Michigan. He was appointed to the Supreme Court of Michigan in 1957; was re-elected two times; and he wrote over one hundred decisions. He resigned to continue his writing —and to fish for trout in his beloved U. P. This is Traver's third novel and eighth book.